CW01159967

LET
THE
BAD
TIMES
ROLL

Alice Slater is a writer and ex-bookseller from London. She studied creative writing at MMU and UEA. Her debut novel, *Death of a Bookseller*, was an instant *Sunday Times* bestseller. It won the Debut Crime Book of the Year Award at Capital Crime's Fingerprint Awards 2024, shortlisted for CrimeFest's Specsavers Best Debut Crime Novel Award 2023 and longlisted for the Authors' Club Best First Novel Award 2024. Alice co-hosts literary podcast *What Page Are You On?* and lives with her husband, their dog Peachy and a lot of books.

ALSO BY ALICE SLATER

Death of a Bookseller

An exclusive signed edition of

LET
THE
BAD
TIMES
ROLL

Signed by the author

ALICE SLATER

HODDER &
STOUGHTON

First published in Great Britain in 2025 by Hodder & Stoughton Limited
An Hachette UK company

The authorised representative in the EEA is Hachette Ireland, 8 Castlecourt Centre, Dublin 15, D15 XTP3, Ireland (email: info@hbgi.ie)

1

Copyright © Alice Slater 2025

The right of Alice Slater to be identified as the Author of the Work has been asserted by her in accordance with the Copyright, Designs and Patents Act 1988.

All rights reserved. No part of this publication may be reproduced, stored in a retrieval system, or transmitted, in any form or by any means without the prior written permission of the publisher, nor be otherwise circulated in any form of binding or cover other than that in which it is published and without a similar condition being imposed on the subsequent purchaser.

All characters in this publication are fictitious and any resemblance to real persons, living or dead, is purely coincidental.

A CIP catalogue record for this title is available from the British Library

Hardback ISBN 978 1 529 38538 0
Trade Paperback ISBN 978 1 529 38541 0
ebook ISBN 978 1 529 38539 7

Typeset in Sabon MT by Manipal Technologies Limited

Printed and bound in Great Britain by Clays Ltd, Elcograf S.p.A.

Hodder & Stoughton policy is to use papers that are natural, renewable and recyclable products and made from wood grown in sustainable forests. The logging and manufacturing processes are expected to conform to the environmental regulations of the country of origin.

Hodder & Stoughton Limited
Carmelite House
50 Victoria Embankment
London EC4Y 0DZ

www.hodder.co.uk

For Alex,
from Leyton to Decatur

Like the tangled veins of cypress roots that meander this way and that in the swamp, everything in New Orleans is interrelated, wrapped around itself in ways that aren't always obvious.
Under a Hoodoo Moon: The Life of the Night Tripper, Dr John
Mac Rebennack

And get the fatted calf and kill it, and let us eat and celebrate; for this son of mine was dead and is alive again; he was lost and is found.
Luke 15:23–24

London: Caroline

Caroline carried her meds in an antique silver pillbox that had belonged to her mother, even though she could never remember whether she'd taken them once the pills were popped from their blister packs. She kept her father's old Zippo in her handbag, although she never had time to refill the gas. She surrounded herself with vintage paperbacks because she liked the familiar way her family's library of broken spines looked on her shelves, but she preferred to scroll social media than read. Her flat was filled with the cassettes and CDs her parents used to pair with a cocktail on a Friday night, but she listened to music on her laptop. She lived her life through a sepia filter, nostalgic for a time she'd never really known, an era that belonged to a different generation. Aesthetics over practicalities. That was Caroline all over.

She planned Daniel's dinner party with the same attention to detail.

Everything had to be perfect: a welcome-home feast for the weary traveller, a thirtieth-birthday celebration surrounded by friends. He'd be jet-lagged, of course, but Daniel always knew how to rise to an occasion, how to perform for a crowd. She could picture his face as he walked through the door, a look of confusion melting into recognition as each guest stepped forward in turn to relieve him of his heavy bags, to gather him into a warm, welcoming embrace, to press a cocktail into his hand. Caroline would remain seated, tranquil as a lily pad.

'You're just in time for dinner,' she'd say, and he'd look at the New Orleans-themed menu and laugh at her cleverness as she swatted away his apologies.

'How'd you know where to find me?' he'd ask, and she'd smile.

'In every life, I'll always find you,' she'd say.

They would drink champagne cocktails spiked with absinthe and stay up late while Daniel regaled them with tales of New Orleans. Maybe they'd even plan a trip together. He could take her to all the bars and restaurants he'd discovered in the city, and they could retrace his steps through the French Quarter side by side. Just the two of them.

She could see it all so clearly.

Caroline didn't know much about New Orleans, so she spent an evening reading articles on the internet, watching informative videos made by earnest amateur foodies. She learned the difference between Cajun and Creole cuisine, po' boys and muffulettas, étouffée and jambalaya. She learned that the famous Café du Monde coffee was flavoured with chicory, and the 'holy trinity' in Louisianan cooking was two parts sweet onion, one part celery and one part green pepper.

She also learned that New Orleans had the third-highest murder rate of all US cities, trailing behind St Louis and Baltimore, and that Louisiana was home to an above-average number of missing persons. Is that why Daniel chose to spirit away to New Orleans? Did it feel like an easy place for a man to disappear?

Caroline's menu came together easily once she understood the culinary landscape of the city. Grilled oysters to start, that was a given. Caroline loved oysters, loved their solitude, their hard exteriors, the secrecy of the full-moon pearls hidden within their soft folds.

For the main course, a seafood gumbo seemed simple enough, served over a scoop of white rice and topped with a tangle of chopped spring onion. A warm, spiced stew – comfort in a bowl.

Dessert had to be something rich and decadent. She considered strawberry shortcake, but settled on the pomp and circumstance of bananas Foster flambéed at the table. With its swirl of rum caramel and melted ice cream, it would be the perfect sweet treat to counterbalance the savoury main.

A Sazerac felt like the classic way to end a feast in New Orleans, but in her heart, in her gut, she knew she must finish with the morbidity of a Death in the Afternoon. Champagne spiked with sugar and absinthe, a taste of green reflections, hallucinations, a legacy of poets and artists touched by madness.

She had the perfect dinner set on hand – the silver-trimmed china from their parents' wedding – but she needed crystal rocks glasses for the aperitifs and champagne flutes for the digestifs. Rattan placemats, organic cotton napkins in deep purple, stitched with gold stars. Delicate oyster forks, green candlesticks pushed into vintage glass bottles, an antique silver chiller to keep the champagne cool.

On Daniel's birthday, Caroline went shopping. She could have procured everything online, but she rather liked the ritualistic process of handpicking each item, although she felt like a housewife trotting around the shops; a Stepford wife with a bright, uncanny smile.

Spanish crisps flavoured with black truffle and a tin of spiced Gordal olives from the deli. A dozen fresh oysters and a heavy bag of fat king prawns from the fishmonger. A fistful of fresh herbs, aromatic as a bride's bouquet, an assortment of vegetables, and a hand of bananas from the greengrocer. Vanilla ice cream, brown sugar, dark rum. Aesop handwash for the bathroom; a Diptyque candle to perfume the air of the flat, to overpower the fragrance of the feast as it came together in the kitchen.

Flowers: she needed flowers, too. Magnolias would be ideal, but she couldn't find any in the local florist, so she settled for a spray of gypsophila instead. Simple, classic.

As she lugged her bounty back to the flat, she felt less like a Stepford wife and more like a scullery maid. The tote bags slid off her shoulders and dug into the palms of her hands, left long red welts as though she'd spent a significant number of hours tied up, left to rot in the boot of a car by a kidnapper. The bright sun burned her eyes, the healed hairline fracture in her tibia ached, and her left shoe gound against her heel, rubbed the skin raw and left a bloody stain on the leather.

The canal was desolate, the water a dark quagmire. Against her better judgement, she had decided to take a shortcut along the canal towpath, which she usually avoided because, even after all these years, she still felt a distinct paranoia about returning to the scene of her first (and, arguably, worst) crime.

The towpath was busy with a crowd of young professionals hanging out by the waters' edge, drinking pints from the trendy canal-side bar and making the most of the first warm day of the year. Some were cooling off by dipping their feet into the water, jeans rolled up to their knees. Vile. Caroline would never submerge so much as a toenail in there. She'd seen the rotten jetsam that collected at the locks, a reeking stew of plastic bottles, crisp packets and scum that baked all day in the sun. She knew what dark histories lurked beneath the water's surface.

The flat was cold and dark. Without Daniel, it felt barren, unlived in. She missed his music, the sound of his voice as he sent endless voice notes to his friends, the sweet smell of Santal 33 as he readied himself for a night out.

It was unthinkable to imagine he might never set foot in here again, might never put away his clean socks on the radiator, might never finish the half-read paperback balanced on the arm of the sofa. No – he would be back in time for dinner. That's what she'd said; that was the deal.

She snapped on the lights, banished the shadows from every corner. As she unpacked her shopping, Caroline listened to the footsteps and music through the floorboards overhead. Her upstairs neighbours were dinner-party people. The savoury scent of their cooking – onions softening in butter, perhaps – dominated the air, and she lit the Diptyque candle to freshen the space. She imagined one pouring wine, the other stirring a Le Creuset of risotto or rigatoni alla vodka. Later, one might dip her wooden spoon into the bubbling dish, and the other might boogey over, her bare feet slapping against the lino, for a taste.

Earlier, they'd played a mix of milquetoast pop, like Fleetwood Mac and ABBA, but now their soundtrack was a lively jazz. If Caroline believed in good omens, which she categorically did not, this would feel like a sign. A nod of encouragement, an endorsement from the universe. Instead, it served as nothing but inspiration: jazz would be the perfect background music to Daniel's dinner party, and she searched the internet for a New Orleans-inspired playlist.

She swept and hoovered, washed the fruit and veg, arranged the flowers in a couple of clean Bonne Maman jam jars and lit more candles. Then she poured the last of a bottle of Sancerre into a glass and took her place at the table to wait.

Her phone rang, the number unknown. Perhaps it was Daniel, letting her know he'd landed safely at Heathrow. She answered the call with a cheerful, 'Hello, darling – is that you?'

London: Selina

One week later

Caroline's invitation wasn't much of a surprise. I'd been seeing a lot of signs in the week since I'd returned home from New Orleans. A pale feather caught in my hair. A cabbage white fluttering in the garden. An empty snail's shell on my doorstep, bleached cream by the sun and no bigger than a thumbnail. White was Daniel's colour, the colour of his shirt, his sunglasses, his vape. Lilies, daisy petals, dandelion seeds. The papery bark of the silver birch. Pearls, the palest sand, bone. It was him; it was always him. It was Daniel reaching out to me, leaving signs to remind me that he was still there, he was still with me, and that I would never be free.

New Orleans was still with me, too. The hum of a bluebottle could be the drone of a sun-drunk mosquito. The light breeze that rattled the leaves of the plane trees could be stirring the branches of the magnolia in the hostel courtyard. A distant pneumatic drill was the dull, melodious whirr of hidden cicadas, and the base note of damp concrete lacked only the top note of spilled rum to complete the perfume of the Big Easy.

In the supermarket, I caught myself looking for the flavours of the city, but the few things that reminded me of my brief time in New Orleans — oysters, absinthe, champagne — felt too ostentatious to bring to an evening like this. It would be a sombre affair, with a simple, wholesome meal at its centre. Something that involved meditative chopping and stirring, minimal clean-up. Wine was the obvious choice, but I worried about showing up with a bottle of red in the face of a delicate saffron-infused risotto, or a white to contend with a rich spaghetti bolognese. A bottle of fizz was probably the safe option for a regular dinner party, but this was no ordinary invitation to dinner.

The crash of broken glass snapped me from my reverie. A woman stood over the crime scene – a bottle had slipped from her grasp and smashed, sending a spatter of red wine all over the plasticky floor, across the white toes of her Converse and up the legs of her jeans.

It was a sign.

Red wine was Daniel's poison. In the muggy heat of the city, I couldn't stand it – room-temperature Merlot held an uncanny resemblance to blood on the tongue – but it was the right choice. I settled on a mid-price bottle of Shiraz, and my hands shook as I fumbled with my phone to pay for it.

Since arriving home, I'd spent so much energy avoiding the topic of New Orleans, it was almost overwhelming to think that I was about to spend an entire evening talking about it. I wanted to talk about New Orleans, though. I did. I wanted to talk about the cocktails I'd drunk, the meals I'd eaten. I wanted to talk about the quality of the air, the dampness of it, the way it curled my hair and made my skin glow. I wanted to talk about Bourbon Street, with its bright lights, cacophony of music and tacky gift shops. The Spanish moss tumbling in knots from the trees like the weather-worn Mardi Gras beads that were draped from so many street signs and railings all over the French Quarter.

These people wouldn't be interested in any of that, though. That wasn't the story they wanted me to tell. They didn't want to hear about the jazz or the drinks or the weather. They wanted to hear about what happened next.

They wanted to know what happened to Daniel.

Menu

Aperitif
Sazerac

⚜

Appetiser
Charbroiled Oysters

⚜

Entrée
Seafood Gumbo

⚜

Dessert
Bananas Foster

⚜

Digestif
Death in the Afternoon

Laissez les bon temps rouler!

Aperitif

Sazerac

⚜

Known as the oldest cocktail in America,
the Sazerac carries the history of New Orleans in its
signature blend of rye whiskey, sugar and Peychaud's bitters.
Served in a chilled rocks glass licked with absinthe.

London: Richard

Richard liked the simplicity of a freshly shucked oyster: a quick, cold swallow of salinity, the brightening zip of lemon, the sharp bite of shallot mignonette. It seemed like a waste to drown their delicate flavour in a punchy garlic butter, to grill them into submission and eat them with a fork like escargot, but that didn't matter now: Caroline's oysters were rotten.

'I couldn't bear to throw it all away,' she said, peering into the fridge as Richard surveyed its contents. Spoiled vegetables, browning bananas, a stinking bag of decomposing prawns. 'I thought he'd be back last week. I did all this shopping for his birthday dinner ... I was just so sure he'd be back.'

Caroline's face was etched with the strain of sleepless nights and frantic, long-distance phone calls. A ripeness clung to her, the smell of unwashed hair and dirty clothes. Richard's attention drifted to the silver scar that traced a path from her eyebrow to her hairline. It was nearly invisible now, faded from amethyst to opal.

'Well, let's get this fridge sorted,' he said. 'You can't leave it like this, you'll get sick.'

'I don't care if I get sick,' she said.

'*I* care if you get sick.'

He peeled a bin bag from the roll and shook it out, then returned his attention to the fridge – a handsome, double-doored Samsung with dispensers for both ice and chilled water. Richard expected such a fine bit of kit to be well used, bursting with fresh produce, glass bottles of spring water and kombucha, artisanal cheeses and deli meats. All Caroline seemed to have to hand, however, were the putrid ingredients for her obsolete menu.

She'd always been the type to live on black coffee, champagne and cigarettes, he supposed. A life sustained entirely on business lunches and pre-packaged salads seemed about right. Perhaps she spent most of her time at someone else's flat? That familiar, shameful feeling of envy rose within him. Best not to dwell on things like that, although it was hard to imagine Caroline in the throes of a romance. She was perpetually single at university, more interested in her studies – and clinging to the shadow of her brother – than finding a lover of her own. In the twelve years they'd known one another, she kept any trysts to herself.

Richard dropped the rancid shellfish, wilted herbs and mouldy green peppers into the bin bag. The overripe bananas would make a fine banana bread, but he couldn't bear the thought of using produce that had sat in such close proximity to rank seafood for a week. They had to go.

The flat still had a sour smell to it, like stagnant water, and Richard found the culprits after a quick search of the open-plan kitchen-diner: several jam jars of gypsophila, the stems slimy with rot. Into the bag with them, too. He rinsed the jam jars in hot, soapy water, then turned back to the fridge to wipe the glass shelves with an antibacterial spray.

His fingertips skimmed the slender shoulders of a champagne bottle, the iconic sunflower yellow label of Veuve Clicquot. He knew this champagne like the back of his hand: its golden hue, a rich silkiness on the tongue, flavours of white tree fruits, pears, apples and peaches; citrussy notes of mandarin and grapefruit; morning-pastry aromas of fresh brioche and warm croissants, a touch of dried fruit to finish. A celebratory champagne. It reminded him of Caroline. It spoke of finishing essays and passing exams, of observing milestone birthdays, special occasions.

Sex. It wasn't the right choice for Death in the Afternoons, where a punch of absinthe would kill those delicate flavours. Again, it was a waste – but they wouldn't be opening any champagne tonight.

'I keep expecting him to walk through the door and pour himself a glass of wine,' Caroline said.

She looked so broken, with dark bags beneath traumatised eyes, and candy-pink nostrils chapped from too many tissues. Should he hug her? Was that the right thing to do? Richard's desire to hold her was the very thing that made him hesitate. It felt too much like an ulterior motive, the behaviour of a desperate loser, a creep taking advantage of a vulnerable woman in her hour of need.

'I can't imagine what you're going through right now,' he said. 'But you need to take care of yourself. When did you last have something to eat?'

She thought for a moment. 'I can't remember.'

'You need to eat,' he said. 'Let me make you something while you grab a shower and get into some fresh clothes, and then when the others arrive, we can talk about Daniel.'

Daniel. Richard's heart ached. When he thought of Daniel, he pictured dust drifting through the silver light of an overhead projector, the smell of fresh popcorn, red wine and cigarette smoke. Late nights in the library; long conversations in candlelit bars.

He opened Caroline's kitchen cupboards, surveying her meagre groceries: tinned olives, expensive crisps, chicken stock, flour, two large brown onions, wrapped in dried papery skins. 'Shall I make some pasta? I can pop to the shops.'

Caroline bit her bottom lip. 'Do you know how to make a gumbo?'

*

Caroline's kitchen knife was blunt, the edge rough with nicks, but it moved quickly in Richard's practised hand, a flash of silver under the kitchen's bright spotlights. The muscles in his forearm rippled and flexed as he diced a twist on the French mirepoix: white onion, celery and, in lieu of the conventional carrot, green pepper.

With neat efficiency, he gathered the peels and seeds and dropped them into the bin, then scooped the diced vegetables into a bowl and put them to one side. He dried his hands on a tea towel as he scanned the recipe on his phone.

Caroline reappeared in a cloud of her signature perfume, dark hair damp. The warmth of the shower had failed to return the colour to her cheeks, but she looked more put together as she lit a scented candle and opened the balcony door to clear the air.

'Feeling better?' he asked.

'A little.' She leaned against the fridge. 'What are you up to?'

'Making the roux,' he said, tipping a dune of flour from a paper bag into a bowl on the scales. 'There's an expression in Creole cooking: first, you make a roux. It means ... well, I guess it's self-explanatory, really. It just means you always start with the roux, because the roux is the most important part of the dish. It binds everything together, creates the base of the stew. Plus, the deeper the colour, the richer and more flavourful the gumbo will be.'

'Wow,' Caroline said, a blank expression on her face. 'That's fascinating, Dicky.'

'Right,' he replied, ears turning pink. 'Well. I thought it was interesting.'

He dumped the flour and several shiny pats of butter into a burnt-orange Le Creuset and stirred until the fat melted into a thin, creamy sauce. Caroline placed a hand on his bicep, and he couldn't help but tense the muscle beneath the sleeve of his T-shirt.

'I need a drink,' Caroline said. 'Shall we open a bottle of something?'

He swallowed. 'Sure.'

'Red or white?'

'Which is open?'

'Neither.'

'Which do you prefer?'

She took a deep breath, as though he were testing her patience. 'I don't know, Dicky. Just pick one.'

'Is the white chilled?'

'It's been in the fridge for about' – she checked the time on her phone – 'an hour.'

The memory of that awful smell of rot and decay flashed through his mind. 'Red, then, please.'

'Fine. Red it is.'

She retrieved a bottle from the rack and uncorked it without much ceremony. Richard winced as she filled two glasses straight away. It should really sit for a while to breathe, but that didn't seem to be of great concern to Caroline. He stirred the roux, and a warm, nutty smell rose from the pan as the velvety mixture turned peanut-butter brown.

'It's a good wine,' she said to fill the silence, prompting Richard to lift his drink and examine the colour in the light. 'Daniel's favourite.'

He swirled it, let the bright haemoglobin red coat the sides of the glass, then took a deep sniff.

'Spicy,' he said, as he considered the wine's bouquet. 'Soft, ripe blackberries. Earthy – hints of leather.' Hints of Daniel. He took a small sip and nodded. 'Châteauneuf-du-Pape? Beautiful.'

As Caroline brought her glass to her nose and inhaled, her eyes filled with tears. He wondered if the scent reminded her of Daniel too.

'Caroline, I can't imagine what you're going through,' he said, turning towards her.

'You've already said that.' She glanced into the pan. 'Don't let that burn.'

When the roux reached the colour of an old penny, Richard added the chopped vegetables and stirred until they were coated in the rich, savoury base. He sprinkled the mixture with Cajun seasoning, poured a litre of chicken stock into the pan, and left his gumbo to simmer. By the time they were ready to eat, it would be unctuous and perfect, although he had a feeling most of it would remain untouched, left to congeal in their bowls.

*

Sage arrived with a dusty bunch of dried lavender and a batch of homemade elderflower cordial, neither of which Caroline seemed particularly taken with. Max had a crate of Camden Hells and a bottle of Jim Beam in his arms, as though preparing for a party.

'Thanks for inviting us over,' Sage said, dragging an unwilling Caroline into a full-bodied hug. 'It's good to be surrounded by your community at times like this.'

Richard could see Caroline's face reflected in the mirror by the door, grimacing at the forced proximity to Sage's blood-red curls. He suspected Caroline did not consider Sage part of her community.

'I owe you an apology,' Caroline replied mechanically, extracting herself from the essential-oil scent of Sage's embrace. 'I wasn't in my right mind the last time we met.'

'Oh God, don't even think about that. Stress does funny things to people.' Sage cocked her head to one side, empathy written all over her face. 'Not that I think there's anything to worry about. I spoke to my spiritual advisor, and she said Mercury's in retrograde.

Miscommunication is king right now – so I think that's all it is. Mixed messages, a lost phone ... something like that.'

Caroline eyed Sage with a dangerous expression.

'Yeah, that'll be it,' Max said under his breath.

'It's Max, isn't it?' said Richard, disrupting the tension with an extended hand.

'Yeah man, good to meet you,' Max said, switching the Jim Beam from one hand to the other to accept Richard's greeting. 'It's Dicky, right?'

'Richard,' he said, correcting Max before the old nickname took hold.

Richard had seen various photos of Max over the years, mostly attached to articles about the band. He'd always thought Max possessed an enviable, effortless rockstar swagger, the kind of striking features that turned heads, but there was a gauntness to his face now. He had the sweet smell of a man drinking to recover from the night before.

While Richard poured Sage a glass of wine, he watched her take in the strangeness of Caroline's apartment. It was modern and open-plan, towering over the city on the tenth floor of a sparkling new build, but Caroline had filled every inch of it with an incongruous mix of old hand-me-down furniture, stacks of battered second-hand books, and threadbare Turkish rugs that had clearly felt the weight of many pairs of feet over many decades.

'You grew up nearby, right?' Sage asked Caroline, accepting a glass of wine from Richard and taking it to the round séance-style table set for dinner.

'We did,' Caroline said. 'My parents lived on the other side of the canal, but we had to sell the house when they died.'

The mention of death lingered, as it so often does, and a brief silence settled over the group. No one knew what to say, no one knew what to do with themselves, without Daniel there to bring them all together.

'Have you heard from Daniel?' Max asked.

Caroline took a deep breath. 'We should sit down.'

Richard swallowed a mouthful of wine and braced himself as he took the seat next to Caroline.

'I've had some worrying news,' she said. 'I don't really know what to make of it.'

'Oh God,' said Sage, covering her face with her hands. 'What's happened?'

'Some of Daniel's things were found in a body of water, about fifteen miles from New Orleans,' Caroline said. Her hands were shaking, but her voice remained steady.

'What things?' Max asked. 'What did they find?'

'His passport and a shirt.'

'I don't understand,' Sage interrupted, bewildered. 'So, Daniel's in New Orleans?'

Caroline closed her eyes and inhaled, and then she spoke slowly, as though she were explaining something very simple to someone very stupid: 'We don't *know* if he's in New Orleans, Sage. That's the whole fucking problem. But there's more. The police said the shirt was like a cheesecloth cover-up, the kind a woman might wear to the beach. It was torn and covered in blood.'

'Jesus wept,' said Max, who had turned a strange porridge-grey colour, as though he were on the verge of passing out.

'Let's not panic,' Richard said, swallowing the urge to vomit. 'Have they run any tests? Do they know whose blood it is?'

'Not yet,' said Caroline. 'It could take a while, apparently, but I said it didn't sound like something Daniel would wear, so I don't think it can be his shirt – or his blood.'

'It's obviously not his shirt,' Sage said. 'That's something, at least? It obviously can't be his shirt.'

Richard couldn't decide which element of this surprised him more: the fact that Daniel had been traced to New Orleans, or that Caroline's original menu of charbroiled oysters, gumbo and bananas Foster was clearly inspired by the city. Typical Caroline: she had based an entire dinner party around a trip Daniel had taken without her.

'So, what happens next?' Richard asked. 'Forensics, that kind of thing?'

'They're going to dredge the surrounding swamp,' said Caroline. 'And see if they can find anything else.'

Sour saliva flooded Richard's mouth. He went to take a sip of wine, found his glass was empty. As he topped up their drinks, he paused. There were five wine glasses on the table.

'Are we expecting anyone else?' Richard asked, and then he felt the vertiginous plunge of a misstep. Of course – she had set a place for Daniel. They each turned to consider the last place at the table, a place set for the ghost at the feast.

'I've invited a psychic,' Caroline said. 'She spent some time with Daniel in New Orleans, and her name came up in the investigation. She's from London, so I asked her to join us.'

*

The psychic was in her mid-thirties, by Richard's estimation. Her heeled boots clicked on the hardwood floor as she followed Caroline to the dining table, eyes darting around the flat, taking in the parquet flooring, the trailing plants, the stained-glass feature window above the front door.

'I bought wine,' she said, in a surprisingly high-pitched voice, as she handed a bottle of cheap supermarket red to Caroline. She kept touching her hair, adjusting the neckline of her dress.

She's nervous, Richard thought.

'That's very kind of you,' Caroline said, eyeing the label.

It took the others a moment to recompose themselves as they absorbed the psychic's striking appearance: long turquoise hair, the roots covered with a wide-brimmed black hat, and a sweet face hidden beneath glamourous gothic make-up. She had large breasts, Richard couldn't help but notice, and a narrow waist accentuated by a black wrap-around dress that was belted just beneath her bust.

She blinked at them all, a rabbit caught in the headlights of their attention. Perhaps sensing her anxiety, Sage placed a hand on her arm. 'Thank you so much for coming – this must be pretty overwhelming.'

'I just hope I can help,' said the psychic. 'Or offer some comfort in these uncertain times.'

'Do you know what Daniel was doing in New Orleans?' Richard asked, although he looked to Caroline as he spoke.

'He was on holiday, same as me,' the psychic replied. 'I didn't think there was anything unusual about him at first. I mean, he was very striking, of course. Very charismatic, fun to be around.' Her voice cracked, and she coughed.

'Sorry – can I get you a drink, Selina?' Richard asked. 'We're just having some wine, or I could make you a cup of tea?'

'A glass of wine would be lovely, thank you.'

Richard fetched the bottle and poured her a glass of Châteauneuf-du-Pape. Given the chance to breathe, the heady aroma of the wine opened like a flower: he detected lichen growing on tree branches, chestnut mushrooms burrowed deep in the frigid winter earth, liquorice held in a paper bag, and rich, overripe blackberries on the brink of rot. It was an incredible, complex wine. He wished he could slip a bottle into his bag, take it home and truly appreciate it – and then he caught himself and felt a tremendous swell of grief. What did the wine matter, at a time like this?

'Caroline told us you're a psychic – is that right?' Sage asked.

'Yes,' the psychic said. 'I've been practising the tarot since I was a teenager.'

'That's incredible,' Sage replied. 'Do you get much work?'

'Enough to get by. I started selling readings online during the pandemic, and it grew from there.'

Sage reached for the psychic's hand and gave it a warm squeeze. 'We really are so grateful you could join us tonight,' she said.

'I just want to help,' said the psychic, 'in any way I can.'

'Did you bring your cards?' asked Sage. 'I'd love a reading – we all would, I'm sure.'

'Oh, absolutely,' said the psychic, digging into her handbag and withdrawing a fat deck of cards wrapped in a square of black silk. 'I often find the tarot helps me organise my thoughts – and you never know what it might bring up.'

Richard frowned. That didn't seem like a productive way to spend their evening – surely there were more pressing matters to discuss? He caught Max's eye, who curled his lip into a sneer as he raised his can for a swig. Caroline's attention was fixed on the psychic though, so he swallowed the desire to protest.

'Like what?' Caroline asked. 'What might it bring up? I genuinely can't imagine.'

'Oh … you know … memories, thoughts, feelings. The cards are almost like prompts for discussion – it's ultimately up to you to decide how to interpret each one, but I can help to guide you.'

'Are people receptive to this kind of thing?' Richard asked, attempting sincerity for the sake of propriety.

'Some are – but I get quite a lot of hate for it, actually,' the psychic said, with a small, self-deprecating smile. 'But I don't mind. I know it's not for everyone, and that's okay.'

The psychic's attention settled on Richard. 'Did you say your name was Richard? Are you the friend from university?'

Richard swallowed. 'Yes. Caroline, Daniel and I studied film together.'

'You too?' The psychic turned to Caroline, surprised. 'I thought you were a little older.'

'I took some time out,' Caroline explained. 'I had to take care of Daniel after we lost our parents. He was only sixteen.'

'And you went to the same university?'

'We've always been very close,' she said. 'We don't have anyone else. Just each other. Grief does that to you – it makes you hold on to things.'

*

In their first year, the siblings didn't seem particularly interested in getting to know their course mates, and the feeling was mostly mutual, although Richard couldn't help but think about the petal-pink rosebud of Caroline's mouth when his mind drifted during seminars, and he often found himself searching for a glimpse of her when he entered the lecture theatre for their three-hour class on world cinema.

Everything about her was a little bit different. Richard liked the way she dressed – in loose summer dresses and an oversized tweed blazer, like a farmer's daughter raised on fresh milk, apples and honey. He liked the way she smelled, too – clean and astringent, of washing powder and a punchy, almost masculine perfume that belonged uniquely to her. She seemed like a real adult. Mature, wise beyond her years. In comparison, Richard felt almost adolescent. He spent most of his first year following in the footsteps of many noble freshers before him: destroying his taste buds with cheap pints, bottles of Smirnoff Ice and various iterations of the 'student special' from the local takeaways that he ate with fumbling, drunken fingers, dropping ribbons of kebab meat and scatters of shredded cabbage as he stumbled home.

Caroline was more reserved than her brother. While Daniel savoured the limelight, she kept to herself and didn't seem to have any friends. She was serious and studious, and seldom spoke up in seminars, despite arriving to each session well prepared, with pages of annotations written in a controlled hand.

In lectures, she took careful notes, filling page after page with a neat cursive, while her brother often turned up late, fiddled with his phone, and never had a pen of his own.

Daniel swept around the Brutalist campus in a black overcoat with the collar turned up, surrounded by a never-ending parade of friends. Intriguingly, Richard occasionally spotted him deep in conversation over coffee or a bottle of red wine with their lecturer Benjamin Taylor, a tall, slender man with salt-and-pepper hair and an infectious enthusiasm for the big screen.

Richard didn't struggle to make friends, but they were friendships of convenience. He rubbed along well with his flatmates, a laddish group who mostly studied either Business or Sports Science, and he shared the occasional pint in the student union with a couple of the guys on his course, but considering they were film students, they weren't particularly interested in talking about cinema, and Richard didn't have much else in common with them. He often felt himself fade into the background in social situations, and knew that in five years' time, none of them would remember his name.

*

'So how did you end up becoming friends?' the psychic asked, placing a white plastic vape between her lips and inhaling a lungful of sweet smoke.

'I helped Daniel with an essay,' Richard replied.

'That's one way to put it,' Caroline said.

*

It was towards the end of their first year. The final essay was due, a 1500-word comparison piece on two films of their choosing from the syllabus. The library smelled of Red Bull and anxiety; it was busy with stressed students cramming for exams and desperately hunting for books that might unlock the secret to scoring a first. Richard wasn't the type to leave things to the last minute, but he was looking for any books that might mention either Claire Denis or Kathryn Bigelow to strengthen his arguments and add a little credence to his work.

'If you're looking for the *Oxford Guide to Film Studies*, I'll murder you for it,' a voice breathed into his ear.

He turned, and there was Daniel, dressed in black, with his curls pulled into a ponytail.

Richard gave him a perplexed smile. 'Well, no – of course not, that's the core text. We've been working from it all year. Don't you have a copy?'

Daniel rolled his eyes and offered a wan smile. 'I kept meaning to pick one up, but I never got round to it. Can I borrow yours? Just for an hour?'

Richard's copy of the *Oxford Guide to Film Studies* was fringed with sticky tabs, the margins thick with annotations. It was the blueprint for his growing understanding of the landscape of cinema, and he'd used it for every essay, every presentation, every seminar, since they'd arrived in Norwich. It was broken in like a favourite pair of boots, shaped over time to fit the specific way his brain worked. Lending it to Daniel would be like handing over the skeleton of his own essay.

'Go on, darling. I'll buy you a drink,' Daniel said, nudging him. 'It's only an hour, don't be so mean.'

Caroline appeared then, with a pair of takeaway coffees and a copy of *Lacan and Contemporary Film* under one arm. Ignoring Richard entirely, she muttered to her brother in a low voice: 'Well, I can see you haven't managed to find it.'

'No, but this handsome young man said I can borrow his,' Daniel said, wrapping an arm around Richard's shoulders. As a rich, musky smell of sweat and body spray rose from

Daniel's armpit, Richard glowed. No one had ever called him handsome before. He knew he wasn't unattractive, but his red hair and petite frame meant he was doomed to be compared to Rupert Grint or Ed Sheeran, which he simply loathed. He'd grown a beard specifically to distance himself from his baby-faced celebrity doppelgängers, but it seemed impossible to shake the association entirely.

'Sorry, darling,' Daniel said. 'What did you say your name was again?'

'Richard.'

'Dicky – my friend, my saviour, my hero. I owe you a drink.'

'Are you on our course?' Caroline asked, and the brief flutter of elation Richard felt at being addressed directly was quickly replaced by the crushing realisation that she had no idea who he was.

'Yeah,' Richard said. 'I think we're in the same seminar, too – Monday mornings?'

'The best seminar,' Daniel said. 'No one can be bothered to show up on a Monday morning, but who goes out on a Sunday night?'

'Like you'd know,' Caroline said. 'You're never there either.'

'Oh, I mean the seminars are a waste of time anyway,' Daniel said. 'Fuck the seminars. Come on, Dicky, let's find somewhere for us to sit.' He must have caught Richard's hesitation, because he recoiled slightly. 'Oh God, I'm so sorry – you obviously have better things to do than hang out with us. I can return the book to you later, if you like? I only need it for a couple of hours, tops.'

Richard checked the time on his phone. The essay was due at midday the following day, and it was already gone eight. As much as he wanted to be helpful, he couldn't risk letting the book out of his sight in case Daniel failed to return it. Richard suspected Daniel wasn't the most reliable of men.

'No, you're alright,' Richard said. 'Let's find somewhere to sit.'

'Well, take your coffee, then,' Caroline said, pushing the disposable cup into Daniel's hand. Richard thought that meant she wasn't going to stay, but, to his unspoken delight, she followed them through the library to a quiet corner in the creative writing department and unpacked a tote bag of books.

Richard studied the titles with keen interest. 'What are you writing about?'

'The role of the psychopath in twentieth-century cinema,' she said.

'What are your comparative texts?'

'*Silence of the Lambs* and *Psycho*.'

'Hitchcock or Van Sant?'

'Van Sant.'

'Huh,' he said. 'Rogue choice.'

She prickled. 'Well, we have to pick texts from the syllabus.'

'Yeah, but the original was a secondary text, so I think it's okay to write about it. You can't examine psychopathy in cinema and not discuss the Hitchcock original – that's wild.'

'Well, I've obviously referenced it,' she said, offended. 'I've *obviously* referenced Hitchcock.'

Richard shrugged off his rucksack and unpacked it, placing his laptop and notebook side by side. 'Obviously.'

'Why, what would you do? Just write about a primary and a secondary text and risk failing for not following the rules of the assignment?'

'Nah,' he said. 'I'd write to Benjamin and ask if it was okay.'

'Well, I can't change it now anyway,' she snapped. 'I've been working on this essay for weeks.'

'There's my darling,' Daniel said, ignoring them both and swooping in on Richard's copy of the course textbook.

'What films are you doing?' Richard asked him, relieved to step out of the bracing limelight of Caroline's attention.

'Oh, I don't know,' Daniel said breezily, flipping through the textbook without really paying attention to the words as they flicked past. 'What's on the syllabus again? What are the primary thingies?'

'I'm not telling you,' Caroline said, opening her laptop.

'She's being such a bitch about the whole thing,' Daniel said to Richard in a stage whisper. 'She knows my taste; I don't know why she can't just tell me what to write about. She wouldn't even lend me her textbook – her own *brother*.'

'But you've been to the screenings, haven't you?' Richard asked.

They had a lecture every Tuesday, followed by a screening of the film. Richard was confused – he usually spotted Daniel there with a coffee in hand.

'He bloody well sleeps through them all,' Caroline said. 'I told him I wasn't going to do his essay for him.'

'Oh, I think it's ridiculous,' Daniel said. 'We don't all need to sit there in the dark like a fucking pensioners' film club. I'd rather watch them in my own time with a glass of wine and a cigarette.'

'But you *don't* watch them in your own time,' Caroline said.

'Well, I'm not going to sit through them all twice, am I?'

'Just the once would do!'

'So – wait, you haven't watched *any* of the films?' Richard asked, amazed.

'Oh, you sound just like *her*,' Daniel said, cocking his head and jabbing a thumb in Caroline's direction. 'First year hardly matters. It's just pass or fail; the actual grades don't mean a thing.'

Caroline took a steadying breath. 'Well, if you pass, I'll buy the champagne. But I'm not spoon-feeding the entire syllabus to you the night before the final deadline. I have my own essay to worry about.'

'I don't need your spoons,' Daniel said triumphantly. 'I have *Dicky*.'

'You have Dicky's *textbook*,' Caroline corrected him. 'For an hour. And then you have to leave the poor boy alone.' She turned to Richard: 'Don't let him drag you down to his level. He'll pull you under to save himself.'

'She's so dramatic,' Daniel said with a fond smile. 'Don't you just love her?'

Caroline rolled her eyes and returned her attention to her laptop screen. After a few moments, she seemed to find her place and began to type. Richard followed suit, and soon he was lost in thought about the subtle beauty of *Beau Travail*.

After an hour or so, Caroline closed her computer and began to gather her books and notes. 'Right, that's me done.'

'You're *not* done,' Daniel said, leaning back in his seat to eye her with surprise. He had been sketching a pair of vampirine lips, complete with bloody, pointed fangs, in the margin of Richard's book.

'I'm *done*.'

'You can't be finished – I haven't even started.'

'Well, that's probably how I've managed to finish and you haven't,' she said, shrugging into her oversized blazer. It drooped at the shoulders, made her look like a little girl in her father's jacket. 'I'll see you back at the house. Nice to meet you, Dicky.'

'Bye,' Richard said, watching her glide through the library, books held against her chest.

'What a dumb slut,' Daniel said, tapping a biro against his cheek. 'How's yours going?'

'Nearly done,' Richard replied. 'I just have to write the conclusion and then cross-reference my sources.'

Daniel sighed, and tipped his chair so he was balancing on the back legs. 'Christ, do you smoke? I'm desperate.'

'I think I have some Marlboro Lights,' Richard said.

'Ugh. Fresh-air fags.'

'Suit yourself.'

'I didn't say *no*. Come on, let's go for a cig.'

The concrete campus was still relatively busy while the last of the day's sun clung to the horizon. Students were dotted on the amphitheatre-style steps, listening to music and waiting for their evenings to start in earnest. Disco lights flashed within the student union bar, some kind of celebration unfolding inside.

'I'd kill for a glass of red,' Daniel said, gazing towards the strobe as he accepted a cigarette from Richard's pack.

'You have an essay to finish,' Richard replied, stowing the pack in his pocket without taking one for himself.

'No, *you* have an essay to finish. I have an essay to start.' Daniel drew on the filter, and blew smoke into the breeze. 'Oh fuck it, shall we have a wine? Go on, just one. The library's open all night, isn't it?'

'The library closes in half an hour,' Richard corrected him. 'Summer hours.'

'Oh well, double-fuck it. I'm screwed anyway – we might as well.' He laughed. 'What are you writing about?'

'Masculinity and the male gaze in *Beau Travail* and *Point Break*,' Richard said.

'Sounds hot – what are they about?'

Richard sighed, and shifted his weight from one foot to the other. He didn't want to share his work with Daniel, but there didn't seem to be an elegant way of sidestepping the question.

'*Beau Travail* is about soldiers in the French Foreign Legion – one becomes irrationally obsessed with the other and tries to kill him.'

'Hot.'

'Well—'

'And *Point Break*?'

'It's about an undercover FBI agent who infiltrates a group of surfers suspected to be a criminal gang.'

'I'm going to be honest with you, darling, they don't sound like they have much in common,' Daniel said.

'I'm interested in the relationship between the male body and the camera,' Richard said, and he went on to explain the way the camera lingered on sweat, salt and sea spray on skin; the way the films explored themes of masculinity, toxicity and domesticity, and the relationships between men in all-male spaces.

Daniel listened with an intense expression on his face, and asked pertinent questions.

'But if they both have female directors, I don't see how the male gaze is relevant,' he said.

'Have you actually read Laura Mulvey's essay on the male gaze?'

'Of course not,' Daniel replied with a lackadaisical shrug, and Richard found himself laughing.

They talked as Daniel finished his cigarette, and when Daniel suggested they went to the library to collect their things, Richard followed. It didn't take much persuasion for him to rent both movies from the AV department, and Daniel bought two bottles of red wine from the Co-Op to take back to Richard's flat, where they watched the films back to back.

As the wine loosened the mood, Richard could feel Daniel slowly teasing the details of his essay out of him, but he found he didn't mind. What did it matter? It was too late for Daniel to do anything with his analysis, anyway. Plus, they were friends now, right? Friends shared wine and batted ideas between them, didn't they? And he was proud of his thesis: the idea that these films were stitched together by the relationship between the camera, the viewer and the place where a seam of fabric met the skin of a man's thigh. He wanted to share his pet theories, his thoughts on the balance between the masculine and the feminine, the roles men played, the masks they wore.

'Are you gay?' Daniel asked, reclining on the sofa.

'No,' Richard said. 'I just really love these films.'

'Shame,' Daniel replied with a smirk, and Richard couldn't help but feel flattered. The thought of being perceived as even marginally attractive by someone as charismatic as Daniel was thrilling.

Richard fell asleep in the early hours, wine-drunk with a head full of the crashing of waves and the crunch of salt beneath army-issued boots. He woke up late, and delivered his essay with a rushed conclusion that he suspected would cost him the first he felt his ideas deserved. He was right: when their grades came in, Benjamin had awarded his essay a 2:1.

Daniel got a first, and when Caroline bought him a case of Veuve Clicquot to celebrate, it was Richard he invited over to share the first bottle.

*

The psychic was shuffling her tarot cards, full attention on Richard. 'Did you mind that he chose to write about the same films?' she asked.

'Of course not. He didn't copy me or anything,' Richard said quickly, and he couldn't help but cringe at how defensive he must sound. 'I inspired him. I just happened to be writing about something that interested him, and then he did his own thing with it. It wasn't a carbon copy of my essay; it was totally different.'

Caroline snorted. 'Come on, Dicky.'

'Did you read his essay?' the psychic asked.

'Well, no – but ...'

'Did he read yours?'

Richard squirmed. 'I guess he read parts of it over the course of the evening.'

'So, he took the foundations of your work and built a new structure on top of it,' the psychic summarised, nodding thoughtfully.

'I wouldn't say that's quite what happened.'

'You're very loyal,' she said, and then her voice softened: 'Did you stay friends after university?'

'Sure,' Richard said, swallowing the sudden, shameful desire to cry. 'We meet up from time to time. Daniel's great. Fun to be around, smart. He isn't perfect – but no one's perfect, right?'

'What grade did you get overall for your degree?' the psychic asked.

'I graduated with a 2:1.'

'And Daniel?'

Richard paused.

'He was on track for a first,' Caroline answered.

'Interesting turn of phrase – did he not get a first in the end?'

'No, he dropped out,' she said. 'He could never see anything through.'

'He bounced between things,' Sage agreed. 'First, it was cinema. Then it was the band.'

'The band was different,' Max said. 'That wasn't his fault, it was just …' A pained expression crossed his face as he searched for the right words.

'A tragedy,' Sage said.

'Yeah.' Max nodded. 'A tragedy.'

'Why did Daniel drop out of university?' asked the psychic.

Richard shifted uncomfortably in his seat. He really didn't see the value of picking apart their past, but Caroline didn't seem to have a problem with the direction the conversation was taking.

'Well, technically,' he said, 'it was because of me.'

*

Richard didn't hear from Daniel over the summer, and by the time August gave way to September, he assumed he'd been forgotten by the siblings entirely. He moved into a house share with some guys from the bouldering society – a medical student and two mathematicians who worked long hours and had little time for fun outside of studying and climbing.

The first film studies lecture of the year was an introduction to classical Hollywood, again with Benjamin Taylor at the helm. Caroline was there when Richard arrived, sitting in the front row with a notebook and fountain pen on the desk in front of her. She fixed Richard with a cool, impassive gaze as he passed her by, but didn't return his awkward wave. There was no sign of Daniel until twenty minutes into the lecture, when the theatre doors burst open with dramatic effect. Coffee in hand, Daniel grinned as he took the seat next to his sister. Benjamin cocked an eyebrow at the late arrival but didn't break the flow of his speech.

Afterwards, Daniel was standing outside, smoking a cigarette. The campus was leaf-strewn with autumn's approach, but it was still warm and light at 5pm.

'Dicky darling, what did you think of the film?' he asked, as though no time had passed since their last encounter several months ago.

'I loved it,' Richard said. 'I've seen *Casablanca* before, but it was such a privilege to watch it on the big screen for the first time.'

'Oh absolutely,' said Daniel. 'I love old Hollywood. It's all so glamorous, isn't it? Oh look, here comes Caroline.'

'Hello Dicky,' Caroline said. She was holding that oversized tweed blazer over one arm, a burgundy leather satchel hanging from her slender shoulder. Her skin was peachy and looked petal-soft to touch. 'Shall we get a drink?'

'Thank fuck – I'm gasping,' Daniel said. 'My stomach thinks my throat's been cut.'

'Of all the lecture theatres in all the universities in all the world,' Benjamin said, coming out of the theatre and locking the door behind him. 'He walks into mine a mere twenty minutes late, with a takeaway coffee that's still steaming.'

Daniel caught Richard's eye and smirked. 'He thinks he's funny.'

'What did you think of *Casablanca*?' Benjamin asked, addressing the whole group. 'You've seen it before, right?'

Caroline and Richard both nodded but, to Benjamin's apparent amusement, Daniel shook his head.

'Well, of course *you* haven't seen it.' Benjamin laughed, pulling a pack of cigarettes from the breast pocket of his shirt and placing one between his lips. 'I've never known a film student to be so uncurious about cinema.'

'I'm not going to dignify that with an answer,' Daniel replied.

'We were thinking about going for a drink,' Caroline said. 'Would you like to join us?'

'Yeah, okay,' Benjamin said, then wrinkled his nose. 'Not the student union, though. Let's go into town.'

Richard followed them to a tiny bar called Christian's, tucked down a side street, a short walk across the city centre. They sat in the candlelit basement, from which they could pop out to a leafy little patio to smoke, and Benjamin ordered a bottle of wine for the table. Day turned to night as Caroline bought a second bottle, and the discussion meandered between film, literature and politics.

'Loved both your final essays, by the way,' Benjamin said, pointing first to Richard, and then to Daniel. 'Although I have to say, I was surprised to see the same pairing twice. What made you guys choose *Beau Travail* and *Point Break*? Did you work together?'

'I just loved the relationship between the camera, the viewer and the place where a seam of fabric meets the skin of a man's thigh,' Daniel said, and Benjamin laughed.

Richard bristled – hadn't those been his words? He opened his mouth, but the fight died on the tip of his tongue. He'd sound petty if he brought it up – and what did it matter? People subconsciously echoed one another all the time, especially people they admired. If anything, it was flattering.

Something shifted that night, though. Daniel said they should do it again some time, and when they said goodnight, Caroline – pretty and tipsy – stood on her tiptoes and gave Richard a kiss on the cheek. The whole evening contained a shade of glamour that he had never experienced before – red wine in a candlelit bar, a spirited discussion with fellow cinephiles – and he floated home. The place where Caroline's lips had touched his skin felt warm, anointed. Almost holy.

The following week, Benjamin suggested they migrate to Christian's after the screening, and the week after that, too, until it became something of a routine. A couple of third years started to join them, and then a PhD student. They were all exceptionally bright, with varying taste in film: Rahim was a Kubrick fanboy, while Bret had a penchant for Japanese and Korean cinema. Natalie was writing her thesis on Dogme 95, and Daniel mostly seemed to watch biopics of musicians and trashy films about the music industry. Caroline liked to say her passion was German expressionism and hyperrealism, but Richard soon learned she had a soft spot for psychological thrillers and horror.

'You should do the master's,' Rahim said to Richard one evening.

'I'd love to,' he replied. 'But I don't know how I'd afford it. My parents wanted me to study science or medicine, and they said if I wanted to waste my life on the arts, I'd have to pay my own way.'

'There's funding if you don't have the money,' Rahim said. 'It's competitive as fuck, like, but Benjamin will help you out with your application.'

Richard glanced across the table, and saw that Daniel was listening.

*

The psychic placed the shuffled tarot deck on the table. 'Who would like to go first?'

'Christ,' Max muttered, snapping the tab on a second can.

'Not your thing?' she said, with the patience of a woman who had perhaps found herself in this position more than once before.

'Not my thing,' Max confirmed. 'If I'd known this was the plan for tonight, I wouldn't have bothered showing up.'

'Hey,' said Sage, hurt.

'That's why I didn't tell you,' Caroline shot back. 'Because tonight isn't actually about you, Max.'

'You can be a casual observer,' the psychic said, turning her attention back to the table.

'Start with Richard,' Caroline said.

'Go on, Richard – it might help,' said Sage.

'I don't know; I think we should be focusing on Daniel right now,' Richard replied with well-practised diplomacy.

'We *are* focusing on Daniel,' Caroline replied.

'Let me show you how it works,' the psychic said. 'You're going to split the deck for me – just separate it into two piles, wherever feels natural – and focus on Daniel. Then I'm going to draw three cards. The first represents your past, the second represents your present, and the third represents your future. Does that sound good?'

Richard looked to Caroline for guidance.

'Go on, Dicky,' she said, eyes glittering with something close to malice. 'You never know what it might *bring up*.'

Resigned, Richard split the deck as instructed, and the psychic drew three cards and dealt them face down on the table in front of him. She turned the first card, and they all leaned in to look at the illustration.

'Ooh, the Ten of Swords,' she said. 'This is a dark one – painful endings, unforeseen betrayal, and old wounds running deep.'

Richard ran an anxious hand through his beard as he studied the card. A man lay prone, his back punctured with a thicket of ten swords.

'Does that resonate with you, darling?' the psychic continued. The word darling lingered for a moment, a shadow of Daniel looming over the table.

Max scoffed. 'He literally just told you Daniel plagiarised his work.'

Richard's mouth felt dry. He took a sip of wine. 'No,' he said. 'Not really. That's not what I said.'

'Aha, interesting,' the psychic continued. 'Well, you don't have to say, but it might be helpful to consider whether you see yourself as the *victim* of a betrayal, or the perpetrator.'

The psychic's eyes were a pale hazel, and they seemed to look straight into Richard's soul. She'd referred to him as *the friend from university*, hadn't she? He wondered why Daniel might have mentioned his name to her, and what – if anything – she knew about their shared history.

'Let's flip another,' she said, turning over the middle card. It showed a child handing another a bunch of flowers. 'The Six of Cups. This is a warm, romantic card. Full of love and nostalgia. It could mean you've met your soulmate, or that love is on the horizon. On the other hand, it could represent unrequited love, depending on what it's paired with. Are you single at the moment?'

'I am,' Richard said, the heat rising in his cheeks. 'Yeah.'

'Is there someone you're interested in, someone waiting in the wings?'

'No,' he said, avoiding Caroline's eye.

*

Richard's friendship with the siblings went from strength to strength over the course of their second year, and by their third year, they were inseparable. As well as hanging out with Benjamin's circle of students at Christian's, they spent their evenings at the Picturehouse, watching movies with miniature bottles of red wine smuggled in via Caroline's satchel, or at the siblings' place.

Caroline and Daniel lived close to campus, and Richard spent most of his free time there, drinking coffees between classes, or whiling away hungover afternoons watching DVDs while Daniel fiddled around on the bass, noodling through the same simple riffs for hours at a time. It wasn't unusual for Richard to crash on the sofa and wake up to the smell of Caroline's strange perfume as she brewed coffee. He grew accustomed to the sight of her bare legs as she padded around in a faded dress shirt, the fabric soft from so many tumbles in the washing machine, and made them buttered pasta or smashed avocado on toast – the only dishes in her repertoire, which Daniel complained about endlessly.

'It's just slime on toast. It's *vile*.'

'*You* cook something then,' Caroline said, biting into a slice of sourdough. 'I'm not your little Wendy Darling, here to see to your every need.'

'I can cook,' Richard said, which was a lie, but he always worried that his place at the table was temporary and he was keen to be helpful whenever he could. Before his next visit, he browsed the internet for recipes he thought Caroline might like, and the next time he came over, he stopped off at the supermarket for eggs, peppers, tinned tomatoes, paprika and a crusty baguette to make a richly spiced shakshuka.

'This is divine, Dicky,' Caroline said, mopping up sauce with a piece of bread. 'You're so talented. You could be a chef.'

Next time, he made a simple spaghetti bolognese, and then attempted a more experimental laksa. He learned how to make curries, soups, pastas and salads, and for a while, happiness was watching Caroline dip a clean spoon into whatever was bubbling on the stove.

As his career as a chef bloomed, he often thought back to those first experiments with flavour. Daniel cheerfully ate whatever was plated up for him, but Caroline seemed genuinely interested, and it became habit for her to send Richard photographs of unusual delicacies she'd seen in town and picked up with him in mind: fresh morels, fat anchovies in olive oil, misshapen heritage tomatoes. It could have remained that way for years to come – a comfortable, casual friendship, the occasional text out of the blue, with a photo of a particularly handsome cheese plate or a question about the best way to poach an egg – but sex ruined it, curdled the comfortable neutrality of their interactions.

It was late one night towards the end of their final year, and Caroline and Richard were sitting at the kitchen table, working on their theses. The pressure was on for Richard: he would use this essay in his master's application, and it would be the paper he'd submit for potential funding.

Caroline seemed unusually antsy; she kept checking her phone and tutting.

'Have you heard from Daniel?' she asked.

Richard was deep in thought, considering whether he needed to read *The Communist Manifesto* in full to reference it in an essay about Lukas Moodysson's *Together*, or if he could get away with skim-reading quotes online to get the gist.

'Hmm?'

'Has my waste-of-space brother been in touch?'

Richard checked his phone. To his surprise, it was nearly midnight. 'Nope, but I guess the Loft doesn't close until three.'

She sighed. Daniel often went out without Caroline and Richard. People liked him; they were drawn to his wit, his charm, his vampiric good looks. He was often asked on dates by a wide range of people, from shy girls to older men, and everything in between, and he always went for the thrill of it all, but he always came home. On Thursday nights, he went to the local gay club, and it wasn't unusual for him to roll in late, smelling of other men's sweat and stale vodka. Caroline hated nightclubs, but Richard joined him from time to time. The looming deadline had, however, killed any desire he had for a night out with Daniel.

'Oh, he isn't out-out,' Caroline said. 'He's with Benjamin tonight.'

'Without us?'

She shrugged. 'They hang out from time to time. It isn't a big deal.'

Richard knew this used to be the case, but he hadn't realised Benjamin and Daniel still saw each other socially outside of those evenings at Christian's. Not for the first time, he wondered if they were having an affair. Richard had asked about Daniel's relationship with Benjamin only once, and his answer hadn't suggested they were sleeping together.

'Oh.' Daniel had smirked. 'He just likes to surround himself with protégés. Haven't you noticed? I'm just another sweet idiot who makes him feel clever.'

'Maybe they went to a late-night screening at the Picturehouse,' Richard suggested.

Caroline rubbed her temples. 'Yeah, maybe.'

'You look stressed.'

'I feel stressed. He never says no to anything – one more drink, one more pub, one more line, and then the next thing you know, he's in A and E having his stomach pumped.'

'Has that happened before?'

She threw him a dark look. 'What do you think? Christ, I need a drink. Could you open a bottle, Dicky?'

Richard found a bottle of white in the fridge. He didn't know much about wine, but the label looked impressive.

'This one?'

'No, open the Veuve. Fuck it. I'd planned for us to drink it tonight, anyway.'

'The champagne? That's a pretty fancy drink of choice for a random Thursday.'

'Well, it *is* my birthday.'

'It's your birthday?'

'Is there an echo in here?'

Richard felt a flood of affection towards her. She was so modest, so reserved. They had spent the whole evening together, and she hadn't mentioned it once. He cracked the bottle of Veuve Clicquot with a celebratory pop and filled two glasses.

'I wish you'd said something earlier,' he said, a jovial scold. 'I could have baked you a cake. Or we could have gone to a restaurant or something.'

'Like a date?' she teased, although the warmth of her words didn't soften the hint of steel in her eyes.

'Like a birthday celebration,' he said quickly, cheeks burning with the heat of stepping into dangerous territory.

The champagne was delicious, familiar to him now after so many popped corks to celebrate the handing-in of essays and the end of so many terms. By the time the bottle was empty, they were both tipsy, and while Richard felt unsteady on his feet, there was a fearlessness in his heart. University was coming to an end soon, and their evenings together were numbered.

'Still no Daniel,' Caroline said, slamming her laptop closed. 'Fuck it, I'm going to bed.'

When she stood up to say goodnight with the customary kiss on the cheek, the bubbles made a bold man of Richard, and he turned his head to kiss her on the lips.

She paused in surprise, but then he felt her body relax into his arms. They kissed in earnest, their lips coming together with a tenderness that made Richard's head spin, and he felt as though he'd had more than half a bottle of chilled champagne to drink. When he ran an uncertain hand down the curve of her hip, she pressed herself against him.

'Can I …?' he asked, and in response she sucked her stomach in, and oh, how warm and how ready she felt as he dipped his fingers between her legs for the first and only time. Beneath that heady, astringent perfume, he could smell a musky, intimate aroma.

She slipped off her underwear and hitched herself on to the kitchen counter, light as a feather. She pulled him closer, tugged at his fly, and let him push into a rush of intimacy as he pulsed his hips, and God, she felt incredible as he groaned and moaned and ejaculated within thirty seconds of entering her.

'Sorry,' he gasped. 'Oh God, I'm so sorry, I'm so sorry.'

His penis wilted, and Caroline climbed down from the counter and adjusted her dress to cover herself.

'It's fine,' she said in a tight voice. 'Don't worry about it.' And then she scooped her knickers from the lino and disappeared into the bathroom. Richard quickly cleaned himself with a square of kitchen paper and fastened his jeans, crushed under the cacophonous rush of shame.

He wished he could turn back the clock and take his time, make her come first with his fingers, and then his mouth, let her experience the pleasure of his touch as much as she liked before he so much as touched his zip. Instead, like an inexperienced schoolboy, he'd grabbed and kneaded and orgasmed in an inelegant frenzy of desire. He hadn't even taken the time to reach for a condom.

The toilet flushed. He wondered if it was too late to rectify the situation – if she might say yes if he suggested they move up to her bedroom, where he could tease off her dress and worship each of her breasts in turn, feel the rolling hills of her hips and the ripeness of her rear in his hands; if he might summon another erection, and let her rock herself into a slow orgasm, while he gazed at the beauty of her body, looked in awe at the pinkness of her areolae.

But no – she came out of the bathroom a different person, fully dressed, the blush of her cheeks muted, the soft animal of her arousal all but gone.

'I'm on the pill, by the way,' she said, matter of fact. 'Sorry – I should have said. When did you last get checked?'

'Caroline,' he said, 'I—'

'No need to apologise,' she said. 'It's fine. And I haven't slept with anyone since my last test, so you don't need to worry about that, but I'd appreciate a message if your next test comes up with anything.'

He burned with unspoken longing. He wanted to say, *Caroline, I've wanted this for a very long time*. He wanted to say, *Caroline, I've wanted this since the first moment I saw you*. He wanted to say, *Caroline, I love you, I've always loved you, I love the very bones of you*.

Instead, he said, 'Okay.'

And that was it: the epitome of a lousy fuck, forgotten as quickly as it began.

*

Richard reached for the wine bottle, remembered he'd already emptied it into their glasses. Caroline was gazing at him across the table, an unreadable expression on her face. It was unlikely she was thinking of their brief union, he thought, and he felt pathetic, like a worm of a man, thinking of the past when what mattered was the present. What mattered now was Daniel.

'Okay,' the psychic said, shrugging her shoulders. 'Let's pull another card and figure it out from there.'

She turned the final card, and the Devil smiled up at them.

'Ooh,' Max said, raising his hands and wiggling his fingers. 'Spooky.'

'That doesn't look good,' Richard said, peering at the spread. A murdered man, unrequited love, the Devil.

'Well, that explains the Six of Cups,' the psychic said, tapping the cards with her fingertips. 'Unrequited love; a feeling you can't ignore. Does that resonate with you, darling?'

There it was again – that incongruous *darling*, an unsettling echo of Daniel.

'No, unrequited love doesn't *resonate* with me,' he said gruffly.

Sage had the decency to keep her face neutral, but Max smirked. *They must know*, he thought. Daniel, or even Caroline herself, must have told them. The shame of it was enough to make a man sweat.

'So, why did Daniel drop out?' asked the psychic.

*

Caroline had dismissed Richard that night, sent him away like a puppy that had soiled the carpet, and he was forced to walk home with nothing but his supreme humiliation for company. He kept relieving that awful moment, the realisation that he was a simmering pot on the point of boiling over, and it was too late to turn down the heat.

He didn't hear from either sibling the next day, or the day after. He sent Daniel a message that went unanswered. He found baby aubergines in the organic shop, but Caroline ignored the picture he sent. He saw them across campus a week later, and Daniel offered a distracted wave, but Caroline didn't cast her gaze in his direction. The invitations to the cinema dried up, and as class had finished for the year, there were no more shared lectures, no more seminars, no more trips to the library or to Christian's. Richard even bought the ingredients for pad Thai one evening, but when he arrived unannounced at their house, no one answered the door.

He finally encountered Daniel in the wild when he was walking home from a late-night screening of *Enter the Void* with the Film Society – the last screening of term, his last taste of being an undergrad. Daniel and Benjamin were walking down the steps of the Art Faculty, which played host to Benjamin's office. It was late for a tutorial, but as Richard picked up his pace to catch up with them, he realised Daniel was crying. It was so out of character, Richard stopped dead in his tracks to watch them from afar. Daniel wiped his eyes, his breath ragged and uneven. Benjamin was talking quietly, but the murmur of his voice carried on the quiet evening air.

'Come on now, none of that,' he was saying. 'I'll always think very highly of you.'

'Let me come back with you,' Daniel said, in a voice thick with sorrow. 'We can't leave it like this.'

'I don't think that's such a good idea,' Benjamin said gently, betraying no emotion. 'But don't worry about the essay; you know I'll take care of you.'

'I don't give a fuck about the essay, Ben.'

'Well, you should,' Benjamin replied sharply. 'Communism in Lukas Moodysson's *Together* is a brilliant choice for your thesis, but for pedagogical reasons I have to intervene. I'm going to be speaking to Richard about this, too – I've been telling you all year to stop working together, and now – unfortunately – too many essays have been too similar, and Frank has noticed. *I* know you're not plagiarising each other, but for pedagogical reasons I—'

'Stop saying *for pedagogical reasons,* for fuck's sake.'

Benjamin glanced over his shoulder then, and saw Richard standing stock-still beneath one of the many streetlights that illuminated the dark campus with pockets of light.

'Richard,' Benjamin said. Daniel turned on his heel to meet Richard's eye.

'I just came from the Gaspar Noé screening,' Richard explained.

'Oh – *Irreversible?*' said Benjamin, in a genial tone, as though comforting a crying student was nothing out of the ordinary, which Richard supposed it wasn't.

'*Enter the Void*,' Richard replied.

'Ah, psychedelic melodrama. Much better than *Irreversible*, in my opinion. Less controversial, too. Could you tell most of the dialogue was improvised?'

Richard shook his head, too stunned by the unfolding scene to speak.

'Mmm – but apparently, Gaspar Noé needed someone to translate the improvised dialogue for him on set. Doesn't sound like a terribly efficient way to write a script to me, but what do I know?'

Richard forced a laugh that sounded hollow.

'Come on, Dicky, let's go,' Daniel said, turning his back on Benjamin to take Richard's arm.

'See you soon,' Benjamin said, waving them on. 'I'm looking forward to reading your theses.'

'Daniel,' Richard said, struggling to keep up with his friend's long strides. 'What—?'

'Nothing,' Daniel snapped. 'Don't worry about it.'

At Daniel's request, they stopped at Bargain Booze for two bottles of red and twenty Marlboros, and to Richard's delight they headed back to the house, where the air smelled of Caroline's perfume, although she didn't seem to be home.

'She's on a date,' Daniel said. 'Can you believe it? Some awful philosophy student. I think she only said yes for something to do.'

Richard tried not to let the hurt show on his face, but he needn't have worried; Daniel was busy unwrapping the cellophane from the Marlboros, indifferent to his pain. He chain-smoked out the kitchen window while Richard picked a film to keep them company.

'Darling, no,' he said, turning from the window and seeing Richard opening a library copy of *His Girl Friday*. 'I'm in no mood for a screwball comedy. I can't take the plucky dialogue – it sets my teeth on edge. Can't we watch *Velvet Goldmine*?'

'I can't see that one,' Richard said, rummaging through the pile. '*Rio Bravo*?'

Daniel rolled his eyes, then proffered his cigarette. 'Take this, would you?'

'I don't smoke Reds,' Richard said, wrinkling his nose and fanning the acrid smell away from his face.

'I'm not asking you to *smoke* it, I'm asking you to *hold* it.'

Daniel disappeared upstairs and came back with a short stack of DVDs, which he dropped on to the sofa. He reclaimed his Marlboro, and Richard picked over his options.

'*Interview with the Vampire* ... *True Romance* ... *Heathers* ... these are all Christian Slater films,' Richard said, not without a hint of disappointment.

'The heart wants what it wants. Now be a good boy and pick one,' Daniel said, exhaling.

Richard crouched in front of the DVD player and busied himself with the task of switching one DVD for another, searching for the right box in which to tidy away *One Flew Over the Cuckoo's Nest*.

'Daniel,' he said. 'Can I ask you a question?'

'No.'

'Are you writing your thesis on *Together*?'

'Oh,' he said. 'That. Well, yes, if you must know.'

'Daniel?'

'Yes, dear?'

'Did you apply for the master's?'

'I did.'

'And did you get in?'

Richard had received a rejection. He'd folded the letter into quarters and put it straight into the recycling bin.

Daniel exhaled tusks of cigarette smoke from his nostrils. 'I did,' he replied.

'Oh,' said Richard. 'Right.'

'Caroline will shit a brick,' he said, flicking the dead cigarette out of the window, without a thought for who might pick it up. 'I daren't tell her. She's sick to death of Norwich.'

Richard swallowed the desire to cry. 'What does that have to do with anything?'

'Well, she'll want to stay here too,' Daniel said. 'We do everything together.'

'It's only a year, though,' Richard said, pressing play and taking his place on the sofa next to Daniel. 'She can manage without you for a year, surely?'

'Well, a year for the master's. At least three for the PhD.'

'You're going to apply for the PhD too?'

He shrugged. 'I might. I haven't decided yet. Fuck, I might not even bother with the master's. What's the point? I feel like I'm just killing time until death anyway.'

Richard felt winded. It was painful to think that something that had meant so much to him could mean so little to Daniel. He curled up on the sofa, and as Louis de Pointe du Lac recounted his death and subsequent rebirth as a vampire on the banks of the Mississippi, Richard drifted into an uneasy sleep.

When he woke up, the lights were low and the air was perfumed with a familiar punchy scent.

Caroline.

She and Daniel were deep in conversation, his head resting in her lap. They didn't notice that Richard had stirred, was blinking himself awake.

'Well, darling,' Caroline was saying, stroking Daniel's hair. 'It's the end of the year now. Just get your thesis rewritten, and then we can run away together. Where would you like to go?'

Richard felt a burning jealousy at the comfortable intimacy between them, at the conversation he'd missed.

'Paris,' Daniel said, voice syrupy with too much wine. 'I'd like to go to Paris and meet a beautiful French boy with brooding eyes. I'd like to ... smoke a cigarette in Père-Lachaise and ... drink espresso ... on the Champs Élysées. You'd come with me?'

'I'd follow you to hell, darling.'

'Or New Orleans,' he said. 'I want to sit in jazz bars and drink red wine with a beautiful woman that looks like Jayne Mansfield, and then find my own Lestat to turn me into a vampire.'

'Decide where you want to go, and I'll look at flights.'

'What about the master's?' Richard said.

'Oh look, Dicky's awake,' Daniel said thickly. 'Hello Dicky, darling. Splendid fucking evening, as always.'

'What do you mean?' Caroline asked, then she turned to Daniel. 'What does he mean? What master's?'

Daniel raised his hands in the air, a drunk's approximation of a shrug. 'I don't know what he's talking about,' he said.

'I should go,' Richard said, uneasy.

'Want me to call you cab?' Caroline asked, and Richard simply said yes.

*

'Our essays were flagged for plagiarism,' Richard said. 'There was a whole investigation, and the university found "undeniable similarities" between our work. *All* our work. They went right back to that first essay, the one about *Beau Travail* and *Point Break*.'

'Did you tell someone?' the psychic asked. 'Is that what the betrayal card means?'

'Of course I didn't tell anyone,' Richard said, cheeks aflame. 'This is the first time I've ever spoken about it.'

'But you still graduated,' the psychic said, with a frown.

'I had to redo my thesis over the summer, but yes. I still graduated. Daniel didn't, though – he just accepted defeat and left.'

'And Benjamin was sacked,' Caroline said. 'It was against university policy to sleep with students, and of course that all came out too.'

'Well – good,' Richard replied, folding his arms. 'He was using Daniel – it wasn't okay.'

With the speed of a striking viper, Caroline slapped her palm against the table, making them all jump. 'Daniel was using *him*. Ben *knew* he was riding on your coattails; he just didn't give a shit as long as it kept Daniel sweet.'

'Well, either way – I didn't tell anyone about the essay,' Richard insisted. '*Any* of the essays. I love Daniel; I'd never do anything to hurt him.'

'You told the university about him and Ben, though,' Caroline said. 'Come on, Dicky. We both know it was you.'

'I don't know what else I can say,' Richard said. He felt deflated, attacked. The heat of Caroline's anger came at him in waves, and there seemed to be nothing he could do but brace himself against it.

'When did you last see Daniel?' the psychic asked, her voice a gentle balm compared to the sting of Caroline's.

Richard cast his mind back. 'About a month ago,' he said. 'We saw *A Streetcar Named Desire* at the Prince Charles.'

'How did he seem?' Caroline asked.

'Fine,' Richard said, frowning. 'Normal. Apart from – well, I didn't think much of it at the time, but now I'm not so sure. We shared a bottle of wine, and he said he was sorry for the way things were between us. He said he wished we'd stayed in touch more, seen each other more often. I was touched, but I didn't think anything of it.' Richard swallowed, and then, in a small voice: 'But what if that was goodbye?'

'Don't be so ridiculous,' Caroline snapped. 'Of course it wasn't goodbye.'

'Don't,' Sage said quickly. 'Don't speak it into the universe.'

Max rolled his eyes. 'He was probably just a bit pissed, mate. Feeling sentimental.'

The psychic reached for Richard's hand, and he let her hold it for a few moments, appreciating the gesture. 'I think the cards are saying it's time for you to let go of the past,' she said softly. 'Learn to live with your regrets, but let go of the guilt. It doesn't suit you. You have a kind soul, a beautiful blue aura.'

'You can see my aura?' he asked, doubtful, but desperate for a slice of kindness to cut through the misery.

Max snorted, but the psychic pressed on. 'I can. It's the colour of a summer sky, the Mediterranean Sea. It shows you have depth, that you're a clear thinker. It really is quite beautiful.'

'Thank you,' Richard said, partly because he didn't know what else to say, but also because somehow, despite his scepticism, he was moved by her response. He couldn't help but like the idea of having a clear blue aura, even if it was nothing but a fantasy.

He'd never betrayed Daniel, but he still felt guilty. After the plagiarism scandal, he'd refused to help Daniel write a new dissertation, and after that, it was as though a wind of change had blown through their relationship. Daniel had never truly trusted Richard again, and their friendship had never recovered. The odd trip to the cinema, the occasional drink, was nothing compared to the way they'd been at university: spending most of their free time together, finishing each other's thoughts as easily as Daniel finished Richard's half-smoked cigarettes. Now, he felt as though he barely knew Daniel at all.

'If you'll excuse me,' Richard said. 'I need to check on the gumbo.'

The psychic looked surprised. 'You're making a gumbo?'

'I've never had it before,' Caroline said. 'It was Daniel's thirtieth birthday last Friday, and I had a whole dinner party planned. I was going to serve oysters, gumbo, Sazeracs … they're popular in New Orleans, aren't they? Sazeracs? You must have enjoyed a few on your trip?'

'Oh, absolutely,' said the psychic. 'It's the official city cocktail. I think I read that on a menu somewhere. In fact, I drank my first one with Daniel, the day we met.'

Caroline's eyes glittered. 'Tell us about that,' she said. 'How did you meet Daniel?'

New Orleans: Selina

The French House was a backpackers' hostel with an old soul, located about a mile as the crow flies from the grand hotels and boutique bed and breakfasts of the French Quarter. It was built on positive energy – I could feel it as soon as I laid eyes on it, the way I'd felt the close heat of a new climate when I'd stepped off the plane.

Planted in the middle of a residential block of mix-matched shotgun houses, the wooden sidings were painted the colour of lemon drizzle cake, complete with a frosted white trim around the window frames, shutters and porch. A trio of flags – a faded tricolour, the stars and stripes, and one I didn't recognise – a black flag with a gold fleur-de-lis – fluttered in the evening breeze, silhouetted against a pale lilac sky.

The cheesy scent of dope adulterated the evening air. I quickly spotted the source of the smell: a blond man sat on the wooden steps leading up to the porch, his long legs crossed at the ankle as he reclined to make the most of the fading sun. The tinny sound of reggae blared from his phone, and the soles of his bare feet were encrusted with dirt, which I quite liked. It showed he was connected to the earth, at one with the ground he walked on. As an empath, I could tell he was a good person, with a kind and gentle spirit.

He raised a lazy hand by way of greeting, revealing a crescent of sweat under the armpit of his pale grey T-shirt. 'Hey, you good? Need a hand?'

'It's cool,' I said, thumping my suitcase up the steps to the house. 'I've got it.'

His eyes were narrowed against the bitter smoke that curled from the tip of the joint between his lips. 'Nice accent – you're British?'

'I like to think I'm a citizen of the world,' I replied.

'That's beautiful, man – I love your vibe.' His attention drifted to the slice of stomach where my vest didn't quite meet the waistband of my shorts. 'Hey, courtyard later for a smoke? You in?'

'Yeah, maybe,' I said, giving him a final lingering glance as I pushed open the front door and made my way inside.

It smelled like incense, with a faint thread of garlic and onions, as though someone deep in the bowels of the house had just started dinner. I put my bag in front of a desk wedged at a diagonal beneath a darkly varnished staircase, the banister thick with knots of cheap plastic beads, all caked in grey dust.

'God fucking dammit, man.'

A young woman with an aura the colour of peaches appeared from the depths of the house and marched to the front door, where she stood silhouetted in the frame, hands on hips.

'Yo Gabe, I told you to quit smoking that shit out front – we have neighbours, you know.'

'It's out, man, it's out,' Gabe said, laughing and raising his hands in surrender.

'It's *rude*. I'm sick of telling y'all.' She turned and noticed me for the first time. Snapping into a customer-service cadence, she placed a palm on her heart: 'Oh my goodness, I'm so sorry, ma'am – I didn't see you there. You here to check in?'

She squeezed passed me to slip behind the desk. Her hair, plaited into braids as thick as pixie sticks, gave the sweet smell of jasmine shampoo.

'You're gorgeous,' I said, and she melted into a smile.

'Ah, you're too cute. This your first time in New Orleans?'

'Yes, but I've always felt like it might be my spiritual home.'

'Well, you sure aren't the first. D'you have a reservation with us, baby?'

She shuffled through sheaves of paperwork and unopened post, eventually unearthing an iPad smeared with fingerprints. Her nails – frosty-white talons studded with little pearlescent beads, like chips of icing from a wedding cake – clicked against the screen as she found my booking and entered my passport details into the system. The wall behind her was covered in a collage of postcards from all over the world: Tokyo, Niagara Falls, Oslo, Whitby. Some were brand new, while others were so faded their colours had paled to cyanotypes: impressions of landmarks in shades of seafoam and mint green.

'Okay, you're all set.' She handed me a plastic key card. 'I'm Kenna, but there's a whole bunch of us you'll get to know. Come on, let me show you where you're at.'

I followed her through a TV room, in which a dozy couple relaxed on a battered green sofa as a horror film played on a large flatscreen TV. A werewolf howled, fangs bloody, and the girl covered her face with her hands. The walls were papered with foreign currency, a bricolage of euros, sterling, yen and pesos, taped from floor to ceiling. There were coins, too, dark and tarnished, glued to the doorframes. The whole place felt like a scrapbook.

'There's somebody on reception twenty-four-seven, so if you ever need anything, any time, just come on by,' Kenna said, pushing open a fire door that led to a kitchen painted a cheerful saffron yellow and covered in strips of torn masking tape. On closer inspection, I realised each piece of tape held a Sharpied name and a string of numbers: *Carla (22) 01.07.22. Diego & Flaca (5) 9.28.18. Miguel (11) 04.17.23.*

She stopped at an industrial-sized fridge and tapped the door with her nails. 'No alcohol in here, okay? Just groceries – and make sure you label everything with your name, room number and departure date, otherwise it'll either get jacked or thrown in the trash.'

The screen door slapped against its frame as we descended rickety steps. The sun was low, the evening air warm and tender as a lover's breath. Beyond a covered decking area, which was crammed with mismatched furniture and an old, weather-worn piano, a courtyard garden was illuminated with golden market lights. A few travellers read paperbacks, wrote in journals and smoked cigarettes on a scattering of picnic benches. Within a ramshackle food truck, a chef listened to bounce as he stirred an industrial-sized pot, and a greenish concrete pond played host to a small alligator statue baring its blunt teeth. Several paths snaked off from the main courtyard, signposted with hand-painted signs and arrows: *dorms, private rooms, pool.*

'You need anything, I'll be at reception until ten, then Krish will be taking over. Krish or Nicky, I don't remember. Dinner is from whenever it's ready until whenever it sells out, and break-fast is served in the courtyard until one – cash only, though, 'kay?'

'Until one? That's amazing – I usually have to set an alarm to catch a hotel breakfast.'

Kenna threw back her head and shared an easy laugh with me. 'Yeah, well, this is New Orleans, baby. We're not gonna make you get up at the crack of ass for *anything*.'

Cool and clean, my room was a sanctuary. I'd splurged on a private rather than a dorm, so I could have my cake and eat it: the social benefits of a hostel, the luxury of my own space. The fading sunshine streamed through the window, warming the tiled floor and bedsheets that felt fresh off the line and smelled like summer. I draped myself over the bed and soon drifted into an uneasy sleep, where I dreamed of churches, incense and cloisters thick with ghosts.

*

I woke up several hours later, confused and disoriented, with a dry mouth and a headache. The room had grown dark around me. I could hear voices outside, though, and as I'd promised myself to make the most of every moment, I decided to change into fresh clothes and see if Gabe, the barefoot stoner, was out there. I was an excellent judge of character, and I'd sensed good energy coming off him like a rich, heady perfume. Maybe I could scab a drink or a smoke from one of my fellow travellers in exchange for a tarot-card reading to tide me over until I could find a supermarket and buy some supplies of my own.

I changed into a slinky black dress and boots, hooked silver earrings into my lobes and dabbed some barely-there make-up on to my face, which looked pale and jaded from the long flight.

The atmosphere in the courtyard was lively, full of hyped-up college kids on a weekend break mixing with the more laid-back, international crowd. The darkness was punctuated by candle-light, and the warm air was perfumed with blooming magnolias, melted citronella wax and marijuana. Exquisite.

A few people were chilling on the decking, reading or talking in quiet tones, and one girl was sitting at – but not playing – the piano, ivory keys yellow as smoker's teeth. Hand-painted signs were screwed to the walls behind her, offering abstract platitudes like **BE NICE OR LEAVE** and **NO DRINKS OR DRUNKS ON THE PIANO**.

Gabe was strumming a lazy tune on a battered-looking acoustic guitar, an unlit cigarette pinched between chapped lips. He caught my eye and nodded a stoic greeting. He was among a loose group hanging out on the picnic benches, smoking cigarettes, passing joints and sharing a few six-packs of beer, the tables littered with empty bottles and stray caps. The group were bohemian and relaxed-looking. Each voice spoke of a different city, a different country. I gathered from the variety of accents that they must have met here, in the hostel. I liked that, and decided this was the best place for me to be.

A laddish pair from New Zealand were having a heated debate over how they should spend the rest of their evening.

They both paused to watch my hips swing as I slipped between the benches to choose a seat near – but not too near – Gabe, then they resumed their conversation. One felt it was time to call it a night, while the other kept talking about a place called Frenchman – I wasn't sure if this was a bar or a club – to a young woman with long blonde hair who was carefully peeling the label from her beer bottle and pasting it into a journal.

'Best music in the city, girl, best music in the city, I swear.'

'I'm not going anywhere without my friends,' she said, writing the date next to the label in girlish bubble writing.

'Frenchman, girl, I'm telling you.'

'Nah, dude, forget it. We're maggoted already.'

I unwrapped my tarot cards, imagining I could ingratiate myself by doing ad hoc readings in return for a space at the table and a bottle or two of the beer they were all drinking – an unfamiliar brand called Abita.

The girl with the journal glanced up when I started to shuffle the cards. After a few seconds, she pointed and said, 'Hey, you any good?'

'I'm not bad,' I said. 'I'll do you a reading for a beer?'

'Oh, they aren't mine,' she said, pointing to the Kiwis. 'Those guys gave it to me.'

I wasn't picking up on the best energy from the lads, so I just shrugged. 'Okay, don't worry about the beer. Do you want a reading anyway?'

'Sure.'

'What would you like to know?'

She frowned. 'I thought you were just gonna tell me my future?'

'Nah, it isn't really like that. It's more conversational. Do you have a particular question? Or we could just do a three-card spread and take it from there?'

'Um,' she said.

'It's okay,' I said. 'I'll talk you through it.'

I neatened up the shuffled pack and offered it to her. 'Cut the deck for me, please, and focus on whatever's on your mind. It can be anything. No rules.'

'Like this?' She reached forward, picked up half the cards and set one pile next to the other. Her nails were manicured a shimmery lilac.

'You're a natural,' I said, peeling three cards from the remaining half-deck and placing them face down in front of her. 'So, the first card represents your past. Let's see what we have.'

I couldn't help but smile as I flipped the card. Easy. 'This is one of my favourite cards,' I gushed, and she leaned forward to study it, bringing with her the sweet smell of hairspray. 'The Eight of Wands. This is a fun call-to-adventure card.'

Someone snorted, interrupting our flow. I glanced up to see Gabe had stopped strumming, and instead was looking our way with an ugly sneer smeared across his face.

'Well, isn't that kind of obvious?' he said. I blinked at him for a shocked second, and he took my silence as a prompt to continue. He turned to his friends. 'We're in New Orleans – of course Jenna's past includes *a call to adventure*. That's true of literally every single person sitting here right now.'

My cheeks glowed with the humiliation of being negatively perceived.

'Hey man, guess what – I can tell the future too,' one of the Kiwis said, while Gabe lit his cigarette and laughed. 'Huge-ass beers in the French Quarter. Who's keen? Gabe? Amy? C'mon man, its Saturday night. Let's get fucked up.'

'We *are* fucked up, bro.'

A woman – Amy? – with a red wolf cut sucked on her vape. In a tight voice, she said: 'Leave her alone, she's not doing any harm.' As she exhaled, the space between us smelled like blue raspberry Slush Puppies, and this felt like a sign. When I was little, holidays were long weekends in family campsites that, if we were lucky, had a working Slush Puppie machine that would turn our spit swimming-pool blue and make our mouths taste like artificial raspberries. Luxury to me was a slushie machine and enough loose change to indulge. I remember telling my sister Katie this once, and she'd laughed and said, 'We must get you on to frozen daquiris. You'll lose your mind – you'll feel like you're on holiday every night of the week.'

I was on holiday now. I didn't have to put up with this shit.

I smiled at the girl with the journal as warmly as I could, given the curdling energy in the courtyard. 'Hey, listen: you cut the deck yourself. That's *why* I asked you to cut the deck – so the card you pull is *your* card. I didn't choose it for you, and I didn't twist the meaning, or trick you into picking a card that matched what little information I know about you. You can google the Eight of Wands if you like, and you'll see there's more than one way to interpret it – maybe a different interpretation will resonate with you even more? Who knows. That's the *real* magic of tarot.'

'Ahh! So you *just so happened* to get a card that says the only shit you know for sure about this chick? What an incredible coincidence!' Gabe jeered, and around him, some of the others laughed too. The expression on his face was shocking – an ugly, contemptuous smirk.

'The cards don't *say* anything,' I replied tartly. 'I just interpret them. Sure, if I think I know *how* a card might resonate with a particular person, I'll use that information as part of the reading. If we were at home, I wouldn't necessarily have read this card in the same way, but that doesn't mean anything. It's storytelling, not clairvoyance.'

'What a crock of shit,' he said, shaking his head.

'Look man, huge-ass beers,' said one of the Kiwis. 'Who's in?'

The others began to stir, finally convinced to continue the night elsewhere. They drained the dregs of their drinks and started to collect empty bottles. The girl – Jenna – picked up the Eight of Wands and made a move to slip it into her journal.

'Hey, sorry – you can't take that. The deck won't work if it's missing a card.'

'Oh, my bad.' She pushed the card towards me on the bench, then indicated to her half-drunk bottle of Abita, the label now flayed and pasted into her journal. 'Here. You can have the rest of this, if you like – I don't like beer anyway.'

The girl drifted towards the dormitories, and I watched the Kiwis, Gabe and Amy leave without me, a hollow feeling in my heart. I shuffled my cards for company instead.

'That Gabe guy sucks; don't even worry about it.'

I turned to see Kenna, the woman from reception. Her braids were hanging loose now, framing her face. She was distributing a fresh batch of citronella candles around the courtyard, lighting them with a taper and swaying to the thin bass that was leaking from somewhere deep within the main house.

'He's been driving me *crazy*. Arrogant, doesn't listen to a thing anyone else has to say, has an opinion on everything, always has to have the last word. You know the type.'

'Yeah, I certainly do. I didn't pick that energy up from him earlier though.'

'You didn't? *Girl*. He stinks of it. Just another entitled asshole.'

She'd circled the entire courtyard and was now placing her last candle on the table in front of me. She sparked the wick with her taper, and a lemony smell that reminded me of camping filled the air between us.

'You looked kinda bummed, though,' she said.

'It's nothing ... he just ruined my moment,' I said. 'I was chatting to that girl, and he just bulldozed the whole thing. And then they all left for the French Quarter without me.'

'Fuck that guy. Why didn't you go anyway?'

'Well, it's late. And they didn't invite me.'

'Ptsch,' she said, a gentle reprimand. 'You can't wait for an invitation around here; you have to be your own invitation.' She pointed to my cards. 'Hey, do me for a beer?'

Her eyes twinkled with the reflection of the dancing candle flames.

'I have a beer,' I said, raising Jenna's half-drunk bottle.

'And you're gonna stop at one? On your first night in New Orleans? Nah, hold up.'

She disappeared for a moment and returned with a six-pack of Purple Haze and twenty Camel Crushes.

'I never got into vaping,' she said, lighting a cigarette and taking a drag. 'I don't get why people are out here smoking cotton-candy this and cherry-cola that.'

'Same,' I said. 'I prefer tobacco. It feels more natural.'

She laughed, and tapped the table between us, nodding at the cards in my hands. 'Well, that's one way to put it.'

I shuffled the cards, and the soft ripple sounded like home. I placed the deck between us, and she expertly cut the stack without being prompted. With that, I flipped her first card.

Tomorrow will be a new day, I thought. *And whatever happens, I'll be my own invitation.*

*

I'd only been asleep for a couple of hours when a disturbance interrupted my peace. It was the cacophonous cries of a drunk. The voice was so close and so loud, I thought a man was in the room with me, standing over my bed. It took a few seconds for everything to come into focus, for me to realise I was in my hostel room and the disembodied voice was on the other side of the door, out in the courtyard.

'I'll tell your fortune, you motherfucking bitch.'

Disorientated, I reached for my phone, but my groping hand met nothing but cool cotton sheets. The light was thin, a blue dawn bleeding through the darkness.

He paused, and a wracking cough split the silence. It was Gabe, I was sure of it, although his voice was hoarse, his words smeared together with too much liquor. As my eyes grew accustomed to the dark, I saw his shadow looming on the other side of the curtains.

'I'll tell your motherfucking fortune.' My heart leapt as he slapped my bedroom window, making the glass rattle in its frame. 'But—' He took a deep breath and sang the next few words at the top of his lungs: *'I keep my visions to myself.'*

'Can you shut the fuck up, please?' Another voice, distant and thick with sleep, sliced through the night.

'Come to bed,' a girl whispered, her syrupy Californian accent ringing clear as a bell beneath Gabe's sloppy rendition of Fleetwood Mac's 'Dreams'. 'Come to bed, baby, come on.'

The pair banged around for a while, fussing with their key card as they struggled to get their door open. Just as my fear of the man's looming shadow began to fade, a series of distant animal grunts and gasps filled the void, the sound of bed springs bouncing under their combined weight.

An Italian broke the silence. 'Please, there are people trying to sleep.'

'Fuck you!'

'*Vaffanculo*! You are like – like *animals*.'

'Sorry man, we're sorry,' the girl called out, trying to keep the peace.

I covered my head with my pillow and tried not to cry.

*

A small queue of tourists wearing matching 'I ♡ Nashville' T-shirts stood around the front desk, waiting to be checked in by a hip-looking guy with dark stubble and wooden beads around his neck. A girl in a pink boob tube sat at the communal PC, looking at pictures of alligators and sipping a can of diet Mountain Dew.

When it was my turn, the man at the desk greeted me with a warm smile, as though we were old friends. 'Welcome to New Orleans. Can I get you checked in today?'

'Oh, I'm already checked in, but ... I was just wondering if it would be possible to switch rooms?' I asked, and then I burst into tears.

'Hey girl, don't cry!' he said, and he looked genuinely pained to see me so upset. 'What's up, has something happened? Are you okay?'

'I'm really sorry. It's nothing, I'm just exhausted ... I got woken up in the middle of the night, and ...'

'That's dorm life for you,' he said kindly, reaching over the desk to hand me a tissue. 'I can check to see if we have another free bed, but I have a feeling we're fully booked.'

'Oh no, I'm not in a dorm,' I said. 'I'm in a private room, but it leads off the courtyard and it's just ... so loud. I feel so exposed.'

He tapped the iPad screen, and a deep furrow appeared between his brows.

'I'm sorry, we're totally full – but hey, stop by after three and I can let you know if there's any cancellations? Although, I'll be real with you – all the private rooms lead off the courtyard, so you may as well stick it out. The dorms are pretty wild.'

*

Bad vibes clung to me like old cobwebs. I'd always found that. Energy tended to tangle in my hair, muddy my aura, dull my shine. I needed to cleanse the night away with a hot shower, shake off the negativity and practise a little gratitude.

My en suite was small and dingy, with no window of its own. A cheerful glass vase of condoms sat on the counter, and someone had drawn a crude map of the USA in Sharpie on the yolk-coloured wall. An 'X' was labelled with the words 'Welcome to the Deep South,' although the mark was placed somewhere near Corpus Christi, Texas.

The shower was clean, though, and while it only sprayed lukewarm water in thirty-second bursts, it performed alchemy on my mood. As I lathered my hair, I was scrubbing the night before from my soul, and by the time I'd towelled dry and put on some fresh clothes, my head felt clear, the day full of promise.

I ordered huevos rancheros from the food truck and fixed myself an instant coffee in the kitchen, stealing a little creamer from a bottle marked with an illegible name. Outside, Gabe had appeared, and was playing 'Redemption Song' on his phone, an unlit cigarette hanging cowboy-style from the corner of his mouth. He gave me a cool nod, as though nothing had transpired between us at all.

'Good night?' I asked, and he just cocked his head to one side and closed his eyes.

The Kiwi lads smoked in silence, one bent over a map on his phone, the other picking between his molars with a blunt finger. The woman with the red wolf cut sat alone at an empty bench, battling a hangover with her head resting in her arms. A chipped mug of coffee cooled on the bench in front of her, a rolling tide of steam rising on the chilly morning air. I wondered if she was the lucky girl who'd spent the night with Gabe. Perhaps he was giving her the cold shoulder too.

I mulled over the possibilities of the day while I ate my breakfast – a paper plate of steaming black beans, a fried egg and salsa piled on a soggy tortilla. The egg white was rubbery, and the overcooked yolk crumbled against the tines of my plastic fork. I spat a half-chewed mouthful into my hand, surreptitiously returned it to my plate and rinsed away the taste with a swig of lukewarm coffee.

I had a spread of flyers for local tour companies to pick through: guided ghost walks around the French Quarter to learn more of the city's dark past, and true-crime tours that focused on its ugly present. Vampires, voodoo, serial killers, cemeteries. Boat rides through the bayou to see the alligators, where Spanish moss hung like ghostly beards from the tree branches, the swamp water the colour of milky tea. While I had the hostel Wi-Fi at my disposal, I booked a tasseography reading at Deja Brew for the following day, and then I decided that my only priority was to escape the rancid energy of the courtyard and introduce myself to the city.

*

The streetcar shuddered its way down Canal Street, past derelict buildings daubed with graffiti, unremarkable shops, and mundane municipal buildings: a flat-roofed nail salon, an insurance broker's, an auto repair shop, a dinky Chinese restaurant, a hospital whose many windows reflected a sky thick with clouds.

The driver kept up a running commentary, hardly pausing for breath: 'I'm heading down to the river front, y'all, hold on tight. Bourbon Street? That's me. Café du Monde? That's me. Jackson Square? That's me.' Whenever the doors opened, she greeted anyone who dithered with a cheerful reprimand: 'You coming with me? Then let's keep it moving, let's keep it moving, let's go, let's go, let's go.'

The French Quarter was much further from the French House than I'd thought when I'd booked my room, but eventually the great oaks that lined the street gave way to towering palm trees, and I knew by way of the driver's bright chatter that we'd arrived at the very edge of the old town.

My first taste of Bourbon Street was both drab and garish, a cesspit of cheap indulgence and tacky excess. I had to swallow my disappointment: the streets that had known the feet of so many mystics, voodoo priestesses and spiritualists before me smelled like vomit and disinfectant, and the vibrant neon signs that made the place look so appealing in photographs were muted in the cold light of day.

It was still early, a little before noon, and everything of interest seemed to be quiet, apart from the occasional bar or brunch spot. A few people were milling around, looking at maps on their phones or sucking on paper straws pushed into oversized Styrofoam cups. It felt like arriving early to a dinner party, when the host was still setting the table, the candles unlit.

The pavements were wet and stank of a strong floral bleach. It was clean like a crime scene, aside from a milky, almost spermy liquor that collected in the deep cracks and potholes of the road, garnished with extinguished cigarettes, crushed to-go cups, and strings of cheap plastic beads. I couldn't study those pockets of stagnant fluid too closely without feeling nauseated, and I shuddered to think what could have happened the night before to necessitate such a scrub down the morning after.

Inside gaudy cocktail bars, great washing machine-like mixers stirred sticky slushies packed with e-numbers and laced with grain alcohol. Bored-looking bar reps hustled for punters in the street outside their clubs, shifting their weight from one foot to the other, staring into the middle distance, their eyes reflecting purple, green and gold from the abundant souvenir shops. A sign above one club made the sinister promise of 'barely legal' dancers within. *Barely legal*. What a repulsive phrase. What a repulsive desire. I swallowed an unwelcome thought: what a repulsive place.

My head ached from lack of sleep, so I dipped into a tiny diner with a Pride flag sticker in the window for a caffeine fix. It was populated by an eclectic crowd: a few bleary-eyed stragglers, perhaps still out from the night before, trying to force down sobering coffees; a surly college-aged girl with a shimmer of blonde hair milking a bottomless soda; and a found family of queer kids sharing a plate of pancakes, three forks digging into one syrupy stack. I recognised them from the hostel – one was Jenna, the girl with the journal, whose cards I'd read the night before. She looked younger by the light of day, and I felt oddly protective of her, glad she hadn't followed those men into the French Quarter. I tried to catch her eye, but she remained focused on the plate in front of her.

A server with the words 'pure love' tattooed on his knuckles poured me a filter coffee. Halfway through my first cup, I made eye contact with an Italian drag queen with a desolate aura: face painted for the gods, her make-up was cakey and dramatic, but her bloodshot eyes betrayed the evening's revelry. Over rapidly cooling eggs and a bottomless Diet Coke in a red plastic cup, she shredded her napkin and chewed her bottom lip as I shuffled the deck. Her face visibly paled when I offered her the cards to split, but she went ahead and pulled the Three of Cups.

'The community card,' I said, with a bright smile. It was a relief to deliver some good news to someone who looked like they needed a dose of hope. 'You have good people around you – but you need to keep them close.'

She relaxed, her shoulders loosening. 'Oh, baby – I was so certain it was going to be some *terrible* card, like the Death card or the Devil or something like that.'

'None of the cards are terrible,' I said, patting the deck fondly. 'But this is a particularly nice one to pull, I think.'

By the time I'd finished my coffee, I was in a better mood, and as I made my way further down the street, things began to change: the buildings were decorated with wrought-iron balconies, hanging plants, plastic skeletons, and banners in purple, green and gold. I kept seeing these colours together, and wondered if they represented the local football team. I made a mental note to ask Kenna when I got back to the hostel.

Bars of the old world soon replaced those of the new: cheap, pounding slushie shops gave way to oyster bars, seafood grills, jazz clubs and divey-looking pubs that were shadowy even in the midday sun. The air smelled like hot oil, Cajun spices, fresh pony shit, and rum, and I breathed it in and was thankful.

The tarot proved to be good company for the rest of the afternoon. A talking point, a bridge to connect me to the strangers I found myself sitting alongside. People in New Orleans were open to talk, interested in those around them, and keen for a free reading.

In Café du Monde, over cups of chicory-spiked coffee, I drew the Ten of Cups for an artist with a sketchbook in his lap and a patina of smudged paint on his clothes.

'This is a real gratitude card,' I said. 'I recommend you take a look at your life, and appreciate all you have right now, in this moment.'

'I was thinking of leaving my wife,' he said, distracted eyes drifting to my cleavage.

'Well,' I said. 'Don't do that.'

In a Vietnamese café, over a spicy lemongrass tofu bánh mì, I drew the Three of Wands for a girl on the next table. An untouched bowl of pho congealed in front of her, great coils of fragrant steam rising from the broth.

'Ahhh, this is such an interesting card,' I said. 'It can feel intimidating, because it's all about having a clear view of oncoming obstacles, but—'

'Is it good or bad?' she asked.

'Well, it's neither one nor the other. Every experience has both pos—'

She shrugged, and turned back to her pho, signalling the end of the exchange.

In a courtyard garden, the humid air warm and lush as a greenhouse, I drew the Nine of Pentacles for a mumsy-looking tourist from Omaha, Nebraska, over bright red Hurricanes in white plastic cups.

'Is that bad?' she asked, chewing on her thumbnail.

'It's a wonderful card,' I said. 'It's the card of abundance. It's a card that says you've worked hard for your money, so you should enjoy it. If there's an expensive purchase you've been putting off, it says *go for it*. Or, if that isn't quite right, maybe it's saying you should treat yourself while you're on holiday. Go for a really decadent meal, buy a luxury souvenir, or go on an expensive day trip.'

She turned to her husband with the air of a woman who'd made up her mind. 'Honey,' she said. 'We're booking the steamboat jazz brunch.'

Wherever I went, I kept seeing the same man, a striking man in a white cheesecloth shirt. Dark, shoulder-length curls, hollow cheeks and Scorpio energy. His aura was electric pink – independent, charming, fun-loving – and I felt inexplicably drawn to his vibe each time our paths crossed: I saw him at the Pharmacy Museum, staring with great interest at a case of small glass vials inscribed with the word *poison*, and again in a lapidary, fingering obsidian pendants. He caught my eye and I looked away; I caught his eye, and he looked away. He was prone to styling his cascade of hair with an absent hand, gathering it first to one side, then the other. I don't know why, but I felt embarrassed to keep seeing him, and I shrank away from the sight of him whenever I caught sight of those familiar curls from the corner of my eye.

*

On my way to Erin Rose, a man in a dirty black beanie blocked my path with an appreciative whistle. 'I love your shoes, girl, let me take a look at those shoes.'

Surprised by the unexpected interruption, I stopped in my tracks, and he made a show of studying my feet. They were just a pair of scuffed black boots, nothing special.

'Listen, I'm psychic, baby. I get these visions, and I got a vision right now. Bet I can tell you where you got them shoes.' He pointed to my feet. 'Bet I can name the state, the city and the exact *street* you got them shoes. I'm psychic, baby, it's a gift. But hey, listen – will you be honest with me like I'm being honest with you?'

'Um.'

He was speaking too quickly for my jet-lagged brain to process what he was saying, and I blinked as he smiled a lizard's smile, revealing a mouthful of toffee-coloured teeth.

'If I can tell you where you got them shoes – like the street, the city and the state you got them shoes – will you be honest and tell me if I'm right?'

'Sure,' I said. I'd ordered them online, so I didn't think it was likely he'd get that right if he was already thinking of a specific street in the US.

'How much d'you wanna bet? Ten bucks? Ten bucks and I'll tell you where you got them shoes?'

'I don't have ten bucks,' I said. That reminded me, I needed to find an ATM. Above us, the sky was a deep, thunderous grey, and the air smelled like a brewing storm. I'd need to be quick, before the weather broke.

'You have ten bucks,' he said. 'No one's coming to New Orleans without ten bucks in their pocket, and hey – if I'm wrong, I'll give you ten bucks more, and then you'll have twenty. How about it, baby? Do you feel lucky?'

Just then, a firm hand fastened itself around my arm and dragged me down the street. A cloud of expensive-smelling perfume engulfed me, and I turned to see my saviour: the striking man with the mane of dark curls.

'Christ, are you brand new?' he whispered as I let myself be whisked down Bourbon Street.

'Huh?'

Behind us, the would-be psychic was shouting a few outraged *Heys!* in protest, but he didn't seem invested in a pursuit.

'It's a *scam*, darling.'

We were already several paces away, but the stranger hadn't let go of my arm. His expression glittered with mischief.

'Well, yeah. I mean, I didn't think he was psychic,' I said, although I had been curious. 'I just wanted to know where he thought I'd bought them.'

'You have to listen to the way he's phrasing it: he didn't say he knew where you *bought* them, he said he knew where you *got* them. When you agree to play along, he'll tell you where you have them right now: "You got them on your feet, right here on Bourbon Street in New Orleans, Louisiana."'

His accent was English – southern, with a lick of private school – but he recited the scammer's line in a decent approximation of a New Orleanian accent.

'Ha,' I said. 'That's cute. But I don't see how it's a scam – it's just a silly bet. And I wouldn't have given him ten dollars – I literally don't have any cash on me.'

'Aha!' The stranger laughed, revealing perfectly straight white teeth and attractive dimples in his cheeks. 'It's misdirection, darling – a cheap trick to grab your attention. Once you're relaxed and laughing along at his clever little joke, he'll spray your boots with shoe polish and charge you twenty dollars to clean it off.'

'That's like asking for a penny, getting turned down, and asking for a pound instead.'

'Trust me, darling, you don't want to get involved in all that. I *saved* you – and you're welcome, by the way.'

I laughed. 'Thank you.'

'My pleasure.'

We'd reached the corner of Bourbon and Conti when he finally let go of my arm. A teasing smile was still fixed on his face, as though he expected me to say something more, and briefly, wildly, I wondered if *this* was all part of an elaborate scam, and he was about to ask for a reward for his trouble.

'Well,' I said, flustered. 'I'm heading to Erin Rose.' I'd been on my way to a place famous for its frozen Irish coffees, but in my confusion, I couldn't remember which street I was meant to turn down, so I just pointed vaguely down Bourbon.

'Ah, I'm heading this way,' he said, pointing towards Conti. 'Take care of yourself, darling. Unless …?' He grinned, and raked his curls away from his face with one hand. 'Unless you want to buy me a cocktail as a thank you for saving your sad little boots from death by shitty polish?'

'Yeah?'

'Well, it seems fate keeps bringing us together. Shall we succumb to her desires and let her have her way with us … Sorry, what was your name, darling?'

'Selina,' I replied.

'My new friend Selina,' he said. 'It's a pleasure to meet you. I'm Daniel.'

Daniel led me through the French Quarter, first past the tacky chains of Bourbon Street with their gargantuan slushie machines, tropical murals and sticky floors, and then past a lively karaoke joint, a tiny jazz bar, and the candlelit smuggler's inn. They all looked appealing to me in their own way, but Daniel took a right, and then a left, zig-zagging further and further away from the well-beaten path of 'I ♡ New Orleans' T-shirts and green plastic hand-grenade cups. The streets grew quieter, the crowds thinning to only the occasional passer-by. Drops of rain began to polka-dot the pavement, and I wondered if this stranger had a specific place in mind or if he was leading me to an isolated spot to – what, rob me? – when he seemed to find what he was looking for: an airy cocktail bar with bouquets of dried flowers hanging from the ceiling. The bottles behind a gleaming counter reflected the dancing honey of candlelight.

The menu was the wildest thing I'd ever seen. Alongside cocktails with esoteric names, there was a list of psychic services and a special page dedicated to custom-made vampire fangs.

'Well, here's trouble.' A handsome man in a pinstripe waistcoat gave Daniel's shoulder a light squeeze as he walked past our table. His short black hair was slicked back like Gomez Addams, his eyes ringed with black liner.

'The resident psychic,' Daniel said, cocking his head towards the stranger's retreating back. 'If you fancy getting your tea leaves read, just ask Patrick. He's the best – unless he tells you anything scandalous about me, in which case, he's a liar and you must disregard every word. Anyway, what would you like to drink, darling?'

'I actually have a tea-leaf reading booked for tomorrow,' I said, flipping through the menu. 'Not here, though; some place in the Quarter.'

The words blurred on the page, and I couldn't work out what any of the drinks were. *Corpse Reviver #2. Bloodiest Mary. Spiritous Hot Toddy.*

'I'll just have a – a beer.'

Daniel sighed, his whole body contributing to a display of outrage. 'Oh darling, come *on*. You can't sit there with a beer while I slam a whiskey cocktail. It's ... unchivalrous. What do you like, come on. Rum? Gin? What's your poison?'

'I really don't know,' I said, turning a page of the menu. 'At home, I usually drink prosecco.'

'Well, you're in New Orleans now,' Daniel chided. 'Let's commune with the spirits together.'

A server appeared in front of our table, and Daniel closed the menu and fixed him with a charming smile. 'Two Vampire Sazeracs please, darling. Thanks so much.'

'Excellent choice,' the server said, scribbling on his notepad and tucking the pen behind his ear. 'I always go for a Sazerac.'

'And I always trust the locals,' Daniel replied, a frisson of flirtation passing between them.

I watched the bartender work his magic, taking bottles from the shelves and tipping spirits and tinctures into two rocks glasses, then squeezing lemon peel over the surface of each drink with a flourish.

While we waited for our drinks, the weather finally broke. Rain lashed against the windows, bounced on the sidewalk, flooded the roads and formed puddles in the potholes. Tourists squealed and laughed, made a run for it as they battled with umbrellas, while street tarot readers hastily packed up their tables.

'Oh man, it's really coming down,' I said.

'I guess you're stuck with me,' Daniel replied, just as the server delivered our drinks. 'Cheers – to alligators and straight dudes. Two things I don't fuck with.'

We clinked glasses, and I took a tentative sip. It tasted like paint thinner, with a sweet sharpness as the rye flooded my tongue.

'Ugh, isn't that divine?'

'Yep,' I lied, failing to hold back a grimace. 'Divine.'

'Well, perhaps it's more of an acquired taste, but it'll grow on you.' He laughed. 'So anyway, tell me about you. What brings you to New Orleans, Selina? Work or pleasure?'

'Pure, unadulterated pleasure.'

He leaned forward and adopted a conspiratorial tone. 'Fabulous – I *love* pleasure. Tell me more.'

'Well, I guess I've always been drawn to New Orleans. I love the witchiness of it all. It feels like a place steeped in magic – like I said, I'm getting my tea leaves read tomorrow at this little place called Deja Brew, and I'm thinking of booking a ghost walk around the French Quarter. I just want to make the most of every single second, you know?'

'Oh, I know. I love this city. I love everything it has to offer. The food, the music, the nature, the art – *everything*. But don't book a ghost walk. They're a total rip-off, and the guides lie through their teeth. I'll be your guide, if you like. How long are you in town for?'

'Just two weeks,' I said.

'Delightful. And you're travelling alone?'

I nodded.

'Me too,' he said, raising his glass. 'I'll cheers to that.'

We clinked again, then sipped our drinks, letting the whiskey warm our blood. Daniel swept his hair from one shoulder to the other, and I admired his profile: a fine, straight nose; a full, biteable bottom lip.

'Hey, can I ask you a question?' I asked.

'Anything – and make it as personal as you like. I'm an open book.'

'Are you a Scorpio, by any chance?'

He threw back his head and laughed. 'Ahh, I should have known you were *that* girl.'

'What girl?'

'Oh, you know – *that* girl. That horoscope-reading, crystal-healing, tarot card-dealing, incense-burning girl. No – don't be embarrassed, I think it's wonderful. I *love* that girl. My best friend in the world is that girl.' He leaned forward and raised an eyebrow. 'And I'm a Gemini, for my sins, but don't you *dare* judge me for it.'

'I'd never judge a Gemini!'

'Sure, half your best friends are Geminis, right? Well, you're in the minority there, darling. Everyone hates us for being two-faced little cunts, and they're not wrong.'

'I *love* Geminis,' I said, digging into my bag for my tarot cards. 'And you're right – I'm *so* that girl. I've been doing card pulls for people around the Quarter all afternoon. Do you want one?'

'Oh, go on then,' he said. 'Do your worst.'

I placed the shuffled cards on the table between us. 'Split the deck for me, then.'

He cut the deck roughly three-quarters of the way down. I flipped the exposed card to reveal his pull, and he slapped a hand on the table. 'I knew it. I fucking *knew* it.'

Death. A skeletal knight on a pale horse, a black flag clasped in his bony grasp. At the horse's hooves, the corpse of a king lay prone, his crown toppled. A gilded bishop and children in flower crowns prayed side by side, all equal in Death's gloomy shadow. It was a solemn card, granted, but in the distance the sun was rising – a new day on the horizon.

'It's more about a fresh start—' I began, but a sudden cacophony of loud electronic beeps echoed through the room, and everyone picked up their phones in unison. 'What the fuck was that?'

I reached into my handbag to find mine. On the screen, a notification glowed.

> **Emergency Alert!**
>
> National Weather Service Alert: A FLASH FLOOD WARNING is in effect for this area until 10pm CST. This is a dangerous and life-threatening situation. Do not attempt to travel unless you are fleeing an area subject to flooding or under evacuation order.

I turned the screen towards Daniel, and he smiled serenely as he swallowed the last of his drink. 'I guess we should order another.'

Postapocalyptic images from Hurricane Katrina rolled through my mind: surging waters and broken levees; people wading through flooded streets; stranded New Orleanians painting pleas for help on the rooftops of their submerged homes.

'But – are we safe?'

'It's fine,' he said. 'Look – let's ask Patrick. Patrick, darling, can I borrow you?'

The resident psychic glided towards us and placed a hand on Daniel's shoulder. 'You rang, dear?'

'Did you just get an emergency alert?'

'Sure did. Welcome to New Orleans, honey. Y'all should get another round.'

'No, it's okay, I still have loads,' I said quickly. The barman seemed to be occupied: he was carrying a thick-bristled broom across the bar to brush a rising seam of rainwater away from the front door. The psychic smirked and made his way to the door, where he stood for a moment to admire the rainfall.

'Anyway,' said Daniel, tapping his fingers on the tarot card between us to get my attention. 'The fucking Death card. Trust me to get the fucking Death card on my first go.'

'Daniel, I'm really worried,' I said, biting my thumbnail. 'Are you sure we're safe? That alert ... I've never seen anything like it.'

'Trust me,' he said. 'It's just the way things are. The storm will pass – the alert is more for people driving, or close to the water. We'll be fine here. Now come on, tell me my fortune.'

I exhaled and refocused my energy on the card between us. 'Okay, no need to panic,' I said. 'It's so misunderstood, but I actually think the Death card is an exciting card to pull. It can mean loads of cool things – like a transformation, or a fresh start, or the end of something significant – not necessarily death.'

'Hm.' He narrowed his feline eyes into a studious squint. '*Can* it mean death, though?'

'I suppose it could,' I said, choosing my words carefully. 'In that it can mean a sudden change.'

'Like death?'

'Well, death isn't always sudden,' I said quietly, thinking of my grandmother. Six weeks in hospice, the light slowly fading from her eyes.

'No, but even if you can see it coming, it's still an immediate change,' he said, a distracted expression on his face, as though he might be remembering someone in particular too.

'Either way, it isn't predictive,' I said quickly. 'Tarot guides us through our choices, through the highs and lows of life, but it's not a torch lighting up the whole way. It's more like a candle keeping us safe, giving us a little clarity about our immediate surroundings.'

'I like that,' he said, draining the melted ice in his glass. 'A candle keeping us safe. I like that a lot. Shall we have another? On me?'

'Oh, no.' I waved my hands in protest. 'Don't worry, you don't have to do that. I'm fine.'

'Well, what else are we going to? We're trapped, remember?' He flashed that devil-may-care grin. 'Besides, I feel like I owe you one,' he said, digging into the pocket of his black jeans and extracting a few crumpled dollar bills. 'I've spent a whole day wandering around town with no one to talk to but myself, and I'm absolutely terrible company. Consider it payment – you're saving me from myself. And for the card reading, of course.'

When Daniel caught our server's eye, he held up his empty glass, tapped it lightly with one finger, and then flicked a peace sign to ask for two more. The server nodded, and the bartender got straight to work. The exchange was so fluid, I couldn't help but admire it.

'Do you believe in fate?' he asked, after a thoughtful pause.

'Absolutely,' I said. 'Do you?'

'I think so,' he said. 'And I think it was fate we met one another today. I kept seeing you all over the French Quarter, and I think the universe was bringing us together for a reason. Unless you were following me, of course.'

'I wasn't following you – I was just doing my own thing.'

'Where were you going when I saved you from the street scam?'

I paused to think. 'Let's see ... Oh, I was going for a frozen Irish coffee.'

He clapped his hands together in triumph. 'Aha! Erin Rose?'

'Yes! Do you know it?'

'I do,' he said, growing animated. 'It's the little Irish dive bar on Conti, right? With all the metal signs pinned to the ceiling?'

'Yes, that's the one.'

'Well, guess where I was going?'

My heart leapt, and a wave of goosebumps prickled my arms. 'No, you weren't.'

'See? We were destined to meet today.'

Just then, our server placed two more Vampire Sazeracs in front of us. 'To us, and to fate,' Daniel said, raising his glass.

'To us, and to fate,' I replied, raising mine in tandem. The whiskey was loosening my mood, lighting a fire in my belly.

'Laissez les bon temps rouler,' he said, and then, catching my blank expression, he clarified: 'That means, *let the good times roll.*'

'Let the good times roll,' I said, glowing with the pleasure of it all. A cold cocktail, a handsome new friend, and the French Quarter opening up before me like a freshly shucked oyster.

As night crept across the Quarter, the bar filled with an influx of women, all laughing and talking quickly, full of high spirits. I noticed the same motif on many of their T-shirts – a blood spatter and the words 'The Murder Girls'. I wondered if a concert had just finished.

Daniel was easy, fun company. We switched from cocktails to beers and ordered a plate of garlic chicken wings that we picked apart with our fingers. We meandered between small talk – where are you from, what do you do for work, how do you spend your free time – and those wonderfully deep, excavating conversations about the big things: love, art, gratitude, death.

'Darling, I have a question for you,' Daniel said, lips shining with beer and chicken grease. 'You seemed to have a little speech prepared when I pulled the Death card. Are many people frightened of it?'

'Yes,' I conceded. 'I think it's quite an unsettling card to pull.'

'Why do you think people are so scared of the Death card?'

I took a long swallow of a raspberry-flavoured Abita while I pondered the question. 'Well, why are people so frightened of death?' I countered.

'I'm not frightened of death,' he replied, patting the breast pocket of his shirt, where he kept a white plastic vape that he sucked on surreptitiously whenever he thought no one was looking.

'Everyone's a little frightened of death,' I said. 'It's the ultimate unknown, right? And that's what fear always comes down to – the uncontrollable, the unfathomable, the unknowable.'

He nodded, in a reflective mood. 'Have you ever lost anyone?' he asked, softly now, voice laced with intimacy.

'I have,' I said. 'In fact, I'm only sitting in this bar, in this city, in this country, because of a recent loss. My grandmother passed away last year, and I inherited a little money.'

*

My mother had called at 6am, the ceiling a washed-out shade of grey. I was lying on my back, thinking about work, and money, and loneliness, letting a pool of sadness settle into the hollow of my heart.

'Nanna's gone, love,' my mother said. 'It's over. She's gone.'

Grief brought synchronicity: after Nanna died, she was everywhere for a while. Late at night, I'd drift to the kitchen for tea or toast, something warm and comforting to hold me while sleep was elusive, and each time, I'd notice the digital clock on the oven was showing me an angel number: 12:12, 01:01, 02:02, and so on. I'd see her, too: in dramatic, pink-streaked stratus sunsets; in the glittering early morning frost; in spiderwebs, gilded with pearly raindrops, stretched between the bare branches of winter-barren trees. I know how that sounds, but I'd feel her in these moments, as though she'd just said my name and I'd turned, expecting to see her.

It was comforting, but it troubled me too. I wondered if she was struggling to let go. Was she at peace, or were these signs that her spirit was restless? I felt untethered for a while, increasingly disconnected from my body, my mind and my psychic gift. My menstrual cycle became unpredictable, my dreams unnerving. My pendulum stopped working, and I experienced a new-found difficulty in deciphering the tarot. Patterns and combinations didn't make sense, and I struggled to interpret the meaning of the cards, as though a sudden mist had rolled through the landscape of my mind, obscuring what was once a clear view.

After considerable research, I found a simple ritual that would encourage her spirit to pass on to the next realm, but I couldn't do it. I couldn't ask her to let go, because the thought of never feeling her presence again summoned a pain I wasn't sure I'd ever be ready to face. Guilt chewed me up, because I was holding on to her soul like a tiny child on her first day of school, clinging to her mother's skirt and preventing her from leaving me in the classroom.

Time is the ultimate caster of spells, though, and the greatest source of magic. By the time a year and a day had passed, I realised Nanna was no longer with me. She had managed to slip from the room unnoticed, when she knew I was busy, focused on the present, and ready to carry on without her.

Nanna didn't have much to her name. She was neither a big earner nor a big spender, and she didn't own expensive jewellery, designer clothes or valuable antiques. All she had were some shares in a little tea shop that she'd bought in the fifties, when she was a young woman with a little money going spare. That's how she referred to it – 'her little tea shop' – and so we were surprised to learn she'd actually put a small amount of money into the very first branch of what later became a popular high street chain selling luxury tea, coffee and hot chocolate. By the time she died, there was a branch in every town in the country. The value of the shares was enough to cover the funeral costs, and my mother split the remainder three ways, between herself, my sister and me. Katie bought a new guitar, a beautiful Fender on which she took great pains to learn how to fingerpick 'Spanish Caravan' by The Doors and strum acoustic renditions of 'Come as You Are' to impress girls at parties. She didn't need such an expensive instrument, but she loved it deeply, and took great care to keep it clean and in tune, learning how to replace broken strings and treat the wood with the keen affection of a new parent learning how to care for her first child.

Craving stability, I'd been trying to save for a meagre deposit on a flat of my own, but the few thousand pounds I'd managed to scrape together were a drop in the ocean in the face of a housing crisis, a cost-of-living crisis, an energy crisis, an everything crisis. Ten grand was more money than I'd ever had, but it wasn't much towards a flat. I prided myself on valuing experiences over things, personal growth over personal wealth, the metaphysical over the material. Wasn't owning property the ultimate material aspiration? Wouldn't a trip to New Orleans be so much more spiritually fulfilling?

*

I blinked, returning to the present. 'So that's why I'm here, I guess – to experience a big fat slice of life. But what about you? Have you ever lost anyone?'

'Oh, darling. Both my parents are gone,' he said, in a crisp, matter-of-face voice.

The story was heartbreaking, but he told it with a stoicism that I admired. Daniel had lost both parents by the age of sixteen. His mother died swimming on a Cornish beach – a riptide had taken her, exhausted her before the lifeguards realised anything was wrong – and his father had died soon after of a broken heart.

'Well, I think his death certificate said "cardiac arrest", but we all know what that means,' Daniel said. 'They were each other's worlds; he couldn't go on without her.'

'What were your parents like?'

'This is the shitty thing,' he said. 'I only remember them through the perspective of a teenager. I know my mother liked to wear kaftans and smoke marijuana. She loved to throw parties and stay up late. The most soothing sound to me is the sound of a party winding down in another room – it was the sound I fell asleep to most nights as a child. My father was a lawyer – he worked himself to death. But my mother was the centre of his universe. He adored her – she was so glamorous. I think she drove him quite mad, really, but that's love for you. It drives people insane.'

'Do you have any siblings?'

He nodded, face clouded with thought. 'Caroline. She's two years older than me, so she was eighteen when we lost our parents. She took care of us both,' he said. 'For a while, anyway. She's … a difficult woman to love, struggles with demons of her own.'

I tried to push for more information, but whatever reserves had inspired him to open up had run dry, and he delicately ended the conversation as swiftly as it began: 'All I can say is, if I found out a friend of mine had been alone in a room with Caroline for an extended period of time, I'd insist they send me their therapy bill afterwards.'

'That's awful,' I said, words steeped in the reverence of such a tremendous, unthinkable grief. 'I'm so sorry for your loss.'

'We were very young,' Daniel said, taking a quick glance around the bar and then stealing a clandestine pull on his vape. 'That's not all, though. I once saw a little boy die,' he said, his eyes dark. 'I was ten. He was only small, maybe six or seven.'

'Oh Daniel, that's terrible. Your poor heart.' I reached across the table, perhaps for his hand, or perhaps just to bridge the gap between us, but he was lost in his recollections and didn't acknowledge the gesture. 'I'm so sorry.'

'He drowned, too,' he said, voice a tremolo of sorrow.

I tried to swallow the lump in my throat. 'I can't imagine how traumatic that must have been. What happened, if you don't mind me asking?'

He took a small sip of his beer. 'He had this little blue bike – he was riding home along the canal near our house and lost control. My sister and I both saw it happen. The water wasn't even that deep, but it was winter, and cold – bitterly, bitterly cold. My father said it was probably the shock of the water temperature – it would have triggered something called a gasp response, which is when you take a deep involuntary breath when submerged in freezing cold water. His little lungs—' He paused, briefly lost in the memory, then continued. 'He was so small, and we didn't know what to do, we didn't know CPR. I was only ten, and Caroline was twelve. God, I'll never forget the way it felt to see his little blue bike being hauled out of the water.' His eyes were glassy and fixed on the candle flame. 'I think it changed us both forever. My sister was never the same after that. And nor was I.'

It was such a moving image, so lonely and so desolate, that my eyes pricked with tears. I used the sleeve of my dress to subtly blot away the sadness, but then I gave myself away with an involuntary sniff.

'Oh no, darling, I'm so sorry,' he said, full of regret. 'I've made you sad.'

'Sorry, I said, wiping my eyes properly. 'This is so embarrassing. Ignore me, I've had too much to drink. It's just – oh, it's just so sad. That poor child, his poor parents. And you – what a shocking thing to see. So traumatising, and at such a young age. I'm so desperately sorry.'

He leaned back in his chair and took a long draught of beer, and I wondered if he was breaking eye contact to disengage from the emotional intimacy of the moment. Self-conscious, I followed suit and drained my drink to pull myself together.

'I need to use the bathroom,' he said. 'And then I'm getting us another round and we're going to shake off this awful, macabre energy. Deal?'

I smiled. 'Deal.'

*

Outside, I smoked a cigarette and watched the rain fall. Across the street, a woman in an American flag vest sheltered beneath a gallery balcony, gazing down the road as though waiting for a bus. When I returned to my seat, curiosity got the better of me, and when I caught the eye of a young woman in a 'Murder Girls' T-shirt, I beckoned her over.

'Hey, are you having a fun night?' I asked.

Her hair had been fried to the colour of cheap vanilla ice cream, and beneath an amethyst-coloured hairband, her roots were long and dark. She was clutching a glass bottle of Mike's Hard Lemonade in Wild Berry flavour, and a smell of ripe, rotten blackberries carried on her breath.

'Can I have a fag?' she said in an East London accent, pointing to the carton of cigarettes on the table next to me. There was something strange about her demeanour – a distracted, glassy look, as though she'd once witnessed something terrible.

'Go for it,' I said. 'How was the gig?'

'It wasn't a gig,' she said, sliding a cigarette from the box. 'It was a podcast recording.'

'Oh, that's cool,' I said, handing her my lighter. 'What kind of podcast?'

'True crime,' she said.

'Oh, wow. So do they talk about like, historical cases or—'

'They discussed a recent cold case.'

'Oh yeah?'

'A young woman in Margate was found strangled to death in her home, but the investigation was bungled because multiple witnesses thought they saw her walking along the beachfront that evening, so no one reported her missing. But it wasn't her on the beach; it was another woman with a similar look who just happened to be there that afternoon.'

'God, that's awful. I think I remember that, though. She was a writer, right?'

'She was.'

'And did they ever find the woman on the beach?' I asked.

'No one ever thought to look for her,' the stranger replied. 'She was just in the wrong place at the wrong time. It's rarely a stranger, anyway. Murder. Stranger danger is bullshit. In murder cases like this, it's usually someone the victim knew.'

'And they have no idea who did it?'

'There's some speculation,' the stranger said. 'But they have no idea.'

'Do you have a pet theory?' I asked.

'I have an idea,' she said. 'Yes.'

She didn't seem interested in sharing her theories with me, and I wasn't going to prompt further discussion of such a morbid subject.

'Would you like me to draw you a tarot card?'

'Uh.'

I shuffled the deck and offered her the pack to split. When she turned the top card, the smiling skeletal face of the Devil peered up at us. For the first time, I felt spooked by the cards.

'This is the card of obsession,' I said. 'Addiction. You see the two figures, the couple chained beneath the Devil? The way they've grown horns of their own? It means, the more time you spend with the devil, the closer to the devil you become.'

I'd been focusing my attention on the tarot card on the table between us, but as I raised my head to look the stranger in the eye, I was met by an awful expression on her face. Her eyes were glassy with tears, but her lips were stretched into a shadowy smile that darkened the room and chilled the air, and I found myself suddenly quite desperate for the interaction to end.

She placed the cigarette between her lips and raised the lighter to spark it.

'You can't smoke inside,' I said quickly. 'You have to take it outside.'

'I'll bring your lighter back,' she said.

'Keep it,' I replied, and she smiled that eerie smile once more before heading out into the night.

The booze must be catching up with me, I thought. The lights of the bar had doubled, dancing before me like so many stars. Perhaps this was the right note to end on – not the disquieting interaction with the girl in the purple headband, but the conversation with Daniel. A poignant discussion in a candlelit bar. I'd wait for him to return, and then insist it was time to call it a night, while there was a break in the weather. That would be a nice way to end my first proper day in New Orleans.

I called the server over, paid our sizeable tab and left a generous tip. There was no sign of Daniel, and I began to wonder if he'd ditched me. It was later than I'd thought, and he'd been gone for some time, although I couldn't say how long. I'd lost track of time entirely.

That's the problem with alcohol. It fosters a false sense of intimacy. Tarot cards in hand, I shuffled the deck and treated myself to a random card pull. The Temperance card – a card of balance and moderation. Loose from a night of drinking, I laughed out loud, and several people turned their heads in my direction. Sometimes, I felt the tarot knew me better than I knew myself.

Still no Daniel. I glanced around the bar. The bathroom was one small gender-neutral toilet, and as I gazed at it, the door opened and a chubby woman in a black-and-gold American football shirt stepped out, drying her hands on her jeans. He wasn't at the bar, and I couldn't see him among the smokers outside – besides, he'd left his vape on the table. Perhaps he'd gone to find an ATM? But no – there was the glow of an ATM in the corner next to the juke box – and the bar took cards, anyway.

Wherever he'd gone, he was taking his time. It was getting late, and I was drunk, and I was tired, and I was ready to go home.

Fuck it.

I borrowed a pen from our server and scribbled a note on the receipt:

Sorry Daniel, got tired of waiting – shall we let fate have her way? See you around, I hope.
Selina xox

I tucked the receipt and the Temperance card under his empty beer bottle and placed his vape on top. I let our server know I was heading out and to please leave them in case Daniel came back, and then I stepped out into the night.

A dizzy rush of alcohol went straight to my head.

The rain had finally slowed to a gentle patter. The pavement was wet, and the evening had turned into a warm and muggy night as moisture seemed to rise from the concrete. I ordered a cab with an app on my phone and it came quickly. There was no traffic; we cut through the city with no delay, sailing dreamlike past bars that were still in full swing, the driver steering us around potholes the size of paddling pools, brimming with rainwater.

My deck was precious to me, well cared for and well thumbed, but I knew in my alcohol-soaked heart that if I left a piece of it with Daniel, fate would intervene. A primordial instinct told me he would keep the Temperance card, and he would find me again to return it.

Appetiser
Charbroiled Oysters

⚜

Freshly shucked oysters on the half shell, topped with garlic butter, breadcrumbs and Parmesan, and grilled until the cheese turns golden brown and the butter froths.

London: Max

Behind the locked door of the bathroom, Max took a swig of lager and contemplated how much longer he'd need to stay at Caroline's. He couldn't give less of a shit about the conversation happening at the dining table. So, the prodigal son was yet to return home, too busy drinking New Orleans dry, too wrapped up in himself to spare a thought for those he'd left behind. He'd been mugged, some cunt had chucked his shit into the bayou. So fucking what? The shirt was a mystery, but life was full of them.

Max swallowed the rest of his beer. He'd crunched the numbers: if he nursed each tinnie for thirty minutes, his supply would last until midnight. On the one hand, he didn't think they were likely to stay that late – he might even make it to the Hawley Arms before close – but on the other, no beer had the chance to grow warm on Max's watch. He had to pace himself.

He set the empty can on the cistern and turned to the sink. Caroline's hand soap smelled like a spa, frothed into heavily perfumed suds between his fingers. He rinsed his hands, dried them on his T-shirt and, under the cover of running water, opened the medicine cabinet for a quick snoop. Caroline was bound to have the good shit via private prescription – Vicodin, Valium, Xanax. Leftover pain meds from her accident last year, old pills she wouldn't miss. Something for later, to take the edge off.

Instead of anything useful, he found blister packs and pharmacy bottles of expired medication, dusty toiletries with retro labels. He picked a cardboard box at random, the corners softened with age. Beta blockers prescribed to an Edward Dumortier. Caroline's father, he guessed. Weird, he thought, to still have shit like this knocking around after all these years. Could an expired beta blocker kill him? Best not find out. He slipped the box back into place.

Max had never thought much of Caroline, had always found her rather wet and dull, a piece of loo roll caught on the heel of her more charismatic brother, but he couldn't help but feel there was a heat to her now. Perhaps it was just the stress, he thought, but while in the past he'd always been indifferent to her attention, it now felt hard to endure, like sitting too close to a bonfire. She seemed angry, and he couldn't blame her: in her position, Max would be pretty fucking angry too.

A gentle knock on the bathroom door made him jump. He snapped the medicine cabinet closed, and a look of the devil returned his gaze in the mirror. He tasted acid, cleared his throat and swallowed a mouthful of water from the tap, but the flavour of bile lingered.

When he opened the bathroom door, Sage was waiting for him in the hallway. He could hardly stand to look at her. All the things he used to like about her, he'd grown to loathe: the awful red hair dye, the nose ring, the year-round festival gear, the pick-and-mix approach to spirituality.

'You were in there for ages,' she said, arms folded like she was about to give him a bollocking. 'Were you doing coke? Or just nosing through Caroline's things?'

'I was reciting ten Hail Marys while taking a shit,' he said, pushing past her.

'I heard you slam the medicine cabinet,' she called, as he made his way back to the ambient hum of the dinner party.

*

The air in the flat had filled with the warm, spicy smell of stew. Max returned to his seat at the table, but he couldn't keep still. He jigged his legs, a nervous energy animating his muscles. As he opened another can of lager, he noticed the psychic was watching him.

'I don't know,' Caroline was saying, chin resting in her hands. 'I woke up one morning, and he was gone. I thought he was on a night out, but he never came home, and then I realised a suitcase was missing. Dicky, darling, is there more wine?'

Richard jumped to his feet, a little dogsbody desperate to please his queen, and returned to the table with a second bottle of bougie-looking red just as Sage sat down next to Max.

'Your turn next,' Sage said, resting a hand on his arm that reeked of Caroline's fancy soap. She never could keep her hands to herself.

'Have you faced the tarot before?' the psychic asked him, scooping up Richard's cards and shuffling them back into the deck.

'Yeah,' he replied, forcing a nonchalant shrug. 'I don't believe in all that, though.'

Hazy memories of summer festivals, house parties in student digs, girls backstage with pints of cider in plastic cups. If she was fit enough, Max would let a girl do anything she liked, from mapping his birth chart to studying his palm to drawing his cards. He'd once let a girl give him a stick-and-poke tattoo of a snake eating its own tail, although now it had blurred to a black ring, an eclipse in reverse on his ankle. A permanent memory of a girl he'd quickly forgotten.

'You don't believe in it at all?' the psychic asked, with a serene suck on the white plastic vape.

'It's all a load of bollocks, babe. Sorry.'

Cotton vapour bloomed from the psychic's lips and draped the table in an ectoplasmic cloud of sweetened smoke. 'Why are you sorry?' she asked, unperturbed.

Max took a beat to consider this. 'I'm not all that sorry, to be fair. I actually think it's dangerous bullshit, if you must know.'

'Dangerous? That's an interesting word to use. Why do you think it's dangerous?'

'Well.' He fiddled with the ring pull of his can, flipping it one way and then the other until it popped off in his hand. 'It starts with crystals and horoscopes, and then it's homeopathy and refusing life-saving medication, and then it's all 5G this and chemtrails that.'

'Well, to be fair, 5G is destroying our minds and chemtrails are destroying our cities,' Sage said. 'Don't you remember when we used to look up and see a big, beautiful blue sky? You don't see that anymore. The sky's always hazy. They're dusting us with chemicals like crops.'

'See what I mean?' Max said.

'I discovered something interesting recently,' Richard said, appearing in the doorway with a fussy little tea towel thrown over one shoulder. 'Do you know what it means for a planet to be in retrograde?'

'Yes,' said Sage. 'It's a reversal of energy. Like, for example, Mercury is the planet of communication, right? So, when it's in retrograde, like it is right now, you can expect more misunderstandings, crossed wires, things like that.'

Richard listened with a faint smile. 'Okay, but where does that idea come from?'

Sage shook her head. 'I'm not sure.'

'When ancient astronomers traced the progress of each star, they noticed that occasionally, some appeared to change direction and move backwards. Hence, retrograde – a reversal. We now know the planets all move in the same direction as they orbit the sun, and this apparent reversal is just an optical illusion based on the different speeds of each planet's orbit, observed from a point in the galaxy that's also in motion.'

Sage blinked. 'So?'

'Oh, I just find it fascinating – the idea that people pin the unpredictable nature of life onto something so easily proved wrong. It would make just as much sense to blame the fae folk.'

'Exactly,' said Max, skimming the words but gathering the general point Richard was making. He drained his can. 'In other words, it's all a load of bollocks.'

'See, this is why I like astrology,' Sage said to the psychic. 'It annoys men.'

'You *would* say that,' Max replied.

'Just let people *live*,' Sage said. 'Our horoscopes and tarot cards aren't doing you any harm.'

Max took a deep breath and steeled himself for another row, but the psychic intervened before he could respond.

'I have a question for you, Max,' she said. 'Do you believe in God?'

'Nah,' he replied. 'I was raised Catholic, but I'm an atheist now.'

'So if you don't believe in God, or anything spiritual, where do you get your morality from? How do you centre yourself?'

A crackle of electric tension ran through Max's body, and he jumped to his feet and helped himself to another can of lager from the fridge.

'Well, babe,' he said, with a cocky grin as he snapped the ring pull. 'I'm a lifelong member of the church of rock and roll.'

*

Max had discovered live music when he was fifteen, because it was the only way he could have a cheap night out without a fake ID. The Garage, the Astoria and the Mean Fiddler were places of worship: the spotlights that dappled the show in jewel-coloured light were the stained glass of church windows; the dry ice that clouded the stage was the swinging thurible that filled a cathedral with the sweet scent of frankincense. The braying crowd was the devoted congregation, and if the stage was their altar, the bands who stood above them, who put their blood, sweat and souls into their sermons, were closest to God.

Being there, in the moment, listening to the music, was somewhere between dissociation and euphoria. Nothing mattered; every worry faded to insignificance. Max found his problems dissolved like a Communion wafer on his sinful tongue as he spat the lyrics, each chorus repeated like a Hail Mary.

His CD collection, mostly shoplifted from HMV, was both his Bible and the soundtrack to his life. Listening to records was like dipping into his own memoir: each significant experience had a band or an album or even just a song attached to it, and those memories could be brought to life with a pair of noise-cancelling headphones and the right track: old friends, ex-girlfriends, holidays, house parties, hangovers.

Max wanted what they had, the bands: he wanted the talent, the fame, the adoration, the girls. Girls in miniskirts, girls who drank beer and burped, girls who played guitar, girls who loved the music, girls who knew the words. He wanted girls, because he didn't like an intrinsic truth about himself: that while he liked girls, his desire didn't stop there.

He couldn't afford a guitar, but he began writing songs when he was a teenager, terrible poetry and angsty, clichéd lyrics. By the time he turned twenty, he'd learned the basics on a borrowed acoustic, and would badger lads at house parties to let him have a go on their Fenders and Les Pauls. His mate Carl had the most beautiful guitar Max had ever seen: a cherry-red Gibson SG with a body that curved into devil horns either side of its slender neck.

'We should start a band,' Carl said, watching Max fingerpick a rough melody of his own creation on the coveted guitar.

'Yeah, alright,' said Max. 'Can I borrow your guitar?'

'Fuck off,' Carl replied. 'I'm the guitarist. You can learn bass.'

'Nah,' said Max. 'Bass is for bitches. I'll write the lyrics, so I'll be the front man.'

'You can't sing for shit,' Carl said, although that wasn't strictly true. Even at twenty, Max had the voice of an angel who'd spent a lifetime smoking cigarettes, drinking whiskey and swallowing gravel.

They found a drummer, a psycho everyone called Sesh due to his propensity for chemicals, and a bass player called Mike. They practised in Carl's living room, writing songs that mostly sucked but sometimes grew into tracks that weren't half bad.

They had nearly made it, the Strangeways. They had so nearly made it.

*

The psychic shuffled her deck, a soft ruffle that filled the silence, and placed the cards on the table in front of Max. Without instruction, he reached over and split the deck in two.

'See, you're a natural,' she said. She dealt three cards face down on the table between them and flipped the first without ceremony.

'Interesting,' she said, drumming her nails against the wood. At such close proximity, he could smell the acerbic edge of wine on her breath. 'The Fool.'

Sage snorted. 'That's rich.'

'Fuck off,' said Max.

The psychic offered a muted smile. 'Don't take it personally. This card represents your past. The Fool is all about childhood innocence, a sense of naivety. It shows a man at the start of a journey, full of optimism and unaware of the dangers that lie ahead. Does that resonate with you, darling?'

'Surely *everyone* relates to this card,' he said. 'We're all born innocent; we're all full of the optimism of youth up to a certain point in our lives, aren't we?'

'And then the soul-crushing weight of adulthood squeezes it out of us,' Richard said.

'I mean, you're not wrong,' the psychic replied. 'Let's draw your next card and see if we can contextualise the Fool.'

She flipped the second card. It showed a man gazing down upon three overturned cups. Behind him, just out of his line of sight, were two more standing upright.

'The Five of Cups. This card represents your present. I get the impression you missed out on something, a big opportunity or chance for success, and you've struggled to move on from it.' She pointed to the two cups behind the downtrodden figure. 'You're missing out on new opportunities in the present because you can't move on from past mistakes. Does that resonate with you, darling?'

Max frowned. Had they mentioned the Strangeways this evening? Yes – Sage had said something, hadn't she? *He bounced between things. First, it was cinema. Then it was the band. A tragedy.*

'Not particularly,' he replied stubbornly. 'No.'

Agile as a snake, the psychic changed tack: 'How did you meet Daniel?'

'Aren't *you* meant to tell *me* that?'

The psychic smiled coolly. 'That's not quite how it works.'

Max realised he was clenching his jaw and forced himself to relax as she turned the third card. It showed a tower struck by lightning, people falling to their deaths.

'Jesus fucking Christ.' He forced a laugh, but sweat prickled his brow. The heat felt claustrophobic. The flat was too warm, and the smell of the psychic's vape mingled with the acrid wine, scented candles and meaty stink from the hob. It was all too much, too overstimulating, and made him feel sick.

'I'm going to level with you,' she said. 'This is a dark spread. It matches your aura.'

'My aura?'

'Your entire body is haloed with a blood-red aura. It's almost difficult to look at you. I felt it as soon as I walked into the room, this spiritual putridity that clings to you. It's overpowering, to be honest. Have you ever done a Ouija board, anything like that?'

Max blinked. 'I have actually, yeah. A long time ago. In fact, it was the night I first met Daniel.'

'That's interesting. Could you tell us about it?'

'Nah, there's no story there. It was just a bullshit game when we were bored one night. I'm sorry, can we roll it back a second – I have a spiritual *putridity*?'

'It's not your fault. Well, it's probably not your fault. It's perfectly common – some of my best friends are spiritually curdled, but I love them all the same. Have you considered an egg cleanse? Perhaps we could ask Caroline for an egg, see if we can clear some of that dark energy. You'll feel ten pounds lighter – it's like colonic irrigation for the soul. Have you ever had a colonic?'

'Okay,' Max said, cutting her off. 'I'll tell you about the night I met Daniel.'

*

Max was twenty-five when he met the devil. He was seeing Melanie Matthews at the time, a peachy-arsed angel in vintage 501s. She worked at a wanky record shop in the dregs of Soho, but she let him hang out and listen to records whenever it was quiet and her boss wasn't there, which was most days. Vinyl was in fashion, but everyone wanted to buy their records from the curated, painfully hip selection at Urban Outfitters.

Mel was different. She was into Elliott Smith, Bon Iver and Jeff Buckley. Serious men with delicate guitars: men who wrote lyrics like poetry, wore their hearts on their sleeves. Max still couldn't hear the gentle strum of 'Needle in the Hay' without remembering, with both fondness and regret, the sweet taste of Mel's strawberry-flavoured lips. He should have stuck with Mel, but he was young and reckless, and the grass looked greener every time his head was turned, which was all the fucking time. He dropped girlfriends and jobs whenever the clocks changed, never happy with what he already had on his plate.

The Strangeways were gigging regularly, getting a bit of traction in the local scene, but once you factored in petrol, booze, fags and what Sesh liked to call 'party favours', they were spending more than they were making, and that wasn't very fucking much.

Time moves slowly when you don't have much to do. It was the hottest summer on record, but didn't they say that every year? Max took Mel to a screening of *Whiplash* at the Prince Charles Cinema, and she lent him paperbacks that he never bothered to read, the titles long faded from his memory. They listened to a lot of music, ate tangerines, and talked about the death All Tomorrow's Parties.

They were hanging out one night at Carl's flat in Camden, listening to Midlake and splitting an extra-large pizza that Mel had paid for.

'Sage is coming over,' Carl said from a brown corduroy beanbag on the floor, eyes glued to his phone. 'That's cool, yeah?'

'Who's Sage?' asked Mel, using a napkin to sponge oil from a pizza slice before taking a small bite.

'Carl's *groupie*,' said Max, with a sly smile. Carl and Sage were sleeping together, although they always acted like they were done with one another until the end of the night, when they'd slink off arm in arm. Max gave Carl shit for it, but he respected Carl's dedication to getting laid.

Max liked to be the biggest personality in the room at any given time, but Sage took up more oxygen than anyone he'd ever met. She held Carl back, weighed him down like an anchor, encouraged him to smoke less and drink less and go to bed early. Sage was, in other words, a fucking drag.

'He mocks it because he wants it,' Carl said knowingly, twisting two halves of a rosewood grinder together and releasing the soft, rotten scent of marijuana leaves into the air.

'He gets it plenty,' Mel replied. She was spicy like that, always had a good comeback. Max laughed and Carl rolled his eyes.

'Christ, spare me.'

Sage turned up with some pretty boy in tow and immediately began to bitch about everything. 'Christ, it stinks of pizza in here. And what's with the sad old bastard music?'

'Hey, don't knock Midlake,' Mel said.

'Ignore her,' Max said to Mel. 'She wouldn't know a decent song if it fucked her up the arse.'

'You're *so* disgusting,' Sage replied, and then she turned to Carl, brandishing large bottles of Jack Daniels and Diet Coke. 'This is Daniel, by the way. I didn't think you'd mind, cos he bought the whiskey. Do you have any clean glasses?'

'Like you don't know where the glasses are,' Max muttered.

'Like I ever hang out *here*,' she shot back, glancing at the damp curtains, the spaghetti of wires beneath the dusty television, the scatter of cans on the floor, the bong collection arranged like glass vases on the mantel.

'And yet, here you are,' Max replied, spreading both hands to indicate her overwhelming presence in the room. 'Once again, here you are.'

Daniel reached for the laptop to scroll through iTunes, and as he did so, Max couldn't help but notice the length of his body, the broadness of his shoulders. Without asking the room for permission, Daniel switched from Midlake to the mellow bongos of 'Planet Caravan'. Max admired the tenacity, if not the music itself.

'Black Sabbath? Is that what the kids are listening to these days?' Carl teased, lifting his freshly packed pipe to his lips. He took a deep toke and narrowed his eyes against the wispy smoke rising from the bowl.

'You're a stoner, darling,' Daniel said. 'I'd have thought bongos would be right up your street.'

'Ozzy Osbourne's an energy vampire,' Sage said, nodding to the laptop and disappearing into the kitchenette. 'Did you know that?'

'What are you on about?' asked Max.

She reappeared with a trio of frothy Jack and Cokes. She gave one to Daniel, one to Carl and one to Mel, then headed back to the kitchen to collect two more.

'He's an energy vampire,' she repeated, handing a drink to Max. 'You ever see what he's like offstage? Hands shaking, can barely string a sentence together. Then when he's on stage, he comes to life – a totally different man. Where do you think all that energy comes from?'

'Uppers,' said Carl.

'It's coming from the audience – he *feeds* off the crowd.' She took a sip of her drink and winced at the ratio of bourbon to mixer.

'I thought he had Parkinson's or some shit,' Max said.

'It's adrenaline,' Carl said, shifting to make space for Sage on his beanbag. 'Performing to a stadium of dedicated fans who know every word to every song – what a rush, man. Can you even imagine?'

'That'll be us one day,' Max said.

'Oh, of course you're in a band,' said Daniel, as if it were the most boring and predictable thing in the world.

'Fuck off,' said Max.

'No go on, tell me. Is it a band like Midlake?' Daniel asked, eyes sparkling. 'Do you write poetry?'

'Who's this cunt again?' Max asked the room.

'No, they're much heavier,' Sage said.

'Rock 'n' roll,' said Carl, and Max surprised himself by feeling embarrassed.

'Oh, listen to you.' Daniel smiled affectionately. 'No one listens to rock anymore, darling. Rock and roll is dead.'

The pipe circulated, and talk turned lazier, more muted, as the marijuana took hold. Sage mixed another round of Jack and Cokes, and Carl swapped Black Sabbath for Idles, then Sage swapped The Libertines for Kate Bush. She lit candles and snapped on a set of fairy lights that snaked around the corners of the room.

'You can never just leave things as they are, can you?' Max complained.

'God, can you just fuck off with your moaning for five minutes?'

'I think it's nice, actually,' Mel said, an arm around his shoulders, leaning in to nuzzle his cheek. 'It's cosier like this.'

As the night wore on, though, Max couldn't take his eyes off Daniel. The sweep of chocolate curls, the David Bowie cheekbones, the hint of hair on his chest as he fiddled with the laptop or ashed his cigarette. He smelled of smoke and amber, and every time he spoke, Max found himself leaning closer to listen to what he had to say.

'I've got work tomorrow,' Mel said, pulling on her jacket with a pout. 'You coming?'

'Nah,' he said. 'I'm on the late shift tomorrow.'

'I thought you were staying at mine tonight?'

'Well, I'm still hanging out, aren't I?' he replied.

Mel dithered for a moment, gaze darting from Sage to Carl to Max. Daniel, she all but ignored. 'Call me tomorrow?'

'Uh huh.'

'Love you.'

'Yeah,' he said. 'See ya.'

She hesitated for a moment at the door, then left without saying goodbye to the rest of the group. Max never saw her again, although she sent a text when she heard about what happened, offered to come to the funeral. He didn't take her up on that, and they never spoke again.

'So, darling,' Daniel said. 'Tell me about your band. I can see you're *dying* to talk about yourself. Do you play the maracas?'

Max laughed, because it was true: he did want to talk about the band. He talked about their basement gigs and self-funded micro-tours to commuter towns, and Daniel listened and nodded and asked questions about merch, managers and record labels.

'We're not there yet,' Max said, swirling the whiskey in his glass. 'Studio time costs a fortune, and we need to hire a proper producer to help mix an EP. We have a shitty demo, but the sound isn't right – it's too DIY, and we're too heavy to pull off a lo-fi vibe. The layers all just bleed together. It just sounds … well, it sounds shit, to be honest.'

'How much would it cost to record a three-song demo?'

'Not sure. I mean, it all adds up – time in the studio, mixing, mastering, distribution … plus I guess we'd need an illustrator or a designer or something like that to pull together a decent cover. Maybe a few grand, all in? I'm not sure.'

'Jesus, that's a lot of money,' Sage said.

'No shit,' Carl replied. By now, he'd picked up his guitar, that enviable Gibson, and was strumming, a cigarette pinched between his lips.

'What do you do for work?' Daniel asked. 'Can't you just save up?'

'I work in a bar,' Max said. 'It's cool cos it's casual, so I can take off whenever we tour, but it sucks cos the pay's total balls.'

'Free booze, though,' Carl reasoned.

'Yeah, free booze when I steal it,' Max replied, with a smirk. 'Anyway, no point worrying about that for now. Our bassist moved to Milton Keynes for work.'

'Fucking sell-out,' said Carl.

'He said he'd travel down for gigs and stuff, but he never fucking does,' Max continued. 'I can play a bit of bass, but I'd rather just focus on singing.'

'Daniel plays the bass,' Sage said. 'He's amazing. You should ask him to join your stupid band.'

'Yeah?' said Carl, not looking up from his fingers as he strummed. 'You been playing long?'

'I learned classical guitar at school,' Daniel said. 'Switched to bass while I was at university.'

The night began to soften and blur, the weed and the bourbon fraying Max's grip on reality. He wasn't sure who suggested the Ouija board. Probably Sage. She loved Stevie Nicks, tarot cards, crap like that. She always carried a crystal in her pocket and threw salt over her shoulder whenever anyone spilled any.

'Surprisingly, I don't have a fucking Ouija board lying around,' Carl said.

'No problem, we can use this,' Sage replied gamely, picking up the pizza box and tipping the bitten crusts onto the coffee table. She tore the flat box in two, and made Carl get up to find her a Sharpie.

'Oh, I know,' said Daniel, catching Max's cynical expression. 'Trust me, it's easier to go with the flow and let her do whatever she wants.'

They watched in grave silence as she carefully printed the letters, numbers and words of a Ouija board on to the lid of the box, which was less greasy than the base. Next, she downed her drink, and placed the glass, still laced with a caramel-coloured foam, upside down in the middle of the makeshift board.

'Okay, let's do this,' she said. 'Put both your index fingers on the glass, like this, but just relax. Don't press too hard.'

'What if we conjure up an evil spirit, like a serial killer?' Max joked.

'You're fine,' Sage replied. 'Just chill and let the board do its thing.'

She cleared her throat and shifted her tone, speaking in a soft, melodic voice: 'Hello, is anyone there?'

Carl released a stoned giggle, and Sage glared at him.

'Stop it – you have to take it seriously, or it won't work.'

It was a laugh at first. Max manipulated the board to spell 'COCK' and then Carl steered the glass to spell 'PUSSY', but after a while, Sage began to get fractious, and they had to promise to play in earnest. No more expletives, no more cheating.

'Is there anyone there?' Sage asked. 'Is there anyone in the room with us?'

When the glass moved, Max felt a chill in his guts because he wasn't doing it, and he could tell by the expression on Carl's face – a quizzical smirk aimed at Max – that he wasn't doing it either. He didn't have a handle on Daniel's sense of humour, though. It could be him, he thought, as the glass drifted to the word *Hello*. Max had to admit it was a little spooky. Darkness pressed against the windows, and the candles danced in their jam jars, sending shadows flickering around the room.

'Hello,' Sage whispered, absurdly, to the glass. After a few moments of careful consideration, she spoke again in that same, soft voice: 'How old are you?'

The fairy lights stuttered. A long pause, and then the glass drifted to number eight, and then to number four.

'Eighty-four?' Sage asked, eyes shining.

The glass responded again with a pregnant pause, and then it drifted serenely to *Yes*.

'This is tripping me out,' Carl said. 'I don't think I like it, man.'

'Shh, be quiet,' Sage replied, a hushed reprimand.

Beneath their fingers, the glass began to gently rotate until they were struggling to keep their fingertips in place. Soon it was twirling back and forth across the board in a gentle waltz. Daniel's face broke into a broad smile.

'In life,' he asked, 'were you a ballroom dancer, darling? A regular little Fred Astaire?'

The glass drifted and stopped. *Yes.*

'Oh my God,' Sage whispered. Tears twinkled in the candlelight. 'Wow. Do you miss it?'

Slowly, delicately, the glass twirled and stopped on the word *Goodbye*.

'Goodbye,' she said, smiling. 'Thanks for hanging out.' She wiped her eyes, and looked to her friends. 'It's important to close each session properly by saying goodbye to the spirit – we don't want them to linger.'

'Goodbye, darling,' said Daniel to the glass. 'Don't keep in touch, though.'

'Bye,' said Carl.

'See ya,' said Max.

'That was magic,' Sage said, with a pretty smile. 'That was really, really magic.'

*

'So, the Ouija board worked?' asked the psychic.

'Of course it worked,' said Sage.

Max shrugged. 'We were all pretty wasted.'

'It's simple physics,' Richard said. 'It's called the ideomotor effect. Your brains were signalling your bodies to place an unconscious pressure on the glass, and uneven pressure from different directions caused the glass to move.'

'To *twirl*, though? Come on. We weren't doing that,' said Sage.

'No, but after the first spin, Daniel planted the idea in your heads that you were talking to the spirit of a ballroom dancer, and you liked that, so you ran with it. You wanted it to be true, so you created a narrative, and then your bodies responded to that desire. It's fascinating, but it's just a blend of psychology and physics.'

'Well, that's what you think,' Sage said. 'But you weren't there.'

'I don't mean to be disrespectful,' said Richard, turning a candy shade of pink. 'I just thought it was interesting.'

'What happened next?' the psychic asked.

*

They continued to play with the board for a good hour, and each time the glass moved, it travelled at a different speed or in a different manner, mirroring the way handwriting varies from person to person. Once, it bounced from letter to letter with the alacrity of a teenager, and later it drifted mournfully around the board, refusing to make any sense.

'Can I ask a question?' Max interrupted. He could feel the energy in the room, a frisson of tension and excitement. 'Are the Strangeways going to be famous?'

Carl snorted, but he didn't take his eyes off their substitute planchette as it slipped gently across the pizza box.

Yes, said the board.

'Knew it.' Carl grinned. 'I fucking knew it.'

'Are we going to be millionaires?' Max asked.

No, said the board.

He frowned. That was bullshit. Everyone knew famous bands earned a fortune from gigs and merch, brand deals and record sales. 'Are we going to make *any* money?'

No, said the board.

'But we're going to be famous?' he asked.

Yes, said the board.

'So, we're not going to make any money, but everyone's going to know our names?' Carl asked, with a perplexed frown. 'Sounds shit, mate.'

'Should Daniel join the band?' Sage asked.

Yes, said the board.

'Alright, very fucking funny,' Max said.

'It's not me,' Daniel said. 'I swear, I don't want to join your diminutive little rock band.'

'Okay, how about this,' said Max, speaking to the glass. 'If I sold my soul to the devil, could I be rich *and* famous?'

'Don't even joke about that,' Sage snapped. 'Don't even fucking joke. That's not funny. And look, if someone's moving the glass, just stop it now; you're freaking me out.'

'I'm not doing it,' said Carl, raising a hand in surrender.

'I swear,' said Max.

'Wait a second,' Sage said, leaning forward to speak to the glass as though it were a mobile on speakerphone. 'How old are you?'

The glass meandered over the numbers, back and forth, back and forth, gaining momentum, moving faster and faster, a great sweeping arc, until it seemed to lose control. It flew from the pizza box and smashed against the wall. Shards of glass bounced across the carpet and sparkled in the glow of the fairylights.

'Fuck!' shouted Max. 'Dammit man, that ghostie was telling me my fortune.'

'*Our* fortune,' said Carl.

'Right, yeah, sorry mate – it was telling us *our* fortune.'

'I didn't like that,' said Sage, shaking her head and tearing the lid of the pizza box into pieces. 'I really didn't like that. Carl, can you turn on the big light?'

'Hey,' Daniel said, wrapping an arm around her. 'You're shaking, darling.'

'I don't think that was a good spirit,' she said, and her teeth chattered together as she spoke. 'And we didn't close the session properly.'

'It's just the weed,' Carl said, flipping on the big light and reaching under the sink for a dustpan and brush. 'You just got a bit freaked out, that's all. Don't worry about it.'

'Do you have any incense?' Sage asked. 'I feel like we need to cleanse the space.'

Max offered to mix another round of drinks, but the spell was broken. Sage swept up the broken glass, while Daniel ordered an Uber and regretfully vanished into the night. Carl put on an episode of *Freaks and Geeks*, but no one laughed at the jokes.

'I think I need to leave,' Sage said. 'I really don't like the energy in here right now.'

Carl made a vague noise of protest, but didn't move from his spot on the beanbag.

'Where do you live?' asked Max.

'I'm moored at Limehouse,' she replied.

'You're what?'

'I live on a boat,' she clarified.

'Of course you live on a fucking boat,' Max said, pulling on his jacket. 'I live in Shadwell – I can walk you home.'

It was Saturday night, and it was late: the late night bars and rock clubs were kicking out, flooding the streets with drunks in high spirits. Clubbers in skinny jeans swarmed the pavement, singing 'Seven Nation Army' at the tops of their lungs, cadging cigarettes off one another, asking for a light.

The pair walked through the moonlit streets, talking about the Strangeways and trying to shake the uncomfortable sense of fear that had settled on their skin like sweat after a stuffy gig.

'Oh God, maybe I should have crashed at Carl's. I really don't feel like staying on my boat alone, either,' Sage said. 'It can be really spooky at night.'

Hello, Max thought.

'Well, do you want to come over and hang out for a bit?' he suggested. 'You still seem really spooked.'

A girl in a pink T-shirt made them both jump as she passed, bellowing some attention-seeking crap about free hugs.

'What about your girlfriend?' Sage asked, raising an eyebrow.

'What girlfriend?' Max replied. 'Oh – you mean Mel? Don't worry about Mel. She's cool, but it's not serious.'

'She said she loved you.'

'She's all talk.'

'What about Carl?' Sage asked. 'I don't think he'd like it.'

'We'd just hang out, no big deal.'

'What about Daniel?' she asked, eyes twinkling. 'You seemed quite taken by him.'

Fucking tease. Max swallowed. 'I'm not trying to *fuck* you, you know. I'm just trying to be nice. I wouldn't go near you with a fucking barge pole.'

'Oh, fuck you,' she snapped. 'You know what, don't worry about it. I'll make my own way home.'

'Fine, fuck off then,' he spat, and he watched her walk away until she was swallowed by the darkness. Who the fuck did she think she was? He hadn't been *taken* by Daniel. Sure, he'd enjoyed his company, but that meant jack shit.

That familiar feeling came over him, that sense of pent-up energy and nowhere for it to go. In his anger, he kicked a wheelie bin, and then swung a balled fist that connected with a lamp post. He yelped in pain as the proximal phalanx of his index finger cracked.

As the sun rose, he climbed into bed, and fell into a restless sleep. He dreamed that a blood-red snake had coiled itself around his arm and was sinking its needle-sharp fangs into the flesh of his finger. In the morning, the finger was swollen, the joints stiff and painful to touch. He couldn't bend it at all, as though the bones had been replaced with a lolly stick.

He leaned his head over the side of the bed and vomited all over the dirty clothes that pooled on the carpet, and then he messaged Carl.

Fell over and fucked my finger up. Can't play bass.

Dickhead, Carl replied. *lets ask sages mate to play tomorrow. if good maybe he can cover you on tour???*

K, Max replied. *you ask him.*

*

The sun had disappeared beneath the horizon, and Caroline switched on a lamp. The honeyed light brought Max back into the room, back into the present.

'So, did you guys get signed?' asked the psychic.

'No,' Max replied darkly. 'Daniel joined the band, but it didn't work out.'

He took a long sour swallow of Camden Hells that burned the back of his throat, made his eyes water. He didn't like thinking about what happened next, and yet it haunted him, followed him like a devil on his shoulder, whispering reminders of the role he'd played in the downfall of his band.

After a long pause, Caroline spoke. 'There was an accident.'

*

The crowd were lively, full of bravado and banter, and when the bar kicked them out, they all piled back to Carl's place for an afterparty. The flat was packed and the booze was flowing – cans of Red Stripe, bottles of Jack Daniels and Jägermeister, little white wraps passed between sweaty hands. Girls were hanging around Daniel like flies around shit, trying to figure out if his sister Caroline was his girlfriend, or if any of the many boys who brought him drinks might be his lover. Max did his best to avoid Daniel's eye, to snub the warmth of his attention.

Sage was ignoring Max in turn. She was wearing a loose green summer dress that made her blood-red hair pop against her milky skin. Every time she squeezed past him to refill her glass or go to the bathroom, he found his hands fit beautifully on the dips of her hips, and although she didn't acknowledge his touch, she didn't discourage it, either. Once, Max felt sure she had carved a desire line through the crowd to pass him on purpose, and when she did so, she placed a small, warm hand on the flat of his belly. Carl seemed oblivious, but Max was sure Daniel was paying attention, watching this performance with a knowing look on his face.

Sesh was on one that night, snorting lines from the back of a CD and downing shot after shot of sambuca, talking a mile a minute to anyone who'd listen.

'Everyone thinks three's the magic number,' he was saying, gurning and chewing his lips, eyes wild. 'Three musketeers, three little piggies, three wise men, three primary colours.'

'Yeah, yeah – what's your point, man?' said Carl, lighting a spliff.

'It's bullshit, mate. Bullshit. *Four* is the magic number – the Beatles, Led Zeppelin, Mötley Crüe, the Red Hot fucking Chili Peppers. Who else, mate, come on, who else? Blur, The Stone Roses, Joy Division, right? Who else?'

'The Strangeways!' a drunken voice called out, and Sesh clapped his hands together with alacrity and pointed in the vague direction of whoever had spoken.

'Fuck yeah – *fuck* yeah. That's what I'm saying. Four. Four's the magic number. Me, Carl, Max and Daniel – it's written in the stars. We just need to scrape together enough cash to get a demo out there, and the rest will come together like *that*.' He snapped his fingers. 'We need a sponsor. We need a motherfucking sponsor and a motherfucking manager, and then we'll be on our way. Sold-out gigs, world tour, our mugs on the motherfucking cover of *NME*.'

'You should ask Daniel to cover it,' Sage said to Carl. 'He's rich as fuck. His parents were millionaires or something.'

Across the room, Max saw that Caroline had tuned in to their conversation.

She was a strange girl. After that first encounter with Daniel, she was always there, turning up to their rehearsals and hanging around from soundcheck to encore at gigs. Daniel knew a lot of people, always summoned a crowd to their shows, but Caroline seemed to place herself to one side, happy to observe without joining in.

'Tour first,' Max said quickly. 'Let's see how the tour goes, and then we can worry about the demo.'

'What tour?' Caroline asked. She was wearing an oversized blazer, the shoulders drooping, making her look like an eleven-year-old on her first day of secondary school. She was pretty enough, but she was often sober and serious, always listening and never smiling.

'We've got ten shows coming up,' Max said. 'Pretty decent ones, actually. There's going to be a scout in Manchester, and we're supporting Extermination Event in Sunderland. If that goes well, they might take us on their European tour.'

'Wow,' said Caroline, although she didn't seem particularly impressed. 'How long will the European tour be?'

'A month?' Max guessed. 'Six weeks, maybe? I don't know, really. We're just taking it one show at a time, seeing what happens.'

'Yeah, but if that goes well, maybe we'll build a fanbase abroad, get to do a European tour of our own,' said Carl.

'Are we out of beer?' someone said.

The party had thinned, but those who were still going were going strong. It was unthinkable to continue the night without another drink.

'I'll walk to the supermarket,' Max said. 'There's a Sainsbury's on Chalk Farm Road.'

'It'll be shut now,' Carl said. 'It's gone two.'

'Time to call it a night?'

They all laughed.

'There's an offie by the tube station,' Sesh said, picking up his car keys. 'I'll whiz there and back in, like, five seconds. Five seconds, I'll just whiz there and back.'

'You're smashed, mate,' Max said. 'We can just walk, it won't take long.'

'Fuck no – it'll take like half an hour to walk there, and half an hour to walk back.'

'Will it fuck. Twenty minutes round trip.'

Max felt a prickle of attention, and there was Daniel meeting his eye from across the room. He lifted a finger and touched the centre of his lip. It was the tiniest of gestures, the smallest moment of connection, but Max's heart responded, beating a rhythm of desire in his chest. There was some debate, the car keys passing from hand to hand, and when they seemed to land in Carl's grasp, Max didn't protest. In fact, he encouraged it.

'You should definitely go,' Max said. 'He's way too fucked to drive.'

'It's cool, I've only had a few beers,' Carl said. 'Anyway, I drive more carefully when I'm stoned.'

'I'm going downstairs for a smoke,' Max said, and when Daniel said, 'I'll come,' he knew things were about to change, things were about to happen. There was a frisson between them, an electric anticipation in the air like the moments before a storm.

They stood in the shadows, and watched a curious fox sniff a bin bag on the other side of the street.

'Listen, I have money,' Daniel said, offering Max a fag. 'I can cover the demo, the tour, whatever you like.'

'Yeah?'

'Sure,' said Daniel. 'It's not a big deal. You need a new guitar, too – I've seen the way you look at Carl's Gibson. Like a teenage girl in love.'

'That's kind of you, man,' said Max. 'Sweet.'

'I can be kind, can't I?' said Daniel, almost teasing. 'And I can be very sweet.'

They smoked less than half a cigarette before Daniel summoned a taxi, and in the back seat of the car Max watched the city lights roll across his face, too shy to touch him in front of the driver.

Daniel tasted of smoke and bourbon, of late nights and jazz bars. Max took him to bed, and the inevitable fuck was nothing like he had ever experienced before. Sex with Daniel was euphoric, his masculine smell and broad, hard body a heady aphrodisiac, moving to the rhythm of the night, a metronome that kept perfect time with the beating of Max's heart, until finally, blissfully, he closed his eyes and experienced true nirvana for the last time before everything turned to shit.

*

In the pale morning light, Daniel was an angel with a messy halo of brunette curls spread across the pillow. Lying flat on his back, one arm was thrown over his eyes, the other stretched across a soft, pale stomach towards the elastic waistband of a pair of black boxers. His nipples were rosy-pink pennies against milky pectoral muscles, and he smelled warm and familiar, like stale sweat, alcohol and a lingering thread of expensive cologne. He sighed in his sleep, a gentle *Hmm*, lost in a dreamworld.

A heavy, nauseating cloud of regret settled over Max. He wondered if Daniel would agree to keep this on the down-low, if he'd recognise what was at stake. He gently tugged the duvet to cover Daniel's exposed skin, and then he slipped from the bed for a coffee and a cigarette while he gathered his thoughts.

It was a cool spring day, the sky an overwhelming blue. He'd have to make something up, he thought. Damage control. He'd have to say he'd picked up a girl, she was all over him, that he was drunk and she'd practically followed him home, practically begged him for it, that she was good to go, and what red-blooded man could turn down a sure thing after a few too many beers? He'd say she was a shit fuck anyway, another broad banged and forgotten. Daniel would understand this couldn't happen again. It wasn't part of Max's plan.

It would all be okay. He flicked his cigarette butt into the breeze, and looked for his phone.

*

Sesh was killed instantly, pitched through the windshield and crushed beneath the tyres of an oncoming truck. Carl was wearing his seatbelt, but he failed a breathalyser test and was arrested on the scene for drunk driving. It was all over the news, and every headline mentioned the band in one way or another – *The Strangeways guitarist arrested in fatal car crash; Strangeways drummer killed in drunk-driving incident* – and every newspaper ran the same picture of the original lineup, their old bassiest Mike in lieu of Daniel, lifted from their website.

Max gave Daniel the cold shoulder, stopped returning his calls. He disappeared inside himself, withdrew from the world. When the case went to court, Max was grateful for Sage's presence by his side, and when the judge sentenced Carl to ten years for causing death by dangerous driving while under the influence, it was Sage who held Max's hand. It was Sage who took him home, coaxed him into the shower and made him milky tea and buttered toast.

He poured his grief into Sage and she poured her love into him, and for two years that's what they did. Two years of tea and toast and sex and tears, and rabid fights that caused the neighbours to bang on the walls and threaten to call the police. He wrote song after song about the band, about the accident, about prison, about Daniel, until he had enough material to record an album, but still no fucking cash to cover costs.

'Ask Daniel,' Sage said. 'You're friends, right? He'll lend you it, I'm sure.'

'We kinda lost touch,' Max said.

'He loves you,' Sage said. 'He's always asking after you. I'm sure he'd be open to reconnecting.'

Max started throwing parties again, trying to gather a new crowd. Daniel came from time to time, always dressed in black with a bottle of red wine and a pack of cigarettes that he chain-smoked. Max made a special effort to talk to him, to ask him questions about things he could remember Daniel mentioning the last time they'd spoken, but a light seemed to have died behind Daniel's eyes, and Max resented him for it. What had *he* lost, exactly? A jaunt around Europe, a bite-sized taste of fame? He was a middle-of-the-road bass player, didn't deserve to be there in the first place.

Whenever Daniel and Sage popped by the bar, Max would undercharge them or slide them free drinks, and eventually their friendship progressed to more intimate hang-outs – pub lunches, beers after work, trips to the cinema with his stuck-up sister Caroline to watch long, dull films in which nothing happened.

'Darling, this is why we love you,' Daniel said, accepting a large glass of red for the price of a lime and soda, and Sage grew pink with pleasure, perhaps at the thought of her best friend and her boyfriend finally becoming friends in their own right.

*

Shame crept over him now, at the memory of how it had all unfolded. Max had invited Daniel and Sage for drinks in Camden, and as they passed the stretch of road that took Sesh, ruined Carl and destroyed the band, talk naturally turned to the accident.

'We were so close to getting signed,' Max said, which wasn't strictly true, but he knew Sage wouldn't correct him and Daniel wouldn't question it. 'We could have gone all the way, man. Manager, record deal, sell-out shows, the whole fucking lot. And one stupid decision took it all away. Fuck. Sometimes, I don't think I'll ever recover from it.'

'It's tragic, darling,' said Daniel, pushing open the door to the Oxford Arms. He was wearing a pair of black aviators and a black granddad shirt and, Max thought begrudgingly, looked more like a rock star than Max did.

'You're still on your healing journey,' Sage said, catching the barman's attention with a wave. She was always full of shit like that, and Max bristled but didn't rise to it. 'I do think you should see a therapist, though, work through some of your grief with a professional. I know this amazing crystal healer called Poetry, and she—'

'Music is my therapist. I've been writing songs about it, actually. Some of them are pretty decent. No – some of them are excellent.'

'Good for you, darling,' said Daniel.

Sage ordered a bottle of red and a pint for Max, and they took their drinks to find a table in the beer garden.

'I'm desperate to record a demo,' Max said, licking lager froth from his upper lip.

'You should,' Daniel said, pouring red wine into two glasses and handing one to Sage. 'What's stopping you?'

'I don't have the money,' Max said. 'I need at least a couple of grand, I reckon, to make a decent go of it.'

'Surely you can find that somewhere,' Daniel said.

'I work in a bar, mate,' Max replied, forcing a laugh to keep the mood light.

'We aren't all trust-fund babies, you know,' Sage teased.

'I'm not a *trust-fund baby*,' Daniel said. 'But I could probably lend you a couple of thousand pounds. I'd need to check with Caroline, though – she holds the purse strings.'

Elation flooded Max. 'Yeah?'

'Yes, I'm a kept woman – but I'll see what I can do,' Daniel replied. 'No promises.'

The sun was low in the sky and the beer garden was getting busier. Daniel got another round in – a bottle of red for himself and Sage, and a pint for Max – and life seemed long and the world seemed generous. Max couldn't help but feel things were finally looking up.

When Sage went to the bathroom, Max decided to take the plunge and atone for his sins.

'Look, Daniel, I just wanted to say I'm sorry,' he said, in a low voice in case anyone could hear them. 'About what happened between us. Before. It was just a one-off, but I didn't mean to hurt your feelings.'

'Oh, darling,' Daniel replied, laughing with a shade of pity. 'Bless you. It was lovely, but do you honestly think you ever stood a chance with me?'

*

'Did you keep in touch with Daniel?' the psychic asked.

'Yeah, we hang out from time to time. I last saw him about a month or so ago. We went to see a band in Camden.'

'How did he seem?' Caroline asked. 'Did he say anything unusual?'

Max took a long swallow of beer, thinking back to that day. 'Yes, actually. He tried to give me a guitar. A cherry-red Gibson SG, like the one Carl had.' Max shook his head at the memory. 'Such a sweet guitar, man, but I said no. It was too much; I couldn't take it.'

'So, you'd accept thousands of pounds off him to record a shitty demo, but you draw the line at a cheap guitar?' Caroline bristled.

'It's not a cheap guitar,' Max said, with a hollow laugh. He picked up his phone and tapped at the screen. 'It had a mahogany body, rosewood fingerboard and a maple neck.' He turned his phone to show them a picture of the guitar, pulled from an online retailer. 'Brand new, it'd be way over a grand.'

'That's Daniel's guitar,' Caroline said quietly. 'He bought it when he joined the Strangeways. I didn't understand why he needed such an expensive guitar when he played bass, but he's like that, isn't he? Spends money without really thinking.'

A swell of sorrow rose within Max as he returned his attention to the picture on his phone screen. It was such a handsome instrument. He'd have to remember to thank Daniel next time he saw him, and apologise for refusing it. Apologise for everything.

'Maybe he wanted to rekindle the band,' Sage suggested.

'Did you guys ever play together again?' asked the psychic.

'Nah,' said Max. 'It was too painful. All I could think about was Sesh, and Carl, and what might have been.'

'That's awful,' said the psychic, in a muted voice that paired well with tragedy.

'I never recorded a demo,' Max said. 'Never went on tour, never got signed.'

'You still play, though,' said Sage. 'You were at a festival last year.'

'That was bullshit,' he replied, his mood darkening. 'Just a pity gig, organised by my ex.'

The psychic turned to Sage, eyebrows raised, and Max rushed to correct her assumption. 'Nah, not Sage – Sage dumped me years ago.'

'Don't say it like that,' Sage said, kindly. 'I didn't *dump* you. We grew apart, that's all. It was mutual.'

'I strongly recommend an egg cleanse,' the psychic said again. 'When I was in New Orleans, I had my tea leaves read by a psychic, and she recommended one to me. I didn't do it right away, and I came to regret it.'

'Was Daniel travelling with anyone in New Orleans?' Caroline asked. 'Did he say he was meeting anyone?'

The psychic shook her head. 'No, he was definitely by himself.'

'The strange thing,' Caroline continued, 'is that he never bought a plane ticket. He obviously made it to the States, but I don't know how. We can't trace the payment.'

'Well, he obviously stuck the flights on a credit card or something,' Richard said.

'I don't particularly want to discuss my family finances with you,' Caroline replied, 'but Daniel doesn't have a credit card. There's no need. I invested my inheritance and bought this flat, but Daniel lives off his. I suppose it'll run out eventually, but for now he's very comfortable.'

'Must be nice,' Max said.

'The police checked his bank account,' Caroline continued, ignoring him. 'He withdrew cash in London and New Orleans, and he used our joint account to a book a hotel in the city, but no flights. We thought perhaps he was meeting someone out there, and they'd paid for his plane ticket.'

'He was travelling alone,' the psychic said. 'I'm sure of it.'

Max took another swig of beer to hide the sneer on his face. Caroline and Daniel were the richest people he had ever met, more minted than a pack of gum. Rich people always had credit cards, and multiple bank accounts with huge overdrafts. When you had money, there were always doorways to more money at your disposal.

'Tell us more about New Orleans,' Sage said. 'After that first night, how did you meet Daniel again?'

'It was the funniest thing,' said the psychic. 'We crossed paths in the French Quarter, spent the next five days hanging out, and then it turned out we were staying in the same hostel. For a while, anyway.'

'Daniel was staying in a hostel?' Max said, surprised. Daniel had once phoned him, incredulous, to ask if he'd ever stayed in a Travelodge. 'I mean, at least motels are camp,' he'd said. 'There's a kind of tragic beauty in a roadside motel. But a Travelodge? Darling, I'm telling you – it's the Pizza Express of hotels. The only thing worse would be one of those ghastly backpackers' hostels where you have to share a room with twenty unwashed strangers.'

The psychic met Max's gaze with an almost imperceptible frown. 'Yes – like I said, it was one of those beautiful moments of synchronicity.'

'Wasn't it the Hotel Monteleone?' Caroline asked.

'No, it was called the French House.'

'Was it a fancy hostel?' Sage asked. 'Like, boutique or whatever?'

The psychic shrugged, sucked on her white plastic vape. 'It was a backpackers' hostel. Cheap and cheerful, I guess. Very New Orleans, but I wouldn't call it fancy.'

'When we were planning *our* trip, Daniel wouldn't let me look at anything below four stars,' said Sage. 'He has expensive taste.'

'Yeah, when we were talking about going on tour, he was a total snob,' Max said.

'I don't know what to tell you,' the psychic said. 'It was just an ordinary backpackers' hostel, and Daniel was staying there.'

New Orleans: Selina

I woke to the sound of running water, distant chatter, and the busy clatter of the courtyard's food truck in full swing for breakfast. It took me a few beats to piece together my night – a stranger, cocktails, apocalyptic rain. My carriage home, a taxi.

I reached under my pillow and groped for the silky wrap that protected my tarot while I slept. With a sinking feeling, I remembered peeling the Temperance card from the deck and leaving it at the bar for Daniel to find. A missing card disabled the whole pack, rendered it useless. What a stupid thing to do.

Luckily, I was in the right place to look for a new set. The French Quarter was home to a number of esoteric shops that sold metaphysical gifts – crystal carvings, angel cards, pre-mixed spell bottles and the like. I had my tasseography reading booked that morning, and I'd be able to pick up a new deck at Deja Brew if I found one that spoke to me.

With sunglasses to protect my tender eyes from the bright sun, I skipped breakfast and hopped on the streetcar to a poky magic shop on Royal Street that stocked dusty mala beads, factory-made dreamcatchers, and overpriced tarot decks. Everything on the shelves had a grimy quality to it, coated in a fine felt of dust that suggested it wasn't the most popular place to shop.

My reading was with a clairvoyant called Miss Celeste-Ray, who looked a little worse for wear as she shuffled out to introduce herself. She had long black hair the texture of candyfloss, dark brown bags beneath her eyes and a constellation of skintags speckling her neck. A strong odour of sour cigarettes clung to her, as though she always wore the same T-shirt to smoke and never washed it, and when she coughed, which she did frequently and without warning, it was a rough, wet rattle from deep within her chest.

I followed her into a private room that had the strange, clinical quality of a doctor's waiting room. Colourful leaflets that advertised crystal healing and spiritual cleanses were pinned to off-white walls.

'All I need you to do right now is think about what's been going on with you,' she said. 'Think about where you're at right now. Think about the goals you've set over this year, and' – a rally of ragged coughs interrupted her spiel – 'think about the people involved. Now, you have all that in your head, honey?'

I thought about finding a place of my own. A quiet sanctuary, a little sunlit flat filled with rattan furniture, tapestries on the walls, pot plants and crystals. I'd like a herb garden to tend, a kitchen in which I could make homemade pickles and jams. Perhaps I'd adopt a cat, a little feline familiar to keep me company while I drank tea and read books.

I nodded, and Miss Celeste-Ray handed me a teacup containing a quarter of an inch of hot tea. It was jasmine and ylang-ylang, and had a heavily perfumed fragrance, like boiled bathwater. Steam curled from the cup and mingled with the sweat that rolled from my temples. Miss Celeste-Ray instructed me to swirl the tea three times with my left hand. 'Take your time, honey. Keep swirling until it feels right to stop. That's it, right on.'

When I felt ready, I handed her the cup, and she placed a saucer lined with a napkin over the top and flipped it upside down. The tea soaked into the napkin, and then she turned the cup the right way up and removed the saucer to inspect the contents.

'Really focus,' she said, holding a handkerchief against her lips as an explosive cough interrupted the stillness of the room.

She held the cup between her palms. There was a silver ring wedged on to every finger.

'Yeesh. I'm seeing a lot of dark energy here,' she said, squinting to inspect the stormy swirl of leaves scattered around the edge of the porcelain. 'I see a serpent, close to the lip of the cup, which suggests a current situation you're dealing with. And I see an owl in your future – a sign of poverty or sickness.'

'Oh no,' I said, peering into the cup. I couldn't see any discernible patterns in the Rorschach of wet leaves.

'I'm going to be frank with you, baby – I sense something has attached itself to you, something with bad intentions.'

'Well, that doesn't sound good.'

'Be careful around new people – you're on vacation, you're meeting folk, making new friends, but be careful.'

I thought of Gabe, the way he'd humiliated me in the courtyard on my first night, then hammered on my door to intimidate me.

She turned the cup in her hands. 'You need a cleanse,' she said. 'Urgently. I can book you in for a cord-cutting ceremony, try and sever whoever or whatever has attached itself to you, or' – another thick, wet cough punctuated her flow and left a tiny droplet of spittle on my hand – 'you could do an egg cleanse. We do 'em here, or you could do one yourself at home.'

'How much is a cord-cutting ceremony?' I said, recoiling a little from the table and subtly wiping her sputum from the back of my hand.

'A hundred dollars, baby, but I can give you a twenty per cent discount as you've already paid for the tea.'

The tasseography reading had cost me thirty-five dollars, not including tip. I looked into her exhausted eyes, at the burst blood vessels threaded across doughy cheeks, at her loose jowls and crooked teeth. She seemed like she could use the money more than I could use her services.

'I'll think about it,' I said, and she handed me her card.

*

The air was close and uncomfortable, pregnant with a storm threatening to break. My skin was grimy with sweat and stale smoke, and I felt unsettled by the psychic's interpretation of my tea leaves. I wanted a shower, but instead I followed my feet to the French Market for a lunch of fragrant jambalaya. Everywhere, I looked for Daniel. I looked for him in the faces of strangers, on the balconies of restaurants, in the doorways of bars.

I ducked into a bar on the corner of Pirates Alley, a little cobbled street near Jackson Square, for a drink. I liked the atmosphere around there: the flagstones, the flickering gas lanterns, the proximity to the cathedral, the frequency of the walking tours, usually led by flamboyant goths, that passed me by. At night, it felt like a good place to cross paths with ghosts, but during the day it was the ideal spot to watch the revelry of Jackson Square unfold.

The bartender was dressed like a gothic pirate, in a frilly white shirt and leather bustier that battled to contain her full breasts. I bought a pack of cigarettes from a vending machine and slipped on to a stool to order a beer.

'Hello, stranger,' a familiar voice said, sliding on to the stool next to me.

'What the hell happened to you last night?'

Daniel grinned as he placed the Temperance card on the bar between us. His plastic sunglasses were holding his mane of hair away from his face. He was wearing the same loose white cheesecloth shirt and black jeans as the day before, but he looked a hell of a lot fresher than I felt.

'I knew fate would bring us together again,' I said.

'Cute little calling card, you total cunt.'

'What happened?' I asked. 'I waited ages for you, but you never came back.'

'Oh darling, I'm so sorry. I realised I'd left my credit card behind the bar in Erin Rose, and I had to dash back for it.'

I frowned. That didn't sound right. I cast my mind back to our conversation about Erin Rose. 'But ... didn't you say you'd been on your way to Erin Rose when you saved me from the shoe-polish scam?'

He smiled easily. 'Can't a man visit the same bar twice in one day?'

'Well, why didn't you tell me? I could have come with you for an Irish coffee.'

'I wasn't thinking straight, darling. You know what it's like when you lose something – you panic, don't you? I'm so sorry, though – it was silly of me. I was gutted when I came back and found you'd gone.'

'Did you get your card back, at least?'

'I did, and I'm going to celebrate the return of both my card and my new best friend with a champagne cocktail. Death in the Afternoon, for the lady? Go on, they're divine, and look – this time it really is fate: I wanted to order one, but the bartender just told me they only serve them in pairs.'

'Why do they only serve them in pairs?'

'I think they use mini bottles of champagne, and one bottle splits perfectly between two glasses. Fancy it? Come on, after the way you ditched me last night, you *have* to say yes.'

'Well, technically *you* ditched *me*,' I said. 'Plus, it's a little early for champagne.'

'It's never too early for champagne,' he replied. 'Besides, I feel like celebrating more than just the return of my credit card.'

'How come?'

'Cos of all the bars in all the towns in all the world, you walked into mine.' He nudged me and I laughed, and he ordered, and I insisted on paying for the round in atonement.

The absinthe turned the golden champagne milky and opalescent, an almost alchemic transformation from citrine to moonstone. The drinks were served in plastic cups, and we sat outside so we could smoke and people-watch.

'Look, I'm sorry for doing a runner last night,' I said. 'I had a really great time hanging out with you, I was just so drunk and tired—'

'Don't,' he said, dismissing my words with a flap of his hand. 'It's way too hot to hold a grudge. But if you ditch me again, darling, I'll fucking murder you.'

*

Mood loosened by the cocktail, we spent the afternoon meandering between the shops dotted around Jackson Square. In a masquerade store, we tried on carnival masks made of leather, lace and feathers. The walls were covered in them, from floor to ceiling: a silver mask shaped like a crescent moon, a matching sun gilded in gold, the pointed Venetian beak of a plague doctor. Daniel picked an alligator mask from the display, its long, rounded snout bejewelled with hundreds of shimmering emerald sequins.

'I wish I had an excuse to buy one of these,' he said, fastening it over his head and turning to admire himself in the mirror. 'But we don't have masquerade balls in England. It would simply gather dust and be a constant reminder that wherever I am, I could be having more fun in New Orleans.'

'You could be a sexy alligator for Halloween,' I said, fingering an ornate harlequin mask in purple, green and gold.

He unhooked the mask and wrinkled his nose. 'And cover my beautiful face? Unthinkable.'

I was particularly drawn to the plethora of occult shops, many of which had resident psychics and sold kitsch souvenirs, glossy books about voodoo and witchcraft, packs of tarot cards, fragrant candles, joss sticks, spell kits, charms and hexes. We admired rows of glass vials containing herbs, spices and essential oil blends, and all manner of talismans that hinted towards a different kind of magic – coffin nails, wolf fur, Dead Sea salt, rail-road spikes. With the return of my beloved Temperance card, I no longer needed a new set of tarot cards, but I picked up little trinkets to remind me of my trip: a dried bean for luck, a jam jar of red brick dust for protection, a black candle that promised to banish negative energy.

Daniel trotted in my wake, fingering bracelets and sniffing incense, a bored expression on his face, but whenever I asked if he wanted to move on, he smiled brightly and said, 'No, no – take your time, darling!'

What I really wanted, however, was crystals. Louisiana wasn't known for its rock and mineral formations, and the only crystals native to the state were agate (which could be found pretty much anywhere in the world), the exceedingly rare and therefore wildly expensive Louisiana opal, and petrified palm wood. The witchy spirit of the French Quarter prevailed, though, and despite this shortage of naturally occurring crystals in the area, the city was still home to half a dozen lapidaries, and many of the occult shops offered crystals either in the form of jewellery – fine pendants, rings and beaded bracelets that promised the wearer good health, fortune or happiness – or a dusty tumble pick and mix, the prices of which often exceeded the average cost online by a landslide.

Eventually, I found a shop I liked. It was bright and modern, with crystals arranged by colour, shelf after shelf of appealing candy-hued rocks: the purple haze of amethyst and lepidolite giving way to the oceanic spectrum of angelite, larimar and pistachio calcite. The serpentine greens of malachite and moss agate followed, then the butter yellows of citrine and lemon calcite, the sunset spread of apricot agate and peach selenite, the pinks of rose quartz and aragonite. I burned, I pined, I perished, and my purse braced itself for a mass exodus.

From a glass case loaded with rare specimens, I picked an eye-wateringly expensive rhodochrosite slice, the size and thickness of a beer mat and nearly a hundred dollars, and a tiny chunk of Libyan desert glass, an impactite formed by meteorites striking the Saharan desert, the size of my thumbnail. I chose a spectrum of ergonomic tumbles, too: juicy orange calcite to promote healing; a chunky apatite tumble for enhanced insight; a small bumblebee jasper, found only in the cracks of Mount Papandayan, to dispel negative energy, and a flashy labradorite palm stone whose stormy grey surface glowed electric blue when it caught the light.

'That one looks like bacon,' Daniel said, reaching into my basket to examine the rhodochrosite slice.

'It does!' I said enthusiastically, running a finger along its jagged edge. 'Like raw streaky bacon.'

'And yet so pink and pretty. What does it do?'

'It heals old wounds,' I said. 'And nurtures love. It balances the heart chakra, and—'

But he had turned the slice over in his hands, and his eyes bugged when he clocked the extravagant price tag.

'It's gorgeous, babe,' he said, almost stiffly, as he returned it to my basket. 'But not *that* gorgeous.'

'Beauty is in the eye of the beholder,' I replied, embarrassed by the indulgence, but defensive too. Money was clearly no object to Daniel – he thought nothing of dropping twenty dollars on a cocktail. I worked hard for my money, so why shouldn't I spend it? We didn't have crystal shops like this at home, and ordering online was always a gamble: crystals often turned up broken, or smaller than anticipated, of dubious quality or questionable origin. There were a lot of fakes – lots of plastic, resin and glass – and a plague of mislabelling: howlite dyed blue and sold as turquoise; amethyst artificially heated and sold as natural citrine. Every purchase was a potential scam. I opened my mouth to say all this, but Daniel had turned to examine an impressive display of satin spar towers that were luminous as moonlight under the bright spotlights of the shop, and I thought better of it. Why spoil the mood by picking a fight?

On my way to the till, a shelf of fat, round spheres caught my eye and, almost defiantly, I stopped to admire them. In particular, I was drawn to a fire quartz no bigger than a snooker ball but two or perhaps three times as heavy. It felt good and solid in the palm of my hand. It was transparent and tinged a streaky orange, with threads of flame red catching the light, almost like drops of blood marbling water. I placed it in my basket without looking at the price.

*

A week into my trip, and I was in love with New Orleans. I'd developed a routine: shower, get ready for the day, record some readings for customers, then wander out into the city where, more often than not, I'd run into Daniel.

At home, I usually worked late into the night, when the long, dark hours encouraged overthinking, over-drinking and a desperate need for a connection. I couldn't keep up the same schedule with the time difference, but spiritual matters often felt urgent and it was important I kept up with requests. I knew from personal experience that if their preferred psychic wasn't available to offer guidance when they were needed most, even my most loyal followers would look elsewhere for a quick fix of comfort, hope and direction – and once they strayed, they might never come back. I couldn't afford to risk losing clients.

I lit candles and incense, with the door closed to the sound of the courtyard. The sweet smoke brightened the air of my hostel room with the earthy aroma of sandalwood, patchouli and dragon's blood. I spread a large square of midnight-blue velvet over the bed to create a backdrop, and weighed it down with a clear quartz point to promote a light, bright energy; a raw chunk of inky black obsidian for protection and to help connect me to the spirit world; and a radiant selenite tower to magnify the energy of the other crystals and keep them beautifully charged while I worked.

Rings next. I always wore the same silver rings on the same fingers while I filmed. I didn't always show my face, so stacks of silver rings, black nail polish and the tattoo on the index finger of my right hand created a recognisable aesthetic so my viewers could always recognise me as they scrolled through their endless feeds.

My hands, my tableau and my equipment were all part of my brand. It was about creating familiarity: the same dark blue velvet backdrop; the same well-thumbed Raider-Waite tarot deck, the edges of the cards softened with time; the same obsidian pendulum on a silver chain; the same polished bones for osteomancy. I even kept my sleeves rolled up and out of sight, so it was impossible to tell whether I was wearing a summer dress or a winter jumper. It meant I could work from anywhere, at any time, and no one would know the difference.

I'd started my business by live-streaming free readings to gain a following. It worked. Soon, my stock was rising, and then I'd got lucky with a high-profile customer – not a celebrity per se, but a lifestyle influencer with a reasonable-sized following who had reposted a screen recording of the card I'd pulled for her. Things had snowballed from there.

It had been the hottest summer on record, and then the coldest winter. The oceans were rising and the forests were burning. A famous comedian was in the news for abusing his power. A police officer was in the news for abusing his power. A politician was in the news for abusing his power. The prime minister was in the news for abusing his power. The local started charging over seven quid a pint, and it was an eight-hour wait for an ambulance. The news cycle ground on. I couldn't escape the weight of it – the violence of war and the terror of the climate crisis and injustice after injustice pressing on me from all sides – and nor could my customers. Soon, I had more followers than the original influencer who'd given me my big break.

I checked my email. A client in Nebraska had ordered an osteomancy reading. She wanted to know if she'd met her twin flame. Unlikely, I thought, as I clipped my phone into its tripod and switched on the portable ring light. I filmed five seconds of footage as I threw the bones and asked her question. They scattered in separate directions. *No.*

'Sorry, angel, but not yet,' I purred into the microphone, a sweet, honeyed voice. She was a regular customer, so I collected the bones and asked a bonus question: 'Will she meet her twin flame soon?'

Again, the bones scattered in disagreement, so I deleted the clip. There was no need to over-deliver on the bad news. I emailed the first clip to her with a gentle reminder that sometimes we get disappointing answers because we're asking the wrong questions. It didn't really matter what I said, though – she'd be back in a few weeks with a new man and the same question, and the answer would most likely still be no. *Is he my soulmate? ... Should I stay with him? ... Will she leave me again? ... Will he cheat? ... Should I give her a second chance? ... Should I trust him?*

Heartbreak was my bread and butter.

I worked through another dozen osteomancy readings – *Will he ask me to marry him in Venice? Should I forgive J? Will she ever love me back? Was it my fault he left? Will I pass my driving test?* – and enjoyed the soothing, hollow rattle of the bones as I tossed them across the velvet. *Yes. No. No. No. Yes.*

Coin tosses next. I had a beautiful silver divination token, shiny like a freshly minted fifty-pence piece, with *YES* printed on one side and *NO* on the other, in lieu of the traditional heads or tails. The binary nature of the reading always felt a little less than satisfactory to me, but clients liked the black-and-white nature of a simple *YES* or *NO*. *Should I study literature? Will I get engaged this year? Should I quit my job? Should I move to Paris? Am I on the right path?*

Finally, I settled into some freebie tarot readings and filmed a dozen single-card pulls, picking questions from the comments section of my last video. I kept things vague, ending on a reminder that I offered full spreads at ten per cent off if they felt like they needed a little more clarity, more direction. They usually did.

It was nearly time to venture into the French Quarter, so I ticked off my final task of the morning: issuing refunds to the clients whose questions I couldn't answer. *Will the cancer come back? Will I get pregnant soon? Will her blood tests be negative?* I sent apologies, well wishes, good vibes and offers to light candles, but I didn't answer medical questions. I had to draw a line somewhere.

*

As the clouds lifted and the sun reached its full potential, broiling the city like a shucked oyster, fate brought Daniel and I together. It wasn't unusual to walk into a restaurant and find him sitting at a table, serenely turning the pages of a paperback with a coffee, or scanning the menu, deciding what to order. We shared lunches of fried catfish po' boys and cups of spicy seafood gumbo, and took long strolls through the French Quarter, streetcar rides to look at the grand mansions that lined St Charles, visited obscure museums about death, absinthe, alligators.

We talked about the small minutiae of the time we spent apart, and had long conversations about our lives back home.

Daniel had a passion for cinema, used to play bass guitar in a band and dreamed of travelling the world, but had never stuck to one thing for long enough to see it through. 'My friends think I'm fickle,' he said, 'but I swear, there's always an external force that derails me.'

Daniel and I were finishing our customary Death in the Afternoons at the Pirate Alley Café, the greenish champagne fizzing in the plastic cup and spreading the liquorice scent of absinthe in the air.

'Do you believe in life after death?' he asked, a contemplative look on his face. He was in a deep, reverent mood. His hair was twisted into a bun on the top of his crown, and every so often he reached to give it an absent-minded squeeze as though testing the firmness of a peach.

'Absolutely,' I said, glancing up from my phone. I'd been idly reading my daily horoscope. It said I should be open to financial gain, and recommended I carry a bay leaf and a nugget of pyrite in my purse to promote wealth and prosperity. I was wondering if a restaurant would give me a single bay leaf if I asked nicely, or if I'd need to wait until one showed up in my dinner.

'I don't know why I even asked,' Daniel said. 'Of course you do.'

I lowered my phone to look at him properly. 'When my grandma died, I could feel her presence for ages afterwards. She'd visit me in my dreams, and ... I can't really explain it, but I'd pick up her energy every so often.'

'Sounds ghastly,' he said.

'No, it was nice. It was almost like hearing a familiar song playing in another room. I'd just get this vague sense that she was close but distant.'

'I'd hate to be visited by my grandmother. She had this crusty old white dog, like Buffalo Bill in *Silence of the Lambs*, and it always used to shit on the carpet.'

'I loved my grandmother. She loved soaps and used to ring me up to chat about them.'

'Old people love soap,' Daniel said, with a knowing nod. 'And talc; they love soap and talc.'

'No, I mean soaps on TV. Like *EastEnders* and *Coronation Street*. I still get this odd thrill of anticipation when I hear the closing beats of an *EastEnders* episode, because part of me expects my phone to ring, with her name on the screen.'

'Hey, did you ever try to communicate with her spirit? Like, with a Ouija board or anything like that?'

'Absolutely not,' I said, shuddering. 'I'd never go near that shit.'

He laughed. 'Are you serious?'

'Deadly. Some doors are best left closed – you don't know what you might disturb if you choose to knock.'

Smiling, he returned his attention to his cocktail, twirling the cup to make the liquid splash against the sides.

'Have you ever done a Ouija board?' I asked.

'Yes – and my friend Sage was convinced a demon attached itself to her boyfriend. His whole life turned upside down afterwards.'

'Do *you* think a demon attached itself to him?'

A brief flicker of irritation crossed his face, but then he softened. 'I don't know, darling. All I know is, never trust a musician, and never trust a woman fucking a musician.'

'Do you believe in the afterlife?'

'No,' he said. 'I like the idea of immortality, but I don't think it exists in a metaphysical sense.'

I placed an elbow on the table and rested my chin in my hand. 'In what sense *do* you think immortality exists?'

'In the poetic,' he said. 'Through art, music, cinema. People can live forever through their oeuvre. Jayne Mansfield is immortal, Marilyn Monroe is immortal, Elvis Presley is immortal.'

'Well, Elvis isn't dead,' I said confidently.

'Oh, don't start. You sound like Sage.'

'You don't seem to like Sage very much,' I said.

'No darling, I *love* Sage. She's a lunatic – my sister can't *stand* her. I like to surround myself with people Caroline can't tolerate for long periods of time. It's the only way I get a break from her.'

'Your life sounds complicated,' I said.

'It's never dull, I can tell you that much.'

I grinned and picked up my phone to resume scrolling. 'Hey, do you want me to read your horoscope?'

'No – read me today's tomorrow, and we can evaluate how accurate it was in retrospect. I think that's a more valuable use of our time.'

'Oh, fuck off.'

We sat in silence for a few moments. The sun was setting. Jackson Square was winding down: the artists were packing up their paintings, the band dismantling their instruments, the psychics folding up their tables and chairs, perhaps to find a new location closer to the action of Bourbon Street, where alcohol loosened both purses and inhibitions.

'Do you really not believe in any kind of afterlife?' I asked.

He shook his head.

There can't be nothing, I thought. *This can't be it.* There must be something else. It seemed spiritually bankrupt to imagine I was simply meat with a shelf life, and when I tried to picture death, I imagined the vast nothingness of a dreamless, endless sleep – but it was impossible to think of sleep that wasn't bookended by the contrast of consciousness.

'That makes me feel kind of sad for you,' I replied.

'Oh, don't bother,' he said, draining his drink. 'I'm beyond pity.'

Daniel led me to a little live music bar on the edge of the Quarter for a light early supper – a dozen charbroiled oysters, topped with garlic butter, grated Parmesan and a crunch of breadcrumbs, served with slices of grilled French bread. We washed down the hot, salty oysters with large glasses of fizzy lager while an old man in a suit and pork pie hat played the blues on an acoustic guitar. The air was warm, and Daniel's hair curled from his face in a halo.

I'd noticed people treated me differently when I was with Daniel. Moths were drawn to his light. He flirted with men and women in equal measure and, in return, people bought us drinks, bartenders slipped us free shots, doormen waived cover charges. Fellow tourists invited us to sit with them, and I'd read their cards while Daniel turned on the charm. If the world was an oyster, it was one I'd always struggled to shuck, but people, places and opportunities opened for Daniel like it was the most natural thing in the world.

He seemed to have an instinct for pleasure, and it wasn't unusual for us to walk into a bar or restaurant and for Daniel to sense something imperceptible in the air and usher us out. He might explain his change of heart with something like, 'They had *tater tots* on the menu,' or, 'It was dead in there, darling, like drinking in a morgue.' I was only too happy to let him call the shots because we'd always end up somewhere better: happy-hour oysters spiked with absinthe for twenty-five cents apiece, for example, or a spontaneous skiffle band holding court in a rowdy dive bar. I learned he liked an atmosphere of exclusivity, and always seemed to know where to find a hidden speakeasy or hole-in-the-wall restaurant. I think his ability to seek out the most joyful way of experiencing the city was why I ended up agreeing to the car.

Over dinner, we were talking about our plans for the rest of our time in New Orleans. Daniel had a wealth of suggestions for things to do, and I found it hard to imagine doing any of them without him.

'If you fancy a swamp tour, I was thinking of renting a car,' he said, dabbing butter from his lips. 'Then maybe we could drive out to Lake Pontchartrain, visit the Abita Mystery House, do a brewery tour, or even just take a stroll through the bayou.'

New Orleans was surrounded by an intricate filigree of brackish, slow-moving creeks that were home to voodoo priestesses and cryptid creatures called rougarous that prowled the swamps, looking to feast on unlucky souls.

'I'd *love* to see the bayou,' I replied. 'But is that safe? Aren't there alligators and snakes and things like that?'

'Sure, but they're more scared of us than we are of them,' he said. 'I'd be more concerned about the ghosts.'

'Ghosts?'

'Well, the swamps *are* haunted,' he said, teasing. 'Anyway, the swamp-tour packages are a total rip-off. You end up spending an hour doing a tour of every hotel in the city to pick up other people before you even make it to the freeway. It's so much more chic to make your own way there and just pay for the boat trip. Thing is, it's hard to find a cab to take you all the way out there, and a fucking nightmare to get one to pick you up. If we rented a car, I think we'd actually save money – plus, then we'd have a car to zip around in. You really need a car in the US, even in the metropolitan areas. And then we could do a few day trips, visit other parts of the city … What do you think? There's so much more to New Orleans than the French Quarter, you know.'

I took a sip of my drink, mulling it over. 'How much are we talking?'

'Oh, not much – a few hundred dollars, maybe. I guess it depends on how long we want the car for, and what kind we get – I'm not pootling around in an old banger.'

'I'm not sure if I can stretch to a few hundred dollars,' I said.

'Well, let me figure out the costs and you can tell me what you think? No harm in that, right?'

'Sure, no harm in that.'

'Perfect,' he said, wiping his fingers on a napkin.

The courtyard was filling up with a late-night crowd, and as the old musician in the pork pie hat ended his set and passed around a metal Miller Lite tip bucket, a jazz trio replaced him on stage. A pretty woman with a husky voice began to sing a soulful cover of Amy Winehouse's 'Back to Black'. As she sang, it was Daniel who seemed to hold her attention.

'It's getting kind of late,' I said. 'Shall we call it a night? Where's your hotel again?'

Daniel took a drag on his vape and exhaled a plume of saccharine smoke over his shoulder. 'Oh, not far from here.'

'Shall I walk you there? I need to get a cab back to mine, but I can book it from the lobby of your hotel.'

'We could share a cab,' he suggested.

'Are you in one of the hotels on the other side of Canal? I'm staying at the French House, in Mid-City, so I could drop you off on the way.'

'I'm staying at the French House in Mid-City,' he echoed.

I blinked. 'You're staying at the French House?'

'In Mid-City,' he said, nodding.

'No fucking way. How long have you been there for?'

'I was staying in a hotel in the Quarter, but I got sick of the noise and transferred. I suppose you'd call it fate, darling,' he said, pocketing his vape. 'Shall we promenade through the Quarter and get some cocktails to go?'

I followed Daniel into the night. He passed through the meandering crowds of Bourbon Street like a ghost, spectral in his white shirt, the sleeves of which were now mottled with dirt.

'It's not bad, is it? I splashed out for a private room,' I babbled, trailing after his broad shoulders as we wound our way between revellers. I realised I was quite tipsy. 'I couldn't bear the thought of a dorm, but it's so much cheaper than one of the grand old hotels, isn't it?'

'A steal,' he replied.

As we weaved our way through the bright lights of the city, everything felt quite magical. The atmosphere was carnivalesque. The discarded beads that glittered in the gutter were regal, the Jell-O-shot girls outside the clubs were beautiful, and the neon lights that brightened the night sky were fairylike. We ducked into a lurid bar for twenty-ounce Styrofoam cups of frozen Hurricanes.

'I do *not* need more alcohol,' I said, handing over several notes to cover both drinks.

'Oh no, let me!' Daniel said, thrusting a hand into his pocket for his wallet.

'Don't be silly,' I replied, reaching for my change and dropping several dollars into the tip jar. 'You can get breakfast in the morning.'

'Deal. Maybe we can go for a champagne brunch.'

I booked us a cab with an app on my phone, and soon we were climbing the porch stairs at the French House. The front desk was empty, and we found Kenna in the TV room trying to wrangle a cacophonous group of lads who were drinking heavily and watching a beachy horror movie in which big-breasted women were being eaten alive by flesh-eating piranhas. She caught my eye and gave me a distracted wave, just as one leaned forward and threw up on the carpet.

'God fucking *dammit*.'

We slipped through the kitchen and out into the courtyard. A group of backpackers were playing a drinking game that involved chugging beer and flipping empty plastic cups on one of the picnic benches.

'Animals,' Daniel muttered.

I picked an empty bench and sparked a cigarette, and soon we were absorbed in the party atmosphere. The Hurricane tasted like sweetened nail-varnish remover and turned our tongues a lurid shade of red.

'So, you're really into all this New Age stuff, right? Crystals and all that jazz?' His expression was neutral, and I couldn't work out if he was asking with good-natured curiosity, or as a challenge, but either way I rose to it.

'It's my vibe,' I said. I still had the bag of crystals from the French Quarter lapidary in my handbag. I kept forgetting to take them out. They weighed my bag down, and I kept meaning to move them into my suitcase for safekeeping, but I liked being able to reach for them when I needed some comfort. I extracted the bumblebee jasper and rolled it between my fingers.

'I know it might seem kind of silly to some people,' I said. 'But it really helps me get through life.'

'How so?'

'I dunno,' I said. 'I'd always thought I'd find life easier as I grew older, but it just seems to get harder, and sadder, and more difficult.'

As I'd moved through adulthood, and left my reckless, carefree twenties behind, where life was easy although I didn't know it, didn't appreciate it, because all the stresses – the bad housemates and cheating boyfriends; the exams, hangovers and minor inconveniences – were like gas, and expanded to fill all the available space in my head. They took on this exaggerated, burlesque form of stress. Trauma felt like the exception, not the rule, and those affected by real trauma were hollowed out by it: the unexpected death of a parent or sibling; a tragic, life-changing accident; a violent assault. And then, in my thirties, I realised that everyone around me was burdened by grief, fear, pain, loneliness. My God, the things my friends were burdened with! Sickness, mental illness, depression, suicide, miscarriages, failed IVF, divorce, addiction, alcoholism, redundancy, bankruptcy, death. Death! Death used to be a rare thing, something that happened to other people, and they were known for it: like that one girl at school whose dad died, or that neighbour we watched grow frail with cancer. The dinner lady who was there one day and gone the next. Our friends' grandparents, then our own grandparents. Now, suddenly it was our parents who were fading, our parents who were either dying or dead or struggling with widowhood, and the adults we'd grown up with were slowing down, growing older, checking out.

'I feel like the tables turned without me noticing,' I said. 'Suddenly, I'm looking around at my friends and realising it's now rarer to have two living, healthy parents. And I realised that life is just pain, and that pain is relentless, and that whatever wealth or success you may have experienced, whatever love and whatever joy, those places will vanish from beneath your feet, your loved ones will leave you in one way or another, and death is ever-present, waiting to humble you, and … Well, yes, I realised I needed something to cling to, a raft in the storm of my deepest, darkest depression. I needed something to help me make sense of it all.'

He exhaled, a sharp little *pfft*. 'I can't imagine only coming to this realisation in your thirties,' he said. 'I'm just about to turn thirty, and I can't remember a time when it didn't feel like everyone around me was suffering in one way or another. Failure, car accidents, disappointments, death.'

'I'm sorry to hear that.'

He paused to smoke his vape for a moment. 'Do you think of yourself as an intuitive person?'

I blinked at this rapid change of pace. 'Yes,' I said, swirling the dregs of my cocktail. 'And I trust my instincts. I feel like you're here for a reason, and so am I. Like maybe you were in need, and you were manifesting some spiritual support – I get the sense you've been through a lot.'

He took a small sip of his drink in lieu of an answer, and I reached for his free hand and gave it a gentle squeeze.

'My parents are gone, my sister is … Well, Caroline's just Caroline. And every friend I've ever had has let me down. My friend Dicky fucked me over at university, my friend Max used me, and Sage – well. I've talked about Sage already.' He shook his head. 'Life is just one long string of disappointments. There's little point in trying to do anything, because something will always get in the way.'

'Look, we don't have to get into it,' I said. 'But everything happens for a reason. I think it's easy for me to imagine that I manifested you, because I was lonely and finding the city hard to be in by myself, but perhaps it was the other way round. Perhaps you manifested me.'

'Perhaps we manifested each other.'

'Perhaps we did,' I said.

Morning drew closer, and as the last of the unwashed backpackers called it a night and staggered, flat-footed and loud-mouthed, towards one of the bigger dorm rooms, I pitied their roommates. Daniel excused himself to use the bathroom, and while he was gone, Kenna appeared as a silhouette in the doorway to the main house.

'Hey, baby, what're you doing out here all alone?' she asked, smiling brightly as she crossed the courtyard to join me. She brought with her the smell of the night – blooming midnight jasmine, a tang of sweat and sandalwood incense.

'I'm not alone,' I said, smiling shyly. 'My friend just went to the loo.'

'Ah, I see,' she said, turning back to the house. 'I'll leave you to it – but come on in and say hey if you get lonely. I'll be on the desk for the rest of the night.'

'Who was that?' Daniel asked, taking his place at the table.

'Oh, that was Kenna,' I replied. 'She works here.'

'And you have a thing for her, right?'

'What makes you say that?'

'You've turned the most delightful shade of pink, darling.'

'Oh no,' I said. 'It's not like that.'

He lifted his vape to his lips, but the light flashed ruby red, cast the picnic bench in a bloody spotlight. 'Fuck,' he said, shaking it and trying again. 'Battery's dead.'

'We'll go to bed soon,' I said.

'You can be anything you like, you know,' he replied. 'There are no rules.'

My mouth felt dry, and I swallowed. 'What do you mean?'

'You can do whatever you like, be whoever you like, sleep with whoever you like. It doesn't matter. You might be a different person next week, so what does it matter what you do today?'

He seemed a little drunk. His Hurricane cup was loose in his hand, and melted cocktail splashed down the front of his shirt, which turned translucent and revealed the outline of a nipple that looked pierced.

'We should go to bed,' I said, just as Daniel twisted the cap from a bottle of beer.

'Those brutes left them,' he explained, handing it to me. 'Might as well.'

'No, really, I've had enough,' I said, gently pushing the beer towards him. 'I'm ready for bed, but … do you want me to keep you company while you drink that?'

'Oh no, you go ahead, darling,' he said. 'I need to decompress for a bit, then I'll head to bed myself.'

He looked a little frayed around the edges, with bruise-coloured bags under bloodshot eyes. I remembered something my sister Katie had once said about alcoholics: they never knew when to call it a night. I felt bad leaving him to drink alone in case I was somehow enabling dangerous behaviour or leaving him in a vulnerable situation. Then again, there were only two beers left in the six-pack, and we were already at our hotel.

'Well,' I said. 'One more won't hurt.'

I reached for the last Abita and cracked it with a sharp *psssst*. *I don't have to drink it all*, I thought. I could just nurse it while he finished his bottle, make sure he got to bed okay, then tip the rest down the sink.

We chatted for a while longer, and when I finished the last of the beer, I was definitely ready for bed. My private room had felt like a small luxury when I was planning my stay, but now it felt like the most decadent decision I could have made for myself. My room, my sanctuary. And now, it was calling to me.

'I'm so tired,' I said. 'I think I'm ready for bed.'

He reached for my cigarettes and shook one from the pack. 'Do you mind, darling? My vape's dead. Don't wait up.'

I checked the time. It was nearly 3am. 'Are you sure? I don't mind keeping you company while you smoke.'

As I spoke, however, a yawn bloomed in my throat that I was too tired to supress.

'I wouldn't dream of keeping you up any longer,' he replied. 'Honestly, you go ahead.'

'Okay,' I said, gathering my bag, phone and cigarettes. 'Sweet dreams.'

'See you for breakfast? It's on me, remember.'

'Sounds great.'

When I reached the door to my room, I glanced over my shoulder. He was just sitting there, unlit cigarette held loosely between his fingers, watching me tap my key card on the lock. It made a gizmo-ish click and the little traffic light turned from red to green as the door unlocked. I paused, and then gave him a little wave over my shoulder as I opened the door. He lifted a hand in farewell, but still he did not light his cigarette, and still he did not make a move towards his own bed. It was a peculiar sight, and as I removed my make-up and brushed my teeth, I thought of him sitting there in the quiet courtyard, a ghostly figure dressed in white, and I felt a bone-deep unease. In my pyjamas, I turned off the overhead light, and, telling myself it was good practice for a woman travelling alone, I placed the latch on the bedroom door and checked the handle to ensure it was properly closed.

*

The aircon was blasting a chill and my tongue felt thick in my mouth. I'd been lost in a strange, disorientating dream, a dream in which I'd killed a handsome black peacock by wringing its slender neck, and, far from mourning its tragic beauty in death, I was merrily plucking its ebony tail feathers in a morbid game of effeuiller la marguerite. *She loves me … she loves me not …*

I had a vague idea that dreaming of dead peacocks held some ominous oneiric significance, but I'd need to look it up to learn the exact meaning of the dream.

I reached for my water bottle, and as I swallowed a warm, plastic-tasting mouthful, I realised it wasn't thirst that had disturbed my sleep, but a soft, urgent tapping at my bedroom door. A shiver of fear rippled through me as it came again, the rhythmic tap-tap-tap-tap-tap of a knuckle on wood. I pulled the covers up to my nose and closed my eyes, willing Gabe to leave me alone.

'Selina … are you awake? It's me, darling. It's Daniel.'

With palpable relief, I slipped from the bedcovers and padded across the room to unlock the door. Outside, the air was warm and close, in stark contrast to my cool, air-conditioned bedroom. Daniel stood before me in his white shirt, looking a little worse for wear, exhaustion painted all over his face. I must have looked similarly bedraggled, as he pulled a desperately pitiful face and said: 'Oh, my poor darling, look at you. I'm so sorry to wake you up.'

'Christ, Daniel, you frightened the life out of me,' I said. 'What's up?'

'Oh darling, it's a nightmare. My bloody key card isn't working, and there's no one at the front desk to help me get into my room.'

I rubbed the sleep from my eyes and blinked at him. 'Where's Kenna? I thought it was a twenty-four-hour reception?'

'I have no idea – there hasn't been anyone to help for the last twenty minutes, and frankly I'm getting sick of waiting.'

'Do you want to come in?'

'May I?'

'Sure.' I stepped aside to welcome him into the room.

'Oh, this isn't bad, is it?' he said, peering at the sink, the rumpled bed, the church pew. 'It's quite nice, actually. Like a little student bedsit.'

'What's yours like?' I asked, perching on the bed. 'Are you in a dorm?'

'Christ, no. Mine's a little bigger than this, though,' he said. 'Sorry, I feel so bad for waking you up, I just didn't know what else to do. I thought perhaps Kenna had nipped to the loo or gone for a smoke, but I've looked everywhere, and I can't find anyone. I tried to sleep on the couch in the TV room, but I felt too ... exposed, I guess? All the drunks and heterosexuals storming through from the French Quarter every ten minutes. I just felt a bit vulnerable.'

'There really should be someone on reception to sort out problems like this,' I said, self-righteous on his behalf. 'It isn't safe – I had this drunk yelling outside my bedroom door on my first night, and it scared me to death. And, of course, we don't even have phones in our rooms, so there was nothing I could do but either confront him or ignore it and hope he'd leave me alone.'

'Oh, you poor darling. That sounds awful. Why don't you switch hotels?'

I sank on to the bed and tucked my legs beneath me. 'Well, I've already paid for this one, so …'

'Let's get a room at the Roosevelt tomorrow, darling. Fuck this place, it's awful. We can share a suite with a balcony, have our own space.'

'I can't really afford to pay for a second room,' I said.

'Don't be silly, we'll demand a refund on this one – it isn't fit for purpose,' he said. 'Besides, I can pay. We can get a two-bedroom suite for a few thousand dollars. I think that would suit us better than this. But for now – do you mind having a roommate? I promise I don't snore.'

'Oh,' I said. 'Um.'

'Sorry – that was rude of me. I can wait it out in the TV room until someone finally decides to do some work.'

'No, it's okay … We can bunk up. Thank God you knew my room number.'

He nodded. 'Thank God.'

'You can sleep here tonight, and we'll decide what to do tomorrow. As long as you don't think it's too weird to share a bed with a virtual stranger?'

'We aren't strangers, darling. Besides, sleeping with strangers is my raison d'être.'

I wriggled to the far side of the bed to make space for him. I liked the idea of a hotel suite. I imagined a view of the city, a clawfoot tub, breakfast in bed, room-service champagne. Daniel and I, dressed up for dinner, stepping from the hotel lobby straight into the French Quarter and strolling arm in arm through the city. No more late-night cabs; no more trekking all the way from Mid-City for a cocktail. Dreamy. But of course, I couldn't let him pay for something like that. I was fine in my little hostel room.

'You're truly an angel. I'll buy you beignets for breakfast. Mind if I borrow your toothpaste?'

'Go for it. It's just in the washbag by the sink. Help yourself to whatever you like, there's make-up wipes and moisturiser in there too if you want to freshen up.'

He left the bathroom door open, and I watched him squeeze a slug of Colgate on to his finger and rub it into a foam on his teeth and gums. While he spat into the sink and splashed his face with water, I located my phone and typed, *What does it mean to dream of killing a peacock?* into the search bar.

A peacock represents beauty and pride in the dreamworld, but it can also be an omen of death and transformation. Killing a peacock indicates a barrier to change: perhaps something or someone is holding you back, or you may be experiencing reservations about a new opportunity, connection or situation.

That doesn't make much sense, I thought. If I was on the brink of transformation, I would welcome it with open arms – and I certainly didn't have any reservations about anything new. That's what I was here to do, to welcome as much newness into my life as possible.

The mattress dipped as Daniel sank into the bed beside me.

'Can't sleep?' he asked, rolling over. In the light of my phone, his face was stubbly and pale.

'I don't know. I feel kind of jittery, I guess – you frightened me, banging on my door.'

'Oh darling, I'm so sorry. I was desperate. Hey, want some melatonin?'

'What on earth is melatonin?'

'It's an over-the-counter sleeping aid you can get here,' he said, sliding out of bed and reaching for his trousers. He extracted a little white pill from his pocket and handed it to me. 'It's a natural sleep hormone – it'll knock you right out.'

I took the pill and dry-swallowed it. 'You really are an angel.'

'Night-night,' he said. 'Sleep tight, don't let the alligators bite.'

'Night, silly.'

I closed my eyes, but I was still thinking about my beautiful dead peacock. I wondered who could possibly be holding me back – and then I wondered if it was me, if I was holding myself back from living my best life or transforming into the best version of myself. Was some tiny part of my heart still closed to the endless, radical possibilities of pleasure?

I thought I'd find it difficult to fall asleep with someone in the bed beside me, but soon I felt the melatonin dragging me under, and then I was gone, and I didn't dream of anything at all.

Entrée

Seafood Gumbo

⚜

A thick, silky stew with a robust flavour, gumbo is the official state dish of Louisiana. Made with the Creole holy trinity of bell pepper, celery and onion, with mixed seafood. Thickened with okra, and served with white rice.

London: Sage

The sky burned with streaks of cerise, pumpkin and ochre as the sun began its slow descent. It was a week past the solstice: summer had finally reached the Northern Hemisphere, and the sun had left Gemini and entered Cancer. It was time to follow one's heart, and Sage's heart was telling her to leave. They weren't getting anywhere, and she could worry about Daniel just as easily at home as she could in Caroline's flat.

No one seemed particularly hungry, but Richard was spooning rice into five bowls. He topped each fluffy white island with a ladle of viscous stew studded with coins of sausage and shell-on prawns.

'It looks delicious, Dicky,' Caroline said, without much enthusiasm.

The rising steam carried a heavy meaty smell that turned Sage's stomach. 'Oh – don't worry about me,' she said. 'I'm vegan – sorry, I didn't expect dinner, otherwise I'd have brought something.'

Richard looked stricken. 'Oh shit, I didn't realise.'

'It's fine, honestly.'

'I'm so sorry – there isn't much in the way of provisions. Did you want to order something? Or I could open some crisps?'

'I can eat later,' she said.

Max dipped his spoon into his bowl of gumbo and stirred. A prawn surfaced, its dead black eyes fixed into a thousand-yard stare, insectile antennae coated in slime. The soup clung to the metal, sticky and mucilaginous as snot, and he seemed to think twice about raising it to his lips. The most exotic thing Sage had ever seen Max eat was a doner kebab, and she couldn't help but smile at the stoic expression on his face as he tentatively tasted the broth.

'Woah,' he said. 'That's actually alright.'

The psychic followed suit and tasted a spoonful of the stew. 'Mmm,' she said, pressing a napkin to her lips. 'That's gorgeous – the texture, it's so velvety. Like butter.'

'Thanks,' said Richard, turning pink. 'I've never made it before – I just followed a recipe online. Did you try gumbo while you were in New Orleans?'

'Of course,' the psychic replied. They talked for a while about the flavours of the city, and the many meals she had shared with Daniel, but Sage was distracted by thoughts of the little paper wrap tucked in her purse. A quick bump would take the edge off the wine, which was making her feel dizzy and sluggish as it hit her near-empty stomach. Caroline wouldn't mind, she thought – or, at least, the old Caroline wouldn't have minded – if she pulled out a wrap of coke. The old Caroline would have fetched a mother-of-pearl straw, an antique silver hand mirror and a gold AmEx to chop and cut. No, not an AmEx – a razorblade.

The psychic looked like she knew her way around recreational pharmaceuticals too. No, it was the men that made her think twice. She could already predict the faux outrage. Max would call her a hypocrite for refusing to be vaccinated while shovelling unknown chemicals up her nose, and there would be earnest talk of young, frightened girls forced to swallow condoms of cocaine to smuggle through customs from Richard. Bad things in faraway places, things she didn't like to think about. Max used to love coke, though, loved to stick his dirty house key into her and Daniel's bag and steal frequent, generous bumps on nights out – but one thing Sage understood about Max was that however much he loved something, however much he loved coke, he loved maintaining the illusion of being in control more, even when things were falling apart.

'When you've finished eating, will you read my cards for me please?' Sage asked.

'No time like the present,' the psychic said, pushing her bowl to one side and picking up her cards. 'It needs to cool down for a minute anyway. You've had your cards read before, right?'

'Absolutely. I love this kind of thing.'

'Fabulous.' The psychic shuffled the deck, small hands deftly handling the oversized cards. It was a beautiful set, each card decorated with images of swords and wands, cups and pentacles. 'You're very close to Daniel, aren't you?'

'He's my favourite person,' Sage said. 'I love him to death.'

'But he didn't tell you he was going to New Orleans?'

'No,' Sage said carefully. 'He's like that, though.'

The psychic's eyes narrowed. 'What was he like?'

The question snagged like a chipped tooth against Sage's tongue, but she couldn't quite place why it jarred. 'Independent, hard to track down,' she said. 'He can go months without calling or texting, and then suddenly he'll reappear with a wild story, and I'll see him every day for weeks at a time, and then he'll vanish again. I don't mind, though. That's just Daniel.'

'Interesting,' the psychic said. She flipped the first card, and they both leaned forward to study it. 'The Sun,' she said, with a soft smile. 'What a gorgeous card – success, radiance, positivity.'

'That makes sense,' Sage said. 'I'm such a sun-worshipper. I feel really grounded when it's warm.'

'As opposed to the rest of us, who love the rain,' Max said.

She didn't dignify that with an answer, and kept her attention focused on the psychic. 'I always try to chase the sun in winter.'

'Did you travel much with Daniel?'

'No,' said Sage. 'We went to a festival together last summer, but that's all we've managed so far.'

*

It was quiet at the campsite, a sultry day spread under a clear sky. Sage placed her sarong in the dappled shade of a birch tree and surveyed the meadow. Sunbathers were dotted across the grass, reading paperbacks, napping, scrolling on their phones, painting their faces with glitter.

A girl with cropped hair and a boyish recline laughed as her pretty companion held a buttercup beneath her chin. 'See, you do like butter! The flowers have spoken.'

'Well, I'm vegan, babe. But yeah, I do miss butter.'

Just beyond them, a silver-haired couple were clinging to each other for balance as they took it in turns to push their feet into their wellies. *Unnecessary*, thought Sage. The ground was perfectly dry.

'... beautiful curation, but it finishes next week,' one said to the other. 'So, if you want to go, I'll get us tickets as soon as we get back.'

'I do fancy it, actually.'

Their chatter was soothing, ordinary. They wouldn't remember these conversations in a week, but they'd remember the way they'd made them feel: cared for, connected, part of the world as it turned. That was the nice thing about this festival. It was for everyone, drawing people from all walks of life.

Daniel flopped on the grass beside her, stretched into a yawn. 'God, festivals are dull.'

'It's barely started,' she replied. 'Where's Caroline?'

'In her boudoir,' Daniel said, referring to the elaborate yurt Caroline had rented for the weekend.

Sage picked a blade of grass and ran it over her leg. 'Is she feeling better?'

'Oh darling, she's faking,' Daniel said. 'She took one look at the port-a-loos and took to her bed.'

'Why did she bother coming?'

'Fear of missing out.'

Sage smoked one of Daniel's cigarettes, surveillant eyes hidden behind dark sunglasses as she scanned the passing crowd. Girls in elf ears and flower crowns held hands and giggled; girls with fake freckles called each other's names, chewed gum with open mouths, already rolling, trading sips for tokes, and stumbling and catching each other and laughing it off. They were feeling themselves in their faux-festival chic, twirling to show off their outfits, all vintage and handmade and shopped locally. Bourgeoisie bohemia. Crowds like this were always generous with their resources, because their resources were plentiful. Privately educated with cushy nine-to-fives, they lived in luxury flats in fashionable neighbourhoods. Their weekends were all brunch and matinees, cocktail bars, fine dining. Then summer hits, and it's all crocheted sundresses and bare feet, sleeping in converted vans that cost tens of thousands of pounds, and spending lavishly on overpriced booze and vegan street food, vintage clothes, and henna tattoos.

'Shall we get a drink, darling?' Daniel asked.

'Might as well.'

Red wine for Daniel, a flat cider for Sage. The afternoon bled into the night, a tie-dye of different memories, different moments blurring together. A huge chill-out tent glowed with a soft purple UV light, the people inside on another planet, all lying supine and staring at papier-mâché decorations painted in garish neon. An evening yoga session, Sage's soft body curved into a pretzel against the dark grass. The first night of a festival was like the first night on holiday in a new city: you had to get acclimatised, figure out who you wanted to be in this liminal land in which everyone – even old friends – felt like both siblings and strangers.

And then there was Max.

Daniel had disappeared into the crowd for another round of drinks – this time, choosing a bar further afield that boasted blush-coloured cider ('It's made with Pink Ladies, darling!' he said brightly, as though that mattered – it tasted like synthetic apples either way) and Sage found a space around the bonfire while she waited for him.

Conversation bloomed between strangers. There was a guitar – there was always a guitar – and a few cords of a song Sage knew but couldn't place. The air was dense with the smell of woodsmoke and grass.

She spotted Max on the other side of the fire. He was alone, drinking a beer and watching a contact juggler with unfocused eyes. The juggler was barefoot, with a long, silky ponytail and a lean, tanned torso felted with dark, wiry hair. His limbs moved with a mesmerising fluidity as he rolled what looked like a crystal ball between his hands.

Max noticed Sage watching him, and patted the vacant hay bale beside him with a goading expression on his face. *Dare you.*

'Hello stranger,' she said, perching on the edge of the bale, the hay warm from the heat of the fire.

'Alright?' He extracted a can from the plastic bag between his feet and held it out to her. 'Go on, it's on me.'

'How generous.' She cracked the ring pull and took a swig. It was hideous, a cheap brand that tasted like it had been squeezed from a bar mop.

'I thought you might be here,' he said. 'I've been looking out for you.'

'Who are you here with?' she asked.

'No one. I'm on the line-up.'

'You're playing?'

'Mm-hmm. Just an acoustic set – some of my solo stuff and some old unplugged Strangeways tracks. We have a bit of a cult following now.'

'So I hear,' said Sage. She checked in on him from time to time, searched for his name online to make sure he was still alive. 'How's Carl?'

'Good. He's out soon.'

'Yeah?'

'Yeah. I asked if he wanted to jam, but I don't think he wants to see me, not really. I don't think he ever really forgave me for stealing his girlfriend.'

'I wasn't his girlfriend,' Sage said quickly, with a flicker of shame.

'Well, anyway. Fresh start, and all that. Found God, wants to do charity work. I barely recognise him.'

'Good for him,' she said, and she meant it. 'I hope it all works out.'

Max took a long draught from his can, a bitter expression on his face. 'He thinks it's crass of me to play our old music, like I'm cashing in on Sesh's death ... but it's all I have left of him.'

'I think it's lovely,' said Sage. 'You're keeping his spirit alive. We're only truly gone when there's no one left to remember us.'

'Yeah, playing the songs we wrote together feels ... I don't know, it feels important. Even if they do kind of suck.'

Sage laughed without much humour. 'I did always think you guys kind of sucked. How'd you get this gig, anyway? Do you have a manager?'

'My girlfriend knows the programmer.'

'Ahh.' There it is. Typical Max, moving from one woman to the next, leeching whatever he could extract from her, then moving on. 'And where is the lucky girl?'

'Well, she's not here, is she?' he said, standing up and brushing stray hay from the seat of his jeans. 'Come find me later. I'll see if I can get you a backstage pass or something.'

'I'm with Daniel,' she said. 'And Caroline, obviously.'

'Obviously.' He looked like he wanted to say something else, but the words escaped him. 'I'll see you around, Sage. You're looking great, by the way.'

At the bar, Daniel was deep in conversation with some girl, a stranger with a bare midriff and dreads. He loved to find lost souls, young people to latch on to him, grateful to meet someone who seemed to know the ropes. Sage didn't mind. She was happy to sit and stare into the flames.

*

'It was awful,' said Caroline. 'I had to leave after the first night. I don't know how Daniel could bear it.'

'We had fun,' said Sage.

And they did — without Caroline there to keep him in line, Daniel was free to misbehave. They decamped to Caroline's abandoned yurt and made the most of the proper shower facilities, where the spray of hot water felt nothing short of miraculous on muscles that were sore from dancing.

A shy young man with a butterfly tattoo on his skinny wrist made Daniel a flower crown of daisies picked from the campsite, and he wore it with pride as he wandered around barefoot, his jeans rolled up to his knees.

'I'm going for a walk with Rowan,' Daniel said. 'You'll be okay, won't you darling?'

'Have fun,' Sage replied.

Alone, she moved through the shoal of festival-goers with ease. The acoustic tent was a hidden gem, tucked away down a long, winding path through the woods, illuminated with LED candles in paper lanterns. There were fewer than twenty people lying on the grass, and none seemed that interested in Max as he strummed through his set. Sage sat near the back, smoked a spliff rolled in strawberry-flavoured paper, and when he came off stage, she wasn't surprised to see him make a beeline for her.

*

Let the Bad Times Roll

'Do you do coin tosses, Selina?' Richard asked, scratching his beard. 'That's something psychics do, isn't it? I haven't made that up?'

'Yes,' the psychic replied. 'They're very popular online – I think people like the black-and-white nature of asking a yes-or-no question. There's rarely any wiggle room for interpretation.'

'I was just wondering, are the fortune-telling coin tosses related to the I Ching? Or is it more like flipism?'

The psychic blinked at him. 'I don't know – I don't really know much about I Ching, and I've never heard of flipism.'

'Ah, well, I Ching is a form of ancient Chinese divination,' said Richard. 'And flipism is ... Well, I suppose it's a form of normative decision theory – making decisions based on probability – although coin tosses lack the rationale element intrinsic to normative decision theory.'

'Oh,' said the psychic. 'Well no, it's not that. It's just a really simple way of asking the spirits for guidance. The coin is just a conduit, similar to osteomancy or a pendulum.'

'Osteo-what?' asked Max.

'Throwing bones,' the psychic explained.

'I see.' Richard nodded. 'So, it isn't based on chance?'

'No,' she replied, frowning. 'Of course it isn't based on chance.'

'So, if you asked if the sky was blue five times in a row, you'd get the same answer every time?' he asked, and although he was effecting a casual pose by leaning back in his seat, he failed to hide the faint trace of arrogance on his face. It was the psychic's turn to blush, and Sage felt angry on her behalf.

'Well, no,' the psychic admitted. 'Of course not.'

'No? And why is that?'

'You can't expect to be taken seriously if you're not asking serious questions,' she replied. 'It isn't a game, or a joke, or an exact science.'

'Well, it certainly isn't a science,' Richard said.

'Science is bullshit,' said Sage.

'Okay,' Caroline said, reaching for Richard's hand and giving it a soft squeeze that seemed to derail him entirely. 'Cool it.'

*

Her bladder ached, taut as a drum. Sage squinted against the bright morning light as she surveyed her situation. She was in some kind of hot-boxed motorhome, an open sleeping bag thrown over her bare legs. Although her sundress was ruched around her waist, she was still wearing knickers. A blessing. She wriggled her dress back into place, and the warm body in the bed next to her stirred. In the pale morning light, the stubble on Max's jawline looked bruise-blue.

Sage's bowels rumbled. She could see the familiar detritus of a late night scattered around the van: empty paper pint cups decorated with the festival logo, a green glass bong, a few dented cans of strong lager.

Max opened his mouth with a ghastly, sticky sound, swallowed and then began to gently snore. Dead to the world. If they were at home, and he wasn't her ex but a stranger, this would be her cue to slink off to a distant, gleaming bathroom, run the taps and use the toilet in peace, freshen up, then slide back into bed with minty-fresh breath for a morning kiss. Instead, all she could do was plan her escape.

She briefly wondered if she should wake him up, but it felt cleaner to just draw a line under the whole thing. She slipped from the bed and scanned the messy floor for her sandals and handbag, then crept into the cold light of day.

The campsite was stirring, and the chill morning air smelled like freshly brewed coffee, bacon fat and the bright grassy scent of a morning joint. Sage picked her way between guy ropes, stepping over abandoned takeaway containers of tofu curry and half-eaten veggie burgers that made her stomach curdle. A man was sprawled on the grass in a bucket hat, passed out but breathing evenly, and a bare-legged girl in an oversized fleece was eyeing him warily as she cleaned her teeth. As Sage passed, the girl spat a golf ball of toothpaste foam on to the ground and rinsed her mouth with a swig from a plastic water bottle.

Daniel was sitting on a camp chair outside Caroline's abandoned yurt, paperback in one hand and cigarette in the other. 'Hello, darling. Rough night?'

'Do I look that good?'

'Well, for a second I thought you were Lana Del Rey doing the walk of shame. Or should I say, the walk of pride?'

'Fuck off.'

'Who was the lucky gentleman?'

'Just some guy.'

She felt like a rat. Bits and pieces from the night before shimmered like a mirage in the peripherals of her mind's eye. Pints of cider, another spliff rolled in that strawberry-flavoured paper, a vegan samosa wrapped in a napkin, destined to be surreptitiously slipped into the bin.

'Oh, by the way – guess who I saw last night?' Daniel said.

'Who?' she asked, feigning ignorance.

'Max,' he said. 'He looked absolutely dreadful, I must say.'

Max. Muscle memory, that old familiar choreography.

'Did he see you?'

'Christ, no. I sacrificed my dignity and ducked behind the port-a-loos.'

'Smart,' she replied, but she thought it strange, and wondered – not for the first time – what had transpired between Daniel and Max. She remembered a spark between them, that night with the Ouija board – but then again, didn't Daniel spark with everyone?

'But listen, darling, if you sleep with him this weekend, I'll kill myself.'

A seedling of shame bloomed into guilt. 'I'm not going to sleep with him,' she said quickly. 'Don't be so dramatic.'

He laughed, and stretched his legs. 'God, this is bliss. We should do this more often. I think it suits me.'

'You've changed your tune.'

'I'm nothing if not fickle.'

'I'm going to South East Asia in the autumn – Vietnam, Thailand, Laos, Cambodia. I've been saving up for, like, a year, and I'm going to book it when we get back from the festival. Why don't you come with me?'

'Oh, I don't know about that,' he said.

'What's holding you back? I know you can afford it, and it's not like you have a career to worry about. No offence.'

'None taken,' he said, and then: 'I'll speak to Caroline.'

'I'm inviting *you*, not Caroline.'

'I know, but we do everything together.'

'Yeah, but she only hangs out with me because you hang out with me, and I don't want her to come along and take control. You're nearly thirty. Don't you think it's time to do something on your own?'

Daniel placed a cigarette in his mouth.

'Come on, I'm serious,' she said. 'You've never had a boyfriend, you've never travelled, you've never done *anything* without Caroline. You're both adults – she'll survive without you for a few weeks, a month. Let's go on a trip together. It'll be fun.'

'I'll think about it,' he said.

*

It was blustery on the tenth floor, and they had to take turns to cup their hands around each other's cigarettes as the lighter's meagre flame battled against the breeze. Max blew a cloud of silver smoke towards the navy sky. 'Are you still living on the boat?'

'Yep.'

'Still working for Rozzy?'

'Nah. I've picked up some freelance proofreading. Arlo started an indie publishing house, mainly to publish his manifestos, but he's commissioned some books on alternative medicine and politics too. It's perfect because I can do it anywhere, but it sucks because I don't feel like I belong anywhere either.'

Max took a drag, must have felt the heat of the burning cherry on his fingertips, as he frowned and looked for an ashtray. Giving up, he flicked the spent cigarette over the balcony's edge and watched it fall. Sage followed his gaze. The balcony was solid brick, and the drop to the water below was at least 150 feet. The canal snaked beneath them, a thick khaki-coloured ribbon.

'Weird fucking night, right?'

'Yeah,' Sage replied. 'What do you make of Selina?'

'Full of shit,' Max said, leaning on the balcony wall and scanning the water's edge. 'She's just mining us for information, feeding it back to us and calling it a tarot-card reading.'

'That's not fair,' said Sage, with a frown. 'She's asking us a few questions to help interpret the cards, that's all.'

'Bollocks. Richard told us that story about Daniel copying his essay, and then she pulls a betrayal card? Richard's clearly still in love with Caroline, and she pulls an unrequited love card? Come *on*. And then the band – you called it a tragedy, and she tells me I was once full of optimism until I missed out on a big opportunity.'

Sage considered this. 'But we're splitting the deck ourselves, so she can't be manipulating the cards. Look, it's like she said – the cards are just prompts. Of course they're matching up to our experiences – that's just how it works. You're letting your cynicism cloud your judgement. Try to be a little more open-minded.'

Max growled with frustration, and then seemed to adopt a different approach: 'Okay, so what do you make of her version of Daniel? Daniel would never stay in a shitty hostel, or smoke a fucking vape.'

Sage nodded slowly, lost in thought. It was true: she'd never known Daniel to stay in budget-friendly accommodation. And the vape? That wasn't Daniel, that wasn't the man she knew. 'Darling, there's nothing less chic than a disposable vape,' he liked to say, usually with a fag pinched between his fingers. Were they really such strangers to one another, or was it possible Selina simply didn't know him at all?

'There are some inconsistencies,' Sage conceded.

'Inconsistencies? Come on, babe. She's *full* of shit.'

Everyone was full of shit, Sage thought, in one way or another. People couldn't be trusted. She had learned that from an early age. Her childhood home was a house of lies, everything unsavoury brushed under the carpet and left to fester. Doctors couldn't be trusted, with their marriage to big pharma. Governments couldn't be trusted, with their secret experiments, mind control and cover-ups. Corporations couldn't be trusted, with their exploitation and their greed. Men couldn't be trusted: Carl would never deign to think of her as more than just a casual hook-up. And how many nights had she woken up at three, four, five o'clock in the morning, with Max's side of the bed still cold, the sheets undisturbed? Where did he sleep, those nights when she'd gone to bed alone and woken up just as lonely? And Daniel – Daniel certainly couldn't be trusted. She loved him anyway, although she wasn't always sure why.

It had started small, with white lies and inconsistencies about inconsequential things. Like, once, they went for lunch at Blessed Be, and Daniel said he'd forgotten his wallet, but later pulled it out to pay for a bottle of wine. She didn't say anything – figured he must have found it after all, and didn't think it mattered that she'd paid for lunch. He was always so generous. It wasn't a big deal.

And then there was his mother. Sage knew a little about Solange Dumortier – she had drowned on a Cornish beach the summer of Daniel's sixteenth birthday. She was glamorous, an artist, a socialite. Beautiful, elegant and dramatic, filling their Islington home with the ripe scent of Absolut, turpentine and

Silk Cut. Sage came across a picture of her once in a thinkpiece about the lack of lifeguards on the English coast, and the photo didn't match Daniel's description at all. A round, smiling face, small eyes hidden behind cheap glasses, with a crop of dark curly hair that looked more windswept than salon-fresh. The piece described her as an English teacher. Well, they've simply got that wrong, she thought, but a shimmer of doubt lingered.

'I feel like all we're doing is raking up the past,' Max said. 'Who gives a shit about what Daniel was like at university, or how he joined the band? Don't tell her anything else, babe. Don't trust her. She probably heard some news report about Daniel and latched on to the story. I bet she never even met him, just thought she might be able to extract some cash from his desperate family. It's sick.'

'Now you just sound paranoid,' Sage said. 'And you look like shit, by the way.'

Max appeared out of place slouched on Caroline's pristine balcony, like a discoloured brick ruining an otherwise uniform wall. She remembered the absent-minded way he used to tease his hair, relying on leftover wax from the night before to keep it artfully unkempt. The messiness looked less curated now, more like an organic result of infrequent showers.

He was a shadow of the man she'd once known, and it was her fault. She'd manifested it — the car crash that killed Sesh, sent Carl to prison, ruined Max's life. Everyone else had messed around with the Ouija board, spelling out profanities and taking the piss, so she had, too. She'd moved the glass, said the band would take off, make them all famous, and the board had pushed back. It was like a monkey's paw: she put words into the board's mouth, and a demon had responded. A stupid mistake had made them famous, but not rich. Infamous.

'Yeah, cheers,' Max said, with a snort. 'Do you have another cigarette?'

'I left my tobacco inside.'

'Come on, then,' he said, turning towards the door and placing his hand on the handle.

'Wait,' she said. 'I think you should take Selina's advice and pay for a cleanse.'

'Christ,' Max said, looking tired. She remembered the fear in his eyes that night with the Ouija board, even though he'd insisted it was all a load of bollocks. And once, drunk, he'd admitted that from time to time, he still prayed to the God he was so quick to deny in the light of day.

'I know you'll never admit it,' Sage said. 'But we both know you haven't been the same since that night. I think we manifested a dark spirit and—'

'Listen to yourself,' Max said. 'You sound fucking mental. We didn't manifest a dark spirit. Get a fucking grip.'

'You haven't been the same,' said Sage. 'Everything fell apart, and you've never managed to gather yourself back together.'

'Sesh *died*,' Max snapped. 'Carl went to prison. I lost my best friends and my band, my entire life, my entire future, in one go. Of course I haven't been the same, Sage. Fucking hell. It's not demons, or dark energy, or bad juju – it's just *life*, and it's fucking relentless, and that's it. There's no man behind the curtain, no fairies at the bottom of the garden. I wish you'd just fucking accept it.'

Sage wiped away the tears that were running down her cheeks. 'Are you worried, though? Like, seriously worried?'

'No,' he replied. 'It's all a load of bollocks. And anyway, I'm fine. I don't need you to mother me to death.'

'I meant for Daniel.'

Max dragged open the sliding door and invited Sage to step through it first. 'I dunno, babe. Daniel's a grown man. He can take care of himself. I mean, why break the habit of a lifetime?'

*

The psychic turned the second card and frowned. 'The Seven of Swords. Betrayal, deception, a card that suggests you've pulled the wool over someone's eyes, got away with something. Does that resonate with you, darling?'

Sage peered at the card, goosebumps prickling her forearms. It showed a man struggling to carry a thicket of swords, glancing over his shoulder as though to check there were no witnesses to his theft. She remembered the feeling of power as she'd pushed that glass – and the sickening feeling of the glass pushing back.

'Nope,' she said, shaking her head. 'Not at all, sorry.'

'Don't worry. Have a think and we'll move on. Sometimes, I find the cards that follow justify the cards that came before them.'

'You know what?' said Sage, clapping her palms together as though in prayer and pointing the steepled fingers towards the psychic. 'I don't think this reading is benefiting me spiritually, and I don't think it's getting us any closer to finding Daniel. I think I'd like to leave it there, actually, if you don't mind.'

The psychic looked faintly offended as she scooped up the cards. Sage couldn't help but wonder what the final card was as she watched the psychic shuffle it back into the deck.

'No problem,' the psychic said. 'We can stop. There's no point if you're not willing to be open-minded.'

'I'm very open-minded,' Sage argued. 'I'm just worried about my friend, and I think it's weird we're all sitting here eating fucking gumbo and making small talk. And if I can be honest, I feel like we've all told you quite a lot about Daniel, but you've barely told us anything useful.'

'Well, what else do you want to know?' said the psychic. 'I've told you how I came to meet him, how we spent our time together ... I wish I had answers for you, but I'm just as confused as you are. He was there, and then he wasn't. But he seemed like a seasoned traveller to me, seemed to know all about the city, how to find the best restaurants, the most exclusive bars. In fact, I was under the impression he'd been to New Orleans before – more than once.'

Caroline shook her head. 'We've never been to New Orleans.'

'And you're sure he's never been without you?' the psychic persisted.

'Positive. The holiday with Sage would have been the first time he'd travelled without me,' Caroline said. 'But obviously, that didn't happen.'

*

Raindrops pockmarked the surface of the canal and played a melodic rhythm on the roof of the narrowboat. Sage loathed the rain. She felt the cold, and was better suited to the souks of Marrakesh or the beaches of Greece than the misery of London in the spring.

As steam curled from the kettle, she dropped a mint teabag into the largest mug she owned. It was a wobbly thing, hand-thrown by her friend Petra during the pottery-class-and-marijuana stage of her divorce, and it was painted the same navy blue as the summer sky at midnight. She poured boiling water into her mug, added a squeeze of agave and stirred, then slid into the dinky diner-style bench with her notebook to run through the itinerary one more time, checking there was nothing left to do before she and Daniel flew to Thailand.

Daniel had upgraded most of their accommodation from budget hostels and guesthouses to swanky hotels and five-star resorts. The prices seemed outlandish to Sage, but she couldn't help but look over the images of suites with sea views and lagoon-like private pools and sigh with a new kind of wanderlust. She saved every penny to spend on adventures, from festivals and weekends away in the UK to more intrepid travel further afield, but she'd never dreamed of spending thousands of pounds on luxury, choosing instead to embrace the thin walls and water-stained shared bathrooms of budget accommodation if it meant she could wake up in Beijing, or Patagonia, or Oaxaca.

She knew something was wrong as soon as she saw Daniel's name on her phone screen. Daniel wasn't one for phone calls, unless the purpose of the call was to locate her on a night out, or to put her on speakerphone to prove a point ('Sage, darling,' he might say, 'please tell this silly boy that you've been to Mongolia – he thinks I'm lying for attention, but if I was going to lie for attention, I'd say something altogether more scandalous.').

'Hello, you,' she said, and then: 'Wait, say that again? I can't understand you.'

'Darling,' he gasped. 'I need you. I'm in A and E. Can you come? Like, right now?'

Sage felt her stomach drop. 'Are you okay? What's happened?'

'I'm at – oh God, what hospital is this?' A muffled conversation, and then: 'Look, I'll send you a drop pin, but it's Caroline – she's been hurt.'

'Slow down – take a deep breath,' Sage said.

'A car accident,' he said. 'It's – oh fuck, I can't breathe. I don't know what to do. It's really bad, darling. It's really fucking bad. Can you come?'

'I'm coming,' said Sage. 'Send me your location.'

*

When she arrived at the hospital, Daniel was standing under an umbrella in the car park, a striking silhouette against the glare of headlights as cars rolled by. He turned at the sound of his name. Sage had never seen him look so dishevelled.

'You don't have a cigarette, do you? I'm gasping. I've smoked nearly a whole pack.'

'I have rollies,' she said.

'Ugh.'

'I'll roll you one,' she said, wrapping her arms around his waist.

'Thank you, darling,' he said, stooping to kiss her on the top of her head. After a few moments, she felt him shudder and realised he was crying. 'The silly bitch,' he said, when he caught his breath. 'They keep saying how lucky she is, how much worse it could have been. Christ, darling. She could have been killed.'

'Come on,' Sage said. 'Let me roll you that cigarette.'

Caroline had suffered a tibial plateau fracture – a lightning-bolt crack to the tibia, just below her left knee – along with a meniscus tear and a traumatic head injury that required twenty-two stitches and several weeks of monitoring in intensive care.

Daniel lit his rollie and exhaled a plume of pale smoke. 'Darling, listen,' he said. 'I know you're going to hate me, but I don't think I can leave her.'

'We don't have to decide that right now,' Sage said.

'Her knee requires surgery. They're saying it could take four months to recover. She can't walk, let alone bathe or feed herself. She needs someone to take care of her.'

'But ...' Sage searched for a tactful way to ask, but she already knew the answer: there was no one else. Caroline had no partner to tend to her needs, no friends to fetch shopping and keep her company, no family to cook her meals. There was that old friend from university – Dicky? – and Daniel had mentioned an aunt once, a stern woman who'd fallen out with their mother when they were children, but Sage had a vague memory of her passing away several years ago.

'We'll go another time,' he said. 'I promise. I daresay Thailand will still be there next year.'

Sage couldn't go another time. It had taken her two years to save for this trip, and the flights and transfers were non-refundable.

'Go without me,' Daniel said. 'The hotels are all paid for. I can just transfer the bookings into your name.'

'Aren't the hotels refundable, though?' Sage asked.

Let the Bad Times Roll

'I have no idea,' Daniel replied. 'But I insist. Go to Thailand, Vietnam, wherever the fuck else we had planned, and bring me back some chic presents. Just go, and promise me you'll have a wonderful time.'

*

In Thailand, Sage spent her days on the beaches, strolling on the sugar-soft sands of Koh Samui and dipping her toes in the glittering ocean. It was difficult to meet people in the five-star hotels Daniel had chosen. In hostels, there was usually a sense of community, and it was perfectly natural to talk to those around you and find common ground. Instead, she ate alone, feasting on buttery mangos, the juice sticky as syrup, sweet coconut rice and chubby little bananas. In the evenings, which were blissfully warm, she flipped through paperbacks and drank cold bottles of beer.

In Laos, she visited temples and waterfalls, rode a slow boat down the Mekong River, and slept with an earnest German man with the most exquisite hands and neat, clean fingernails. And so on, to Vietnam, to Cambodia, to Malaysia, where she visited markets and rode tuk tuks and ate solo meals, surrounded by strangers.

As promised, she bought Daniel gifts: coconut oil soap, Thai peppercorns, Vietnamese coffee, handmade sandals and paper crafted from mulberry tree bark.

When she returned to the everlasting grey skies and pouring rain of London, the bridge of her nose and her shoulders tawny and her blood-red hair faded to a washed-out ginger, she found Daniel moody and dismissive of her gifts.

'I missed you,' she said, as he fingered a packet of durian chocolates with a grimace.

'I'm sure you suffered terribly,' he replied, lighting a cigarette, 'in five-star resorts in the most beautiful locations in the world.'

*

'You didn't have to rub it in his face,' Caroline said.

'I wasn't rubbing it in his face,' Sage replied, hurt. 'I'd missed him, and I was excited to see him. I thought he'd be excited to see me, too.'

'Well,' said Caroline. 'He wasn't.'

'It's not like I didn't make it up to him,' Sage said. 'It's not like I didn't go to great expense to make it up to him.'

'Oh yeah, I'm sure you spent a fortune on those tacky souvenirs,' Caroline said, with a cruel sneer. 'What did you think he was going to do with peppercorns? Cook a pad Thai?'

'He gave me his blessing,' Sage snapped, and all the unspoken injustice within her bubbled to the surface. 'He encouraged me to go without him, insisted I stay in the hotels he'd booked. And you know what? I didn't even like them all that much! Surrounded by American snobs and couples on their honeymoons? No *thanks*. I would have been happier in the hostels and guesthouses within my budget, because at least then I would've had some fucking company.'

'Daniel has always attracted vampires,' Caroline continued, to no one in particular. 'People who suck him dry and pick their teeth with his credit card.'

'Hey,' Richard said. 'That's a horrible thing to say.'

'I'm not talking about you, Dicky,' she replied.

'You wouldn't be talking about Richard, though, would you?' Sage retorted. 'Because it's clear *you're* the one who uses *him*.'

Max raised his hands to calm the brewing storm. 'Alright, let's all just chill out.'

'And for your information,' Sage snapped, '*I* paid for his flights to the US. Happy?'

There was a shocked silence around the table. Caroline blinked, taking in this information like a shot of vinegar. 'You paid for his flights? You knew he was in America, and you didn't think to tell me?'

'He asked me not to tell you,' Sage said. 'He wanted to get away for a while, do something on his own.'

*

It had been a relatively straightforward conversation. They were at the Narrowboat, a canal-side pub that overlooked the murky water, sharing a bottle of red. Daniel was smoking a cigarette, eyes vague.

'Could I ask you a tiny favour, darling?' he said.

'Of course,' she replied.

'Now that Caroline's better, I'd like to go on a trip.'

'Oh, fabulous,' Sage said. 'Where are you thinking? I've got a real craving for Amsterdam. Or how about Prague?'

He ashed his cigarette, nodding thoughtfully. 'I was thinking San Francisco.'

Sage wrinkled her nose. 'I don't think I can stretch to San Francisco this year. Maybe next year, if I start saving now.'

'I was thinking more of a solo trip.'

'Oh,' she said, with a frown. 'Right.'

And then he began talking. He described the long, lonely hours, trapped in the flat while he nursed Caroline back to health. Cooking her meals, bringing her cups of tea, helping her hobble to the bathroom, washing her hair with jugs of hot water over the sink.

'I love her to death,' he said. 'But I'm craving some time by myself.'

'Of course,' Sage said. 'I get it. But what's the favour?'

'Here's the thing,' Daniel said. 'If I book a flight, she'll know. And she'll insist on coming with me.'

A pair of swans swept serenely past them, their white feathers stark against the dark water.

'How on earth will she know?' Sage asked.

'She's like a truffle hound for information. She'll sniff it out. She'll see an email or a confirmation or something. It's easier to just do it behind her back.'

'Are you asking me to book it for you?'

'I'd pay you back,' he said quickly. 'I'd pay you back as soon as I was back in the UK.'

'Why can't you just transfer the money now?' Sage asked.

'She'll see the transaction, one way or another, and ask questions. Trust me – if there was another way, I'd grab it with both hands.'

Sage bit her lip. 'Daniel, I'd love to help you out, but how much are flights to San Francisco? I don't just have a grand going spare.'

'You're a freelancer now, though – don't you put cash aside for your taxes?'

Sage laughed. 'Fuck taxes. I'm not paying taxes just for the government to fritter them away on their bloodthirsty wars.'

He extinguished his cigarette and sighed. 'Right.'

'Oh, don't be mad,' she said. 'If I could, I would. You know I would.'

Daniel said nothing, his face a blank mask. Guilt bloomed within Sage as she remembered the beautiful hotel breakfasts, sea views and room service she'd enjoyed in South East Asia.

'Look,' she said. 'I do have a little money put aside. An emergency fund, in case anything ever happens to my boat. I can book you a flight, but I really need you to pay me back as soon as you can. It's my rainy-day fund, and I need it. I don't have insurance; it's all I've got.'

Daniel's face melted into an expression of pure joy. 'I'll pay you back the second my plane wheels touch down on British soil, darling.'

*

Caroline closed her eyes and exhaled. 'I don't understand. What was he doing in San Francisco?'

'I don't know – riding a cable car, taking photos of the Golden Gate Bridge, getting pissed in the Castro. Why does anyone go to San Francisco?' Sage replied.

'You should have told me.'

'I thought I was acting in Daniel's best interests,' Sage replied.

'Why – am I really such a monster?' Caroline said, eyes filling with tears. 'Am I really so dreadful? I took care of him when we lost our parents – was it too much to ask for him to return the favour when I needed him?'

'I'm sure it wasn't like that,' Richard said.

'I don't think you're taking this seriously enough,' Caroline said. 'He's obviously been hurt – he could be dead for all we know. His passport – and that blood-stained shirt – found discarded in the bayou. Aren't you more concerned? Aren't you scared to death? And yet you're all sitting here, telling half-truths, keeping things from me.'

'We *are* taking it seriously,' Max said 'But you said it yourself – it doesn't sound like Daniel's shirt. He doesn't own a loose cheesecloth shirt.'

'Yes, he does,' said the psychic. 'That sounds exactly like the shirt he wore most days in New Orleans.'

On the Road: Daniel

Daniel thought it was wonderfully mysterious of him to run away to the West Coast. It was like something from a Sofia Coppola film or a Lana Del Rey song. He had this image of drifting between bars, reading beat poetry and taking sailors for lovers, but San Francisco was a city of two faces: craft-beer bars, cottage bakeries and busy farmers' markets on one; fraying tents, dirty blankets and people of no fixed abode on the other. Each morning, he'd buy a takeaway coffee and drink it on the walk back to his hotel, where the rotten scent of strong weed followed on the warm breeze. In the afternoons, a thick fog rolled in from the Bay and cloaked the city in a damp shroud that locals seemed to welcome with a baffling fondness. It wasn't quite how he'd imagined his final days as Daniel Dumortier – one doesn't travel to California in June to feel a chill – so he bade farewell to San Francisco and hitched a lift south with a girl he'd met at a bar in the Castro.

Her name was Dorene. She was a heartbroken lesbian with dreadlocks and an asthmatic cough, and she earned a living transporting people's pets between cities when they moved house. As a result, her car was filthy, covered in dog hair and dirt tracked in by dusty paws, and all the rubbish that accumulates when one spends a significant period of time driving without the judgemental presence of another person for company.

She was heading to Los Angeles with a Burmese mountain dog called Misty. She hinted, more than once, that the beast belonged to some Hollywood A-lister, although Daniel refused to take the bait by asking to whom Misty belonged. The dog was a magnificent creature with paws the size of oranges, but her heavy breath filled the car with a rich, meaty stench that turned Daniel's stomach, and when they reached LA, he was grateful to say goodbye to both Dorene and the mutt.

LA was a Hockney palette of popsicle-blue skies and pastel-pink stucco. The sun was a golden coin, and palm trees stretched over the endless traffic that clogged the roads and coated the buildings in a gunmetal felt of pollution. All the people were either beautifully chic in athleisure wear from Lululemon, sipping their eighteen-dollar Erewhon smoothies with lips so rich with filler they struggled to pucker around their straws, or they were wearing custom Micky Mouse ears and taking selfies in front of the TCL Chinese Theatre, measuring the size of their palms against the handprints of the stars, all that faded fame and glamour immortalised in concrete.

Daniel had always thought he'd suit immortality. A tragic figure, taking lovers and forgetting their names from one century to the next. His sister had once said he burned through people like petrol, as though his life were just one long road trip, and friendships were tanks of fuel that ran dry. Caroline's observations were often cruel but seldom incorrect.

In a retro-futurist diner on Sunset Boulevard, he ordered a Creole chicken sandwich, sweet potato fries and a bananas Foster milkshake, which the menu boasted was spiked, somewhat incongruously, with a rum-infused sake. That was perhaps the first indication that New Orleans was calling to him, although he ended up regretting his selection. He'd ordered in the usual way, shooting from the hip, following his heart without any consideration for the cost. First thought, best thought. It was only when he tasted the mediocrity of the milkshake that he thought to calculate the total, and realised he'd spent over fifty dollars plus tip on a bad lunch. He simply wasn't accustomed to keeping track.

Money was like oxygen to Daniel, and for a long time, spending it with reckless abandon was as natural as breathing. That was, one could argue, how he'd ended up in such a mess.

He'd assumed LA would be a breeze. He thought he'd just blow in like so many tumbleweeds before him, with a suitcase and a flick knife like Nomi Malone in *Showgirls*, and then disappear, perhaps finding a temporary soulmate to take him in and pick up the check while he figured out his next move.

Two things quickly became apparent: first, while Daniel may have considered himself to be a head-turning ten in London, he was no more than a generous six in LA. The people were outrageously manicured, chasing eternal youth with elixirs, speculative treatments, the prick of so many needles. Hanging out in West Hollywood was akin to browsing a cosmetic surgeon's catalogue: everyone from the hostess who seated him to the waitress who took his order was surgically enhanced, lifted, tucked, toned.

Second, LA was a place of desire, and that turned out to be an obstacle too. Everyone seemed to be wary of the needs of others in that God-forsaken city. Those who had something to offer – power, beauty, wealth, connections – were only too aware of the fact that everyone else wanted a piece of it, and striking up conversation was often met with a wall of suspicion. For example, he'd asked a well-dressed man in the hotel lobby if he knew a good lunch spot, and the man had responded by placing a hand over his breast pocket, as though Daniel could steal his wallet right through the fabric of his suit with the power of distraction alone.

When the Creole sandwich arrived, the poor thing was drowning in a wet coleslaw that leaked a milky fluid all over the plate. There was no crunch to the batter, the chicken a wet sponge, and the sweet potato fries were undercooked, limp with oil. A complete waste of fifty bucks.

Two tables over, a young trio caught his attention. They were sharing a plate of thick American-style pancakes, glossy with melted butter and maple syrup, and sipping glasses of iced tap water. They were having a heated discussion, showing each other maps and calculations on their phones.

'It's, like, way more than thirty hours on the road,' said one, a handsome boy with shoulder-length blond hair. He was a beautiful sun-kissed brown, but as he stretched to dig his fork into their communal pancake stack, the sleeve of his T-shirt shifted to reveal pale skin, white as fresh cream. He dragged his thumb over the screen of his phone, perhaps tracing a potential route, and shook his head. 'I don't think I can do more than, like … eight hours a day? Absolute max. So, your math is way off – you gotta add the cost of motels to the gas.'

'Well, flights are like one-fifty apiece,' said another, a pretty girl in a white sundress, red plastic sunglasses holding her long blonde hair from her face. 'If we sleep in the car and don't eat much, I think it'll be cheaper to drive anyways.'

'It's not just the money,' said the youngest of the three, a skinny, bespectacled cherub with a crop of dark elfin hair. 'We have to think about our environmental impact, too.'

'Driving three thousand kilometres and back isn't exactly a choice Greta Thunberg would make either,' the blond boy said with a smirk.

'What about an AmTrak?'

'*Way* expensive.'

'So, if we leave tomorrow and drive eight hours a day … Wait a sec, let me figure this out …' the girl said, pre-empting an interruption by holding up a slender finger. 'Tomorrow … Friday … If we left tonight, we could be in New Orleans for Sunday. The show's on Monday, so that's perfect, right? We'd only need motels for three or four nights, and we'll save money if we share a bed.'

'I dunno, man,' the blond guy said, scratching the back of his neck. 'Eight hours a day for four days straight is a *lot* of driving for one person. And then I'd have to do it all again for the ride home, too.'

'I'm just gonna go ahead and book a hostel in New Orleans,' said the girl, picking up her phone and tapping at the screen. 'You guys can pay me back.'

Daniel performed a quick evaluation of their situation: they were sharing a single plate, which at first glance indicated a lack of funds, but the girl's summer dress looked like something Caroline would buy from Free People for a few hundred pounds. Daniel would have bet his last dollar that the handbag on the empty chair next to her, a woven raffia tote, was from somewhere chic like Loewe, and the espadrilles south of her ankles were Valentino or Jimmy Choo. Those kids weren't poor – not really. They were just young, and perhaps not quite spoiled enough to have an access-all-areas pass to Daddy's credit card.

The waitress began to clear Daniel's table with a flirtatious smile. Her name tag said Karen, which he thought was a shame.

'Do you want a box for that?' she asked, lifting the plate to inspect the hefty remains of his sandwich.

'No, thank you darling – just the check, please. And hey.' He leaned forward and lowered his voice. 'Could you add those pancakes to my bill?'

'For real?'

He offered his most charming smile, and she melted into a soft giggle.

'That's super sweet of you.'

'I can be rather sweet, can't I?' Daniel said.

He paid in cash, slurped up the dregs of his disgusting milkshake, and headed out into the sun to find a conspicuous spot to loiter with a cigarette. Through the diner window, he watched the kids as they crumpled their napkins, pulled wallets from their pockets, and then listened in perplexity as Karen approached their table to explain the situation. The girl in the sundress slipped the receipt into her journal, and Daniel averted his gaze, stared into the middle distance in a pantomime of casual indifference, until they spotted their mysterious benefactor. Then he stubbed out his cigarette and turned to leave.

The bespectacled cherub caught up with him, giddy and breathless, before he'd made it out of the car park. 'Hey man, did you cover our check?'

'Might have,' Daniel replied, with an affectatious shrug.

The cherub squinted against the sun, wrinkled his nose. 'How come?'

'Maybe I'm in need of some good karma.'

He was called Frankie, the blond guy was Bradley, and his sister was Jenna. They were making their way to New Orleans to catch a band, some earnest political punk shit.

'I *love* those guys,' Daniel said. 'My band were meant to gig with them in London, but the tour was cancelled because of the pandemic. Such a shame; we were so looking forward to it.'

'You're in a band?' asked Frankie, with a look of abject awe.

'I was, for my sins,' Daniel said. 'Anyway, that's all behind me now, but I was thinking of heading to New Orleans to catch the show, maybe have some drinks with the guys afterwards … But it's way too far to drive solo, and too expensive to take the train. I suppose I could fly, but I hate taking domestic flights, given the state of the world.'

'Exactly.' Frankie nodded. '*Exactly*. It's like, we can see the impact on the environment in real time, like with the wildfires, the floods, the rising temperatures and the melting ice caps? It's crazy to carry on like business as usual.'

'Exactly,' Daniel said, sliding another cigarette from the pack and offering one to the kid.

'You shouldn't smoke tobacco. It's so bad for you, man,' Frankie said, shaking his head and pulling a chunky gizmo the size of a deck of cards from his back pocket.

'They are? Christ, I had no idea, darling. Should we alert the media?'

'Fuck off,' Frankie said with a shy smile, sucking on the vape and exhaling an expert cloud of white smoke.

'Let me see that thing,' Daniel said, taking it from him to inspect it. It was made of white plastic, and promised the smoker gummy bear-flavoured breath. 'And this is better, is it?'

'It's rechargeable,' Frankie explained. 'See, the little display? It tells you when the battery's low and how much juice you've got left. I know it's not the best, like environmentally speaking, but it's better for you than cigarettes.'

The vape almost certainly contained a lithium battery and was an atrocious choice *environmentally speaking*, but Daniel supposed that was the typical hypocritical whimsy one could only expect from the youth.

He raised it to his lips. 'May I?'

'Go ahead,' Frankie replied, and he watched with anxious attention as Daniel took a slow drag. The smoke was cold and sweet, and flowed freely into his lungs.

'Not bad,' he lied, leaning his head back to exhale a plume of white smoke. Frankie beamed, perhaps from the simple pleasure of validation from someone older and cooler than him.

'Hey – if you make it to New Orleans, maybe you could introduce us to the band?' he asked, almost shyly.

'Maybe,' Daniel said. 'I probably won't go, though. It's such a long way from here.'

'Well – maybe we could give you a ride?'

'Oh, no,' Daniel said. 'I wouldn't dream of intruding on your road trip.'

'You wouldn't be intruding! Wait here, let me talk to those guys. I'm sure they'll say yes,' said Frankie.

'Sure,' Daniel said, pretending to turn the offer over in his mind. 'I guess it'd be cheaper for you guys if I came along – I'd pay my way, obviously. And of course I'd do my fair share of the driving, too.'

'Hang on,' Frankie repeated, all animated with the adrenaline of a plan. 'Gimme two secs to talk to them. I'm sure they'll say yes.'

Of course, they said yes. The children trusted Daniel because he was attractive, queer and seemed like he had money, and they hadn't yet learned that the most beautiful creatures in the animal kingdom were often the deadliest.

*

The sky above the open road was a never-ending wash of brilliant blue. Daniel sat with Frankie in the back seat, where they took turns to smoke the white plastic vape as the desert slipped past the window, an endless, rippling tide of sepia dunes and distant yucca trees.

Jenna was riding shotgun. She'd kicked off her shoes and placed her bare feet on the dashboard, head resting against the seatbelt. Her toenails were painted to match her fingernails in a shimmery, frost-bitten lilac. Daniel couldn't help but imagine a terrible accident in which their car might collide with the vehicle ahead of them on the road – a handsome vintage Mustang with a California licence plate – and her delicate shinbones would be shattered on impact.

'Could you put your feet down?' Bradley asked, perhaps following the same train of thought. She didn't respond, so he tapped her knee without taking his eyes off the road. 'Jen – feet. Please.'

'God, you're so fucking bossy,' she moaned, voice syrupy with sleep, but she shifted her feet to the passenger footwell. 'What the hell are you listening to, anyway?' She gave Bradley a contemptuous side eye and reached for the aux to hook her iPhone to the car's sound system.

'You were sleeping,' he said defensively.

'So, while I was defenceless and vulnerable, you were plying me with subconscious Foo Fighters?' she said. 'That's totally criminal.'

'Hey, I was enjoying that.'

'Well, there's no accounting for taste,' she said, unplugging her brother's phone and replacing it with her own.

'Dave Grohl's a sell-out,' Frankie said.

'You don't know what the hell you're talking about,' Bradley muttered, but he let Jenna switch the music anyway, and peace was reinstated as the seductive southern spirit of Ethel Cain filled the car. All thoughts of Jenna's potentially life-altering injuries – and the Mustang – were soon forgotten.

In the early evening, they pulled up in front of a supermarket for supplies. Jenna and Bradley branched off immediately, bouncing towards the confectionery aisle with all the enthusiasm of children prepping for a sleepover, but Frankie stuck to Daniel's side like a barnacle as he picked up a basket and made his way towards the fresh produce.

'We're on a super-tight budget,' Frankie explained, with an anxious expression on his face.

'Don't worry, darling, I get a discount,' Daniel said, with a wink.

'What does that mean?'

'Come on,' he said, 'I'll show you.'

Frankie followed Daniel to a great chiller of dips, salsas and salad dressings. Daniel opened the glass door, picked up two tubs of guacamole and, while he pretended to read the label of one, he slipped the other into Frankie's bag. They repeated the process with French onion dip, carrot sticks and grapes.

'It's a sticky-fingered discount,' Daniel explained. 'Only for the dirtiest of hands.'

Frankie looked both terrified and thrilled. 'What if we get caught?'

'We won't get caught, darling – everyone does it. The staff don't give a shit. They get paid fuck all anyway. And these big supermarkets literally build shoplifting into their projected profits. It's called *shrinkage*.'

Daniel picked up red wine, bourbon, a rotisserie chicken and a loaf of bread and placed them into his basket. For every expensive item destined to go through the legitimacy of the checkout, two lower-priced items went into Frankie's tote until it was distorted with their illicit loot.

'Just be cool and wait while I pay for this,' Daniel whispered, steering Frankie towards the till.

A dead-eyed girl with pale blonde extensions that clashed with the yellow of a bad bleach job scanned their shopping and delivered their total as though she'd recently been lobotomised. Daniel shuffled through the notes in his wallet, making sure Frankie could see how much cash he was carrying, and pulled out several twenties to cover the groceries.

As they left the supermarket, the excitement within Frankie must have reached a crescendo, as he broke into a run and bounced in the air, clicking his heels together like a triumphant leprechaun.

'Darling, you're anything but subtle.'

Jenna and Bradley were waiting for them in the car. They'd bought a large bottle of Diet Coke, some M&M's and a family-sized bag of Flamin' Hot Cheetos.

'Jenna wanted to get apples, but they were too expensive,' Bradley explained, fingertips already stained electric orange with Cheeto dust.

They drove until they found a place that was to Daniel's liking, a cheap roadside spot called the Paradise Motel, where their headlights glided serenely over just two or three unremarkable parked cars. Most of the rooms looked unoccupied, the windows dark.

'We've driven past at least six identical motels,' Frankie moaned. 'What makes this one so special?'

'I thought it sounded kitsch,' Daniel replied, unbuckling his seatbelt. 'Now, Bradley, my love, why don't you park on the other side of the car park, then go to reception and pretend you're alone.'

'*Parking lot*,' Jenna said.

'How come?' asked Bradley.

Daniel sighed. The thing with young people, he thought, was that he must remember to explain every single detail of his plan, because they didn't have the life experience to connect the dots for themselves.

'Because single travellers get a discount.'

'Well, why do *I* have to do it?'

'Frankie's too young, and we don't want some creepy Norman Bates type to think Jenna's travelling alone in case there's a peephole in the shower. Plus, it's *your* car. What if they ask me for the number plate?'

'Bradley, just *go*,' Frankie said.

'Jenna, come with?' Bradley pleaded.

'But then we won't get the discount, dummy,' she said. 'Stop being such a baby.'

'And make sure you request a room round the back, darling, so they don't see us,' Daniel said. 'Tell them you're a light sleeper with a long drive ahead, and you need peace and quiet.'

With a melodramatic sigh, Bradley dragged himself out of the car and trudged across the dark car park with the air of a man heading for the gallows.

It was then that Daniel heard the sound of tyres crunching on gravel, and saw the blacked-out windows of the Mustang rolling into the car park. The driver switched off the engine, but the doors remained closed. Daniel felt unnerved by the familiarity of the car. What were the chances of both parties stopping at the same motel?

Bradley soon returned, a plastic key card in hand, which Daniel found disappointing. He'd hoped for one of those gloriously retro tags in an ice-cream shade of plastic. Without a word, Bradley slipped into the driver's seat and twisted the key in the ignition. Daniel watched the Mustang until it was out of sight, an uneasy feeling in the pit of his stomach. It was exactly the kind of car Caroline would rent on a trip like this: ostentatious, overpriced, all aesthetics over practicalities.

They located their room and parked up. Bradley shoved the key card into the slot, and the little light blinked green. There was a mechanical twitching sound, but the door refused to open. He frowned, and tried again without success.

'Here, let me,' Daniel said, taking the key card from Bradley's hand. He tapped the lock and pressed against the stubborn door, but it wouldn't budge. He nudged it with his shoulder once, twice, and then a final heavy barge unglued it with a thick lip-smack of a noise, like the unplugging of a blocked sink. Inside, the room was dingy, and there was a strange smell to it, like unwashed skin or forgotten laundry. Sweet and stale, warm but not particularly welcoming.

'I suppose these rooms don't get used much,' Daniel said, peering around with a curled lip.

'It stinks in here,' Jenna said, dumping her rucksack on the bed. The mattress bounced under the weight of her bag, and for a moment it seemed as though the darkness itself rippled and reverberated up the walls. Bradley groped for the light switch, and, as soon as their eyes adjusted to the sudden brightness, they all understood what they were looking at.

Jenna screamed.

Half a dozen cockroaches, each the size of a quarter, had scuttled from the bed, across the headboard and up the wall, skittering across the dust-covered picture frames. In a panic, Frankie, Bradley and Jenna stumbled out of the room and into the night. In the distance, the soft bell of a girl's laughter rang.

*

They couldn't stay there, of course, and it was with a sense of relief that they climbed back into the car and left the cockroaches – and the Mustang – behind as they found alternative lodgings.

Jenna wasted no time in turning their new room into her personal boudoir. She opened her suitcase and sent an immediate tsunami of clothes across the bed while she searched for her essentials, pausing only to fling a silk scarf over the bedside lamp so they were engulfed in a soft, peachy light. Daniel was thrilled to see her set a silk scrunchie, matching eye mask and a pink Ziploc bag of pills on the bedside table before she disappeared into the en suite, where a fruity-scented steam soon seeped beneath the bathroom door. Daniel loved high maintenance women, girls with a touch of Hollywood glamour in their veins.

Frankie tipped the contents of his tote bag over the bed with an almost-feverish excitement.

'C'mon man, we can't afford all this,' Bradley said, picking up the bourbon and studying the label with a scowl.

'Daniel paid for the drinks and the chicken,' said Frankie. 'And I stole the rest.'

He was quick to give himself full credit, but Daniel let him enjoy the attention as Bradley evaluated the loot with a new sense of admiration.

Of course, they had no cutlery to speak of, but that didn't deter the ravenous little wolfpack. The children tore the chicken to shreds with greasy fingers, ripped chunks of bread from the loaf, and used chipmunk teeth to split tomatoes into bite-sized pieces, pale juice running from their wrists to their elbows and dripping on to the motel comforter.

Bags of crisps were popped open, a scatter of Doritos across the bed, and the bourbon rapidly changed hands. Frankie's face quickly turned pink and dangerously lovely. He couldn't be more than twenty, Daniel thought.

They chewed with their cheeks distended, laughed with their mouths full. They were learning the world was their oyster, and it was up to them to decide whether to chew it up or swallow it whole.

Daniel picked up the remote control and began to flip between channels for something to do. A garish reality show, a cheesy infomercial for an exercise machine, a terrible made-for-TV movie. Click, click, click.

Bashful, Frankie presented him with a rather feral-looking sandwich. 'We don't have mayo, so I used French onion dip,' he explained.

'Delightful,' Daniel replied, accepting it with the same praise one might offer a child for producing a deranged finger painting. 'Thank you darling, what a clever and resourceful little friend you are.'

Jenna reappeared, hair wrapped in a towel. She was wearing a long white nightdress, like a Victorian ghost, and Daniel longed to present her with a silver candelabra to complete the image. She eyed the feast spread over the comforter with disdain, opened a bottle of water and began rooting through the pink Ziploc bag stuffed with pharmaceuticals.

'My night-night knock-out pills,' she explained. 'Can't sleep without them.'

'Good for you, darling,' Daniel said, and with the wine in hand, he excused himself to sit on the kerb and smoke a cigarette. He found himself scanning the near-empty car park for the Mustang, and realised he needed to shake the strange sense of foreboding he felt about that car. There was no reason to believe Caroline had followed him to America. After all, he'd had a head start.

Soon, a golden rhombus of light fell upon his solitary smoke, and he felt the warmth of a body next to him. Frankie. Of course it was Frankie.

'You're a bandit,' Frankie said, pointing a loose, accusatory finger. He was drunk, his breath sweet with a vanilla trace of bourbon.

'Excuse me, darling, I think we both know *you're* the bandit around here.'

A loose laugh, and then Frankie leaned his weight against Daniel, head resting on his shoulder. Danger, Daniel thought. Amber alert.

'I'm not a bandit.'

'What are you, then?' Daniel said, swallowing a mouthful of wine and letting Frankie take the bottle from his hands. A marionette line of red slipped from the corner of the boy's mouth to his chin and Frankie, the sweet little puppet, wiped it away with the back of his hand.

A small pause, a nervous swallow. 'I can be yours, if you like.'

Daniel cleared his throat. 'Come on now, none of that.'

'I mean it.'

'You're too young to belong to anyone, let alone an old hag like me.'

'I'm twenty-one,' Frankie said, a defiant expression on his whiskey-pink face.

'No, you're not, darling. How old are you really?'

'… Twenty?'

'And you'd swear on your mother's grave, would you?'

'Well, nearly twenty.'

'*Well*, that makes me nearly a decade too old for you.'

'Daniel?'

Please don't, Daniel thought. Please don't do this. 'Mmm?'

Frankie swallowed again. 'Will you kiss me?'

Young hearts are so tender, young egos so easily bruised. Snubbing Frankie's romantic advances could land Daniel in hot water, but it was unfathomable to do anything but demur. Frankie was young, far too young, and for all his sweetness, Daniel carried no desire for such a youthful shade of vulnerability. A predicament: he couldn't abuse the poor boy in the name of the grift, but delicate matters called for a light touch. If Frankie felt the humiliating burn of rejection, Daniel might find it doubled and passed back to him. He saw himself stranded alone in the middle of nowhere.

Daniel placed a hand on the boy's cheek, felt the coolness of his smooth skin beneath his palm. 'You're cold,' he said, and he kissed Frankie delicately on the nose.

The slightest encouragement seemed to stoke the embers of Frankie's desire, and he responded by lunging for Daniel's lips. Daniel had to use both hands – one still clinging to the near-empty bottle of wine – to extract himself from Frankie's hungry embrace.

'Come on, darling,' Daniel said, standing up in one smooth motion and offering Frankie a hand. 'Tomorrow, this will all seem like a bad idea, and we'll be glad we didn't do it.'

'You taste disgusting, anyway,' Frankie said, wrinkling his nose. 'Like a million cigarettes.'

'That would be the million cigarettes I've smoked.'

Daniel let them back into the room. Jenna was tucked in bed, hair wrapped in some kind of heatless curl contraption, eye mask and earbuds in place to cocoon her from the light and sound of the television. Bradley was sitting on the floor and squinting bleary-eyed at his phone. Daniel excused himself and disappeared behind the safety of the bathroom door. He urinated, then took his time shaving, rinsing his face with cold water. He washed his armpits and crotch with grainy pink liquid soap and towelled off with a stiff, grey-white flannel. He cleaned his teeth and combed his hair with his fingers, and then left the water running while he sat on the lid of the toilet and counted to one hundred. When he emerged from the en suite, the television was off, Frankie was in the bed between Jenna and Bradley, and all three were breathing evenly.

Daniel found a spare pillow and blanket in the wardrobe, and settled on the floor to watch the ceiling turn from blue to gold.

*

Arizona, New Mexico, then Texas. Each roadside motel was the same as the last: a concrete swimming pool that may or may not be in use, an ice machine that may or may not be in working order, a vending machine that may or may not be well stocked. Cookie-cutter art on the walls; a watercolour of stains on the ceiling tiles above the bed, the shades varying between iced tea, autumn leaves and rust.

They watched infomercials for exercise equipment, art supplies and cleaning apparatus, and googled the nearest diners, in which they shared portions of chips ('French fries,' chided Jenna) and drank bottomless Diet Cokes from plastic cups.

Jenna hoarded scraps of paper – sweet wrappers, receipts, business cards from motels – and glued them into a bulging diary that she called her 'junk journal'. 'So I can look back and remember everywhere I've been,' she explained.

'Smart,' Daniel said. 'You don't want to forget which Walmarts you've ticked off your list.'

Inspired by Frankie's moxie, their little raccoon hands went to work at every opportunity: from supermarkets to gas stations, the children lifted bottles of liquor, single cans of beer snapped from six-packs, chocolate bars, Twinkies, pre-packaged chopped fruit, crackers. Whatever their greedy hearts desired was theirs for the taking, thanks to the five-fingered discount that so many miscreants had made use of before them. Daniel felt like a regular little Fagin with his motley gang of orphans.

Frankie kept a timid distance, his feelings laid bare like the exposed nerve of a chipped tooth, but at night, if he managed to find his way next to Daniel in bed, his scrawny arms reached for comfort. Daniel pretended to sleep, let Frankie curl into his back like a prawn. There was no harm in that, if the endurance of the boy's hope kept Daniel's place in the car safe.

*

They were halfway across Texas, trying to decide how much further to drive before sunset. Bradley was keen to press on, to make it as close to the Texas-Louisiana border as possible so they'd have less distance to cover the following day. Daniel was bored of driving, wanted to smoke a proper cigarette and have a shave and a shower.

'Do we need gas?' Jenna asked. She was up front in her white summer dress, a delicate hand catching the breeze through the open window. Deep in her teenage-runaway delusions, she was playing the role of a Lisbon sister who'd made it out, a starry-eyed optimist who'd escaped the neatly mowed lawns and white picket fences of suburbia for the open road. As a fellow fantasist, Daniel admired the vision.

Bradley glanced at the dashboard. 'Nah, we're good.'

'There's a gas station coming up,' she said. 'In, like, a mile.' She chewed the skin on the back of her knuckles. 'We still have a ways to go. I think we should top up while we can.'

'I want to buy cigarettes anyway,' Daniel said.

'You shouldn't smoke those,' Frankie said. 'They give you cancer.'

'Chance would be a fine thing,' Daniel replied.

At the gas station, Jenna tried on different pairs of sunglasses from a rack on the counter, while Daniel bought twenty Camel Crushes. The attendant didn't notice Jenna peel the price tag from a pair with white plastic frames and place them on top of her head as though they'd always belonged to her, but Daniel did, and he respected the tenacity.

As they crossed the forecourt together, a familiar sight caught Daniel's eye. It was the Mustang, parked by a gas pump. There was no sign of the driver, but the presence of the car unsettled him.

'Hey, look,' Jenna said, as they climbed back into their car. 'There's that girl again.'

Daniel's stomach dropped. Through the window of the gas station, a girl who bore a striking resemblance to Caroline was at the counter paying for gas. She had the same dark bob, but her face was obscured by an absent-minded hand as she fiddled with an earring or a lock of hair.

'You've seen her before?' Daniel asked, mouth dry.

'Mmm. She was staying at that motel in Arizona,' Jenna said. 'The first one, with the roaches. I met her at the vending machine and we got talking, while you were arguing with Bradley about trying to get a refund on the roach room. Hey, can I smoke one of your cigarettes?'

'Not in the car man, come on,' Frankie complained.

'What do you mean you *got talking*?' snapped Daniel. 'What did she say?'

'I dunno, just girl talk. She asked if I had any tampons, and it just went from there. Who I'm travelling with, where we're going, that kind of thing.'

'So, a total stranger grills you about your travel plans, and you just tell her?' Daniel asked, incredulous.

'It wasn't a big deal,' Jenna said, defensive. 'Girls are never strangers to each other the way men are strangers.'

'That's so dumb. What if it was all a front for a human trafficking ring?' Frankie said, always there with a helpful interjection.

'Maybe she saw I was travelling with three men and wondered if *I* was being trafficked?' Jenna shot back.

'We can make it to Lake Charles tonight if we push on for a few more hours,' Bradley said.

In the rear-view mirror, Daniel watched the stranger climb into the driver's seat of the Mustang and peer over her shoulder, checking her blind spot before she jerked the handbrake and pulled out. There was a brief moment in which their eyes met, and her face morphed from that of his sister to a stranger and back again. Her face was a blank page. It wasn't Caroline. It could be Caroline. There was too much distance between them, and Daniel's resistance to eye tests meant he viewed the world in soft focus, often missing the details.

'Was she English?' he asked Jenna, pulling out as soon as there was a gap.

'Hmm?'

'The woman, the one that asked you about tampons. Was she English?'

'No, she was American. Why d'you ask?'

'No reason,' Daniel said. 'I thought I recognised her, that's all.'

*

It took another full day to reach the border of Louisiana and Texas; a day of heat haze shimmering on the empty tarmac, of spitting sunflower-seed shells and counting down the miles as the car breezed past swampland, the trees roped with trailing kudzu.

Another state, another town, another supermarket. They reached Lake Charles late, when the black velveteen sky was freckled with twinkling stars. Bradley wanted to push on to New Orleans, but Daniel saw little point in arriving at midnight a day ahead of schedule. It would be a nightmare to find somewhere to stay at that hour, and he hadn't yet decided if he wanted to ditch his little gang of miscreants when they reached the city.

As usual, Daniel lit a cigarette halfway across the car park, so he had an excuse to hang back while his savage children stormed the Bastille of Walmart and scattered, each with their own mission: Bradley on protein, Jenna on produce, Frankie on carbs. Daniel's role was to secure the booze through legal channels, and it was from his vantage point in the liquor aisle that he watched his team's downfall.

Frankie was responsible for their ruin. From what Daniel could tell, the boy's new-found confidence had clouded his judgement, and he'd attempted to stroll out of the supermarket with a whole baguette under one arm, casual as you like, with all the indifference of a pint-sized gentleman carrying an umbrella. Daniel could only assume the security guard had noted the gang's arrival to the store, because both Jenna and Bradley were also detained in quick succession.

With clammy hands, Daniel took a bottle of golden reposado tequila to the till and stuck it on his credit card. He watched with an affectation of mild curiosity as the trio were escorted past him by a meaty security guard. Jenna was a picture of misery, tears rolling freely down her cheeks. Bradley was red-faced with fury, although whether his anger was directed at Frankie's indiscretion or the wider situation was unclear. And Frankie – sweet, foolish Frankie – looked shellshocked. As they passed Daniel, Frankie raised his head and caught his eye. He gave a brief, imploring look, and Daniel glanced away.

'You know 'em?' the cashier asked.

'Nah,' Daniel said, taking his change. 'Shame, though, isn't it? I feel bad for them. They're just kids, after all.'

*

It wouldn't have been prudent for Daniel to wait in the vehicle and risk association by proxy with the little larcenists. There was nowhere else to go – no diner, no dive bar, no chain restaurant in which to take shelter.

If this were a film, perhaps he'd have tucked the car keys on the front wheel and bummed a ride with a trucker or hitched a lift with a lonely salesman, but the reality of the situation was that it was late, it was dark, the car park was empty, and Daniel's suitcase was locked in their motel room. The smart thing to do was to climb into the rental and drive away before the Mustang caught up with them.

The kids would be all right. They were cosplaying poverty with wallets full of cash and emergency credit cards from their rich

Los Angeles parents. Jenna and Bradley would call Daddy, and he'd send a car to scoop them up. They would be absolutely fine.

Daniel drove to the motel to collect his bag, but there he faced an immediate obstacle: Bradley had the key card to the room in his wallet.

The teenage goth on reception was passing the long and lonely hours by colouring her fingernails with a Sharpie. The resulting black was dull and flat, and it reminded Daniel of necrosis.

'Hello, darling,' he said, switching on the Hugh Grant charm. 'I wonder if you can help me – I appear to have lost my key card. Room twenty-two?'

'You're not the guy who checked in,' she said, with a healthy hint of suspicion.

'I'm sorry?' Daniel asked, buying himself some time.

'I said, you're not the guy that checked in.'

'No, my friend checked us in.'

'Where's he at?'

'He's ... picking up some drive-thru,' Daniel said.

She dragged the keyboard and mouse towards her, began clicking around on the computer.

'Says here it's a solo room.'

'It does?'

'Did y'all lie to get a discount or something?'

'I wouldn't know anything about that,' Daniel said. 'Like I said, Bradley checked us in.'

'Says here he's travelling alone.'

'Well, didn't you take his registration?' He pointed out the window, towards the car in the car park. 'Look – there's the car. I don't know anything about a discount. He was meant to check us both in. It's just an innocent mistake – I can pay the difference right now.'

'Thought you said he was getting drive-thru?'

Daniel blinked. 'I'm sorry?'

'How's he picking up drive-thru if you have the car?'

Fuck. There was no dignity in being outwitted by a teenager in a *Buffy the Vampire Slayer* T-shirt. 'I don't like the way you're talking to me,' Daniel said. 'Can you please call your manager?'

'I *am* the manager,' she said, folding her arms.

'You know what? This is ridiculous. I'll just wait for him in the car.'

But Daniel didn't wait for him in the car. Instead, he drove with the bottle of tequila between his thighs, taking the occasional swig until his eyes began to itch, and then he pulled into the parking lot of a roadside Denny's to sleep. The ghostly white lights of passing trucks illuminated the car's cabin, and he couldn't help but picture all manner of bandits lurking in the shadows. When the sun rose, he swilled out his stale mouth with tequila and hit the road to meet his fate – and fate came in the shape of Selina.

Dessert

Bananas Foster

⚜

Bananas flambéed in dark rum and drizzled in a rich caramel made from melted butter, brown sugar, cinnamon and banana liqueur, served with a scoop of melting vanilla ice cream.

London: Caroline

The psychic's words were heavy on Caroline's heart. *That sounds exactly like the shirt he wore most days in New Orleans.*

Sage was crying. 'I'm sorry I didn't say anything sooner,' she said, reaching to touch Caroline, who withdrew her hands in response. 'I just didn't think there was anything to worry about until now. You've never travelled – you don't understand how spiritually nourishing it is.'

Spiritually nourishing. Caroline closed her eyes and counted to ten. She had never considered Sage to be a great thinker. In Caroline's estimation, Sage travelled not to experience other cultures, but to experience different versions of herself. She used to talk about the way the sun browned her skin and made her freckles pop, the way a diet of papaya salads and daily swims in the ocean made her jawline sharp and her stomach concave, but never about the history or culture of a place.

'Let me pour you a brandy,' Richard said, in a soft voice that turned her stomach. 'You've had a shock.'

Caroline studied his profile. Dark ginger hair, square glasses and a neat beard that, for all she knew, could conceal a weak chin. In all the years they'd known one another, she had never seen him clean shaven.

He fetched five tumblers and filled each with a honeyed measure of Courvoisier. Max knocked his back like a shot of tequila, but the others cupped their hands around their glasses, stared into the amber depths as though the liquor held the answers to their questions.

'I know this must be difficult,' the psychic said to Caroline. 'I can see how much he means to you. You have one of the most melancholy auras I've ever seen.'

Caroline counted five things she could see. Her brandy glass. The candles, burning low. A drop of gumbo on the table. A pouch of tobacco. The psychic's white gummy bear-flavoured vape.

'It's black, streaked with indigo,' the psychic continued.

Four things she could touch. The table beneath her hands. Her chair. The sleeves of her dress. Richard's hand.

'Tired and low, but sensitive too. Full of pain.'

Three things she could hear. The psychic's inane ramblings. Sage's lies. Richard's longing.

'We're all trying our best to piece together this complicated puzzle.'

Two things she could smell. Melted wax. Cajun spices.

'When did you realise Daniel had gone?' the psychic said.

One thing she could taste. Dread.

*

The project managers at Caroline's office liked to go out for lunch on Fridays. The end of the work week brought a collective sense of conviviality, and they usually went to a local gastro pub for large glasses of cheap wine and flabby burgers that oozed grease and cheese, to pick at their insecurities and gossip about their colleagues.

Jazz was holding court, a glass of room-temperature Chardonnay in hand, telling a long-winded anecdote about some difficulties she'd been experiencing with a client. The rest of the team were hooked on the story, but a tremendous sense of ennui had settled over Caroline, and she was grateful for the distraction when a text from her brother flashed up on her phone: *Hey, where's my passport?*

She typed back a quick reply. *Why do you need your passport?*

Going out later, might need ID.

You won't need ID, darling, she replied. *No offence, but you look your age.*

All the same, I'd feel better if I had it.

'She's such a bitch,' Jazz said, squeezing a packet of ketchup on to her plate. 'We've been locking horns all month over the budget. She wants it to be a champagne experience on prosecco money and I'm just like, I can't turn water into wine babe, so up the budget or get over it.'

'They always want something for nothing,' Simone chipped in.

Dad's bureau, Caroline typed back. *Make sure you put it back when you get in. Where are you going, btw?*

'Anyway,' Jazz continued. 'Ralph pulled me to one side after our last meeting and was like, "Jazz you can't speak to a client like that. I know she's awful, but you need to be professional."'

'I can't believe he said that to you,' Marissa said. 'Were you really that bad?'

'I mean, yes,' Jazz said. 'But it was a *really* tense call.'

Speaking of age, Caroline typed. *Do you know what you'd like to do for your birthday? I was thinking maybe a dinner party? I'll do everything, just tell me who you'd like to invite.*

He left her on read, but Caroline thought nothing of it. She returned her attention to Jazz's dull monologue and picked over her salad until it was time to return to the office.

After work, everything was as it should be. Daniel's bedroom door was closed, but there was a stillness to the air, a silence thinning the lifeblood of their flat, which suggested he had gone out without her. She fired off a quick text – *Thanks for inviting me* – and made herself a simple dinner of buttered pasta and freshly ground black pepper, then poured a glass of Sancerre and settled on the sofa to watch Dario Argento's *Suspiria*.

In the morning, Daniel's bedroom door remained shut. Caroline fixed a bowl of muesli and brewed coffee, then listened to a podcast about Val Lewton as she did the washing-up. After breakfast, there were still no signs of life from her brother, so she left him to sleep off whatever cocktail of alcohol and narcotics he'd swallowed the night before and went for a gentle run. It went against the advice of her doctor, who'd recommended she wait a full year before returning to sport, but Caroline had never been too concerned about the opinions of others.

Signs of summer were breaking through the gloom of early June: a blue sky, the first warm day of the year. It was almost a pleasure to feel the ache in her muscles, to inhale the clean, fresh smell of the changing seasons. She paused to catch her breath and send a message Daniel. *Are you in tonight? Shall we have drinks on the balcony?*

He hadn't replied by the time she'd jogged to the supermarket, but she picked up a bottle of dry vermouth for martinis anyway, plus a jar of fat Nocellara olives and a plump lemon to flay for twists.

When Caroline returned home, there was still no sign of Daniel. She checked they had vodka in the freezer – they did – and that they had enough ice for cocktails – they did not. She filled the ice-cube tray, took a shower and changed into a summer dress. It wasn't quite the weather for bare legs, so she chose a pair of tights and one of her father's old woollen jumpers to keep her warm.

By the time the clock struck four, she was growing impatient for company. She stood outside Daniel's door and knocked, but there was no answer.

'Jesus, what kind of night did you have last night?' she asked, turning the handle and letting herself in, but the room was empty. She sent him a quick message: *Where are you?*

Evening turned to night, and still there was no word from Daniel. After a full twenty-four hours of silence from her brother, she noticed his suitcase was missing from its place above his wardrobe, and his toothbrush was no longer in the glass by the sink of his en suite.

You fucking cunt, she thought.

*

'And that's when you called me,' said Sage, dabbing her eyes with a napkin.

'Yes,' Caroline said. 'Fat lot of use you were.'

'I was just acting in Daniel's best interests,' Sage said.

'You were lying through your teeth,' Caroline spat back.

*

The café was cold and white, anaesthetised by an aggressively bright sunshine that was rendered toothless by the arctic blast of air-conditioning. Dozens of plants hung in the windows, and there was a fridge full of leafy pre-packaged salads and freshly squeezed juices the colour of swamp water. It felt more like a garden centre than a café.

'Thanks so much for meeting me,' Sage said, and then she inexplicably placed an unwelcome hand on Caroline's cheek. 'Have you heard from him at all?'

Sage's fingers were cold and dry, and Caroline jerked away from her touch.

'No,' Caroline replied. 'Nothing all week.'

'You said he took his passport, right? So maybe he simply grew tired of London,' Sage said, scanning the chiller of salads. She picked a vegan superfood salad called 'I am Nourished', which was studded with dried goji berries and jewel-like pomegranate seeds.

Maybe he simply grew tired of you, Caroline thought. Sage was part of a collective of bohemian yuppies that lived in warehouses in Hackney, or artsy flats full of velvet sofas and Turkish rugs in Primrose Hill. The last time Caroline had seen her, she was living on a narrowboat, and their conversations – which, in Caroline's case, were infrequent and kept as short as possible – revolved around tedious complaints about mooring regulations and septic tanks.

Caroline picked over the sandwiches, looking for the least vegan-friendly option, but it wasn't the kind of place to sell schnitzel, or foie gras, or anything of that calibre of squeamish cruelty. The most decadent choice available was a vegan cheese-and-ham toastie called 'I am Comfort' and a salted caramel oat-milk latte called 'I am Warmth', spiked with an extra pump of sugar syrup. Comfort and warmth.

Give me strength, Caroline thought.

The server was built like a javelin, with long blond hair fastened into a neat ponytail and pale skin that glowed with the radiance of a Rivendell elf. He wore a silver ankh around his slender neck.

'Hello ladies,' he said. 'What are you thankful for today?'

'Um,' said Sage. 'I guess right now I'm thankful for …'

'Alcohol,' said Caroline. 'I'll take a rosé spritz.'

The server smiled. 'If you're in the mood for something sparkling, may I recommend our Spiritual Spritz?'

Caroline shot him a venomous look, and his serene smile wavered.

'Sure, a rosé spritz, coming right up,' he said. 'And for you, my love?'

Sage stared at the chalkboard above his head, scanning a handwritten list of smoothies. 'I'd like an ... I am Beautiful?'

'I am Beautiful, right on. May I recommend you take it with a scoop of blue spirulina?'

'Lovely, yes please.'

'And may I suggest you ladies split a portion of the I am Whole as a starter today? Vegan coconut calamari. My favourite dish on the summer menu, and it's perfect between two.'

'Sounds great,' said Sage.

'We're fine,' Caroline cut in.

'Sure, no problem. I'll leave you ladies to take a seat, and I'll get started on those drinks.'

A customer with long, shaggy hair glanced up from his paperback as Sage passed him, and then he actually turned his head and craned his neck to catch sight of her backside as she shimmied towards a table.

'If he'd suggested the Kool-Aid, would you say yes to that too?' Caroline asked, as they settled into their seats.

'I know it's kind of goofy, but I like it here,' Sage said. 'I think it's cool. It's different – it's *mindful*. They want you to really think about what you're thankful for, and to focus on your blessings.'

'It's a fucking cult,' Caroline said. She took a bite of her toasted sandwich, which was cold and smeared with a raw vegan sham of a burrata, made from some kind of almond-based paste that tasted more like cyanide than cream.

Sage shrugged. 'I like it.'

Out of everyone she knew, Sage was most likely to end up drinking the Kool-Aid, so to speak. She had cult-follower spirit, the type to abandon everything at the behest of an unwashed man in a hemp shirt and a pseudo-bohemian philosophy scraped from the internet.

A waitress with a shaved head and a nose ring arrived at their table with a lapis-coloured smoothie and a fizzy spritz. Caroline accepted her drink and took a generous sip. It was made with a natural wine, cloudy like pink lemonade.

'Look, I know you must be worried sick,' Sage said, extracting a pot of dressing from her salad box and shaking it with a well-practised hand. 'But I think everything's going to be just fine.'

'You aren't even the slightest bit concerned? Daniel went out one night and never came home. It's been over a week. He's *missing* – and you don't seem to care.'

'Well … with all due respect,' Sage said. 'Daniel's an adult, and he's only "missing" from your perspective. I'm sure he knows exactly where he is.'

Caroline took a deep breath, a vertiginous flare of anger clouding her vision. 'Look, I'm glad you're finding this amusing, but I'm an absolute wreck. I can't eat, I can't sleep, I can't work. I'm in pieces. If you know something, *anything*, about my brother's whereabouts, you have to tell me, Sage. You *have* to tell me.'

'Look, it's really none of my business,' Sage said.

'If you don't tell me what you know, I'm going to register him as a missing person with the police, and I'm going to give them your name as a person of interest.'

Sage squirmed in her seat, perhaps imagining what uniformed police officers might make of her marijuana-scented narrowboat. 'I don't think there's any need to get the police involved.'

'Do you know where he is or not?'

Sage picked up her wooden fork and stirred her salad leaves, face a blank mask. 'I don't know where he is, and, to be perfectly frank, I think we should just respect the fact that he doesn't want us to know. He packed a bag – it's not like he's been abducted.'

In one smooth motion, Caroline jumped to her feet and tossed the rosé spritz into Sage's smug face.

*

Caroline took a sip of brandy. It burned her throat, warmed her blood. Sage looked as though she expected another, more heartfelt apology, but Caroline didn't regret throwing the drink. If Sage wanted to be treated with respect, she had to earn it.

'The dinner party you were going to throw for Daniel was New Orleans-themed,' Richard said, frowning. 'Sazeracs, oysters, gumbo ... but you didn't find out he was in New Orleans until the police called on his birthday?'

Caroline shook her head. 'No, I knew he was in New Orleans. I got a notification that a bill had bounced from our joint account. When I checked, he'd drained it. He'd booked a hotel, bought a bunch of clothes, and withdrawn some cash in New Orleans.'

'Why didn't you tell me?' asked Sage.

'Well, you obviously weren't worried, so what did it matter?' Caroline replied. 'Anyway, I called the hotel and cancelled his reservation, and then I called the bank and cancelled his debit card too.'

'What hotel?' the psychic asked. 'The French House?'

'No, I don't think so. Anyway, I booked him a flight from New Orleans to Heathrow and messaged him to say he'd better walk through the door on his birthday with a fucking smile on his face.'

'And he didn't reply?' asked Sage.

Caroline's face briefly crumpled, but she regained her composure. 'He didn't.'

'Can I ask you a question?' asked the psychic. 'How did you find me?'

Caroline felt her eyes glaze over with the trauma of the memory. 'The police got in touch with me,' she said, 'when they found his belongings in the bayou. They mentioned you by name, and you were easy to find.'

*

The days passed Caroline by in a blur of messages, phone calls, social media posts. She knew Daniel had left of his own accord, but she didn't know why.

On Daniel's birthday, Caroline held the phone to her ear and stared out of the window. A flat grey sky, the kind of shitty weather that didn't speak to any particular time of day, any particular season. It could have been a bleak afternoon in early autumn, or a miserable morning in spring. It wasn't the kind of weather that made her think of midsummer. Unremarkable in every way but one.

She knew by the tone of voice on the other end of the line that the news was going to be bad. The family liaison officer asked if she was sitting down, if there was anyone with her, if there was anyone she could call for support, and it felt more straightforward to just say, *Yes, yes, yes.*

Daniel had been reported missing in New Orleans, and his bloodstained things had been found floating in the swampy waters of a national park. His possessions might not have been found at all, the officer said, if it wasn't for the car.

What car?

Caroline felt sick, squeezed her eyes closed and imagined a gloomy body of water, thick and green with algae, midges clouding the air. She pictured him floating supine in the swamp, palms up like a masculine Ophelia, with a white cheesecloth shirt spreading through the water, flowers in his hair. But no – that couldn't be right. There was no body, just a bloodied shirt, his waterlogged passport. The heat, she supposed, and the scavengers. The insects. It didn't bear thinking about.

The evidence suggested he may have 'disturbed the wildlife' – that's the phrase the family liaison officer used. Caroline knew what that meant, though. Ripped apart, torn limb from limb, dismembered by the snapping jaws of alligators.

There was a ringing in her ears.

The lab in New Orleans was backed up, and it could take months for forensics to identify the DNA, the family liaison officer explained. If they could confirm the shirt belonged to Daniel, it still wouldn't be enough to declare her brother dead, but a different outcome was unlikely. The evidence pointed to death by misdemeanour, but without a body, without a witness to confirm it, Caroline saw no reason to believe it – and nor did the coroner.

'We need you to identify the shirt,' the family liaison officer said.

'It doesn't sound like something Daniel owned,' Caroline said, phone hot against her ear. 'Can I ask who reported him missing in New Orleans?'

'An English woman,' the family liaison officer said. 'Selina Green. Does that name ring a bell?'

'No. I know all his friends. He's never mentioned a Selina.'

The family liaison officer had the good grace to sound embarrassed. 'Well, she says she's a psychic. It's best not to think too much about it – strange people come out of the woodwork with cases like this.'

'Cases like this?'

'Well, when there isn't a body, there's room for speculation. I should warn you, there may be some activity on the internet if the story breaks. Conspiracy theories, that kind of thing.'

'Right,' said Caroline. 'I understand.'

The flat looked the same. Strange. The clocks hadn't stopped, the lights hadn't dimmed, the mirrors hadn't covered themselves in black crepe. On the balcony, a pigeon cooed. A car horn knelled somewhere in the distance, far below. A plane cut through the sky, a scar of vapour in its wake. The cruelty of an indifferent world.

She'd have to cancel the dinner party. What a banal thought. She almost laughed.

In the bathroom, Caroline's reflection wore a blank expression. She felt disconnected from herself, dislocated from the moment. She was reminded of all those old archival pictures from the Great War showing soldiers in shock. Shellshock – wasn't that what they called it, because they didn't know what post-traumatic stress disorder looked like, didn't have a name for it? That had always baffled Caroline. How did no one know what trauma looked like? Back in the day, they were all traumatised, weren't they? How could a person live through the violence of history and not be traumatised by the horror of it? The French Revolution, the burning of witches, the transatlantic slave trade, the Black Death. All the tortures of early medicine, like amputations with no anaesthetic and childbirth without the clinical safety of hospitals – how could the grisly history of humanity unfold without a record of trauma?

Caroline had a talent for compartmentalising her emotions. When their father died, just six months after their mother, she'd drawn up a list – and then she took to the phone, started organising. She spoke to the coroner, the funeral director, the bank, their solicitor, beginning the arduous process of making the necessary arrangements.

She adopted the same practical mindset now.

Her first task was to call Richard, Max and Sage to cancel the birthday dinner.

'Any news?' asked Sage.

'No,' said Caroline.

'Keep in touch,' Sage replied, as Caroline disconnected the call.

Her second task was to locate this psychic. If there was one thing Caroline excelled at, it was tracking people down online. When her driving examiner had failed her on a technicality, Caroline had managed to find a picture of his daughter in her wedding dress within two hours of getting home. She was going to leave a nasty message about the bride's fleshy upper arms, which were pale and speckled with acne-like keratosis pilaris, but then she realised the wedding hadn't happened yet. Seeking the approval of strangers ahead of her *big day*, the bride-to-be had shared a photo of herself in her wedding dress with an online community of women who based their entire personalities on being brides (baffling, Caroline thought: you're a bride for less than twenty-four hours – you may as well aspire to be a moth). Recognising an opportunity, Caroline saved the picture until the night before the stranger's wedding, and then she sent it to the groom. The meltdown that followed was incredible – all that planning, all those hours wasted in bridal shops, wrestling into silk and chiffon, all ruined by a seventeen-year-old with a grudge.

Had the bride personally wronged Caroline? No. But Caroline felt better knowing she'd hurt someone close to the driving examiner, that she'd spoiled his daughter's wedding dress and hopefully ruined her wedding day, just as he'd spoiled Caroline's day by failing her for running one tiny little red light like a fussy old pedant.

With shaking hands, she searched for more information about this Selina Green character. The first hit was a profile on an online directory of psychic mediums, where grifters with names like Psychic Sammi and Dr Spring Soul Flower flogged their wares to the desperate masses. Caroline read the profile feverishly, her phone gripped in her hand.

Hello angels ✿♡✿ I'm Selina Green, an intuitive tarot reader, nature-lover and empath with over ten years' experience in the art of spiritual guidance. Now, I'm here to offer you the benefits of my clairvoyance. From money and careers to love and relationships, I blend ancient and modern techniques to deliver clarity, answer your questions and help you find the right spiritual path. Let's work together and connect.

The psychic had a reasonably large online platform, with thousands of followers lapping up her metropolitan-gothic style. This wasn't what Caroline had been expecting. She'd imagined a flamboyant nutter with a tangle of crispy greys, scratchy-looking eyeliner, drab outfits covered in cat hair. This woman was modern, successful and undeniably very beautiful. Caroline wouldn't look twice at her in Soho House, apart from that awful turquoise dye job.

She stayed up late that night, watching videos of the psychic's online readings and browsing through all the comments until the early hours. It seemed she lured people into her web with free readings, answering simple questions with the flip of a card or the toss of a coin, then, once their appetite had been suitably whetted, she charged a premium for a more in-depth, personal interpretation of the tarot.

And her fans lapped it up. People shared all their darkest secrets with this stranger, this so-called psychic. Worries about their marriages, fears about their future, all typed into the comments section under each video. They worried they would never amount to anything, worried their lives lacked meaning. It was clear these people were vulnerable, and the psychic was a leech, sucking as much money as she could from the wounds of their desperation.

As the sun rose, Caroline's flat filled with light and her heart filled with darkness. It seemed there were two possibilities, and they both left her boiling with rage. Either this scammer had latched on to the story and had never met her brother, or she was somehow involved in his disappearance. Perhaps she was even directly responsible.

Daniel had a knack for collecting people who could be useful to him. Even as a little boy, people had gone out of their way to please him, to give him sweets or toys or special preference, in the hope they might get to witness the sweet sunshine of his smile, the aria of his boyish giggle. Plus, he had always been drawn to pretty things. Caroline could easily imagine him following this woman into the bayou to do sun salutations or smoke peyote and – well. It didn't bear thinking about.

He'd grown accustomed to living life on easy mode. Richard, their eager-to-please little Dicky, had been Daniel's free ride through university, and of course their lecturer Benjamin Taylor had been seduced by his youth, beauty and wit. Caroline hadn't taken any pleasure in reporting their relationship to the university, but if she didn't teach Daniel a lesson, she was concerned he'd leave Norwich without learning anything at all. Of course, had she known his intentions were to leave her behind and pursue a master's, she'd have intervened sooner, but that was her lesson to learn.

She didn't make the same mistake twice. Daniel was a mediocre bass player, and an expensive instrument covered the sins a cheaper model would have exposed. She knew she couldn't bear the thought of following him on tour with those Poundland Pete Dohertys, couldn't hack the ruckus of a tour bus, but if she wasn't there to keep an eye on things, who knew how high his star would rise, and then where would she be?

She hadn't hoped for death when she pressed the car keys into Carl's sweaty hand, had merely intended to call the police and report them for dangerous driving, but it just goes to show that fate's hand is one that can be easily led. If anything, she thought, the Strangeways should be grateful for her divine intervention. Thanks to her, Sesh had achieved rock-and-roll immortality, had gone the way of Marc Bolan, Eddie Cochran and Razzle of Hanoi Rocks. Carl had survived the crash, and lived on in infamy. Vehicular manslaughter wasn't quite as glamourous as possession, drunk-and-disorderly charges or vandalising a hotel room, but she had once seen his mugshot in a rogue's gallery in a rock bar, alongside Ozzy Osbourne, Vince Neil and Sid Vicious. You couldn't buy that kind of notoriety.

Caroline could admit to herself that the car accident – not the crash that ruined the Strangeways, but her own brush with death several years later – was a little much, but desperate times called for desperate measures. Sage had frozen her out of their travel plans. Caroline couldn't stand the thought of Daniel spending weeks soul-searching in South East Asia. What if life on the road suited him? What if he decided not to come home?

Always meticulous, she did her research. The majority of incidents in which a car struck a pedestrian took place late at night, and there were statistically better outcomes when the victim was young and wealthy, and the accident occurred near a hospital.

On a serene Wednesday evening, she pieced together a funereal outfit of all black and stepped into the path of a speeding car about five minutes' walk from a large metropolitan hospital with a robust A and E. In any experiment, however, there were variables that could not be predicted or controlled. Caroline had relied on the driver being in possession of at least two brain cells and the ability to hit the brakes soon enough to spare her from a full-impact collision, but unfortunately, she'd chosen to put her life in the hands of a serial texter.

The human body was simply not built to withstand a collision with four thousand pounds of steel, glass and rubber, but several factors spared Caroline from certain death: her centre of gravity was above the height of the bumper, which meant her legs were swept in the direction of travel, and her torso was flipped against the windshield. The car wasn't going fast enough to propel her into a full roll, which could have broken her neck, and she remained on the hood of the car instead of being flung into the air. She found all this out later, though – she couldn't remember a thing between stepping off the kerb and coming to ensconced in a hospital bed, with Daniel by her side.

'Hello, darling,' he said, reaching for her hand and then recoiling at the sight of the intravenous cannula that pierced the skin. 'You gave me quite the fright. And look – Dicky sent f lowers.'

Caroline couldn't remember much else from that visit. He smelled like fresh rain. She could remember that. An almost tinny fragrance clinging to his skin and hair. She floated in and out of consciousness, her thoughts coasting on a milieu of morphine-induced dreams. In one particularly vivid narrative, she was a great grizzly bear, roaming the mountains and valleys of Yellowstone, protecting her cub.

When she awoke, those familiar protective instincts were stronger than ever.

*

The first was a little boy riding a blue bicycle, and it happened like this. It was late December, and winter had taken London, turned her skies grey, frosted her parks and frozen her puddles. The chilly afternoon was giving way to evening, and Caroline had convinced her little brother to walk home along the canal – an act of rebellion, as this was explicitly forbidden by their mother.

Night was closing in from all sides. She felt giddy as she walked, keeping a swift pace and enjoying the bounce of her messenger bag against her thigh. Daniel alternated between running ahead, overcome with the joy of novelty, and lagging behind to study the graffiti, or throw rocks to crack the ice on the water's surface.

Once you got past the thatch of narrowboats with their glowing portholes and little chimneys that billowed steam, and the canal-side pub in which beleaguered adults drank foaming pints of bitter, and the Victorian warehouses that had been converted into multimillion-pound flats, it wasn't unusual to see evidence of debauchery in the bushes that lined the towpath: vodka bottles, crushed beer cans, condom wrappers, dirty needles, miscellaneous scrunches of soiled fabric. Caroline liked to scan the puzzling detritus, little keyholes into an adult world she didn't yet understand.

She was perhaps twenty paces ahead of Daniel when she heard the gentle fanning of spokes as a bike approached them from behind. A mean voice cried out: 'Moo-oove!', and as she turned to trace the source of the noise, she saw a little boy, no older than Daniel, cycling towards them on the towpath. Instead of slowing down to pass her brother safely, the child raised a hand and slapped him as hard as he could on the back of his head. Daniel burst into tears, shocked by the indignity of the attack.

Caroline felt a flash of white-hot rage. They were on a stretch of the canal that curved like a horseshoe, and from Caroline's position, she couldn't see any adults keeping watch over the brat. His front wheel wobbled on the uneven paving stones, and in the split second it took for Caroline to recognise the opportunity, she had already done it: she took a step back, and, as he cycled by, she lunged forward and pushed him into the frozen canal. The gossamer-thin ice cracked like a skull hitting concrete and then he was under, and then he was gone, bike and all, in a matter of seconds. Caroline thought he would bob to the surface, and she watched with a detached curiosity as a stream of silver bubbles mapped his whereabouts in the murky depths. Weren't canals rather shallow? He was too small, perhaps, to find his footing, or too weak a swimmer; or the water was too cold, the shock of it too destabilising.

The commotion that followed was an exciting brouhaha. As Caroline started to scream, several panicked adults rounded the corner, running towards the sound of her cries. The crocodile tears flowed easily – she was a natural! – and a man grabbed her by both arms as she stuttered her way through an explanation, pointing at the ragged hole in the ice.

'He came off his bike – I tried to grab him, but it was too late, he was going too fast and—'

Several of the men jumped into the frigid water to fish out the child, but by the time he was retrieved, his face was a chilling shade of alabaster, his lips ultramarine, as though he'd just finished a blue raspberry ice pop.

Caroline had to bite her lips together to stop herself from smiling as a resuscitation attempt was performed. A man with a saviour complex, perhaps the boy's father, was on his knees, compressing the little chest with his great big hands, and as he counted the beats of his rhythm, Caroline counted the jolly cracks that suggested broken ribs.

A woman wearing an eye-watering amount of perfume put her hands on Daniel's small shoulders and steered the child away from the drama. 'Let's let them get on with it, sweetheart,' she said, rubbing his shoulders and bringing him into Caroline's care. 'We don't need to watch, do we?'

Fury mushroomed from the depths of Caroline's wicked little heart. Who was this woman? Who was she to deny Caroline – the architect of this tragedy – the best view in the house? Caroline fixed her attention on the cracked ice while the woman whittered on about the whereabouts of their *grown-up*, as though, at twelve years old, Caroline needed to be chaperoned at all times by an adult. Caroline was small for her age, and she was often mistaken for a child much younger than her years. Occasionally, she found it advantageous to lean in to this, and even at twelve, she could pass for nine or ten.

'Our mummy's at home,' Caroline said in a baby voice, hamming it up with a shy little sniff. 'We were on our way back when he fell.'

'On your own?' the woman asked, eyeing her. She was, no doubt, wondering what kind of mother – sorry, *grown-up* – would let children of their age walk home alone along the canal at sunset.

The woman bit her waxy lipsticked lower lip and glanced over her shoulder. Behind them, a crowd had gathered around father and son, who were posed in a tableau of tragedy. In the distance, a siren broke the stillness of the wintry air, and the father glanced up, as though he were expecting a speedboat to come crashing through the ice to his rescue.

As fun as this was, it was probably time for them to take their leave. Daniel was crying, his lashes dark with tears.

'Come on, then,' Caroline said. 'Mummy will be worried.'

The woman wasn't listening to her anymore. It was as though she'd only just realised what Caroline had known all along: that as soon as the little boy and his bicycle had hit the ice, it was over. He was gone. The lights had dimmed, and the child was dead.

Caroline grabbed Daniel by the hand. Together, they took off at a sprint, and no one called after them.

*

Following the psychic online turned Caroline's fury into an inferno, scorching the last of her sweetness to tar. It burned with the capsicum heat of a Carolina Reaper. She felt deranged – like she could start a fire, kill a man, lead a vengeful mob to rip the psychic limb from limb. She wanted to gorge herself on liquor, vandalise something precious, steal something meaningful. She had all this anger, and nowhere for it to go.

Caroline fantasised about booking a private reading with the psychic. The thought gave her chills. Would she be able to face her? Would she be able to keep her cool, or would it all just come tumbling out, a rush of anger and poison, arsenic on her tongue? Caroline didn't think the psychic would clock the family resemblance between herself and Daniel. They looked similar in pictures, but Daniel was always so striking, with his tumble of dark curls. He was bohemian and lackadaisical, in contrast to Caroline's sharp, well-groomed image. People often remarked on their differences and seldom recognised their similarities.

Late one night, she rewatched *Léon*, the nineties film in which Jean Reno plays an illiterate assassin with a heart of gold, and she thought, *That's how it's done, hire someone slick and take her out, nice and clean.* But she knew it wasn't a realistic aspiration.

In her darkest moments, Caroline dreamed of buying a gun and shooting the psychic between the eyes herself. The great thing about the internet was that you could get anything you liked if you knew where to look. You could get a single doughnut hand-delivered by an artisanal bakery. You could buy weed, space cakes, THC gummies, LSD, magic mushrooms, cocaine – even heroin, if you really wanted it. You could buy credit card info, PayPal details, and all sorts of personal information. You could buy unthinkable things, too, pictures and videos of despicable acts that turned Caroline's unusually strong stomach. If you could think of it, and you had the money, anything could be yours. Pepper spray, knuckle dusters, flick knives, handguns. Anything.

In the end, she simply sent her a message.

Dear Selina,

I hope this email finds you well, with an open heart and mind. I'm Daniel's sister, Caroline. As you can imagine,

Alice Slater

I'm struggling to piece together the circumstances that led to my brother's disappearance, and I wondered if you'd be able to help shed some light on his state of mind when you met him in New Orleans.

Fate is a powerful force, and I believe you met one another for a reason. My brother is a very special person, and I just know you must be special too if he decided to share his time in New Orleans with you. Please consider joining myself and several of Daniel's close friends for dinner this Friday – we'd like to talk about the trip and anything that Daniel may have said that could help us find him. I have included my address below.

I can't tell you what it would mean to meet you. I have so many questions.

Yours,
Caroline xox

New Orleans: Selina

I slept like the dead, and woke up sweating, legs tangled in the twisted bedsheet. It took me a moment to orientate myself, my brain slowly warming up. Daniel's side of the bed was empty, the sheets cool, and my limbs felt heavy as I heaved myself into the bathroom to clean my teeth and freshen up.

When I found my phone, I was shocked to see I'd slept through most of the day. It was nearly three o'clock in the afternoon, and I had a bunch of unread messages from home. A dozen customer orders. My mother, checking in. My flatmate, asking some inane question about the water bill. There was also a message from my bank, and as I read it, the floor tilted beneath my feet with a vertiginous sense of fear. *Dear Miss Green*, it said. *Account log-in detected in Manchester, UK. If this was you, you can ignore this message and your transfer will clear within 24 hours. If this was not you, please call our fraud prevention helpline between 8am and 8pm.*

Your transfer will clear? What transfer? A tidal wave of panic. The message had come through at four o'clock in the morning – that meant nearly twelve hours had passed since the fraudulent transfer attempt. What if it had already cleared? I closed the message and logged in to my bank account. Everything looked normal – my current account held what was left of my travel money, and my savings account remained steady at ten thousand pounds, with no pending transactions – but would a pending transaction show if it was a bank-to-bank transfer? I wasn't sure.

I needed to speak to the fraud team asap, but – I counted the time on my fingers – it was already 9pm in the UK. By the time the fraud department reopened, it would be too late. The transfer – whatever it was – would clear.

My legs ached as I pulled on some clothes, like I'd spent the night swimming laps in my sleep. The air felt heavy, every movement a tremendous and exhausting effort.

Daniel was sitting at one of the picnic benches in the courtyard, smoking his white plastic vape. He looked well-rested and fresh-faced behind a pair of white plastic sunglasses, although he was still wearing the same white cheesecloth shirt, now with a light pink stain down his chest.

'Good morning, darling,' he said. 'Or should I say – afternoon? You were out cold; I couldn't wake you up. Anyway, I got coffee and beignets, although the ice in your coffee has melted.'

'Daniel, I'm freaking out,' I said, and I showed him the message from my bank. He frowned as he scanned the words.

'Oh, shit,' he said. 'That can't be good. Have you called the fraud helpline?'

'It's closed,' I said, distraught. 'I slept through the whole day, and now it's closed and I'm going to lose everything. Oh God, I can't breathe.'

'Shhhh,' he said, reaching for my hand. 'It's okay. You're not going to be the first person on the planet who's been in this situation. How much do you have to lose?'

'Ten grand,' I whispered, although this figure didn't seem particularly significant to him, as he merely shrugged.

'Well, look – let's set an alarm to remind us to call the fraud helpline when it opens. And in the meantime, why don't you transfer your money to another account for safekeeping? Do you have an account with another bank?'

'No,' I said. 'I just have a current account and a savings account, both with the same bank.'

'Hmm,' he said, drumming his fingers on the bench. 'That's not ideal.'

'I suppose I could speak to my sister – see if she could take it?'

'Well, the bank might freeze your current account, and then you might need to access your savings,' he said. 'She'll go to bed within the next couple of hours, and you won't be able to message her if you need cash.'

'Fuck, this is a nightmare,' I wailed.

'Do you have a credit card?'

'Yes, but the rates are terrible. It's just for emergencies – and I'm terrified of using it, in case something happens, and I can't pay the bill.'

'Well, look – I have a spare bank account you could use,' he said. 'There's nothing in there at the moment, and I can give you the card and app log-in, so you'd have total access. Would that be helpful?'

'Oh …' I said, unsure. 'I don't know about that.'

'Sorry, no – of course. Stupid suggestion. I'm sure if this dodgy transfer goes through before we can sort it, your insurance will cover it.'

'Oh God,' I said, fingers working my temples to massage away a brewing headache. My mind felt foggy, unfocused. Would travel insurance cover something like this? What other insurance was there? 'I don't know what to do.'

'Don't worry about it,' Daniel said. 'Ten grand is nothing, in the grand scheme of things.'

'It's everything I have,' I said. 'Oh God, I can't breathe.'

'There,' Daniel said, reaching into his wallet and handing me a bright orange card. 'Consider it yours until you can speak to your bank. All the information is on there – download the app and I'll log you in.'

'Are you sure?'

'I don't need to rob you, darling. Between you and I, I'm a very wealthy man.'

I picked up my phone, logged in to my bank account, and moved every penny into Daniel's account. 'And you're sure I can keep this?' I said, turning the debit card over in my hands.

'I never use it,' he said. 'I prefer to use my AmEx, for the points.'

'Okay,' I said. 'Okay. Thank you. I promise I'll reverse the transfer and give you back the card as soon as I've spoken to my bank.'

'It's nothing, I'm just glad I could help. Now, be a darling and eat your beignet. You've had a shock – you need to keep your blood sugar up.' He pushed the paper bag across the table towards me.

'Mmm – Café du Monde?'

'Oh Christ, no,' he said. 'Total tourist trap, darling. We can do better than that. I went to this little place on Royal Street. They've probably gone cold now, but I'll get some more tomorrow so you can try them fresh – as long as you don't oversleep again.'

I bit into a square-shaped doughnut duned with icing sugar, which plumed into the air between us and created a constellation of powdered stars down the front of my dress.

'How is it?' he asked.

'Good,' I said, licking sugar from my lips. I felt jittery with adrenaline, couldn't stop my teeth from chattering.

'I found a great deal at a car rental place in Mid-City. Look, darling – very reasonable.' He showed me a list of calculations on his phone, but the numbers all blurred together.

'I don't know,' I said. 'I'm worried about money. I think it's best if I just leave it for now. Sorry to ruin your fun.'

'Oh fuck it, let's just do it,' he said. 'I'll pay. I want to see the gators. We'll get a cab to the rental place, shall we? I can't be doing public transport without a drink in me.'

'Have they sorted your key card yet?'

'No, apparently it's a problem with the lock itself,' he said breezily. 'Sorry about the shirt – everything's trapped inside my room. Can you bear to be seen with me?'

I hoped he'd bring up the idea of a suite at the Roosevelt again, but he sipped his coffee and smoked his vape, and didn't seem to remember his drunken offer.

'Oh God, that's so unlucky,' I said.

'You might say unlucky,' he said. 'I say touched by the devil.'

*

It took an hour of negotiations to secure the car. A jobsworth with a curdled aura, whose pit-stained shirt smelled of overripe blue cheese, said there was a problem with Daniel's credit card. It didn't seem to be working, and each time the clerk tried to run it, we were met with an error message and a request for a phone call to his bank.

'It won't be open,' Daniel repeated, his voice tight with frustration. 'I told you, I'm from England. It's an English bank. It's the middle of the night over there right now. Can we just try it one more time?'

The guy on the desk ran the card for a fourth time and shook his head. 'I dunno, man, it's still saying we should call them. Do y'all have another card we could try?'

Daniel glanced in my direction. 'Do you have my card, darling? Just for the rental; I'll pay you back once I've spoken to my bank.'

'Oh,' I said. 'Um.'

'You can take a debit card, right?' he said to the clerk, who shook his head with all the solemnity of a funeral director.

'No, sir. I'm afraid it has to be a credit card.'

Daniel took a deep breath and exhaled slowly. 'Can we pay in cash?'

The clerk continued to shake his head. 'No sir, we need a credit card for insurance purposes. Perhaps your friend has a card you could use?'

They both looked at me, and Daniel raised his eyebrows. 'Darling?'

'Oh no,' I said, 'I can't. I mean, I do have a credit card, but it's for emergencies.'

'This *is* an emergency,' Daniel said. 'If I don't see an alligator today, I'll die. Go on, darling – I'll cover it, I just need to call my bank when the phone lines open.'

'Could I see your driver's licence, please, ma'am?'

'Oh, I won't be driving,' I said quickly.

It was more complicated than I'd thought, though – the credit card on file had to belong to the driver, which meant if we covered the cost with my card, only I would be insured to drive the car.

Overcome by the humidity and acrid smell in the office, Daniel waited outside, vaping and scuffing his boots on the kerb, while I dealt with the paperwork.

'I've never driven abroad before,' I said, peeping my head outside to debrief. 'And I feel like shit. I'm not sure I'm up to it.'

'You'll be fine,' Daniel reassured me, squinting against the sun. He lowered his glasses on to the bridge of his nose. 'It's good to challenge yourself from time to time.'

'I'm really worried about charging this to my credit card,' I said. 'Like, with the situation with my bank.'

'I'll pay you back as soon as I'm on Wi-Fi,' he replied. 'Don't worry, darling. It's clearly a problem with my card, not my account.'

*

The car's interior had baked in the afternoon sun, and the black seat felt uncomfortably hot against my bare legs.

'Turn on the air, would you, darling?' Daniel said.

I peered into my phone, dragging my finger over the map, scanning the distance we had to travel to make it to the specific swamp tour Daniel had chosen.

'Selina?'

'Hmm?'

'The air con?'

'Oh …!' I started the car, and a welcome blast of icy air engulfed us. I leaned forward to fiddle with the fan to make sure I was receiving the optimum chill, and then pulled out of the car park and let the satnav guide me to the freeway.

Soon, the neat little clapboard houses gave way to the open road, and the sky above us was a limitless and optimistic shade of blue.

'Where's your phone?' Daniel asked.

'It's in the cupholder.'

'What's your passcode?'

'Why?'

'Because someone needs to DJ.'

'It's two-two-two-seven-seven-seven,' I said.

'Fabulous.'

He fiddled around with my phone for a few minutes, a gentle tap-tap-tapping of his forefinger on the screen. Eventually, a dark eighties new-wave song spilled from the tiny speaker and filled the car with a vampiric melody. Daniel settled back into his seat with a tranquil smile.

It was a longer drive than I had anticipated, and it was already so late in the day. The sun beat down upon the car as we trundled through the heat haze towards the swamp. By the time we reached our destination, my dress was stuck to my back and the sun was low in the sky. Even Daniel looked wilted, his dark curls losing their shape, the bridge of his nose a dusky pink where he'd caught the sun as he'd napped against the passenger window.

'Alright, y'all, let's go see some gators,' Daniel said, as he unclipped his seatbelt and adjusted his sunglasses in the passenger mirror. Stepping into the sunshine, he gasped, and in his best impression of southern belle, he said: 'Oh my stars, it's hotter than the devil's tail out here.'

Arm in arm, we strolled towards a sun-bleached visitor centre surrounded by a scatter of picnic benches. A weather-worn sign, hand painted in flaking purple, green and yellow, said 'Welcome to Gator Country'.

In the gift shop, surrounded by cartoon alligator keyrings, fridge magnets and T-shirts, I bought us two tickets for the 6pm tour. There was a basket of alligator teeth on the counter, conical in shape with rounded tips, each the size of my little toe.

'Not so sharp, are they?' Daniel said, picking up a tooth. I took one from the basket and found it surprisingly light to hold. It was rough, brittle to the touch and completely hollow.

'Well, I wouldn't wanna find out,' the woman behind the counter said with a chuckle, handing me two pink raffle tickets with my change. 'Listen out for your ticket colour, okay folks? There's one boat going ahead of y'all today, so listen out for pink, not yellow. Got it?'

'Two in the pink.' Daniel winked. 'Got it.'

We found an empty bench to wait for our boat. Children chased one another, erratic as flies buzzing around a picnic, while their parents watched on with calm indifference to the chaos, fussing with buggies and backpacks, dispensing snacks and anointing small, impatient faces with wet wipes and sun cream.

In the distance, a man's voice called out, and several heads turned at once to catch his words on the breeze. 'Yellow tickets, y'all. Yellow tickets! Everyone with a yellow ticket, step right up.'

'Yellow,' I repeated, unnecessarily.

Daniel didn't respond.

'What shall we do later?' I said. 'Now that we have the car, we can do whatever you fancy – we could drive somewhere for dinner.'

Daniel lowered his sunglasses to make eye contact: 'But if you drive to dinner, you can't have a drink.'

'It's possible to enjoy a meal without being absolutely lathered, you know.'

'But you're in New Orleans,' he said.

'Pink! That's pink tickets, ladies and gents. Pink tickets, this way please.'

'Come on,' he said. 'Let's go. I want a good seat.'

Our captain was a solid-looking man with the round cheeks of a schoolboy and the teeth of a heavy smoker. He took our tickets from my outstretched hand and ushered us on to a small, flat-bottomed boat called *Swamp Thing*.

As the boat shuddered from the dock, the captain began his monologue in a strong Cajun accent. 'Good afternoon, ladies and gents. I'm Captain Paulie and I'll be your guide this afternoon. First of all, I'd like to welcome you to the heart of alligator country, the Manchac Swamp. Now, ladies and gents, I know gator attacks are rare and all, but I'm gonna need to ask you to keep your hands inside the boat at all times, and please hold back from feeding the wildlife unless you wanna be dinner. Hopefully we're gonna see some gators today – I seen a big ol' boy on my last ride, so we'll cross our fingers and keep our eyes peeled for Chuck, alright?'

I tuned him out, enjoying the gentle rumble of the boat as we moseyed further into the swamplands. The bayou was dreamlike in its serenity, hemmed by ghostly grey cypress trees and the jagged branches of ancient oaks, all decorated with ivy and trailing silver veils of Spanish moss – a bridal flourish that carried the faded air of Miss Havisham.

An overhead speaker projected the captain's voice as he talked us through the different types of wetlands. 'Now, a marsh is an underwater meadow,' he explained. 'A swamp is an underwater forest. And a bayou – this right here – is a winding body of slow-moving water.'

'Look!' I hissed, placing a hand on Daniel's shoulder and pointing to the bank, where a trio of fat-bottomed racoons were up to no good, their tiny humanoid hands busy in the underbrush. Moments later, a wild pig snuffled through the trees, causing the racoons to scatter. Cormorants, cranes, herons and egrets were all introduced by Captain Paulie and met with muted enthusiasm from the tourists on the boat.

'Now, I bet y'all are asking: are gators dangerous? Let me answer this with a question. Do we have any folks here from Florida on the tour today?'

A couple of studenty girls near the front raised their hands. 'I'm so sorry to hear that,' he quipped, to be met with an outraged cry. 'Alright, alright – tell me this: how many people do you think are killed by gators in Louisiana each year?'

One, a blonde in a white vest that showed a flash of hot pink bra, cocked her head to one side and looked to her friend. 'Like, maybe three per year?'

'Less than Florida, anyways,' the brunette said, and while they both laughed, I didn't really get the joke.

'Yeah,' the blonde agreed. 'Less than us, for sure.'

'Well, the answer is actually zero,' the captain replied with a smug smile, holding up his hand and making a doughnut shape with his finger and thumb.

There was a murmur of polite surprise, and then a toddler made a loud 'Baba!' sound, only to be shushed by his mother.

'In the State of Louisiana,' the captain went on, 'alligator attacks on humans are extremely rare – so rare, in fact, that we have just one known fatality under our belts since records began.'

'Why are they so rare here compared to Florida?' a voice piped up. It was the mother of the child, who now seemed to be harbouring futile dreams of freedom as he squirmed in her arms.

'Well, let's get one thing straight: fatal alligator attacks are rare in Florida too,' he said, and then, with a quick grin to the college girls: 'I don't wanna be accused of hating too much on Florida, but gators find themselves in residential areas more often over in those parts. But here in Louisiana, they mostly stick to the bayous, and we have a team of licensed hunters that take out around a thousand gators a year that are flagged as aggressive. Now, if you go pulling on a gator's tail, you might meet a swift end, but on the whole, they don't bother us and we don't bother them.'

'That's wild,' said the girl with the hot pink bra.

'Now, who believes in ghosts?' the captain asked, and around three-quarters of us raised our hands. Not Daniel, though. His mood had dipped, and he was staring dully at the water with a bored expression on his face.

'Now, let me tell y'all about the legend of Julia Brown. She was a local healer, and some folk even said she was a witch. She predicted a great hurricane was gonna strike the town of Frenier, and folk didn't like the sound of that. But that ain't all she predicted. Days before her death, she took to sitting on her front porch, rockin' back and forth, back and forth, singing the words, "When I die, I'll take the whole town with me," over and over again, and folk grew kinda scared of her, as you can imagine. Anyways, she died alright, and she was buried on September twenty-ninth, 1915. Now, what do y'all think happened next? That's right, a hurricane hit Louisiana that very same day. Out of a town of four hundred people, only twenty-two souls survived. Why? Well, most of the townsfolk had gathered to see old Julia Brown get good and buried, and that's right when the storm hit.

They say on a quiet night down here on the swamp, you can hear those drowning souls crying out, real vivid, but when folks go looking for them, they can't find nobody out here. Some people claim to have seen a lady dressed in all white, right there on the bank. They say that might well be the ghost of Julia Brown. Now, I personally have never seen or heard nothing I can't explain out here, but if I ever do, I'll find someplace else to earn a living, if you know what I'm saying.'

He chuckled, and everyone on the boat laughed too, and I felt a knot in my stomach tighten, a deep, writhing knot of eels, as I scanned the bank, convinced I'd see a wisp of white between the tangled trees.

'Now, folks, the reason I'm telling you this story is because of this right here on the left.'

Across a grassy marsh, a lone white cross popped against the shadowy treeline.

'Y'all, this is supposedly the burial site of Julia Brown, the old voodoo priestess herself. Here's the thing: you can't just bury somebody in the swamp in Louisiana. Nothing stays buried out here. Everything comes back up eventually.

'Now, here's what I think could have happened. People worship the burial sites of voodoo queens – it happens every day to Marie Laveau, you can go check out her tomb in St Louis Cemetery No. 1, see all the lipstick crosses painted on it and all the beads and candles and tchotchkes people leave for her. I think these surviving townsfolk might have been so scared of Julia Brown's spirit, and so scared of people worshipping her grave, they created a fake burial site for her out here and buried her body someplace else. But that's just me.'

The boat rumbled on over opaque brown water, and the captain paused his rambling to point somewhere ahead of us.

'There we go, ladies and gents. Can you see that big boy over there?'

At first, I couldn't see anything at all, and then a long, rounded snout and an avocado-skinned tail grazed the surface of the water. The alligator was at least as long as I was tall, and was swimming rapidly towards us. Everyone on the boat twisted in their seats to get a better view, and the toddler started to cry as his mother squeezed him more firmly in her lap. The captain responded by tossing something that looked like an egg into the water. It turned out to be a marshmallow.

'Now, these living dinosaurs first appeared on Earth over thirty million years ago,' the captain said, chucking another marshmallow into the water. 'They can leap five feet into the air, and reach speeds of thirty-five miles per hour on land.'

Daniel stared resolutely at his phone.

'Do you have any reception?' I asked.

'No,' he replied.

In the water, the alligator snapped its jaws and swallowed the floating marshmallow. I turned to Daniel again, to share the moment, but he remained uninterested in the alligator.

'Ah!' I leaned over and plucked a small white feather from his shirt. 'This has to be sign of some sort, right? Of good things to come?'

'Sure.'

I returned my attention to the beast floating in the water. Its cold reptilian eyes glowed yellow against the pea soup of the swamp and, in a certain light, it looked like it was smiling.

*

We stopped in a late-night supermarket and bought guacamole, tortilla chips, and a bottle of red wine at Daniel's request, but I already knew I wasn't going to be sharing his supper.

When we arrived at the French House, Daniel wheedled for me to drive us into the Quarter, but I said I was tired, that I needed to have a shower and take some time to myself to decompress.

He stalked off towards the French Quarter alone, the white of his shirt vanishing into the darkness of Canal Street as he chased another bar, another cheap drink, another lonely soul to draw into his light, a lost moth attracted to the flame of his charisma.

Alone at last, I crossed the busy courtyard with my head down, and disappeared into the privacy of my room with palpable relief.

I felt better after a purifying shower. Sitting on my bed, wrapped in a towel, I shuffled my deck and drew the tarot. The Knight of Swords. *A man on a mission*, I thought. A confident visionary who'll stop at nothing to get what he wants. Did that track? I stared at the card, rolling the different interpretations through my mind. The Knight of Swords was an assertive card, but it also served as a warning: slow down. You may not be thinking things through before taking action.

Perhaps the Knight of Swords was telling me to slow down, consider everything carefully before taking a leap of faith. Perhaps the tarot was telling me to ask Daniel for my money back before he was lost to the next adventure.

I picked a black velvet mini dress to wear, and coiled my damp hair into a bun on top of my head. I moisturised and added a shimmer of pearly highlighter to my clavicles, slipped my feet into black leather sandals. I felt pretty, and I was in the mood to carve my own path through the city. A solo glass of white wine, a jazz bar. Perhaps I'd take a taxi to one of the candlelit courtyards uptown, and pick at a cheese plate beneath the stars, write in my journal, read a book. Be alone. I hooked my handbag over one shoulder, and checked I had everything I needed for an evening in New Orleans – my key card, my tarot deck, my journal, my paperback, my phone, my cigarettes. That's all a girl needs, I thought. A stranger in a strange place with nothing but her thoughts for company.

Daniel was waiting for me in the courtyard with a single black rose, a cheap fabric flower glued to a bottle-green plastic stem. His white shirt was covered in blood, and his nose was swollen and bruised.

'A peace offering,' he said, twirling the rose between his fingers before handing it to me.

'Oh my God, what the hell happened to you?'

'Oh, this.' He touched his nose gingerly with his fingertips. 'I took a shortcut down a side street and was jumped by a group of thugs. It's nothing – it looks worse than it is.'

'It looks painful. Do you need to go to hospital? Did you report it to the police?'

'The world is full of scoundrels,' he said. 'I'm okay. It isn't broken or anything.'

'You poor thing,' I said.

'Let's go to dinner. Let me treat you. You spent all day driving me around, it's the least I can do – if you can bear to be seen with me in this state.'

'You don't have to pay for dinner,' I said.

'I want to,' he said. 'You look gorgeous, darling. I want to show you off. Although I should probably change my shirt first. I bought a new one in the Quarter.'

He reached into a plastic bag, pulled out a champagne-coloured silk shirt and changed right there in the courtyard. He put the bloodied shirt in the plastic bag and hung it from my door handle. 'I'll grab that later,' he said. 'I can't be bothered to go all the way back to my room right now.'

'Hey, I've been thinking,' I said, watching him fasten the buttons of his new shirt. 'That message from my bank was probably just a scam thing, right? A phishing thing or whatever.'

'Hmm,' he said, adjusting the collar and smoothing the satin against his chest. 'What do you think? I usually only wear black, but something about the heat makes me crave lighter colours.'

'I like it,' I said. 'Very handsome. So anyway, could you maybe transfer my cash back please? I think I'd feel better having it in my savings account.'

'Are you sure?' he said. 'Wouldn't you rather speak to your bank first?'

'I'll risk it,' I said.

'Okay, darling, I'll sort out a transfer at dinner.'

'Can you just do it now? While we're on the Wi-Fi?' I asked. 'I'd feel better if it was done.'

'Oh, absolutely,' he said. 'Let me do it now. And then dinner?'

'Sure,' I said. 'Okay.'

'Perfect,' he said, fiddling with his phone.

*

He was trying to prove something that night, or so it seemed. We started with a dozen oysters – six fresh, six charbroiled – in a lavish oyster bar in the French Quarter, washed down first with icy shots of Chartreuse and then with glasses of white wine so fine it was almost green in the glass. We mopped up the butter and brine left in the shells with chunks of bread, which soaked up enough of the alcohol to keep us feeling balanced. When the server delivered two steaming plates of pasta – creamy blackened chicken alfredo for Daniel, and angel hair topped with barbecued Gulf shrimp in a rich lemon butter sauce for me – I groaned with pleasure, picked up a fork and twirled a knot of pasta around the tines. I hadn't realised how anxious the money situation had made me, but now that we were out together, chatting and laughing, I felt my mood lighten.

Next, we drank a bottle of red wine in a jazz bar, watched a saxophonist seduce the room with sultry renditions of Louis Armstrong hits. I checked my banking app from time to time, but the money was yet to hit my account.

'It's taking ages,' I said.

'Well, I suppose it's the middle of the night in the UK now.'

'Surely it's all just automatic, though,' I said.

'I suppose a transaction of that size, in a foreign country, might have raised an alarm.' He shrugged. 'It will be okay

– perhaps my bank blocked the transaction. I'll check in the morning.'

'Can't you check now?'

He laughed. 'It's the middle of the night, darling. Look, I know you must be worried but I promise, it will be back in your account in no time. Come on, you'll feel better after a cocktail.'

It felt easier to just go with the flow, let his current take me wherever he pleased. I followed him into a candlelit bar in an old Creole cottage, where the air felt ancient, the atmosphere cobwebbed with spirits.

'What's so special about this place?' I asked.

'It's a vampire bar,' he said. 'No electric light – perfect for haunting the shadows. Hey, you order for us – I'm going to deal with this music situation.' With that, he made a beeline for the jukebox.

I ordered us a pair of rum and Cokes, and then found a free table to wait for Daniel. One more night like this, I thought, and tomorrow I'd do my own thing. I'd wake up early, have a long shower and head out for a solitary breakfast. There was still so much I wanted to do. I wanted to visit the Singing Oak in City Park, a grand oak tree whose branches echoed with the dulcet tones of dozens of windchimes. I wanted to see the Music Box Village, and Mardi Gras World, and the Backstreet Cultural Museum, and the doll collection in the House of Broel, and I wanted to pay my respects to the voodoo queen Marie Laveau.

At the jukebox, Daniel's face glowed. A cool-looking dude in skinny jeans and winklepickers approached him, and Daniel turned on the charm. He touched his injured nose with a shy smile, and then they turned to the jukebox together and Daniel let the stranger use his last credit. He nodded in approval at whatever song had been selected, and then wrote his phone number on the back of the man's hand. It was all so smooth, so effortless. It was enviable. I wished I had the courage to be so bold.

'There's something so romantic about writing your phone number on a man's hand,' Daniel said, sliding into his seat and taking a rum and Coke. 'It feels like something a Jane Austen character would do.' He thought about that for a moment, and then laughed at himself. 'Well, obviously not that, but you know what I mean.'

He was in a good mood, cheeks aglow with the buzz of romantic attention, and he had no intention of letting the night end there. We finished our drinks, and then I let him take me to a hidden cocktail bar above a Jackson Square restaurant. The room was opulent, draped in red and decorated with Egyptological ephemera, masks and great sarcophagi gilded in gold.

'It's a secret séance room from the 1920s,' he said, leaning too close, his breath hot against my ear. 'The owner gambled the place away in a game of poker. Heartbroken, he killed himself right here, by jumping from the balcony. They still reserve a table for him, to soothe his restless spirit. A glass of wine is poured every single night for an empty place setting. Isn't that spooky?'

'Gosh,' I said, in a breath.

'Can you feel any spirits in here with us?'

The room was warm, the lighting soft. Around us, couples leaned in, breathy words whispered over strong cocktails. There was a thin thread of melancholy in the air, though, and I felt all the heartache of the room, all the lost souls and missed opportunities, all the sour hearts and bitter regrets.

'Yes,' I whispered, and then: 'Can you?'

'Yes,' he said, so close that the tip of his nose touched my cheek. 'I can feel rum.'

I burst into bright, unexpected laughter. The alcohol was turning my mood into one of lightness and colour, memories fading as soon as we moved from one bar to the next. Cocktails in the séance bar led to Hurricanes in Pat O'Brien's; Hurricanes led to a vampire speakeasy, hidden in the upstairs parlours of a jazz bar. Daniel, laughing, taking my hand, twirling me in the street. My limbs loose, my soul weightless.

I wasn't being fair to Daniel, I thought. So what if he was a little strange, a little pushy, a little too fond of the bottle? He was being so good to me, letting me hang out with him, a near stranger. He was a good person, a trustworthy person, struggling with his own demons. And weren't we all? I felt such warmth for him in that moment, like I never wanted the night to end.

And then, I blinked and we were in a dive bar halfway back to the hotel. The locals laughing, Daniel's arm draped around the neck of a man who seemed pleased to be in such close proximity to his hips. Daniel holding court, insisting we were up for another, up for anything. I belched and tasted the petrol-tang of vodka and garlic.

'Drink it first, then we'll tell you what it is.' The barman offered a baleful smile, and there was something of the devil about him, his oily expression laced with malice. Two shots were placed in front of us and, despite my better judgement, I knocked one back. A sharp, smoky whiskey mingled with something warm, thick and creamy. An involuntary gag.

'It's Scotch and mayonnaise,' the barman said, cracking into cruel laughter. 'We call it a Smoker's Cough. Get it?'

I got it. Gag reflex: the sweet phlegm-like shot regurgitated across the bar to whoops and claps from the demonic crowd.

'Straight back up!'

'She puked *immediately*, bro.'

'Can't take it, man.'

I turned to Daniel, my chin wet with rancid alcohol.

'Enough,' I said. 'I'm going home.'

Everything was a tumble. Disembodied voices, shadows waxed and waned, figures loomed from the darkness, gas lanterns flickered. Incense smoke curled from bars of the old world, ectoplasmic. We crossed paths with ghosts – a pirate in a tattered frock coat, a naked figure on a rooftop, a woman dressed in white.

Julia Brown, I thought. *She'll take the whole town with her.*

*

My mouth tasted sulphurous; my stomach set to a rolling boil. It felt like a very fine, cold knife had been plunged into my brain. Still half asleep, I groped under my pillow for my phone, but felt nothing but the soft, cottony bedsheets.

The evening seeped into focus with a belch that tasted like cinnamon-flavoured vomit. I remembered candlelit drinks in Jean Lafitte's Blacksmith Shop, and good conversation, light conversation. Daniel fed dollars into the mediocre jukebox, his hair loose and lovely in the warmth of the bar. Had we eaten? The oysters and the pasta, yes, but later? A vague memory of sipping something savoury, and then – oh, God. I cringed at the thought of having been so drunk, so out of control. It wasn't me. It wasn't me at all.

With a start, I realised I could feel the presence of another body in the bed. I turned to see a tumble of dark curls spread across the white pillow. Daniel. His hair was loose and knotted, the ringlets frizzed to static, and he was asleep, his breathing heavy and even. His eyelids were mottled grey with faded make-up, and his jaw was thick with stubble.

Why was he here? Why had I let him stay? I tried to think to the end of the night, but memory was a slippery thing, and the more I stretched for it, the less I could grasp. With great horror, I realised that I couldn't remember how we'd got home, let alone how we'd ended up in bed together.

I don't know you, I thought, recoiling from the intimate warmth of his body. *I don't know who you are.*

He had one hand resting on the pillow, and his neat polish had flaked to craggy islands of black varnish on each finger. There was a repulsive crescent of dirt underneath each nail. An irrational firework of anger burst within me, and I battled the impulse to shake him awake, demand that he leave. I considered slipping out of bed and vanishing into the courtyard like a shame-faced lover after a regretful one-night stand, escaping the expectation of breakfast and awkward small talk in the cold, sober light of day, but I didn't like the idea of leaving him unsupervised in my room with my things.

My things.

I needed to find my phone, see if the transfer had finally come through.

The mental image of his unkempt fingers digging through my bag popped into my head. I did a quick inventory of the room and found it. My purse was accounted for, stuffed haphazardly with crumpled ones and fives that indicated many larger notes had been broken, the change instantly forgotten, but I couldn't find my phone anywhere.

Daniel's black jeans were crumpled on the floor. With a surreptitious glance to his sleeping form, I dipped my hand into his pockets and pulled out his wallet. Inside, there was a great wedge of green dollars and half a dozen credit cards from different banks.

I tucked everything back into the wallet and returned his things to his pockets, then drew the curtains, spilling golden light over his serene face. His eyelids remained closed, but his features had lost their dreamy softness. Eventually, cat-like, he opened his eyes and looked directly into mine with a calculating intelligence that betrayed him. I wondered how long he'd been awake.

'Good morning, sunshine,' he said, rubbing his face and sitting up in bed. 'Shall we go for a walk along the boardwalk today?'

I'd always thought of a boardwalk as a kind of seaside promenade, like Brighton Palace Pier. A Ferris wheel, the smell of hotdogs and popcorn on the breeze, perhaps an old wooden roller coaster or a ghost train rattling by. My stomach lurched at the thought of it. I was still standing by the window, and I couldn't bring myself to relax. I wanted to ask Daniel to leave, but I found I couldn't; the words failed to launch.

'But shall we get some breakfast first though, darling?' he asked. 'I'm starving.'

'Have you seen my phone?' I said.

'Your phone? No – is it not in your bag?'

'No. I can't find it anywhere.'

'It'll be in the last place you look,' he said, and then he relaxed against the headboard of my bed, unlocked his own phone and sucked on his white plastic vape.

'I need a shower,' I said.

'Go for it,' he said. 'Then we can decide what we feel like doing today.'

I stood for a few moments more, frozen by my own inaction, as he tapped away at the screen of his mobile. He glanced at me, then his eyes popped open with surprise.

'Oh, darling, I'm so sorry – let me give you some space.'

He slipped from the bed and plucked his trousers from the floor, stepping into them and zipping up the fly. He inspected the blood-stained cheesecloth shirt, then thought better of it and slipped into the champagne silk one instead, then excused himself to use the bathroom.

He reappeared holding my phone. 'It was on the floor by the toilet. Shall I order us some breakfast? Huevos rancheros, right?'

'Sure,' I said.

He opened the bedroom door and disappeared into the courtyard.

I locked the door behind him, and lay on the bed, sinking into my hangover, but the sheets smelled like Daniel and I baulked at the scent of his unwashed hair. My stomach lurched, and I made it to the bathroom just in time to catch a spatter of frothy yellow bile in the gleaming white sink. A memory of vomit from the night before came to the surface of my mind, and I cringed again with embarrassment.

I needed to cleanse my energy. A long shower under a hot, heavy spray left me feeling cleaner and fresher but no better.

The floor tiles were cool against my cheek, and it was there on the bathroom floor that I lay, waiting for the nausea to fade. At some point, there was a gentle knock on the bedroom door and then the rattle of the handle.

'Selina? Selin-a! Are you okay? Your eggs are here.'

Time passed. I must have rolled over, because the next time I opened my eyes, I was facing the toilet. Another knock, more urgent this time.

'Selina, are you okay in there? Should I get someone?'

'I'm fine,' I called.

'Selina? Are you in there?'

'I'M FINE!' I shouted, louder this time, and the pain in my head spiked in response.

'Okay darling, I'll be out here if you need me.'

He wasn't going anywhere without me, I realised. I dragged myself upright and the floor tilted beneath me. On all fours, I crawled out of the bathroom and into my bedroom, where I climbed under the sheets and passed out.

Hours passed, hours in which I slipped in and out of consciousness, dreamed I was wading through the swamp. My slow progress was witnessed by a dozen alligators in the middle distance, only the lamp-like glow of their eyes visible, a cosmos of deep red stars in the darkness, caught in the soft warmth of my torch.

It was time to get up. My head, tender as the New Orleans nights were long, ached as I sat up and stretched until the bones in my back popped. Tentatively, I peeped out the window, but the courtyard was empty.

Daniel had finally gone. With a sinking feeling, I realised he'd left his passport on the bedside table, and his bloody cheesecloth shirt was thrown over the church pew.

He would be back, and I would never be free of him.

Digestif
Death in the Afternoon

⚜

Invented by Ernest Hemingway, this refreshing, effervescent cocktail blends the sweet anise-flavour of absinthe with ice-cold champagne, creating a green-tinged glow. Served with a single red rose petal floating on its surface.

London: Selina

Dinner was over. Most of the brandy glasses were empty, and the candles were half-inch nubs, burned right down to their final gasping flames. Richard's gumbo was rich and gummy, with a smoky, briny flavour, like a tearful conversation in a late-night bar, a drift of cigarettes on the air. No one had the stomach to finish their bowl though, and the lingering savoury smell made it difficult to breathe without feeling nauseated.

The atmosphere around the table was rancid, the energy curdled. Caroline's aura had faded and her mood was spiky. She seemed agitated, as though the conversation hadn't gone the way she'd hoped. She picked up one of my tarot cards and examined it in the dying candlelight with an expression of mild disgust.

'So,' she said. 'This is how you make your living, is it?'

'I get by,' I replied.

'I bet you do,' she said, placing the card on the table. 'How did you *get by* in New Orleans – did you pay your way? Or did Daniel foot the bill?'

'He scammed me out of quite a significant sum of money, actually,' I said.

Caroline smirked. 'Oh yes – so you said. How much was it again? Ten thousand pounds?'

'More than that,' I said. 'He talked me into covering the cost of the rental car, too.'

'Bollocks,' said Max.

'I'm not lying,' I said. 'I can show you my bank statement.'

My mouth was dry, but I couldn't bear to touch the brandy on the table in front of me. I didn't think it wise to have anything more to drink. I'd nursed a single glass of wine all evening, while the others had opened bottle after bottle, had allowed themselves to be taken by the alcohol. They had grown sloppier, less focused, and the conversation felt less polite, less patient, and more hostile.

Caroline looked amused. 'You gave him ten grand? You silly bitch.'

A hot sear of dislike burned within me. 'I suppose ten grand isn't much to you,' I said coolly. 'But to me, it's a life-changing amount of money.'

'Daniel didn't need to rob you,' she said. 'I think I've made that perfectly clear: he had plenty of money of his own.'

This was going nowhere. 'I can show you the transfer on my phone.'

'I don't doubt he offered you a solution in your time of need,' said Caroline. 'But that doesn't make him a thief.'

'I don't know what else to tell you,' I said.

'I know what you can tell me: you said he'd left some things in your room,' Caroline said, changing tack. 'Did he come back for them?'

'Yes, I think so,' I said, recalling my final days in New Orleans. 'I wasn't feeling very well, and I thought something to eat might help settle my stomach. I couldn't face the French Quarter again though, and I certainly didn't feel up to driving, so I took a cab to a Creole restaurant in Crown Point and had a quiet dinner by the bayou. Before I left the hostel, I put Daniel's things into a plastic bag and left it hanging from the door handle of my room in case he came back while I was out. I had a Caesar salad and an iced tea, but then I couldn't get a cab to pick me up from the restaurant – Daniel had warned me this could happen, but of course I'd forgotten. I'm so used to London, being able to get a taxi at the drop of a hat. Luckily, some kind locals gave me a lift back into town. I was feeling much better, so I stopped at a bar for a drink. I kept an eye out for Daniel, but we didn't cross paths again.'

Caroline closed her eyes and took a steadying breath. I knew all the irrelevant details about where I'd been and what I'd eaten were annoying her, but as we crept closer to the heart of the story, I couldn't help but fill the silence with these unnecessary elaborations.

'So did Daniel pick up his things or not?'

'The plastic bag was gone when I got back to my room, so I'd assumed he'd stopped by,' I said. 'I didn't see him though, and he didn't leave a note.'

'Someone else could have taken it,' Sage suggested. 'Right? Surely it isn't a good idea to leave valuables hanging from a door handle in a public space?'

'Sure,' I said. 'Maybe. There wasn't really anything valuable in there though.'

'And when did you realise Daniel was missing?' Caroline asked.

'The next day,' I said. 'I realised something was wrong when it was time to return the car.'

*

A bright sunshine beat against the curtains, giving buoyancy to a light headache. My lifestyle in New Orleans was catching up with me: too much sun, too much alcohol, not enough water, not enough sleep. I rolled over to find my water bottle, and I was almost surprised to see Daniel's side of the bed was empty.

There were still traces of him in the room: his energy was fading, but his vape was still charging on the nightstand. I craved nicotine but I couldn't face the thought of going outside for a cigarette. After a moment's hesitation, I unplugged the white gummy bear vape and took a tentative puff. It tasted sweet, like the air around a candy floss stall at a funfair.

With no plan in mind, I got dressed and cleaned my teeth. Daniel's toothbrush was sitting in a glass in front of the bathroom mirror, and a cheap disposable razor sat on the edge of the sink. A pair of black boxers were draped over the towel rack, handwashed and left to dry several days ago.

As I spat minty foam into the sink, it occurred to me that we needed to return the rental car. I wondered if I'd find Daniel in the courtyard nursing a coffee, or if he'd finally given up on the French House and decamped to the Roosevelt without me.

*

'But then I couldn't find the car keys,' I said. 'I checked my pockets, emptied my handbag, looked under the bed, searched every corner of the room. Finally, I reached for my phone with a mind to ask Daniel, but I realised I didn't have his phone number, didn't follow him on social media. I had no way to contact him, and just had to pray that I'd find him in the courtyard.'

'But he wasn't there?' Sage said.

'No,' I said. 'He wasn't there. Outside, the courtyard was quiet, and Daniel was nowhere to be seen.'

*

A few travellers were picking over breakfast and sipping from chipped mugs. Jenna, the girl I'd pulled a tarot card for on my first night in the city, was sticking scraps of ephemera into her journal, and a guy with finger-length dreads and an Urban South T-shirt was already on his first beer of the day.

I checked the kitchen, the TV room and the lobby for Daniel. I even padded out to the swimming pool, where the water was covered by a dirty pool protector, punctuated with dead leaves. The concrete poolside smelled faintly of urine, but there was no one there.

'Hey baby,' Kenna said, grabbing my attention as I walked past her on the deck. She was relaxed, curled cat-like in an armchair on the decking, a cigarette in one hand and a battered paperback in the other. She turned a page of her book – *The Alchemist* by Paulo Coelho. 'How you doing today?'

'I don't suppose anyone's handed in a set of car keys?' I asked.

She lowered her paperback and folded the corner to mark her page. 'I don't think so. Want me to check?'

'Oh no, don't worry – I can see you're busy.'

She laughed. 'Do I look busy? Come on girl, I got you.'

I followed her through the empty kitchen and TV room to the front desk. Andreas, the guy with the beaded necklace, was taping a postcard to the wall: a picture of the Eiffel Tower surrounded by a collage of red, white and blue flowers.

'Cute,' Kenna said.

'I think it's from those beer-pong chicks. Remember, the girls with the vanilla-flavoured cigarettes?'

Kenna shrugged. 'Yeah maybe. Hey, has anyone found a bunch of car keys?'

'Not that I know of,' he said.

She rummaged around under the desk and pulled out a large Tupperware container that had seen better days. There were a few bank cards in there, a baseball cap, a pink leather purse, and a couple of orphaned earrings rattling around at the bottom, but no keys.

'Sorry baby, I guess not. I'll keep an eye out for you, though.'

'Thanks,' I said. 'Oh, I wonder if you've seen my friend Daniel – the tall guy, with the shoulder-length hair? Do you know who I mean?'

'Can't say I do,' she said, with a frown.

'I'm always with him,' I said. 'He's around six foot tall, with dark curly hair. Usually wears a loose white cheesecloth shirt, with black jeans and white plastic sunglasses? Wait, I think I have a picture.'

I unlocked my phone. It was the last picture I'd taken, a snap of Daniel walking along the boardwalk, the encroaching bayou looming on either side of the rickety wooden path.

'You can't see his face here,' I said. 'But he's quite striking.'

'And you're travelling together?' she asked, puzzled. 'I don't remember him at all.'

'No – we met here,' I said. 'We've been hanging out.'

'Ahh, I get it. Well, I'm sure you'll see him around.'

'It's just ... We need to return our rental car today, and I can't find the keys anywhere. If they haven't been handed in, I think maybe he grabbed them by mistake.'

'Did you try calling him?'

'No,' I said. 'I don't have his number or anything. I don't know what to do – we're going to get a fine if we don't return it by eleven.'

She checked the time on her phone. 'It's only nine-thirty. You've got some time. I have to say though – people come and go all the time around here. He might have moved on.'

'He talked about switching hotels, but I don't think he'd leave without saying goodbye,' I said, shaking my head. 'It would be really out of character.'

'How d'you know it's out of character? You've only known him for what, a week?'

'It's been ten days,' I said, eyes filling with tears. 'Look, I know how it sounds... but I'm a really good judge of character. I trust him, and I trust my gut. I'm just worried he grabbed the keys by mistake, and hasn't realised yet.'

'Well, if he's a guest here, we should have his number on file. I can't give it to you, but I could try calling him if you like?'

'Oh, that would be a lifesaver – thank you so much.'

Kenna tapped on the iPad, her long nails click-clacking against the glass screen.

'What did you say his name was?'

'Daniel,' I replied.

'Daniel who?'

I blinked at her. 'Du ... Du-something. It's French.'

'You don't know his last name?'

'I can't remember it,' I said. 'Hang on a sec.' I dug through my handbag, and extracted my purse to check the name on his debit card, but it wasn't there. With a sinking feeling, I remembered handing it to him in the car rental office. Had he given it back to me? I couldn't remember, hadn't thought to ask.

'Do you know his room number?' Kenna asked. 'I can pull the reservation that way.'

'He ... Well, no. Not his original room number. He's been crashing in my room for the last few nights. There was a problem with his key card the other night, and it was super late and ...'

Kenna offered a sly smile, eyebrows raised. 'Oh, *I* get it.'

My hands were shaking. 'No, it's not like that.'

'Hey, no judgement here,' she said.

'We're just friends – he was in a tight spot and I helped him out. That's all there is to it. We've been inseparable all week.'

'On your dime?'

'No, it's not like that,' I said again, blushing at the memory of the bank transfer. Then it occurred to me: Daniel's name would be on my bank statement. I logged into my banking app. 'Dumortier,' I said. 'It's Daniel Dumortier.'

'Great, let me check that for you,' Kenna said, tapping away at the iPad. She paused and gave me a strange look. 'Huh, that's weird.'

'What?'

'Well, it says he's in room twenty-two.'

I shook my head. 'No, that can't be right – that's my room. I've been here since last Saturday.'

'I know, but the only booking we have for a Dumortier is for room twenty-two,' she said. 'According to this, he checked into your room two days ago.'

A sickness bloomed deep within my soul as the truth dawned on me. There had never been a problem with Daniel's key card. There was no key card. There was no reservation. He'd sweet-talked his way into my room, just like he'd sweet-talked his way into my bank account.

'The car's still there, right?' Andreas said, turning to collect another stack of postcards from the desk.

'It should be,' I replied. 'He's not insured to drive it.'

'I'd check on that if I were you,' he said, picking up a postcard of a mountain range and taping it next to the Eiffel Tower. 'Cos this situation don't sound right to me.'

'The cops won't do shit, though,' Kenna said. 'You've got to report it for the insurance, but they won't do shit about it. Cars get busted into all the time and nothing ever happens. Want me to come with?'

'Oh no, you don't have to,' I said.

'Come on,' she said, pushing a pair of sunglasses on to the bridge of her nose. 'Let's go.'

The sun was a pat of melting butter, and the soupy air was thick as gumbo.

'Where'd you park?' Kenna asked, glancing up the street.

'A little further down South Lopez,' I said, and we began to walk. Kenna kept up a breezy stream of conversation, and I answered her on autopilot, barely listening to anything she said.

'Are you sure you parked on South Lopez?' she asked, eyeing me.

'Let's keep going,' I said. 'I'm sure it was down here somewhere.'

With each block, I manifested Daniel's return: Cleveland Avenue. The car will be there, and when I get back, Daniel will be waiting for me at the hostel with the keys. Palmyra Street. The car will be there, and Daniel will be waiting for me at the hostel. Banks Street. The car will be there, and Daniel will be waiting.

Kenna and I made it all the way to Tulane Avenue before I accepted that the car was not there. Daniel would not be waiting for me at the hostel, and all signs suggested the car wasn't there because he had taken it.

*

Caroline looked furious, as though she had just been slapped in the face. 'Are you *honestly* suggesting my brother stole a shitty rental car?'

'I'm not suggesting anything,' I said quickly. 'I'm just telling you what happened.'

'Did you report the car missing?' Richard asked.

'No, not right away,' I said. 'Eleven o'clock came and went, and I googled things like *What happens when your rental car is stolen?*, but the circumstances were too unusual for the generic search results to be of any use. I couldn't bring myself to call the rental company, and instead I just hoped Daniel would emerge with a wild story, like an emergency trip to the hospital, or something like that, and we could simply pay the fine and that would be that.

'At lunchtime, I grew tired of waiting around, so I borrowed a pen from the front desk and left Daniel a note with my phone number. I explained about the car, and said I'd gone to the French Quarter to look for him, and to call me immediately if he got back to the hostel first.

'I went to the Roosevelt, but they wouldn't tell me if he'd checked in or not, so I just searched the French Quarter methodically, first walking down Burgundy to Esplanade Avenue, then up Dauphine to Canal, and so on, and so on, searching Chartres, and Decatur, peering into shitty dive bars and high-end restaurants, showing Daniel's photo to bartenders and shot girls, maître d's and bouncers. No one had seen him. No one even *recognised* him. It was like he'd never existed at all.'

After an hour of searching the Quarter, I ducked into the Abbey and ordered a shot of Fireball and a bottle of PBR. I sank half the beer in one go, and then I opened my banking app, but there was still nothing. No transfer had come through.

I went to check Daniel's account – the one he'd let me use – but I'd been automatically logged out. I felt a froth of regurgitated beer at the back of my throat. Reality dawned like a sunrise, casting my deep-rooted fears into the harsh light of day.

Daniel had taken my money, taken the rental car and vanished.

On reflection, why hadn't I just sent the money to my sister for safekeeping, and used my credit card if I needed emergency access to cash? That's what it was there for, that's why I had it. He was just so charming and spoke with such confidence. I hadn't been thinking straight. I had been disorientated from oversleeping that day. Groggy, confused, and panic-stricken, I'd been grateful to let someone take the wheel and steer me through such uncertain waters. It was stupid of me, and I felt embarrassed. I was meant to be a good judge of character, in tune with the energies of others, and yet Daniel had completely hoodwinked me.

I took the streetcar back to the French House, my face pressed against the window. I studied each of the pedestrians as we passed, looking for Daniel's familiar gait within a sea of strangers.

In the courtyard, Jenna was standing in front of my bedroom door, holding the note I'd left for Daniel. She was talking animatedly to two young men. Their energy crackled like hot fat in a frying pan, and an angry heat radiated from the trio.

'Hey, you can't take that,' I said, snatching the note from her before she could squirrel it away in her journal. 'It's there for a reason.'

The blonde boy turned to face me with a look of thunder and pointed at the piece of paper in my hand. 'Hey, this Daniel guy – is he a tall English dude with dark brown hair by any chance?'

'Yeah, that's him,' I said. 'He's my friend – I've been looking for him all morning. Have you seen him today – like, in the last few hours?'

'That motherfucker,' he spat, turning to his friends. 'I *told* you guys we shouldn't trust him. I *told* you he was full of shit.'

'What are you talking about?' I said. 'What's happened?'

They told me their story over cups of coffee. It was difficult to follow, as they kept talking over one another, picking up each other's threads and circling back to fill in gaps, but I got the gist.

'He's a thief and a liar,' Jenna said, shaking her head. 'We should never have trusted him.'

*

Alone in the courtyard, I nursed the cold dregs of a coffee. My journal was spread open on the table in front of me, a pen held loosely over the blank page.

An oppressive heat was thickening the air, and the rain of last week was fading into a distant memory. In the food truck, Andreas was cleaning the grill, nodding along to a bounce track playing on the tinny overhead speakers.

I felt dead inside, drained and discarded like a plastic Hurricane cup in a Bourbon Street gutter. This wasn't how my holiday was meant to end. I was meant to find peace here. England felt far away and, while I was in New Orleans, I could almost pretend everything at home was okay. I could pretend my grandmother was still alive, and everyone was happy. The weather was beautiful, and the planet was safe, and justice was being served to those who deserved it. I could pretend we had a prime minister we trusted, who cared for the country and was leading us into a healthy economy. I could pretend the NHS was stronger than ever, with waiting times reduced to nothing, and healthcare workers were well paid. I could pretend the food banks had closed, and the warm hubs were a distant, dystopian memory. I could pretend the future was bright, full of promise.

Instead, things would never be the same again. The woman who'd arrived in New Orleans, wide-eyed and excited for the trip of a lifetime, was gone forever. I'd followed my instincts, trusted my intuition, and been bitten.

I needed to refocus my energy and find some spiritual guidance, so I pulled my daily tarot card, and my mood dipped even lower.

The Tower.

I'd told Daniel there were no bad cards to pull, but that was a lie. The Tower was a card that frightened me. Chaos, death, destruction. It showed a lightning bolt of insight, an explosive revelation, a cold shock of truth striking a crumbling tower while those inside fell screaming to their deaths. It was pain, it was disruption, it was a sudden, life-altering change.

I tapped my pen against the page, but I couldn't bring myself to commit to paper the words in my head. My holiday was over, and soon I would be returning to all the pain, fear and uncertainty of home, with a new shadow hanging over my wretched soul.

Just then, two NOPD officers entered the courtyard, and I felt like I'd jumped into a plunge pool of iced water. With a sinking feeling, I watched Andreas raise a hand and point in my direction.

The meatier of the two spoke first. He had ruddy cheeks, a ginger moustache, and small piggy eyes fringed with thick blond lashes. 'Miss Selina Green?'

'Yes?' I said, lowering my pen. His gaze followed the movement to the tarot cards spread on the table in front of me, and then he glanced to his partner. He reached into his pocket and flashed a badge.

'I'm Officer Duplain, this is Officer McNichols. We'll only take a minute of your time, ma'am. We just need to clear a few things up.'

'Oh,' I squeaked. 'Sure, okay.'

'We'll only take a minute of your time,' Officer McNichols repeated. 'Would you mind coming with us?'

'Is this about the car?' I asked, gathering my tarot cards with shaking hands. 'I reported a stolen car about an hour ago.'

'We just need to ask you a few questions down at the station. That okay with you, Miss Green?'

'Absolutely,' I said.

The police station was a twenty-minute drive from the hostel, nestled in a block of drab municipal buildings, the Orleans Parish Prison and, incongruously, a modest fountain and a flat concrete memorial, which I later learned was to commemorate the birthplace of Louis Armstrong.

'Now, could you confirm the registration for us?' Officer Duplain's forehead glittered with sweat as he squinted at his notes.

'I'd need to check on my phone – it was a rental.'

'We have time.'

My hands were shaking. I opened the confirmation email from the rental place, and shared the number plate with Officer Duplain. He wiped his brow with a damp-looking handkerchief and exhaled.

'Well, the good news is we found the car,' he said. 'It was reported by a ranger in the parking lot down by Jean Lafitte National Park.'

'Oh, thank God for that,' I said, leaning back and rubbing the tension from my face with both hands. 'Thank God for that. And the driver?'

The officers exchanged a brief glance, and McNichols tapped in. 'Now Miss Green, when you reported the vehicle missing, you said you believed you knew who took it?'

'Yes, I think – I think my friend took it. I couldn't find the car keys and put two and two together.'

'And which friend would that be?'

'Daniel Dumortier. We were staying at the same hostel and rented the car together, but he disappeared, and I think he took the car with him.'

'Can you talk me through the last time you saw Daniel?'

'Um. Sure. We went out Monday night and had a bit of a wild one, and then I saw him briefly on Tuesday morning, but I spent most of the day alone in my hostel room. He knocked on my door a few times, but I didn't answer because … because I wasn't feeling very well. I haven't heard from him since.'

They exchanged a glance, and Officer Duplain nodded. 'Alright, and what time would you say he knocked on your door?'

'I can't think,' I said. 'It must have been … well, some time after midday. One, maybe two o'clock in the afternoon.'

'Well, which is it, Miss Green? One or two?'

'Two,' I said. 'It must have been around two.'

'And can anyone confirm that?'

I blinked. 'I don't know. Like I said, I didn't answer the door. There's always people in the courtyard though, so someone may have seen him, but I couldn't say for sure.'

He took a deep breath and sighed. 'There's no easy way to say this, Miss Green, but we have reason to believe Daniel may have walked into the bayou and disturbed the wildlife. I'm sorry to say, the ranger who found the vehicle was in the process of locking up the parking lot for the night, so he went ahead and checked the boardwalk for any folk still out walking. He spotted bloody clothing floating in the water, and a passport belonging to your friend. We're dealing with a possible alligator attack.'

The lights were too bright, the hum of the station beyond too loud.

'Would you like a glass of water, Miss Green?'

'No,' I said. 'No. I'm fine.'

*

'I need a cigarette,' Caroline said, rubbing her face with her hands. 'My fingers feel numb – could someone roll one for me?'

Max peeled open his plastic pouch of tobacco and fished out a pinch, but the alcohol had slowed him to the speed of a somnambulist. As though in a dream, he plucked a Rizla from the cardboard booklet and dropped a sprinkle of tobacco fronds on the table.

'You've had too much to drink,' Caroline said.

'I'm all right,' he replied thickly, words bleeding together.

'Where's Sage?' Caroline asked.

'Bathroom,' I replied.

'Oh, for God's sake. Dicky, darling – could you do it?'

'I don't know how,' Richard said apologetically.

'Here,' I said, taking the tobacco from Max. 'Give it to me.'

I rolled a neat cigarette for Caroline and handed it to her.

'Come and keep me company while I smoke this,' she said.

'Shall I come too?' Richard asked.

'We'll be fine,' she replied. 'I want to talk to Selina by myself.'

Outside, Caroline hitched herself on to the narrow ledge of the balcony wall. Behind her, the dark city glittered and winked with a hundred tiny windows, a hundred glimpses into ordinary Friday nights. Takeaways and television, first dates and impromptu gatherings. Ordinary dinner parties where the candles had burned low, the wine bottles empty, dessert plates all but licked clean.

'Are you sure you're okay to sit up there?' I said, holding out a hand. 'It doesn't look safe.'

'Oh, what does it matter?' she replied. 'No one gives a fuck about me anyway. Daniel certainly doesn't.'

She lit her cigarette, and blew a veil of soft grey smoke into the air between us.

'I'm sure that isn't true,' I said.

'He's all I have, you know.'

A soft golden light shone through the balcony doors and cast her in an eerie glow. All evening, Caroline had seemed dazed – a strange patina of something unreadable clouding her features. She was existing somewhere deep in her head, and it was hard to get a proper reading of her mood.

'I know,' I said. 'He told me as much.'

'What else did he tell you?' she asked, almost goading.

'He told me he loves you very much,' I said, and she burst into bitter laughter.

'You fucking liar.' She sucked on the cigarette, and tilted her head back to exhale. She swayed dangerously, and I couldn't help but picture her falling backwards, disappearing into the darkness.

'Christ,' I said, reaching for her again. 'Please be careful – we're really high up, you could fall.'

'Do you always say whatever you think people want to hear?' she asked, disregarding my concern.

'I don't know what you mean,' I said. 'But you're making me feel really uncomfortable. Get down, and then we can talk properly.'

'Do you want to know what I think?' she continued. 'I think you're a parasite, drawn to the scent of death. I think you heard about my brother's disappearance and inserted yourself into the investigation to try and extort money from me. I think you're a leech, sucking as much as you can from the dead at the expense of the living.'

'Caroline,' I said. 'That's absurd. I spent ten days with Daniel in New Orleans, and then he robbed me.'

'Prove it, then,' she said. 'You spent ten days together – prove it. Show me a photo of the two of you together.'

'We didn't take any,' I said. 'We were just … living in the moment.'

Let the Bad Times Roll

'Every single word that's come out of your mouth has been a lie,' she said. 'Daniel smoked Marlboros and stayed in five-star hotels. He wore Ray-Ban aviators; he would never touch white plastic sunglasses. In fact, he only ever wore black. He never wore white at all.'

I felt light-headed, dizzy. 'I don't know what to say,' I said. 'I don't know what else I can say to you. I can show you the bank transfer – but I'm not here about the money. I'm here to help. The police can corroborate everything I've told you. He manipulated me, he convinced me to transfer my savings into his account, and then he stole our rental car. I don't know what happened after that. I don't blame you for doubting the story, but I've no reason to lie to you.'

I glanced inside, desperate for someone to come to my rescue. Richard had his head in his hands, eyes fixed on the table as though he were reading a difficult exam question, the answer eluding him. Sage was at the kitchen sink, her back to us as she filled a glass with water. Max was nowhere to be seen – perhaps in the bathroom, pulling himself together.

'I'd like to know what you think happened,' said Caroline.

'I've been thinking about everything I've heard tonight,' I said. 'Before he left, Daniel made peace with Richard, and tried to give Max his guitar ... doesn't that sound like he *knew* he wasn't going to come home?'

Caroline wiped her nose with her hand, eyes glossed with tears. 'And then what, he marched into the bayou and grabbed an alligator by its tail?'

'There's more,' I said. 'His energy—'

'Can we please keep this conversation grounded in reality?' Caroline interrupted. 'I don't want to hear about his *energy*, or his aura, or his fucking star sign, okay?'

'Fine – his mood, then. His mood was often dark. He talked a lot about death, and the afterlife, and he'd sink into these bouts of silence from time to time, even when we were doing something fun like a swamp tour. It was as though a cloud settled over him, and briefly blocked his light.'

'Are you suggesting Daniel was suicidal?' Caroline said. 'Don't be so ridiculous. I'd know if Daniel was thinking about ending his life. Trust me: he hasn't got a care in the world.'

'I don't know about that,' I said. 'He was reckless – walking around late at night on his own, didn't seem to care that he was mugged. And he seemed adrift. He was on the brink of turning thirty and hadn't achieved anything with his life. He didn't have any goals, or plans for the future. And I know he was having trouble sleeping. He gave me a sleeping pill one night: he said it was an over-the-counter sleeping aid, but it knocked me out for nearly twelve hours. It *must* have been prescription.'

'What does insomnia have to do with anything?'

'I think he was in some kind of financial trouble,' I said. 'You keep saying he had plenty of money, but why did he ask Sage to book his flights? Why was he staying in a cheap hostel instead of a fancy hotel? Why did he use your joint account if he was trying to keep his whereabouts a secret from you – why didn't he just use his own money? And why did he trick me into giving him my savings?'

'You tell me. You're the psychic.'

The cherry of her cigarette flared as she inhaled.

'I think he had a lot of demons,' I said. 'I think he was a deeply unhappy man, and I think he didn't care whether he lived or died.'

'Why do you keep doing that?' she said, eyes narrowed with suspicion. There was a hard, glassy expression on her face, as though something sinister had just clicked into place.

'What?' I said, wrong footed.

'You keep referring to him in the past tense.'

A gust of wind stirred Caroline's hair and sent a prickle of goosebumps over the surface of my skin.

'No, I don't,' I said quickly, but she grabbed my wrist and squeezed.

'Do you know something you're not telling me?' she said.

'Stop it,' I said, twisting out of her grasp. 'Of course not – I'm just as invested in finding him as you are.'

'Well, you don't sound like it,' Caroline said. 'You sound like you know exactly what happened to Daniel. Did you do something to him? Did you hurt him?'

'Of course not,' I said again. I tried to take a step back, but found myself pressed against the balcony door.

'Here's the thing, Selina. Until my brother's body is found, I will continue to push for a deeper investigation. I'll hire a whole team of private investigators, and I'll do whatever it takes to uncover the truth. And if you don't tell me what you know,' she said, her tone dark. 'I swear to God, I'll choke it out of you, and the last psychic vision you'll have will be the sight of concrete rushing towards you as you fall to your fucking death – do you understand?'

I understood. Caroline had found a loose thread, and one sharp tug would unravel my whole story. I couldn't let that happen. I'd learned in New Orleans that I was more capable of protecting myself than I'd ever imagined. In a fight, flight or freeze scenario, I'd learned I was a fighter. Beneath my gentle timidity, there was a survival instinct that outtrumped my morals.

I glanced over my shoulder. Inside, the others were still preoccupied, lost in their own thoughts, paying no attention to the girls on the balcony.

Caroline looked confused, and then alarmed, as my hands connected with her shoulders. For a brief second, her centre of gravity was in a state of flux, and she pawed at the air for something to anchor her, but it was too late. She tipped backwards, and then she fell, and then she was gone.

I screamed her name, and then screamed it again, and then there was Richard scrambling to drag the heavy glass door to one side as I grabbed the empty space where, moments before, his paramour had been.

'That didn't happen,' he said, panic giving way to shock. 'That didn't happen. That didn't just happen. Oh my God.'

'I told her to get down,' I gasped. 'I told her it wasn't safe, but she wouldn't listen.'

'Call an ambulance,' Richard shouted. 'Someone, anyone. Call a fucking ambulance.'

*

Everything that followed happened in a blur of blue lights. There were sirens, a commotion down below. The buzzer screaming; Max vomiting into a plant pot. A swarm of uniforms. A stocky paramedic with a shaved head made Richard lie on his back with his legs elevated, his skinny white ankles resting on a dining-room chair. A woman with eyelashes laden with clumps of blue mascara wrapped me in a fire blanket.

'He's probably in shock,' I said, pointing to Richard. I meant to say it softly, just to Sage, but it came out as a shout and several people turned to look. There were a lot of people in the room, an ambient hum as they spoke into walkie talkies and wrote things down. The crackle of so many radios sounded like the whirr of cicadas.

Someone had switched on the overhead light. Everything appeared in technicolour – the piles of books with their frayed spines, the paintings on the walls. The dirty half-full gumbo bowls by the sink, the candlewax pooled on the scratched wooden table, the empty brandy glasses.

It didn't feel right. Caroline had seemed particular about creating the right atmosphere, I thought. She wouldn't like for the overhead light to be switched on.

'Should we switch off the light?' I asked, and Sage frowned at me, placed a cold hand on my cheek. Her wrist smelled faintly of flowers.

'Your lips are pale blue,' she said, and then I suppose someone turned off the light, because everything went blissfully dark.

*

The lobby smelled expensive, like the duty-free section of an airport. A cocktail of fancy fragrances lingered in the communal spaces, ghostly echoes of the building's residents as they made their way home from Michelin-starred restaurants, gallery openings, book launches, West End shows, the opera. It's strange, the things one notices.

The police were still scattered around, waiting for the coroner, but we were free to go. It wasn't a crime scene, after all. A few questions, an exchange of details. No crime had been committed. No one had heard Caroline's final accusations. Our last conversation had been lost to the wind. On paper, it was just one of those things. A tragic accident.

Sage took my hand in hers and gave it a squeeze. 'I'm moored nearby,' she said. Flakes of mascara were scattered around her bloodshot eyes. 'Do you want to come back for a cup of tea? You're still shaking.'

I shook my head. A layer of dark energy was clinging to the surface of my soul, like duckweed floating on a pond. All I could think about was returning home for a long, hot shower, letting the scalding water cleanse my aura and rid me of every second of this awful night.

'Do you want me to walk you to the tube station?' asked Richard. His teeth were chattering, his lips dry and pale. 'I have my bike, but I can wheel it.'

'Are you okay to cycle home?' asked Sage, touching him lightly on the arm. 'You've had a shock.'

A tear rolled down his cheek, and he wiped it away. 'I don't know. I feel sick.'

'Come back to mine for a while,' said Sage. 'Sober up, gather your thoughts. We shouldn't be alone right now.'

A realisation dawned. 'I think I left my tarot cards on the dining table,' I said.

'Here, I grabbed them for you,' Sage said, reaching into her bag and handing me the deck. It felt solid in my palm, thick and heavy.

'We could book you a cab,' said Max. The shock seemed to have sobered him up. 'Do you have far to go?'

'It's okay,' I said. 'I'm okay.'

'You'll come for a bit, won't you?' Sage said to Max, and he nodded.

'Yeah, course,' he said. 'I'll come back for a bit.'

'Hey, Selina,' said Richard. He was frowning, as though trying to remember a dream. 'Can I ask a question?'

'Sure,' I said, although the last thing I wanted to do was stand around in this lobby and prolong the night. It was over. There was nothing more to say.

'You mentioned you had a picture of Daniel,' he said. 'On the boardwalk.'

My fingertips were tingling, limbs light and weightless. The lobby felt small, the ceiling close. I had the sudden urge to swallow a shot of whiskey, smoke a cigarette, slap myself. Anything to break the wave of panic rising within me.

'Did I?' I said, attempting indifference.

'You said you were showing it to people, to see if anyone recognised Daniel.'

'Oh yeah,' said Sage, eyes welling up with tears. 'Could you send it to us? I'd love to see it.'

'Of course,' I said. 'I can send it to you now.'

'So, you *did* go to the boardwalk with him?' Richard said.

'Did I say boardwalk?' I said. 'I meant the swamp tour. It's just a picture from the swamp tour.'

'Oh,' he said, shaking his head. 'Right. Sorry. I'm still trying to piece it all together.'

'I'll send it to you,' I said to Sage. 'When I'm on Wi-Fi.'

The moon was just a fleck of light, a silver sequin high in the sky. We followed the road for a while until we reached a gate that led to the canal. It was manned by a police officer in a high-vis jacket.

'Sorry folks, towpath's closed. There's been an accident.'

'We know,' said Sage. 'My boat's moored in the other direction, just past that bridge.'

The officer considered this for a beat, then nodded us through.

'You'll be better off walking the street way,' Sage said, as she realised I was following them.

'I just feel like walking along the canal for a while,' I said.

'There's a good energy around here,' she said, and then she offered me a hug. 'I've followed you online. If we hear any news about Daniel, we'll let you know.'

'Thanks,' I said, accepting hugs from Max and Richard. 'Take care of yourselves.'

The towpath was a dark seam along the water's edge, but the golden portholes of the narrowboats, and their gentle scent of woodsmoke, gave me the illusion of safety. It was dark, but I wasn't alone. Guilt was my companion, keeping pace with every step.

I pulled the tarot deck from my bag, peeled the first card from the pack and turned it over. The fucking Death card. I almost laughed as I dropped it into the water. The Devil went next, his smiling face shining against the liquid black. The Six of Cups. The Fool. I scattered my cards like breadcrumbs, dismembering the most valuable tool of my trade, card by futile card.

New Orleans: Daniel

Daniel parked the car in a lonely lot on North Rampart Street, just on the edge of the French Quarter. With any luck it would be towed – or even better, stolen – and the problem would take care of itself. His fingerprints were all over it, of course, but he didn't think that would matter much. From what he understood, the New Orleans Police Department were not particularly moved by stolen cars.

He performed a quick survey of the detritus left in the back seat, and shoved everything that could be of use into Frankie's tote bag – a tangle of loose clothing, a couple of dog-eared paperbacks, Jenna's white plastic sunglasses. Tragically, her pink Ziploc was locked away in the motel room back in Lake Charles, but he found a prescription bottle of sleeping pills rolling around in the passenger footwell. Frankie's gummy-bear vape was still charging in the USB port, and although there was something rather melancholy about it – the touch of innocence, perhaps – he took that too.

The car park smelled like damp concrete. It was a muggy evening, and an overcast sky threatened rain, but the adrenaline of Daniel's arrival in New Orleans had left him feeling like a shaken bottle of champagne ready to pop. He checked the map on his phone, and began to walk in the right direction for Royal Street. Soon, he saw the red neon sign of the Hotel Monteleone glowing against the clouded sky.

A charming relic from a different era, it was a beautiful hotel situated in the heart of the French Quarter. Crystal chandeliers cast a gleaming light against display cases filled with the books of famous novelists who'd once slept within these hallowed halls. Daniel's boots made a satisfying click-clack against the polished marble floor, and heads turned as he made his way towards the front desk. A teenage girl perched on a hardshell suitcase studied him with naked longing as he passed.

The concierge was quite the feast for the eyes. Floppy blond hair, the aquiline nose and sharp jawline of a Greek god, contrasted with a Clark Kent-esque pair of spectacles. The golden name tag pinned to his jacket said *Philip*. His fingers bounced on the keyboard with brisk authority as he asked for photo ID and a credit card.

'I'm afraid there's a problem with your card,' the concierge said. 'Would you like me to run it again?'

Daniel forced a genial smile as he made a show of peering at the card in the young man's hand. 'Ah – did I give you the AmEx, darling? So sorry, my mistake. Try this one instead.' He slid a World Elite Mastercard across the desk.

'Certainly, sir,' the concierge said, but soon he was shaking his head. 'Do you have another card we could try?'

'Of course I have another card,' Daniel snapped. 'Here, try this.'

By now, a small queue had formed behind him. The concierge swiped the card, and then glanced at Daniel with an astute look. 'It's saying we should call your bank.'

'Well, there's no need for that,' said Daniel, finally handing over the card linked to Caroline's account. 'I'll do it myself in the morning. This is fucking ridiculous.'

The concierge bobbed his head as though he were dodging a blow, but this time the payment seemed to go through.

Daniel swept his hair away from his face and feigned melancholy. 'I'm so sorry, darling; I'm not in my right mind. I'm travelling for a funeral.'

'I'm sorry to hear that, sir,' the concierge said, a creeping flush colouring his tanned cheeks. He cleared his throat, and Daniel almost felt bad. He imagined the concierge saw him as a tragic figure, alone and anonymous, a stranger with nothing but grief for company in a glamourous hotel room in New Orleans.

'Would you like to make a dinner reservation for this evening, Mr Dumortier?' the concierge asked, pushing his glasses against the bridge of his nose – a nervous habit, Daniel assumed, since they didn't appear to slip.

'No thank you, darling. Can I ask – if I book a car for tomorrow, can you charge it to my room?'

'Certainly, sir,' the concierge replied. 'I've put a hundred-dollar hold on the card, so any expenses, including taxis, room service or drinks at the bar, will be taken from that at the end of your stay, and any remaining funds will be released.'

'Perfect. And if I go over a hundred dollars?'

'We'll just charge it straight to your card, sir.'

'Fabulous.'

He handed Daniel another generic key card. He was growing so tired of the lack of aesthetically pleasing keys. There was something so wonderfully gothic about being given a proper key to a hotel room. He imagined that if his beautiful corpse were to be discovered face down in the bayou, the key to his room would be the first clue to his identity, perhaps along with a matchbook or a beer mat from a local bar in his pocket, the phone number of some scoundrel scrawled on it in ballpoint pen. A plastic key card didn't fit the bill as nicely as an iron key with a handsome tassel.

'Would you like me to book that car for you now?' the concierge asked.

'No need; I'll call down later.'

A bell hop appeared with one of those large golden trolleys. He was striking, with blue eyes that popped against lightly tanned skin. He glanced, with a look of uncertainty, at Daniel's tote bag. 'Would you like help with your luggage, sir?'

'No thank you, darling,' Daniel said. 'I travel light.'

*

The room was small but elegant, a king-sized bed made up with crisp white sheets. After so many days on the road, he thought he'd collapse straight into bed, but New Orleans was already working its magic on him and he didn't feel tired at all. In fact, Daniel felt fully charged, electrified, as he sucked on Frankie's gummy-bear vape and planned his next move.

In his final act of decadence as Daniel Dumortier, he was here to commit an abundance of sin. It felt like a sinful, debauched sort of place, a place where, under the cloak of darkness, anonymity and the smeared neon lights of the city, one could get away with murder.

In New Orleans, Daniel planned to gorge himself on rich dishes that rarely graced the pedestrian menus of Soho: blackened catfish, fat muffulettas, beignets piled high with powdered sugar and washed down with chicory-spiked coffee. He wanted to experience Cajun fine dining in ancient restaurants, where ghosts walked in the shadows of the servers and the air was fragranced with a hundred years of roux, mirepoix and garlic; and he wanted to eat salty fried catfish po' boy sandwiches with bottomless root beers in anonymous diners. He would welcome the evenings with chilled cocktails: Sazeracs, Hurricanes, Death in the Afternoons.

Daniel was going to worship nature: the sprawling live oaks, the Spanish moss, the alligators and the encroaching bayou, and he was going to pray to the old spirits, to Barons Samedi, La Croix and Cimetière. Perhaps he'd have his palm read by a lost soul, some pretty little transplant from out of state who'd found his way to the French Quarter like so many drifters before him, drawn to the music and mysticism of the city.

And he was going to fuck. God, Daniel was going to fuck. He wanted to wake up in grand hotel rooms with champagne hangovers, and in squalid hostel bunks with a head clouded by cheap cocktails and bad weed. He wanted to wake up in Garden District marital beds that smelled of absent husbands and distant wives, in artists' studios in the Marigny, his naked body daubed with oil-paint fingerprints, and in musicians' shotgun homes in the French Quarter, skin anointed with red-wine kisses. He wanted to fall briefly and hopelessly in love with a different person every night, and leave a string of lovers behind in a city that wouldn't remember his name when he was gone.

Daniel stood for some time by the window, peering down at the glittering city beneath him, at the little shops and art galleries of Royal Street, at the people like termites crawling in the streets below.

He needed a drink and a change of clothes. He called room service for a glass of champagne, but the apologetic concierge explained they only sold Dom Pérignon by the bottle. No matter – a bottle would do.

Then, with a wish and a prayer, he rooted through his tote bag of stolen loot to find something to wear. He unrolled a beach towel, which sprayed sand all over the carpet. Wrapped inside it was a pair of palaka-print Mickey Mouse ears and some silver sandals, marked by the ghostly imprint of bare feet. The souvenir ears and sandals went straight into the wastepaper basket. Next, he tugged on a pearl of white fabric and, like a hanky plucked from a magician's sleeve, it grew until he was left holding a baggy white cheesecloth shirt. Pinching it by the shoulders with the tips of his fingers, he held it up to inspect it properly. A faint whiff of chlorine suggested Jenna – or perhaps her mother – wore it as a cover-up by the pool. It was at least two sizes too big for Daniel, but he could make it work. It had a kind of vampiric, dandyish quality to it that he rather liked.

There was a gentle knock on the door. He tipped the young woman who delivered his champagne twenty dollars for the trouble, and poured himself a glass of wheat-coloured bubbles.

In the bathroom sink, he rinsed the chlorine from the shirt with a squirt of complimentary shampoo. He twisted it into a knot to sluice as much water as he could from the fabric, then dried it off with the hotel hairdryer. It was still a little damp around the collar and cuffs, but it looked suitably sexy tucked loosely into his black jeans, and he was pleased with the overall look.

His phone screen was cracked, and a garnet of blood bloomed from a tiny cut on his finger as he unlocked it, but it was still functioning. He searched online for a designer boutique and filled a basket with essentials: a pair of leather Alexander McQueen trousers, a black Valentino shirt, Saint Laurent shorts. Calvin Klein underwear, silk pyjamas. Perhaps he was flying too close to the sun, but what else could he do? In for a penny, he charged it all to the joint account and arranged for it to be delivered to the hotel. Then he poured himself a second glass of champagne, drained it, and headed out into the night.

*

Daniel had expected the following days to pass in a hurricane of jazz, jambalaya and joie de vivre, but he quickly discovered how difficult it was to move through the world with so little access to cash. His current account was deep in the red, there was nothing left in his savings, his credit cards were maxed out, and he knew it was only a matter of time before Caroline froze their joint account if he kept spending so lavishly. He withdrew two hundred dollars from an ATM to tide him over until he could find himself a sugar daddy, a Ken or a Patsy.

Sugar daddies were self-explanatory: older men with expensive taste. They looked after themselves, always paid for dinner and took great pleasure in taking care of handsome men like Daniel. He liked them well-groomed and understated in tailored suits from Savile Row. In New Orleans, they would be in the grand hotel bars, the Michelin-starred restaurants and the country clubs. Difficult spaces to navigate without much cash to hand.

Kens were boyfriend material. Somewhere between twenty-five and thirty-five, with decent jobs. They were interested in travel, going to the gym and fine dining. They were easy to find on dating apps, and usually preferred to invite men like Daniel back to their luxury apartments for a roll in Egyptian cotton sheets and a morning Nespresso with a cigarette on the balcony, where he could admire the inevitably incredible view. He logged in to Grindr and changed his location, but he'd worry about combing through potentials later.

A Patsy was a glamorous woman with an eye for beauty, drawn to pretty things. As a pretty thing himself, Daniel was often surrounded by girls who loved his cheekbones and his chocolate-coloured curls, and were happy to pick up the tab if the laughs and the compliments were flowing. Daniel made Patsies feel a little more beautiful, a little more interesting. The ideal Patsy was pretty but a touch insecure, someone who struggled to make friends easily and hated to be alone.

New Orleans was a communal city, a city best suited to sharing with others, and it was easy for the untrained eye to miss the shrinking violets behind the bawdier holidaymakers – the stag and hen dos, the milestone birthday celebrations, the college sports teams, the girls' trips and the lads on tour. Couples, too – there were couples everywhere. Retired couples strolled through the Quarter with gaudy plastic hand-grenade cups, empty-nesters dipped into jazz bars, honeymooners wandered with their hands in each other's pockets.

It was enough to make anyone feel lonely.

*

Daniel spotted a likely-looking Patsy before she noticed him. A lost soul with a tumble of turquoise hair, an hourglass figure in a black bodycon maxi-dress and heeled boots. Despite her striking appearance, she seemed alone and terrified, scuttling between cafés, bars and restaurants like an anxious crab. As he tracked her through the French Quarter, he painted a picture of who she was in his mind's eye, and in turn who he needed to be to win her over and gain her trust. She spent money like it was going out of fashion, dropping dollars on coffees and cocktails without a second thought. In fact, she reminded him of Sage – drawn to the occult, she favoured gauche witchy shops with in-house psychics, selling votive candles, mass-produced amulets and tacky spell books.

Daniel followed his Patsy into Pat O'Brien's, where he spent fourteen of his precious dollars on a premixed Hurricane cocktail while she talked to a middle-aged couple, and then he trailed her to the Pharmacy Museum, where he spent five of his precious dollars on entry, then a Vietnamese café, where he spent thirty-five of his precious dollars on filet mignon pho and a jasmine iced tea.

She was clearly open to interactions with strangers, many of which she instigated with a deck of tarot cards, a conversational prop that she deployed whenever she found herself alone and in need of some company. Instead of scrolling on her phone or writing in a journal, she shuffled her cards until she caught someone's eye. At first, Daniel thought this would be his way in: a tarot-card reading between strangers, a drink purchased in return until they were locked into rounds, getting tipsy and lowering their inhibitions, sharing their secrets, a synthetic intimacy inspired by too many cocktails. It quickly became apparent, however, that this wouldn't work. Every time Daniel stepped out of the shadows and into the light of her attention, the psychic shrank away from his presence and blushed.

She was anxious, holding her handbag close to her body, focused entirely on her surroundings as though she expected to be robbed at gunpoint any moment – but, bless her, she was stupid too, and he saw his opportunity when she was accosted in the street by a shoeshine scam.

'Well,' she said, her tailfeathers ruffled by the strangeness of the confrontation. 'I'm heading to Erin Rose …' And then, the sweet, silly thing pointed down Bourbon Street, which was the wrong direction for the dive bar famous for its frozen Irish coffees.

'Ah, I'm heading this way,' Daniel said with exaggerated regret, pointing towards Erin Rose, which he knew to be just out of sight on Conti Street. 'Take care of yourself, darling … Unless …?' A devilish grin.

From there, it was easy to lead his lamb to slaughter, to steer her away from the crowds of Bourbon Street and to a more secluded bar to ply her with tacky Vampire Sazeracs, segue into a conversation about fate, the stars and the metaphysical. She didn't seem to remember mentioning Erin Rose, and when Daniel pretended that had been his destination too, her eyes misted with thoughts of inevitability, destiny, chance. Daniel could feel the trust between them growing. It was written all over her face.

And then, of course, the storm hit and they were trapped. The alcohol flowed as raindrops the size of blueberries beat against the cobblestones of the French Quarter, and their connection deepened. When Daniel finally came up for air, he had six missed calls from a local number. It was almost certainly the Hotel Monteleone, which could only mean Caroline had cancelled his card and reported the transaction as fraudulent.

Daniel was facing several problems: firstly, it wasn't prudent to return to the hotel he could no longer afford. Secondly, Caroline now knew his exact location. Thirdly, and most urgently, he and Selina had a sizeable tab, and Daniel had no way to pay it. No cash, no card, no credit.

Selina's gaze was unfocused, and Daniel thought how easy it would be to slip into the night and ditch her with the check, but it seemed like such a waste to dine and dash after putting in so much work. There had to be another way.

Daniel excused himself, and then, when he was sure she wasn't looking, he ducked outside. The rain had finally stopped, and the air was fresh and damp as he scoured the streets for a likely target.

In a busy slushie bar that seemed to appeal to yahoos, he swiped a roll of notes from an open handbag, but when he counted his loot, it only came to thirty-seven dollars. The petty theft was exhilarating. Next, he slipped a wallet from the pocket of a bleary-eyed college kid who was more focused on the honey-skinned Jell-O-shot girl than his possessions. Daniel whipped out a fistful of notes, sequestered them into his back pocket, and then dropped the wallet on the floor at the boy's feet.

'Hey, this yours?' Daniel said, sweeping it off the floor and handing it to him. 'You wanna keep an eye on that.'

'Oh, shit bro …' The kid gazed at the wallet in his hand with a look of drunken confusion. 'Hey, thanks so much, I owe you big time, man.'

'De nada,' Daniel said smoothly, patting him on the back.

Across the street, he walked into a busy karaoke bar and repeated the process, and again in a pizza slice shop, and again, and again, until he had at least three hundred dollars to his name – enough to cover the cocktails and a night's stay somewhere shitty, although he already had his sights set on Selina's hotel room.

When Daniel got back to the bar, however, he was distraught to find his lamb had deserted her post. She'd been kind enough to leave a note pinned under Frankie's vape, but no phone number or email address. The sarcastic little tarot card – Temperance! In New Orleans, of all places! – was salt in the wound.

All that work, and nothing to show for it – but at least she'd picked up the tab.

*

It was late. Daniel couldn't stomach the thought of more alcohol, so he picked a direction and started to walk. There weren't many people out at that hour. A few hospitality workers were milling around, smoking cigarettes and locking doors, as the dregs of Bourbon Street weaved their way through the dark streets towards their hotels. The occasional homeless person camped in the many vacant doorways, accessorised with sleeping dogs, trolleys, piles of rags and handwritten cardboard signs asking for food, water, cash.

Lack of cash didn't suit Daniel. He should've been born the child of a rock star, with a name like Techno, River or Slim, living in a sprawling mansion in Beverly Hills or Bel Air, with a summer house in Palm Springs, and regular vacations to beautiful beaches in Bora Bora, Fiji, the Maldives. His birth certificate should have been the only backstage pass he'd ever need, with access-all-areas to every show, from sleazy gigs at the Whisky a Go Go to sold-out stadium tours, Glastonbury, Coachella and

Lollapalooza. Instead, Daniel was penniless, a waif drifting through an unknown city, with nothing but a tote bag of other people's shit to his name. His heart sank: he didn't even have the tote bag anymore – it was trapped in the Hotel Monteleone, along with his spare T-shirt. All he had was the ridiculous shirt on his back, his passport, wallet, phone, a couple of sleeping pills and Frankie's vape. He didn't even have a phone charger.

Off the beaten track, there were a few bars that were open all night, but that wasn't what Daniel's heart desired. After about fifteen minutes of directionless meandering, he ducked into an all-night diner – a tiny place that was completely empty – and stopped at the ATM to squeeze the joint card for one last drop. He pressed the buttons to withdraw a thousand dollars, but the card declined. He repeated the process, this time requesting a more modest hundred dollars, but again the card refused to cooperate, so he took a seat at one of the Formica tables and picked up a menu.

The diner felt like a slice of classic Americana. High chrome stools with red pleather seats lined a gleaming white bar. Behind the counter, a man with locs tied into a heavy-looking bun scraped unidentifiable matter from the grill, and a guy with a neck laced with blown-out tattoos and stretched ears killed time by flipping through the jukebox.

In California, a diner like this might offer egg-white omelettes, avocado toast, fruit plates, turkey bacon, wholegrain muffins. On the East coast, a standard American breakfast fare of pancakes, French Toast and waffles was to be expected, served with eggs over-easy, streaky bacon and maple syrup – a meal fit for a lumberjack. The menu here was pink and laminated, and it was both short and miserable – grits, hashes, slops. Daniel ordered a dignified black coffee and a plate of eggs from the waiter with the blown-out neck tattoos. The lack of nametag only added to the impersonal misery. The waiter nodded and said, 'Yes sir,' in a way that was quite disconcerting, as though he was a computer responding to his programming instead of a man taking the order of a gentleman.

When the coffee arrived, it tasted burnt. The eggs were undercooked and snotty; the toast cold and the single-serve butter warm. A cockroach skittered across the black-and-white lino floor. Daniel wished he had one of Jenna's paperbacks to pass the time, but they were trapped in the hotel. Instead, he simply sat and watched the clock.

He thought about how different his trip would be if he had some company, and a kaleidoscopic view of alternative realities unfurled in his mind's eye. Caroline would follow him from place to place, a silent and judgemental companion. Richard would take him to all the best places to eat, planned with military precision, each menu meticulously researched, tables booked in advance. Sage would drag him to voodoo temples, vegan cafés and juice bars, and make friends with NOLA-natives to sample the local strains of marijuana.

And Max. In a different life, he and Max might walk through the city hand in hand, dipping into jazz bars and blues clubs to share bottles of red wine and listen to jam bands do their thing. Perhaps, in this fictitious universe, Max might share his bed each night and still be there for breakfast each morning. An outrageous fantasy.

Time ticked by, and as night became day, the French Quarter began to stir. The light turned gold. It was a pleasant morning. Children monkeyed around and chased one another, collected leaves from the pavement, turned to show their mothers. Teenagers left trails of vape smoke in their wake as they shared AirPods and filmed each other on their phones. They had their whole lives ahead of them, Daniel thought. They could study, start a band, travel, or they could drop out, be reckless, choose a different path.

He'd have been content to sit there all morning and people-watch, but as the diner began to fill with a breakfast crowd, the server with the neck tattoos placed the bill on the table in front of him.

'You can stay,' the man explained. 'But I need you to close out, and then you can open a new tab with the morning server.'

Just then, a familiar trio appeared outside, and Daniel's heart froze. He should have known something like this would happen. He'd taken for granted that his petty felons wouldn't make it to New Orleans, would run home with their tails tucked between their legs, and yet here they were. Daniel withdrew into the shadows, and held his breath. By some miracle, the little Pride sticker in the window must have failed to catch their attention, and they drifted by without turning their heads.

*

It was another hot, muggy morning, and Daniel's forehead was quickly dappled with droplets of sweat. He felt it would be too much, too *obvious*, to surprise Selina at her tea-leaf reading, so instead he hovered in the shadows across the street, ready to turn on his heel and pretend to be inspecting the paintings in an art dealer's window as soon as she emerged.

He couldn't bear loitering in the street, though. The French Quarter no longer felt safe: at any moment, he expected to turn and find himself face to face with the Californians. He couldn't risk the commotion of a public display or – even worse – make himself vulnerable to an arrest. He'd stolen their car, after all.

He hoped Selina would see him first, so the initial interaction would be on her terms, but of course, in all her innocence, she refused to cooperate. When she left the teashop, she walked briskly down the street towards Decatur without so much as a glance in Daniel's direction. He followed her through the French

Quarter at a healthy distance, waiting for the right opportunity to make a move.

Sweat soon soaked into the armpits of Daniel's shirt as Selina wandered through the French Market, eyeing menus and contemplating her options before choosing a sad little cup of jambalaya for lunch. She took a seat at one of the wrought-iron tables to eat while optimistic pigeons pecked at the paving stones around her feet. Daniel walked past twice, gaze deliberately averted, but if she saw him, she kept it to herself.

She finished her jambalaya, dropped the empty cup into the bin and continued on her way, oblivious to the devil in white that was in hot pursuit. At first, Daniel thought she intended to walk around Jackson Square, but just as he made the decision to go anti-clockwise to her clockwise and meet her in the middle, she stepped down Pirate's Alley and into a little absinthe bar.

Perfect.

She was sitting on a bar stool, flipping through the menu, when Daniel took the seat next to her.

'Hello, stranger,' he said. 'What the hell happened to you last night?'

Her face was a picture of delight. She could hardly contain her joy at their chance reunion. Daniel insisted they order Death in the Afternoons, which she paid for, bless her heart, and they sat outside so she could smoke.

Now that he'd found her, Daniel wasn't going to let her out of his sight again, so he wasted his afternoon traipsing around the tourist traps while she got her cards read by fellow cranks, then bought mass-produced charms and factory-made spell kits stamped with 'Made in China'. Money was clearly no object for her, and she thought nothing of dropping hundreds of dollars on crystals mined by some of the world's poorest people in the deadliest of conditions, contributing to deforestation, water contamination, soil erosion and habitat loss, and violating international human rights and child-labour laws, just so she could wear a rock around her neck and tell people she was carrying 'New Orleans energy' with her wherever she went.

*

Daniel thought about death a lot. He often wondered if he already owned the outfit he'd die in, if he'd already met the person who'd hear his last words. Who would be the last person to see him alive? Under which sky would he take his last breath?

When Daniel was a much younger man, he used to fantasise about his funeral. He had found it soothing, especially when he was angry or upset with someone, to imagine everyone he'd ever known in mourning. He'd picture everyone he'd ever desired dressed in black, lamenting the passing of his free spirit, his beautiful face, his lean body. He'd be the one that got away, the tragic Romeo to so many Rosalines. It was cathartic – until it clicked that he wouldn't be there to see it.

That's how it started, though – a seed planted in the field of a much wider fiction. Daniel had always wanted to disappear, so it seemed like the most natural way to deal with the financial situation in which he'd found himself. He wanted to simply unpick the stitches of his life and remove himself from it, as seamlessly as a surgeon removing a kidney, and transplant himself into a different kind of existence.

Occultist Aleister Crowley faked his death in 1930. Writer Ken Kesey faked his death in 1965. Pro-wrestler Jerry Balisok faked his death in 1978. There was a precedent for this kind of thing – it was chic.

There weren't many ways to be declared dead without a corpse though. It seemed the ideal scenario would be 'missing, presumed', but that was easier said than done. If a man says he's going out for a pint of milk and vanishes without a trace, there's a seven-year period that must pass with no evidence of life – no sightings, no contact, no digital footprint – before his family can begin the process of declaring him dead. Daniel couldn't see himself living off-grid for long enough for that to be an option, and he couldn't see Caroline applying for a Declaration of Presumed Death, anyway. She had trouble letting go.

There were scenarios in which the seven-year period could be skipped, though: if there was enough circumstantial evidence to suggest loss of life, such as being lost at sea, or caught up in a natural disaster or a terrorist attack. Daniel had always thought his portrait would look rather striking on a missing person's poster, but he could hardly wait for an act of man or God to come along at his convenience.

Daniel had a vague idea sketched out for his death. He pictured a lonely stretch of bayou, a scrap of bloodied clothing, a few bloodstained, identifying possessions strewn around the location. He weighed up the likelihood of the New Orleans Police Department getting the blood stains tested. Relatively high, as a British tourist? Or relatively low, as a suspected animal attack with no criminal angle?

Presumably it was routine to check these things. Daniel imagined the bayou was a popular location to dispose of bodies; it was a place where the humid climate would be quick to melt flesh from bone, where skeletons were promptly picked clean and dismantled by opportunistic scavengers and alacritous insects.

He couldn't google it, couldn't contaminate his internet search history with anything suspicious. He needed to speak to an expert. There was a morbid little museum about death in the French Quarter, and an alligator museum on Magazine Street. Daniel wondered if he might be able to find the answers he needed there: was this plan plausible? Would some well-placed gore be enough? And how long would it take for him to be declared dead? A week? A month? A year? Would the case grow cold? Would a question mark be placed beside his name for the rest of his days?

'If I pay for your ticket, will you come to a museum with me?' he asked.

'Sure, I love museums,' Selina replied, happy as pie. 'When I was a kid, the Natural History Museum was always my favourite. I loved the life-sized blue whale.'

'Fabulous,' he said, sliding Jenna's white plastic sunglasses on to his nose. 'Let's go, it isn't far. And then we can go for dinner?'

'Perfect,' she said.

The sun broiled the air, and heat seemed to radiate from the pavement as they walked side by side through the French Quarter.

'What kind of museum is it?' she asked. 'There's quite a few I've been meaning to check out, but they all close so early.'

'Oh, it's pretty small and niche – a museum about death and local funeral practices. I know it sounds morbid, but New Orleans has a fascinating relationship with death, don't you think?'

She wrinkled her nose, unconvinced. 'Will it be gruesome?'

'Not at all,' he lied. 'From what I understand, it's strictly educational, nothing trashy. And if you hate it, you can just duck out, and then we'll go for fried oyster po' boys when I'm done. Deal?'

'Deal,' she said, and when Daniel offered her an arm, she was only too pleased to take it. He wondered how long it would take for Selina to report him missing, or if she would think nothing of him entering her life and leaving it just as quickly. He'd need to find a way to ensure her compliance.

While he picked up their tickets, a framed photograph caught Daniel's eye. It was propped on the till point, perched between plastic tubs of Le Musée de la Mort pin badges and seventy-five-cent stickers. The black and white picture showed the aftermath of a deadly-looking car accident: a handsome

Buick crumpled into a knot, a smear of blackened viscera on the silver moonlit tarmac.

Selina was studying it too, with a horrified expression on her face.

The man behind the till, an aging goth with labia-like ear lobes that had been stretched many moons ago, noticed her discomfort and leaned forward. 'It's the car accident that killed Jayne Mansfield,' he said, handing Daniel a fistful of change and two black tickets. 'She died on her way into New Orleans. Fun fact: people always think she was decapitated in the wreck, but she was actually scalped.'

'She wasn't scalped,' Daniel said, in a cool detached voice. 'In the photos, where it looks like she was scalped – it's just her blonde wig.'

'No man, her upper cranium was severed. She was scalped.'

'Her skull was crushed.'

Selina tugged on the sleeve of Daniel's shirt, and he followed her towards a red velvet curtain marked 'Entrance'.

'Look with your eyes and not your camera,' the aging goth called after them. 'No photography inside.' Catching Selina's eye, he flicked his tongue in a lizardy impression of cunnilingus. Daniel was not a violent man, but he squeezed his hand into a fist and imagined how satisfying it would be to punch him.

The exhibition offered a strange contrast between the grotesque and the humdrum: a juxtaposition of garish true-crime paraphernalia – crime-scene photos, crude artwork by inmates, letters from serial killers – side by side with the everyday bureaucracy of the death industry: coroners' paperwork, receipts for coffins, a range of complimentary fans and matchbooks collected from funeral homes. It seemed nothing was too dark or dreary to be included, as long as it related to death.

'I don't like the energy in here,' Selina said, squeezing Daniel's arm. 'It feels marbled with an overwhelming melancholy, like fat through a steak.'

'I won't be long,' he said, patting her hand. 'Let's just take a quick look around.'

Daniel studied the other visitors as they examined post-mortem videos and cases of bloodstained clothing with the same polite curiosity as shoppers walking around Whole Foods. He couldn't decide which guests interested him more: the goths, with their blue hair and piercings, flaunting a callous gallows humour, or an ordinary-looking middle-aged man who seemed to be alone, licking his lips as he eyed a grainy autopsy video.

Selina let go of his arm and rushed through most of the exhibition with her eyes averted, stomach clearly turned by the muted violence of it all.

'I really don't like this,' she said, as Daniel studied a white metal bunkbed rescued from the Jonestown Massacre compound. 'It's creepy.'

'Think of yourself as a tourist observing the dark underbelly of other people's passions,' Daniel said. 'You're Louis Theroux, darling, and this is just another strange pocket of human idiosyncrasy.'

'I *am* a tourist,' she replied. 'Just ... not this kind of tourist. I think I've had enough of other people's passions. I'm going to wait outside.'

It was too much for her, but – more importantly – it didn't fit with the version of Daniel that he'd curated for Selina: her soulful new friend, talking wistfully about death and the afterlife, would never have placed her in such a morbid situation. The whole thing had unsettled her. It didn't make narrative sense for his character to be drawn to a place like this, and his only option was to pretend he was equally appalled.

In the final room, a large taxidermy alligator, over twelve feet long, dominated the floor. Its skin was like a dusty handbag, its great mouth frozen mid-snap. Selina, intent on a hasty exit, didn't pause to admire the beast. Daniel took a quick photo of the display case, which contained some information about murder, deaths and missing persons in the bayou, to study later.

A bleached-blonde girl in a black *Murder Girls* T-shirt placed a gentle hand on the alligator's blunt snout. 'I'm sorry you had to die,' she whispered in an East London accent. 'I'm so sorry you had to die.'

*

The days rolled by, and Daniel spent them side by side with Selina. She was easy to spot in the crowded French Quarter, with her cascade of turquoise hair and wide-brimmed black hat, but if that failed he usually found her at Pirate's Alley Café where they lingered over Death in the Afternoons while they decided where to go for dinner.

'Have you ever done a Ouija board?' she asked.

'Yes,' Daniel replied, remembering the lingering taste of Jack Daniels, the smell of Max's sweat. 'My friend Sage was convinced a demon attached itself to her boyfriend. His whole life turned upside down afterwards.'

Sage had manipulated the board, pushed the glass to flatter the musicians with promises of fame, and Daniel had pushed it right back, contradicting her deceitful claims with a promise of poverty. It was spiteful of him, and he regretted it later, but he was too proud to admit to the role he'd played in changing the tone of the evening. Everyone took everything too seriously.

'Let me take you to dinner,' he said. 'I know the most gorgeous little place, tucked away from all the tourist traps. They shuck oysters in front of you while a band plays. You're going to love it.'

Selina believed he had a knack for finding local spots less frequented by tourists, but in truth he was picking places he knew his little motley crew couldn't afford. Between dodging hook-ups, scouring the crowds for Caroline, and keeping tabs on the trio,

Daniel was growing tired of being on the lam. There wasn't much sand left in the egg timer of his life as Daniel Dumortier, and he didn't intend to spend his final days robbing Peter to pay Paul.

Selina *oohed* and *ahhed* over the menu in a courtyard bar. The oysters arrived with a slice of toasted baguette, tattooed with deep char lines from the grill. Daniel forked an oyster onto a corner of bread, bit and chewed. The warm flesh melted on his tongue, buttery, salty and delicious.

He insisted on paying the tab. It was important she thought of them as financial equals: rich people hate to feel taken advantage of and are deeply suspicious of poverty, but they never seemed to mind paying for each other.

Over the plate of charbroiled oysters, Daniel steered the conversation to talk of renting a car. Of course, in theory he had access to a car parked on North Rampart Street, but it felt wise to remain limber and switch vehicles – plus, he needed a car that was legally associated with Selina to ensure her involvement in his scheme.

After dinner, she mentioned the name of her hotel: the French House, in Mid-City. It sounded quaint. Quiet luxury, black coffee and pastries for breakfast, croissants with real butter. Perhaps a little late-night bar might serve French 75s and chartreuse cocktails. Daniel had once read that if you drank enough Chartreuse, it turned your eyes bright green. He fed her a story about switching hotels, and she was delighted to learn they were rooming in the same inn.

When they pulled up in front of the French House, he quickly realised his mental image had been romanticised: it was a vile-looking hostel designed to appeal to backpackers. This was a blow. Daniel had assumed it would be a breeze to convince Selina to hang out in her room while they finished their drinks, perhaps find some reality TV to laugh at, and then ply her with drinks from the mini bar until she passed out. A hostel meant dorm rooms, single bunks, too many bodies packed into too little space. The sour tang of body odour, the yeasty smell of unwashed genitals.

The front desk was covered in a deluge of rubbish, but it was fortuitously unmanned, so Daniel followed Selina past a bacchanalian scene of depravity in a dirty living room, through a kitchen that wouldn't look out of place in a state prison, and into a grim little courtyard decorated with garbage. It was teeming with louts playing some god-awful drinking game, but Selina seemed happy to take a seat and hang out for a while.

Daniel's bladder was swollen, aching with a desperate need to urinate, but he couldn't think of an elegant way to ask where the nearest bathroom was without revealing that he didn't have a room of his own, so he simply slipped away and pissed against the fence of the swimming pool. The water was a ghostly eggshell blue, illuminated by white porthole lights, and he imagined sinking into it, letting the chlorine disinfect his skin.

When he returned to their picnic bench, Selina looked frayed, but she had a good heart and didn't want to leave him by himself as he opened another beer. This was a misstep – he'd hoped she'd go to bed and leave him to figure out his next move in peace, but she didn't: she begrudgingly opened the last beer and toasted their good fortune. This was an absolute nightmare – and the alcohol was starting to compromise his faculties. He found himself rambling, saying too much.

'Do you think of yourself as an intuitive person?' he asked, drunk and goading.

'Yes,' she replied earnestly. 'And I trust my instincts. I feel like you're here for a reason, and so am I. Like maybe you were in need, and you were manifesting some spiritual support – I get the sense you've been through a lot.'

Daniel took a gentile sip of beer and she smiled serenely, pleased with herself. He tried not to let his irritation show.

We're both people, darling, he thought. *We have object permanence. I still exist when you leave the room, when you fall asleep, when we part ways. You didn't just magic me into existence at your convenience.*

'Perhaps we manifested each other,' he said instead, and then he helped himself to one of her cigarettes as she finally made her way to bed. She paused at her bedroom door, though, and glanced back at him, sitting alone in the now-empty courtyard. He waggled his fingers in a regal wave, and, after a few moments, she raised an uncertain hand and waved back. Daniel waited a few beats in case she reappeared, then tucked the unsmoked cigarette into his pocket and headed into the main house.

At the desk, a small blonde was eating a bag of Zapp's voodoo-flavoured crisps, zombified in the glow of her mobile phone.

'Hello, darling,' he said. 'I was wondering – do you have any spare beds at the moment? I have a friend coming to town and—'

'Totally booked,' she said, without looking up.

'Tomorrow too?'

'Totally. Booked.'

'Totally?'

'We might have some space next week,' she said. 'Are you in a dorm or a private?'

'Private,' he replied, plucking an answer from thin air.

'Well, if you don't mind bunking up, you can let your buddy crash with you, but you'll lose your single-occupancy rate … Although, I'll be totally honest, we don't check anyways. People come and go all the time; it isn't a big deal.'

'Okay, fabulous,' Daniel said tightly. 'Thanks so much.'

The courtyard was empty now, the moon high in the sky. He was all the way in Mid-City, and it was closer to morning than night. Cruising for an alternative place to stay felt futile – and besides, he wasn't sure if he had the energy to turn on the charm and sleep with someone.

Like a stray in need of a warm bed, he tapped on Selina's door, and when she opened it, she was still half asleep, confused and disorientated. It was easy to feed her a line about a damaged key card and sweet-talk her into letting him stay in her room for the night.

Settled side by side in bed, he offered her one of Jenna's sleeping pills, and then she was out like a snuffed candle, dead to the world, while he tried and failed to figure out the password to her phone. It was less elegant, but ultimately much easier, to simply use her thumbprint to unlock it, so he could call his phone with hers, and send her an SMS.

*

In the morning, Selina looked like a dead mermaid, her hair spread across the pillow in a faded turquoise tide. Did Jenna's sleeping pills mix well with alcohol? Daniel had no idea, hadn't thought to check. After a few moments though, her throat seemed to unglue itself and she emitted a confident snore.

With a sense of relief, Daniel pulled on his jeans and Jenna's shirt, which was in desperate need of a wash, and creeped out into the courtyard. A few sad-looking figures were eating a miserable breakfast, grimacing through their first cigarettes of the day.

In the lobby, a man was sprinkling a large vomit stain with some kind of acerbic powder.

'Hey, how's it going today?' he said brightly, as though cleaning up a stranger's sick was a neutral activity.

'Hello, darling,' said Daniel. 'My girlfriend and I are staying here at the moment, but we only have one key card. I wondered if perhaps I can pay a little extra for a second one?'

'Oh, let me see if I can fix that for you. What name was the room booked under?'

'Selina – we're in room twenty-two.'

'No worries,' he said, pulling up the iPad. 'What's your girlfriend's surname?'

'Did you say there was a fee? Can that be charged straight to the card we provided?' Daniel asked. 'Otherwise, I think I'll need to pop back to the room and—'

'Oh, hang on, I think I've found her. Selina Green?'

'Yes, sorry, Selina Green. That's her.'

'No problem, that's fine. I think your girlfriend might have booked a single occupancy, but I'll let it slide. Let me fire up a second key card. What was your name?'

'Daniel Dumortier.'

'There you go, man – you're all set. I've added you to the room, so you're legit.'

'Fabulous,' said Daniel. 'Thanks so much for your time.'

It was a thirty-minute walk into the Quarter. The roads were quiet, the morning thick with warm, stagnant air. Daniel had been dipping into a lot of pockets, flying a little too close to the sun, and he was considering his next move when a harassed-looking woman caught his attention by slamming her car door.

'I don't give a shit,' she said into her phone, pressed between her ear and shoulder. Her hands were full: she was juggling a handbag, a paper bag stamped with Café Beignet, a cardboard drinks holder containing two iced lattes, and her car keys. She put her breakfast on the roof of the car and locked it by squeezing the fob on her keys, then struggled to get the keys back into her handbag while she continued to berate whoever was on the line. 'No, Larry, I'm totally serious – if you invite her, I'm not bringing the kids, and you can explain why we're not there to your mother.'

Distracted, she turned towards a nail salon and disappeared inside. Daniel gave it a minute, then swiped the drinks and paper bag of beignets from the roof of her car and headed back to the hostel.

Things were looking up – although perhaps not for Selina.

The sleeping pill had left her groggy and unfocused, and the fallout of the banking scam was detrimental to her mood. It was with a great sense of tedium that Daniel guided her hand to the only sensible solution: she should place her money somewhere safe, and worry about it later.

*

The swamp tour was more illuminating than the Musée de la Mort, although it did little to lighten Daniel's disposition. Alligator attacks were rare, and deaths were unheard of in Louisiana. As the captain prattled on, Daniel grew increasingly despondent. His idea of death by alligator was beginning to feel more like a flight of fancy than a viable plan.

'There we go, ladies and gents,' said the captain. 'Can you see that big boy over there?'

An alligator with a head the size of a MacBook had risen from the depths of the swamp, its cold, blank gaze fixed on the boat. The captain tossed marshmallows at the beast, and reeled off facts like he was regurgitating a Wikipedia page.

'Has an alligator ever attacked a tour?' Daniel asked, more to amuse himself than to glean any useful information. The captain chuckled like he'd cracked a joke.

'No, sir,' he replied. 'These old dinosaurs are used to humans and very placid. Like I said, if you were to grab him by his big ol' tail there, he might have something to say about that, but to date we've never had an accident on a tour – and knock wood, we never will.'

'Is it always this busy?' Daniel asked. 'Around here?'

'Pretty much,' the captain replied. 'We have tours right up until midnight most nights. The night tours are spooky as hell, and you get a ten per cent discount if you show them your ticket from today.'

It would never do. He needed to find somewhere more remote, more isolated, than a busy tour route.

'Right,' Daniel said. 'Something to think about, I guess. I was hoping to find somewhere a little more peaceful to really take in the scenery.'

'If you're looking for peace and quiet,' the captain said. 'You can hike through the swamp on a bunch of man-made walkways. Check out the Bayou Coquille Trail – although watch out for gators!' He laughed.

'The Bayou Coquille Trail,' Daniel repeated. 'Sounds wonderful – thank you, darling.'

On the way home, they stopped at Rouses and picked up some snacks and wine for later. Daniel couldn't help but think of his little motley crew – how his darlings would have squirrelled Nerd Clusters and Hershey's Kisses into their pockets – but he was feeling too pumped to linger on any sense of regret. He'd looked up the Bayou Coquille Trail, and it seemed ideal. Isolated, where man and nature could meet face to face. It was the perfect path towards death, towards freedom, and he wanted to celebrate with a drink, but Selina was in no mood to party.

'I'm exhausted,' she said, parking up about a block away from the hostel on South Lopez Street.

'You just have to push through it, darling,' Daniel said. 'Once you're out, you'll be leading the conga line to the bar.'

'I've been driving all afternoon,' she replied, climbing out of the car and waiting for Daniel to do the same. 'I feel disgusting.'

'Well, why don't you have a shower while I open the wine, and then we can see how we feel?' he said, offering a charming smile.

Selina shook her head, and locked the car as soon as Daniel slammed the passenger door shut. 'No, I need to chill out for a bit. Maybe I'll see you later?'

Daniel was smart enough to recognise a sinking ship.

'Fine,' he said, tartly. 'Enjoy your sad little shower – and here, take the wine. Maybe it'll loosen your mood.'

He handed her the Rouses bag and turned towards the French Quarter. Nights in New Orleans were always young, after all, and brimming with promise.

*

A mix of different melodies poured from the bars and mingled in the street, a cacophonous cocktail of jazz, rock and pop. Daniel breezed through the crowd, past the street performers and the party-goers that clogged the roads, which were closed to traffic at that hour. He was already playing the role of a weary local, sick of the tourists.

So many versions of Daniel Dumortier had already lived and died: the little boy, the teenager, the son, the scholar, the musician, the nomad. Why not be reborn again? New Orleans felt like a good place to start afresh. He could get a cash-in-hand job washing dishes or mixing cocktails for tourists. He quite liked the idea of that. The taciturn bartender with a mysterious past. What would he call himself? Dante. Dorian. Damien. Something dramatic, laced with a touch of gothic tragedy.

In a boutique, he bought Selina a peace offering: a black synthetic rose. He rather liked the drama of a grand gesture. He'd wine and dine her, spoil her rotten with oysters and champagne. In the morning, they'd drive to the nature reserve and check out Daniel Dumortier's final resting place – and, if it proved suitable, he'd borrow the car, plant the evidence and take a taxi to a motel to hide out while his death unfolded. The car would be linked to Selina, and she would be able to piece things together for the police. It was perfect.

He was winding his way back through the Quarter, lost in thought, when Frankie landed the first punch. Daniel felt a flash of white-hot pain and a disorientating tilt of the ground beneath his feet as a shock of blood gushed from his nose and soaked into his shirt.

'You fucking asshole,' Bradley spat, while Frankie massaged his fist.

'Hey, hey – be cool, man.' A burly man appeared between them and blocked Frankie with one thick arm. 'What's going on? What's up?'

'He stole our car!' Jenna shouted, attempting to smack Daniel with her handbag. 'He stole our fucking car and ditched us in a Walmart parking lot.'

'I've never seen them before in my life,' Daniel said to the man, tilting his head back and pinching the bridge of his nose. A thick slug of blood crawled down the back of his throat and he gagged.

'I'm calling the cops,' Frankie said, digging through his pockets for his phone.

'I've no idea what they're talking about,' Daniel said to the man, who didn't seem thrilled by the developing story. 'They're clearly underage and can't handle their liquor.'

'Fuck you,' Bradley said.

'Call the police, darling,' Daniel said. 'And I'll have you arrested for assault, with this kind gentleman as my witness.'

The man shook his head and backed away with his hands in the air. 'Hey man, I can see you got this under control,' he said, and with that he melted into the crowd.

'Nice aim,' Daniel said to Frankie, gingerly checking whether his nose was broken. 'Where did you learn to throw a punch like that?'

'Fuck you,' Frankie replied. 'You ditched us! How could you?'

'You were arrested,' Daniel said. 'What did you want me to do, darling, pay your bail? Send a cake to the county jail with a file baked into it so you could plan your great escape?'

'You stole our fucking car,' Bradley said.

'I did no such thing,' Daniel replied. 'I left it in the parking lot with the key balanced on the front wheel, and then I took a cab to the nearest hotel. If some scoundrel of ill repute found the keys and took the car, I can only apologise – I genuinely thought it would be safe until you were able to retrieve it.'

'Bullshit,' said Bradley, but Frankie's face was softening.

'The world is full of thieves and liars, but I can assure you I'm not one of them,' said Daniel, and then he placed a hand on the small of Frankie's back. He felt the boy melt into his gentle embrace. 'Now, come on – let's get some cocktails to go and you can tell me all about your adventure while you buy me a new shirt, and we'll say no more about that punch.'

As they walked through the Quarter, Jenna pointed across the street. 'Hey, there's our friend.'

Daniel's stomach dropped as he followed her gaze, but it was merely a stranger. A young woman with a black bob and an uncanny resemblance to Caroline; a young woman who'd driven from California to Louisiana in a handsome Mustang; a young woman who'd asked a girl for a tampon, got chatting about their respective journeys, with no ulterior motive. As they passed each other by, the young woman paused to exchange a few bright and breezy words with Jenna.

'Now what in the hell are y'all doing here?' she said, laughing, with that unmistakable Southern twang rounding out her vowels.

'Hell if I know,' Jenna replied with a smile.

Daniel felt a brief pang of sorrow: for a few short moments, he'd thought he was about to encounter his sister, and that would have derailed everything. Now, he was struck by the realisation that he may never see her again, and although he'd grown suspicious of the way bad luck seemed to follow him, the way Caroline always seemed to be there when things took a turn for the worse, he loved her all the same.

*

Fresh and well-rested, Selina was an angel in a black mini dress. She smelled of cheap soap and her legs shimmered with lotion. Daniel held the flower by its stem and twirled it between finger and thumb. The bloody nose was a boon, and he played the stoic hero as he span a yarn about an attempted mugging, and she accepted the plastic rose with a smile.

'Let's go to dinner,' he said. 'Let me treat you. You spent all day driving me around, it's the least I can do – if you can bear to be seen with me.'

'You don't have to pay for dinner,' she said, but she was smiling.

As he changed into the champagne-coloured shirt Frankie had chosen for him in the French Quarter, Selina began to moan about the ten grand he'd taken from her. A mere hour alone with her thoughts had been enough time for her to get anxious, and she wanted it back. He unlocked his phone, opened his banking app, and tapped the screen a few times for authenticity.

'There,' he said. 'That shouldn't take long to come through.'

Daniel booked a taxi to an oyster bar in the French Quarter, and ordered oysters, Chartreuse, grassy glasses of white wine, decadent plates of pasta. He whisked her to one of the oldest jazz bars in the Quarter, where the music was loud enough to drown out any chance of further discussion.

As soon as she mentioned feeling tired, he switched it up again, this time leading her by the hand to Jean Lafitte's

Blacksmith Shop, where he knew the ghostly history of the bar would delight her. He sent her to order their drinks while he fed dollars into the jukebox, choosing songs he thought she might like. He was flipping through the CDs when he felt a firm hand on his shoulder. He was surprised to see the hand belonged to a pretty goth with long box-dyed black hair and a silver hoop in one ear.

'Hey, aren't you the dude who found my wallet the other night? In the Toulouse Dive Bar?'

'Ah, yes,' said Daniel, desperately trying to place the man's face. 'Yes, I remember you.'

The man's face darkened. 'Look man, be straight with me – did you lift the cash?'

'Did I – what?'

The pretty goth leaned forward, a scent of aggression on his breath. 'Did you take my fucking money?'

'I don't know what you're talking about,' Daniel said quickly. 'I'd never do something like that – I don't need to pick pockets, for God's sake. Look at me.'

The stranger's pale blue eyes travelled from Daniel's face to his lips to his satin shirt, and to Daniel's relief, his gaze lingered with a subtle look of curious longing.

'I had nearly a hundred bucks in there,' the man said, his conviction waning.

'I'm so sorry,' Daniel said, and then he touched his bruised nose and winced. 'I was mugged this afternoon myself. You really do have to be so careful around here.'

'Damn,' the man said, his voice softer now. 'That looks painful.'

'Well, it certainly didn't tickle, darling.' Daniel cocked his head towards the jukebox. 'Do you want to use my last credit? Go on, you look like a man who deserves a treat.'

The man flipped through his options, and chose Joy Division's 'Love Will Tear Us Apart'.

'Excellent choice,' Daniel said. 'And hey – I don't know if this is your thing, but if you fancy a drink later, let me give you my number?'

'Sure,' the man said, and he allowed himself a shy smile as Daniel wrote his phone number on the back of his hand.

With that bullet artfully dodged, it felt wise to push for a change of scenery. Daniel led Selina from one bar to the next, lowering her inhibitions, buttering her up. It was only when she regurgitated some god-awful novelty shot all over a dive bar's gleaming wooden counter that he finally booked them a cab back to the French House, and she thought nothing of him following her into her room.

*

Selina slept all morning and most of the afternoon, although on this occasion there was nothing more than alcohol in her bloodstream. She emerged late in the day, her unwashed hair wound into a bun the size of an apple, and looked visibly deflated at the sight of Daniel standing guard at the picnic benches.

'Last chance to visit the boardwalk,' Daniel said, lifting his hand to rattle the car keys. 'We have to return the car tomorrow.'

'I'm too hungover to drive,' she said. 'It isn't safe.'

'I'll drive,' he said.

'You're not insured.'

'I'll drive carefully, then,' he said, flashing her a devilish grin.

She swapped her handbag from one shoulder to the other, as though it were terribly heavy. 'Have you spoken to your bank?'

'Yes,' he said. 'They said it can take three to five business days for a transfer of that size, so your money should be with you soon. Come on, it's getting late.'

She didn't move.

'Look,' Daniel said, growing impatient. 'You can come with me or you can stay here, but I'm going either way.'

'I'll come,' she said. 'I'm driving though.'

*

The car park was small and empty. Laminated signs warned visitors against feeding the alligators with strangely accusatory language:

> *Please do not feed the alligators. If YOU feed an alligator, that animal may eventually attack someone, perhaps by grabbing that person's hand, thinking the hand itself is food since the food YOU fed the alligator came from YOUR hand.*

Daniel patted his pockets. 'Damn, I think I left my vape charging in your room. Do you have a cigarette, darling? I'm gasping.'

'The car park closes soon,' Selina said, reading an information board warning against car thieves and asking visitors to refrain from skateboarding, dog-walking or disturbing the wildlife.

> *STAY ON THE TRAILS. This is a wild area and many hazards exist beyond the trail's edge – poison ivy, fire ants, briars, poisonous snakes and alligators. Every step off the trail destroys a tiny part of the natural environment and your footprints could encourage other visitors to do the same. DO NOT FEED OR DISTURB THE WILDLIFE.*

'This won't take long,' Daniel replied, heading towards a sign that said *Bayou Coquille Trail*, an arrow pointing towards a dense coppice of trees. 'Cigarette, please?'

Selina passed them to him. He took one and slid the carton into his breast pocket.

'Hey,' she said. 'Those are mine.'

'Sorry darling, force of habit. Do you have a light?'

'No.'

'Fuck.' He twirled the cigarette between his fingers, then placed it behind his ear to save for later.

The Bayou Coquille Trail was a gentle hike along a wooden platform that wound its way through the cypress swamp, leading to the bayou. There were no lights to guide their way, and no handrail to offer support.

On either side of the narrow path, the swamp stretched into shaded darkness thanks to a thick canopy of cypress trees. It was hard to believe the surrounding meadow was swampland and not a regular field, that the grass wasn't growing on solid ground, but on several feet of water. In some places, it looked as though you could walk right across it, like it was sturdy enough to support your full body weight. Only the occasional glimmer betrayed the glittering presence of water.

Selina seemed spooked, and gasped at a sudden splash somewhere in the murky depths beneath their feet. Perhaps their footsteps had disturbed a water snake, or a baby alligator. It was difficult to tell. Soon, she seemed lost in a reverie of fear, probably imagining exactly what Daniel was thinking: they were so close to the water, so close to the wildlife. Every step brought with it a sense of danger, a sense of potential harm.

'Daniel,' she said, tugging on the sleeve of his shirt. 'Let's turn back. It's getting dark.'

They had only been walking for fifteen minutes. She was no fun.

'Hey, Selina,' said Daniel. 'Remember that ghost story we heard on the swamp tour? I can't shake the image of Julia Brown materialising in the gloom and walking towards us across the swamp.'

'That's not funny,' she said.

'Remember what our tour guide said? Nothing stays buried out here,' Daniel continued. 'Everything returns to the surface eventually.'

'Stop it,' she said.

'Wait,' Daniel said, grabbing her arm. 'Did you see that?' He pointed towards the bank.

'I'm turning back,' Selina said. 'I really don't like this.'

'I'm serious,' he whispered, continuing to point towards the bank. 'Don't you see it? There, between the trees.'

Selina was trembling as she followed his gaze to a thick thatch of cypress trees that lined the wetlands. 'I don't see anything,' she said.

'There,' he insisted. 'Don't you see it? Maybe you need to stand here, come on.' He gently steered her into position, so she was standing with her back to him. She followed the path of his outstretched finger into the distance.

'It's ... it's ... a floating psychic!' he cried, making a sudden movement as though preparing to push her into the water.

Selina screamed, hand on her heart, as Daniel broke into peals of laughter.

'I'm sorry darling, I couldn't resist. You need to relax – there's nothing out here that can hurt you. Well, nothing but the alligators.'

'Fuck off,' Selina snapped. 'I'm *not* laughing. I'll wait for you at the car.'

She turned to go, and a mean thought popped into Daniel's wicked heart. 'Race ya,' he said, and he was off, light-footed, running on the balls of his feet, leaving her in the middle of the swamp, surrounded by the rustles and clicks of the wildlife.

'Daniel!' she called after him, but he was nimble, impish, skittering across the rotten planks with an almost manic glee as he looked for somewhere to hide, somewhere he could crouch hidden amongst the looming flora, ready to jump out and scare her to death.

Epilogue
London: Selina

Daniel's body was found a few weeks later. The newspapers reported his death as a tragic accident, his injuries 'consistent with an alligator attack'. Apparently, the medical examiner requested the help of a bite-analysis expert from Florida to evaluate the evidence, although reports were prudent with the gruesome details.

There were a few question marks hanging over the case though. At the time of death, Daniel was wearing a champagne-coloured satin shirt. No one could explain the bloodied cheesecloth shirt found in a separate location, although forensic reports concluded the bloodstains did indeed belong to Daniel.

That was the first mystery. The second was the duality of locations: Daniel's final resting place was in the water surrounding the Bayou Coquille Trail, but the car was parked near the Barataria Preserve, a twenty-minute walk towards Crown Point. Presumably, nature had had its way with him, and a combination of the slow-moving water and intrepid wildlife had moved the body from one place to another, but it was difficult to imagine.

Sage reached out, but I declined her invitation to attend the funeral. I just wanted to move on with my life, I said. I wanted to forget about Daniel, forget about New Orleans.

Richard married a primary school teacher, had two boys, and opened a gastropub in Streatham. He didn't post much about his life online, but a digital food magazine wrote a glowing review of his menu: familiar dishes rendered with a British make-do-and-mend attitude: Sazeracs mixed with bourbon, Hurricanes made with Barcardi, pineapple juice and grenadine. Oysters, grilled with garlic butter and parsley. Gumbo, simmered with smoked sausage. Banana bread, served with vanilla Chantilly and a rum-caramel sauce. The thought of it turned my stomach.

Max's music career enjoyed a brief death bloom when a cover of one of the Strangeways' better tracks went viral. An amateur true crime creator had unearthed Daniel's connection to the band, and she used the song as a backing track on a video about Daniel's disappearance. The exposure wasn't enough to drag Max into cultural relevancy, but I'm sure the royalties were welcome.

Sage sold her narrowboat. It was too much for her, living in such close proximity to the location of Caroline's death. She was private person, distrustful of social media, so I didn't know much about her life. I liked to think she was still travelling, perhaps drawing tarot cards for strangers in exchange for a little company. It's funny, isn't it – the habits we pick up from others.

And then there's Daniel. He's still with me, a hand around my ankle, a noose around my neck. Every so often, I catch a whiff of his cologne – a rich, spicy smell of leather and wood, violets and amber – and the whole trip blooms within me. The jazz bars, the endless rain followed by the oppressive heat. The relief of finding a friend in someone like Daniel, that relief boiling into anger when I realised what kind of man he was.

I can't listen to jazz anymore – he's in the tremolo of every trumpet, the rasp of every snare, the pluck of every double bass.

He's the taste of champagne, oysters, absinthe. He's purple, green and gold.

In my waking hours, he's everywhere, but at night I dream of him too. Each night the same as the last: I'm forced to relive an identical sequence of events, over and over again, like a ghost from the future, unable to intervene in the incidents of the past.

It happens like this. A desolate vein of the bayou, a winding wooden path. The sun is low in the sky, and a thick canopy of cypress trees blocks the light, so the swamp stretches into darkness.

Daniel strolls along the boardwalk, hands in pockets, taking in the isolation, the maraca-shake of hidden cicadas. He's wearing the champagne-coloured shirt, the satin one that clings to his broad shoulders. Somewhere in the dark leaves above his head, the soft, hollow melody of a hooting owl accompanies each step. He walks for a long time in silence, enjoying the serenity, the peacefulness of being alone in nature.

Something startles him – a sudden splash beneath his feet, or the sharp snap of a twig. Perhaps he'd been thinking about ghosts, hauntings, and supernatural happenings in the area, and worked himself into a panic, or perhaps he was thinking about alligators, snapping turtles and water snakes. Either way, he turns to retrace his steps, and a primal sense of panic inspires him to run.

In the gloom, he doesn't see a rotten plank. So easy to stumble, so easy to fall. There's no handrail, after all. Nothing to break his fall until he hits the water.

There's a movement on the bank. A racoon, perhaps, or a wild pig. It takes a second to understand the image in front of him: the avocado skin of an alligator, a big girl, the length and width of a casket. Alarmed, Daniel splashes and kicks as he tries to find his footing in the shallow water, but it's so easy to get tangled in the mess of duckweed and saw grass that thickens the water in great knots.

The alligator watches the commotion, cold eyes blank and yellow as natural citrine. Before Daniel can cry out, she lunges with tremendous speed and a tidal wave of swamp water engulfs him, swallows the desperate sound of a guttural scream.

Sometimes, in the dream, it's quick. A well-placed snap of the neck that cracks the silence of the bayou with the force of a whip. Sometimes, it's slow. He's dragged under the surface of the water, and a cloud of blood turns the khaki swamp a dark red, the kind of burgundy that comes from deep within. A few moments pass, and then he emerges once more, his beautiful face a picture of agony, his fine features perverted into a pale mask of shock. And then the alligator, jaws locked on Daniel's flesh, twists into a death roll, dragging him underwater for the final time.

What are you doing? he says, not to the alligator, but to me. *What are you doing?*

I can't speak in the dream. There's no one to answer his call.

There is no alligator. I look down, and I'm clenching the round orb of a fire quartz sphere, threaded with red, coated in blood. The first hit is instinctive, an action born from panic. The wound on his temple bleeds, and as I think of everything Daniel has taken from me, I bring the sphere down once more.

Acknowledgements

I'd like to thank my editor Jo Dickinson for scooping me up as a fledgling debut and waiting so patiently while I smashed out the infamously difficult second novel. So much love and gratitude to my agent Zoe Ross for all your kind words and endless encouragement, and thank you to Olivia Davies for taking the reins so expertly in Zoe's absence. I'm a lucky gal.

Many thanks to the teams at United Agents and Hodder for all your hard work: Kate Norman in editorial, Juliette Winter in production, Helena Fouracre in marketing and Niamh Anderson in publicity. Lewis Csizmazia, thank you for another gorgeous, colour-popping cover. Tara O'Sullivan and Annabel Maunder, thank you for whipping the final draft into shape with your copy editing and proofreading skills. Ellie Wheeldon, thank you once again for another banging audiobook. I'd also like to thank Beth Wickington for being there during the first few rough drafts, and helping me to figure out what the hell I wanted (and didn't want) to write.

I'm so grateful to everyone who read and loved *Death of a Bookseller*. There are too many authors, influencers and booksellers to name individually, but shout out to James Bainbridge and the team at Waterstones Walthamstow, and special thanks to Jordan Taylor-Jones and Dan Stone at The West Kirby Bookshop – my friends, my darlings. Thank you.

A thousand thank yous to my first reader, muse and beloved friend Emily Hatzar. You're an angel, a blessing and a delight. I

Acknowledgements

can't wait to sit side by side at the bar in Erin Rose and toast this book with a cold PBR.

Thank you to the tour guides, psychics and bartenders of New Orleans, particularly at the Toulouse Dive Bar, for being so generous with their time, local knowledge and salacious gossip, and to Liz at The Great American Alligator Museum for answering my strange questions about alligator attacks. Kaylee Wood, thank you for answering my most morbid questions about blood and forensics. Charlie Childs and Richard Wintle (via Tom Wintle!) thank you so much for answering my questions about police procedure. Any errors on the page are mine.

Many thanks to NOLA-natives and beloved friends Nisha Ranshi and Phil Saunders for driving me around town, answering my questions and being the best pals a gal could have. Phil, thank you for sharing your knowledge of Zippos, guitars and muscle cars. I owe you so many Sazeracs.

Much love to my colleagues at big group for the continued support. Thank you to Josh Hayman for letting me borrow his late grandmother's tea shop story, and special thanks to Adam Wilsher for all the pints, laughs and love.

So much love and gratitude to my family, scattered all over the world, who offer nothing but unwavering support: particular thanks to Mom, Pete and Hank. I love you to bits.

My mates are the wind beneath my wings. I'm so lucky to have you all. I promise I'll be more fun at parties from now on.

And finally, this book is dedicated to my husband, Alex Clements. I love the very bones of you.

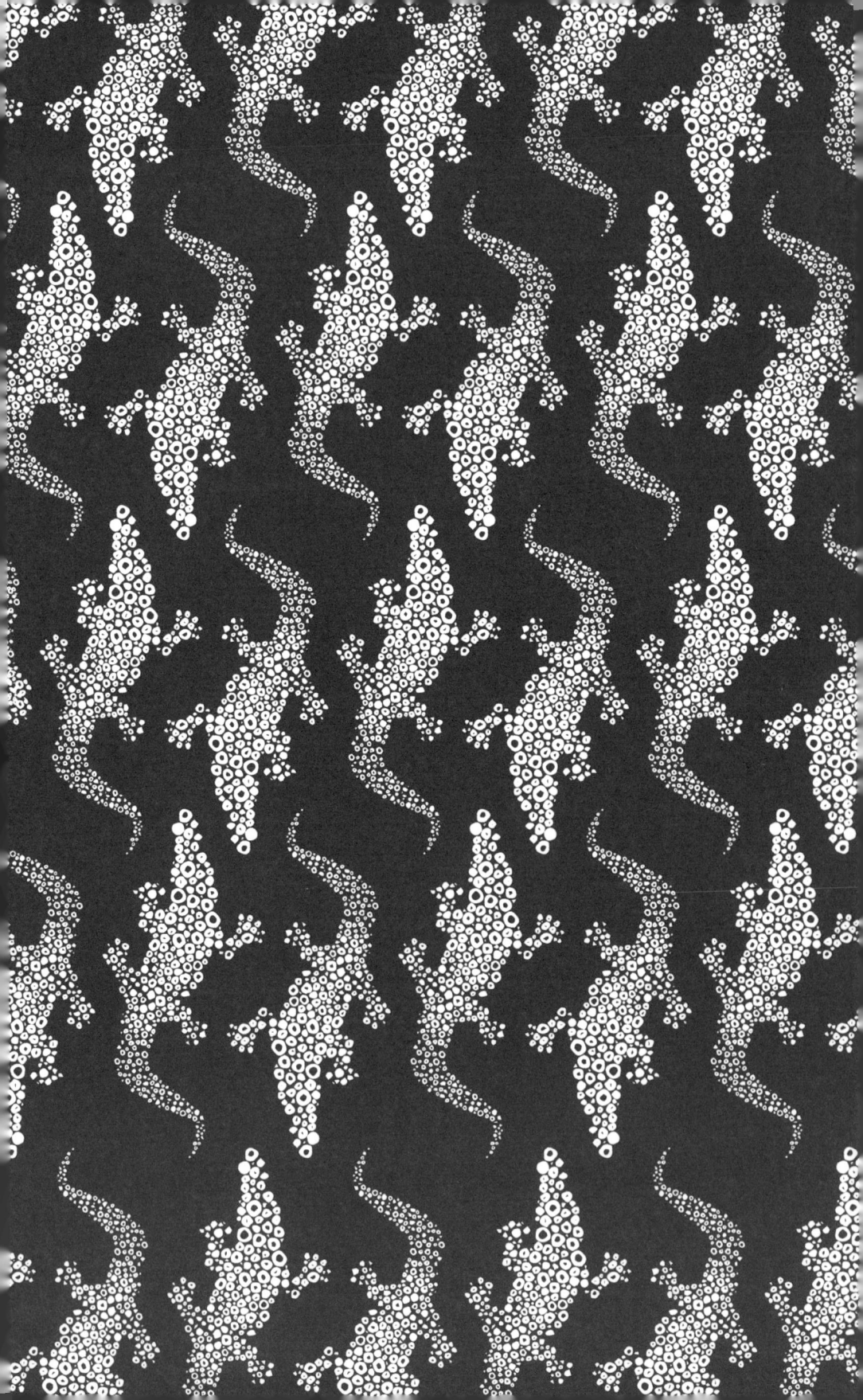